THE TRAIN

Part I: Escape from Hell's Kitchen

Keith Schafer

THE TRAIN

PART 1: ESCAPE FROM HELL'S KITCHEN

Text copyright © 2013 Keith Schafer. All rights reserved

To Those Who Have Guided the Way

To my persevering family, who perused numerous, less sophisticated versions of this book, and despite that, still encouraged me to continue on: to Heather, William, Jeralee and Lee, Glenna and Sharon, your optimistic support and pride in my efforts will always hold a special place in my heart.

Particularly to my wife, Cathy, who has read and reread numerous versions of the book, edited and re-edited them, who diplomatically pointed out flaws and inconsistencies, and who is one of the models for a character in this book, you continue to offer me more support and encouragement in our life together than I ever deserved, or could have imagined.

My special thanks to my son, Lance, a more accomplished writer than I will ever be. Your frank and insightful feedback, encouragement, editing and publishing assistance has been the deciding factor in whether a flawed manuscript remained stuffed in a drawer or became something worthy of introduction to a broader audience.

Thanks also to Jon Humfleet, the gentleman who created the artwork on my behalf for the book's cover.

I dedicate this book to my mother and father, who never had the opportunity to read it, but who sacrificed greatly to give me the skills to write it, and from whose extended families and acquaintances in Jadwin, Salem and nearby environs added the experiences and special color to shape its narrative.

Chapter 1

The train appeared dark and sinister to the children in the fading twilight and coal-polluted air as it rumbled to a stop along the station platform where they huddled, its cars twisting back and away like some giant, evil snake. The locomotive halted with a final screech, its stack still belching smoke and embers that drifted over and around the cars, shrouding them in their own stinking cloud. Even at rest, its engine idled in a low rhythmic growl.

The youngest of the children shrank back from the edge of the platform, reluctant to go near it. All the children were weary, as were the other passengers who had been waiting too long for this tardy monster.

After a few minutes, the locomotive whistle screeched loud, long and impatient, causing the older children to jump and the younger ones to whimper and huddle among themselves for what comfort they could find. Even the normally raucous older boys fell silent, staring at this beast they would soon ride to places they did not know. None had ridden a train before.

A tall, thin female, still in her youth, stood among them, distinguished from the other children by her height and her beauty.

She stood quietly, as if in a daze. To the nearby passengers who observed her, she seemed deeply troubled.

In addition to the older girl, a slightly portly, middle-aged woman, obviously in charge and all business, accompanied this group of little pilgrims. She would supervise them on their strange journey and deposit each along the way in unfamiliar places with people they did not know--but only if they were lucky.

A handsome, stately-looking young man assisted the woman in herding the hesitant children toward the open compartment doors. He shook hands with some of the older boys and hugged a couple of the little girls gently. He offered each a word of encouragement and good luck. As they began to board, he lifted the youngest up to the top of the passenger compartment steps. He did not personally board the train. He would not be traveling with them.

The girl received glances from other passengers as she prepared to board. Even in the twilight, she had great beauty. The handsome man spent extra time with her before she boarded, bending down and giving her a long hug and kissing her on the forehead. He offered her some sort of encouragement but it didn't seem to help.

The whistle screeched again and the conductor yelled one last "ALL ABOARD!" The girl reluctantly climbed the steps, pressed from behind by a final group of passengers who were frustrated by the delay and anxious to find a seat as far from the children as possible, hoping to get a little sleep, fearing that would not be likely. As passengers made their way along the aisles, more than one glanced warily at the children, expecting noise and disruption that would make an already bad trip worse.

The tall girl had not previously been on a train. Her only travel of a distance had been by ship. That trip had been difficult, but she suspected that this one would be worse. Then she had been shepherded by a family who loved her. Now, even in her group, she felt alone.

As she slid into a straight-backed bench with its cracked leather seat, two small, frightened children bolted from their seats and ran over to huddle beside her. After some commotion, they settled tightly against her, so close that she felt claustrophobic.

The train made loud hissing sounds, then shuddered as it lurched forward, pulling away from the station. The girl stared out the window at a crowded, polluted city that had offered only sorrow as its parting gift.

Her eyes caught movement in the shadows of the building across from the terminal. For an instant she thought she saw a familiar shape. She strained hard to see, trying to cut through the deepening shadows to pinpoint the shape, but she had no luck. As the train gathered speed, her view of the station blurred. She shrank back in the seat wearily.

Although she looked older, she was barely thirteen years old; but in her mind, she already felt old. Despite the little companions clinging tenaciously to her, she was close to no one on the train.

It had not always been so. Her parents had been gone only a little while, a time that now seemed a distant past. She thought of her father as the train picked up speed, its rhythmic motion taking her farther away from him and her mother, and the person that she cared most about now. Her breath caught at the thought and she almost cried out in pain.

Her father had been a big, happy man who had adored his daughter and loved his wife. He had brought them to America, this land of unlimited promise, to pursue a simple dream. They had finally reached the island of the great lady statue with her welcoming beacon. The girl was eleven years old then, an innocent time, a protected time that was not hers anymore.

Her family had moved into a small apartment in a miserable, run-down building near the Hudson River in an area of Manhattan called, Hell's Kitchen, a place harboring far too many people in far too little space. But she was not afraid. Her father would take care of her. He always had. He promised that their stay was temporary and she believed him, because what he said had always come true.

He was luckier than most due to his size and ebullient personality. He quickly obtained a good job at the shipyards. The family hoarded every cent they did not need to survive, building that crucial reserve necessary to buy land out west on which to farm. Not a week went by without a conversation about what it would be like when they realized their dream.

Only a month before he died, he told them proudly that their dream was very near now, that they almost had enough to make the move. By this time next year, they would be in the country, where she could have that pony she always wanted and his comely wife, who now seemed to cough endlessly, would have fresh air to breathe to help her recover quickly.

He told his daughter that, unlike him, she would become well-educated and would someday give him lots of grandchildren to spoil. He would live long and always be there when she needed him. He was an optimist to the end.

It was a bright, unusually fresh, September morning when she heard a knock on their apartment door. She had planned to go outside if her mother permitted. She answered the door. It was her father's boss, the dock foreman, a kindly man who had met them only once, but who immediately liked the family, especially the girl. He had three daughters of his own, but none quite as pretty as she. This day, his face was somber and she knew immediately that something wasn't right. A sense of foreboding enveloped her as he spoke.

"Is your mother here?" He was looking past her into the shabby apartment.

"She is resting, sir. I'll go get her." She turned and opened the bedroom door. Her mother, lying on the bed, had already heard the voices. She slowly got up, trying to straighten her hair with her hands and brush out the wrinkles from her dress as she made her way toward the apartment door. The girl remained in the bedroom, partially hidden behind the door, listening anxiously.

The foreman, with great urgency, said to her mother, "You must come with me to the docks immediately."

Her mother froze momentarily, searching his eyes. Then she turned to the girl and said, "You stay here and don't open the door to anyone. I'll be back soon." Then she was gone.

But even though it was only a short distance to the docks, it was already too late. Powerful as her father had been, he was no match for that two hundred fifty pound barrel of rum that had broken loose from the straps of the loading crane and fallen twenty feet, crushing his back and skull. He had just bent over to push another barrel out of the way and never saw it coming. He heard the warning shout of a fellow dock worker as it hit him, driving him forward into the barrel he was trying to move. He died in seconds. His last conscious thought was of his daughter.

With the help of the foreman, they prepared his body as best they could and bought a modest burial plot on the northern edge of Hell's Kitchen where they traveled with him two days later on that final trip. The weather had turned wet and chilly. A mixture of drizzle and rain fell from the sky throughout the slow procession to the graveyard. As the girl rode on the back of the wagon beside the coffin, she couldn't help thinking that this was not the trip that her father had promised, and she was ashamed for thinking it.

Foreman, mother, daughter, undertaker and grave digger were the only ones at the gravesite. The casket made a splatting sound as the men lowered it to the bottom of the grave where muddy water had already pooled. The girl dropped a single rose into the grave on the casket as it rested low in the mud.

The undertaker asked them if they wanted to say something before he filled in the dirt. Her mother, in shock, could say nothing. He looked at the girl. She looked down into the cold grave and shuddered, sick to her stomach, fighting back the tears. All she could think to say was, "Goodbye father. We will miss you and always love you. We are sorry you had to go so soon."

The foreman patted her shoulder and said he was sure her father was smiling down at her from heaven. Then in silence, they turned away. As they left, she heard the sound of wet dirt landing in hollow thuds on top of the casket as the grave digger filled the hole. She looked back and shivered involuntarily and thought how alone he was down in that dirty wet grave.

The foreman took them back to their apartment. Her mother barely made it home before collapsing from a horrible coughing fit. As she lay in her bed, hacking incessantly, a bloody froth formed around her mouth. The girl got a pan of water and a cloth to wash it away.

Over the next few days her mother's condition worsened rapidly. She continued to cough up the foam, but it was redder now. When she tried to sit up in her bed, her coughs doubled her over. She sent the girl for the doctor, who took most of their remaining money, giving the girl a little medicine to ease her mother's pain and lessen the coughing, along with instructions on how to use it. He did not bother to offer hope. He knew the condition well and realized it would end soon for the mother.

In her last days, her mother drifted in and out of consciousness. The girl used what little money they had left for food and tried to give what comfort she could, but it was not enough. Her mother died in mid-November, two months after the passing of her husband. The girl had eaten little as she had nursed her mother. She was now nearing malnutrition.

The landlord, having seen all this a thousand times before, and not a compassionate man by nature, called the county officials to dispose of the body. There were no family members or friends in the city to which the girl could turn. She fixed her mother's body as best she could. When it was carried out of the apartment, she followed.

The Landlord, who had a drinking habit to support, nailed the apartment door shut after she left. When she returned from the graveyard, she could not get in. She searched for the landlord to ask his help. He laughed and told her she had to leave. She asked to be let in to get her clothes and mementos of her mother and father. He just slammed his apartment door in her face.

She stayed in the hallway until he finally came out again and told her that he was calling the police if she didn't get out of the building now. She frantically knocked on the doors of the few people she had met in the apartment but no one answered. Reluctantly she left the building, not knowing what else to do.

When the landlord was sure she had gone, he had a local pawnbroker come to take away the family's possessions, for which he received a paltry sum. It wasn't much, but such events happened frequently enough in his building to help him cover his habit.

She saw some of the people she knew as they entered the tenement late that day, but when she called out to them, they turned their heads away and pretended she wasn't there. They did not want to become involved in another hard luck case. Their own lives already teetered on the edge.

So on that sad and frightening November day in 1884, as she finally left the front of that dirty, run-down tenement that had been her family's temporary home and walked aimlessly along, to where she did not know, she became just another lost orphan on the streets of Hell's Kitchen.

Chapter 2

No one is really sure how Hell's Kitchen got its name. In 1884, it comprised a crowded, filthy, polluted section of central Manhattan, bordered roughly by the Hudson River on the west, 8th Avenue to the east, 34th Street to the south and 54th Street to the north.

Some say the name was coined by none other than Mr. David Crockett himself, who was at the time a U.S. congressman but would later become more famous by trying, unsuccessfully, to defend an old Spanish Mission in San Antonio, Texas. Crockett, who was visiting Manhattan in 1835, did not take to the Irishmen he met there. Being a person noted for turning a phrase and not bashful about making controversial statements, he opined, "In my part of the country, when you meet an Irishman, you find a first-rate gentleman; but these are worse than savages; they are too mean to swab hell's kitchen."

At the time, Davy was actually referring to the Five Points section at the southern edge of Hell's Kitchen, so called because of a five-pointed intersection of the streets of Orange, Cross, Little Water, Mulberry and Anthony, but his conclusion was apt for the entire area.

Others thought the name came from a particularly notorious tenement on 54th street already known by that name; still others thought it referenced another infamous building on 39th street. There was an area gang of the same name. And, of course, there was the famous London slum, long known as Hell's Kitchen. Many assumed that some Brits migrating to New York simply transplanted the name. Finally, there was a well-known German restaurant in the area called Heil's Kitchen. A bastardization of that name might have given the area its label.

But the most plausible and widely accepted origin traced back to a man named Dutch Fred, a veteran New York policeman, who was watching a riot with his rookie partner on West 39th street near 10th avenue one day. Violent riots happened with regularity in that part of town. The rookie cop was reported to have said, "This place is hell itself!", to which Fred drolly replied, "Hell's a mild climate compared to here, boy. This is Hell's Kitchen."

As far as anyone knew, the first time the region's name entered print was in 1881 when a New York Times reporter, covering a particularly grisly multiple murder in the neighborhood, referred to a tough tenement as "Hell's Kitchen" and further indicated that the surrounding block was "probably the lowest and filthiest in the city". That was saying a lot since there was much competition for that designation in Hell's Kitchen. No matter where the name originated, there was total consensus as to its appropriateness.

Charles Dickens, no stranger to describing slums and the people who lived there--particularly orphaned children--made a point of visiting Hell's Kitchen while in New York. He wrote:

"Poverty, wretchedness, and vice, are rife….Debauchery has made the very houses prematurely old….All that is loathsome, drooping, and decayed is here." Apt as he was at descriptions, Dickens probably understated the reality of Hell's Kitchen. Only London's East End could compare for sheer population density, disease, infant and child mortality, unemployment, prostitution and violence of all kinds.

The area was alleged to have sustained the highest murder rate of any slum in the world. In its time, the Old Brewery, an overcrowded tenement on Cross Street housing 1,000 of the wretched poor, was reputed to have had a murder every night for 15 years.

The area was dominated by rival gangs like the Roach Guards, Dead Rabbits, Bowery Boys, Dutch Mob, Eastman Gang, Five Points Gang, Grady Gang, Hook Gang, Hudson Dusters and the famous Leslie Gang, to name a few.

They were led by colorful characters including, "Dandy" Duck Reardon, Baby-Faced Willie, Chuck Connor, Reddy the Blacksmith, Mose the Fireboy, Hell-Cat Maggie, Jack the Rat, Sheeny Mike, Monk Eastman, Kid Twist, Louie the Lump, Wild Maggie Carson, and Dutch Heinrichs.

In early July 1857 a gang war broke out between the Dead Rabbits and the Bowery Boys that escalated to all-out war involving most of the gangs of New York. The fighting involved up to a thousand gang members and lasted two full days. The police, who were in organizational disarray at the time, were helpless to stop it. The battles were fought on wide fronts with the Dead Rabbits and the Five Points Gang and their associates pitted against the Bowery Boys and their allies to the north. The fronts moved back and forth in pitched battles to gain ground much like large conventional armies. Only when the New York Militia came in to reinforce police did the violence subside. A written report of the time documents the chaos:

"...stones and clubs were flying thickly around, and from the windows in all directions, and the men ran wildly about brandishing firearms. Wounded men lay on the sidewalks and were trampled upon. Now the Rabbits would make a combined rush and force their antagonists up Bayard Street to the Bowery. Then the fugitives, being reinforced, would turn on their pursuers and compel a retreat to Mulberry, Elizabeth and Baxter Streets."

--New York Times, July 6, 1857

Hell's Kitchen was America's greatest ethnic melting pot of the 19th century, beginning with the arrival of newly freed African American slaves, then the Irish Immigrants fleeing the potato famine, then poor and oppressed Germans, and later, the Italians. Theirs was an uneasy coexistence that could occasionally explode.

During the Civil War Draft Riots of July 1863, a white mob hanged African Americans at 32nd and 8th Avenue with white women publicly slashing the bodies with knives as they were hanging. Police dispersed the mob, but 5,000 came back later and hung more blacks until the New York Militia's artillery was called in against them. The mob burned a colored orphan asylum near 44th and Fifth Avenue on the way out, just for good measure.

On other occasions, it was white against white. In July 1881 a crowd of Irishmen hurled bricks from a roof at Orangemen parading up 8th Avenue, resulting in yet another riot. Police called on the State Militia, which fired on the crowd with real bullets. Thirty rioters were killed and hundreds wounded.

And so it went in Hell's Kitchen, which became known as "the most dangerous area on the American Continent." It made America's Wild West look placid.

Part of Hell's Kitchen (now the Clinton area of New York City) was situated along the dockyards of the Hudson River and those dockyards needed workers. In 1851, the Hudson River Railroad opened a station at West 30th Street. That brought factories, lumberyards and slaughterhouses, all needing workers who were not squeamish about hard, nasty labor under dangerous conditions. The people working those low-paying jobs needed places to live and that brought the tenements. By the second half of the 19th century, Hell's Kitchen had become the geographic poster child for the worst form of urban poverty in America.

One could find abandoned children of all ages and nationalities in Hell's Kitchen, although Irish, German and African American children were the most predominate ethnic groups. The youngest children died or disappeared after short tenure. The older ones became known as "street Arabs" or "street urchins".

Cruel as their fate might be, those who survived did enjoy their independence. It was a somewhat perverted version of the Lost Boys of Peter Pan's Neverland. At its peak, the streets of Hell's Kitchen hosted over 30,000 homeless and orphaned children on any given day.

There were attempts to assist the youngest of these children, but the cure was as bad as the bite. The Rykers Island infant hospital, which took babies and infants from Hell's Kitchen, had a mortality rate approaching 90%. The situation wasn't much better in orphanages, whose unregulated owners often took advantage of the children for the small sums of money received from charitable organizations. Most children on the streets came to consider placement in an orphanage tantamount to a death sentence.

The street urchins survived by all possible means: begging, foraging, picking pockets, shoplifting, running errands for gambling establishments, and of course, prostitution. They were a wild, dirty, rowdy lot, generally without manners, urinating and defecating on the edges of the streets whenever the urge came upon them.

Outsiders called them "dangerous classes" and they were correct. An urchin who survived to adolescence frequently wound up in the city's jails or prisons for theft, prostitution or violence. Almost all were actively entrenched in a gang. Joining a powerful gang was the ultimate career goal of most boys on the streets of the Kitchen. Given their options, it was a logical choice.

In their own right, the survivors were ingenious little beggars, and often quite charismatic. They could quickly overwhelm any person who dared show them sympathy. Most adults avoided Hell's Kitchen to spare themselves the pain of confronting this unrelenting tragedy.

Children routinely died on the streets of Hell's Kitchen. On a typical day, the police, returning to their beats two-by-two (they never entered Hell's Kitchen alone), would find a child's body lying frozen or mutilated and call the mortuaries to come get it. It was a hard business. Those in authority either became callous to it or lost their emotional stability.

Caring adults were seldom found in Hell's Kitchen, with the notable exception of the New York Children's Aid Society, formed in 1853. But even it focused only on the youngest of the urchins, and its methods were controversial to some authorities and philanthropists.

There were few private benevolent organizations brave enough to take up the cause of the street urchins, and there was little government intervention. The churches did what they could, but many were in the midst of their own great overseas missionary endeavors, which offered far greater rewards than trying to save the wretched, uncooperative children of Hell's Kitchen, located at their geographic back door. It wasn't just the prophet that was not without honor except in his own country—the same could be said for New York's orphan children.

Upstanding citizens of New York, residing outside of Hell's Kitchen, spoke "in horror" about the conditions of the street children. They believed someone should help, but what could one do in light of the constant influx of all these impoverished immigrants? If only they'd stop coming….

As with most repressive human conditions that defy solution, the ultimate response was to turn away from the situation and blame the victim. Among most New Yorkers, a paralyzing apathy set in, interrupted occasionally by public outcry over some atrocity performed by an escaping urchin, or by the feeble whining of a few do-gooders, or more likely, by a tirade from a campaigning politician laying the blame on America's lax immigration policies.

Newspapers chronicled the massive breakdown of law and order in the urban ghettos, citing the dangers of unchecked immigration, the growing numbers of street gangs, and of course, the horrible condition of the street urchins.

Children living with their parents in Hell's Kitchen often did not fare much better than the urchins. Because of rampant drug use, child abuse and molestation was common. Asbury's book, Gangs of New York, tells of a little girl who lived with 25 people in a small basement room. She was stabbed to death for a penny she had begged. The girl's body lay in a corner for five days before her mother dug a shallow grave in the floor and buried her, likely because of complaints about the smell.

And then there was that unexplained mystery among the Hell's Kitchen urchins themselves. The youngest of the urchins sometimes just disappeared from the streets without explanation. It was common opinion that they had been stolen and shipped to other countries to ultimately become sex slaves. That may have been true in a few situations, but it was not the main truth.

In all, Hell's Kitchen was a festering human tragedy of unfathomable proportion that had reached its zenith by late 1884.

Chapter 3

Most of the children who survived on the streets of Hell's Kitchen did so by joining a youth gang that became their new family. As a rule, the gangs were violent and territorial. They preyed on other urchins not in or affiliated with their own gang, as well as on the old, the disabled and the infirm. They did so for their own survival, but also for their personal entertainment.

The youth gangs offered a form of intimacy otherwise unavailable to the children of the street. Each gang had its own rules governing its relationships and behavior, both internally and externally. Each provided structure, stability and social companionship. Most were connected to adult gangs, sometimes of the same name, who used their youth divisions for efficient recruitment. Two of the youth gangs, the Bowery Boys and the Five Points Gang, were the most feared in Hell's Kitchen, and thus the most admired by the street urchins. To be a Bowery Boy or a Five Points gang member was to be king of the hill.

But the two gangs were also mortal enemies. Each had aligned itself with an adult gang of the same name, and each had strongly differing beliefs and political affiliations. The Bowery Boys were generally anti-Catholic and anti-Irish. The Five Points Gangs were the opposite. Thus the enmity was personal, religious and ethnic.

These gangs were so violent that even the police avoided confrontation whenever possible. The gangs, both adult and youth divisions, were also associated with the larger criminal underworld of New York City and even with "legitimate" political organizations like Tammany Hall.

Youth gangs were paid a bonus each time a member was recruited to the big leagues. The youth leader also received a monthly stipend to be used for gang maintenance. On top of this, youth gangs generated their own resources through burglaries, robberies, child prostitution, extortion and other crimes that yielded booty.

On average, a youth gang leader served three years before "graduating" into the adult gang or criminal underworld, depending on his skill level. He was always the best-known member of the gang. It was the job of the youth leader to assure that gang members had safe havens and adequate food. Gangs took over abandoned buildings, living dormitory style. Every gang member was loyal to his leader, in part because he or she knew that his or her personal comfort and safety depended on that leader's generosity.

Youth gangs selected members carefully and recruited the bravest and toughest recruits when possible. Initiation rites required committing a criminal act. The routine sport of the gang was theft and violence in all forms.

Lesser gangs in Hell's Kitchen allied with the Bowery Boys or a rival gang. There was safety in affiliation. An assault on anyone in the alliance called down swift retribution from all associated gangs and protected members across gang lines.

The police knew the pecking order of the gangs well and used that status to enforce compliance to certain unwritten rules. For instance, if a gang member or unaffiliated individual crossed geographic boundaries into neighborhoods outside Hell's Kitchen for thievery or rabble rousing, or caused any unacceptable grief to a respectable citizen in or outside Hell's Kitchen, retribution was usually swift and sure. In such instances the appropriate gang leader would be notified by a police liaison, after which the offending behavior would quickly cease, and often, so would the life of the offending urchin who had crossed the line. The street and river borders of Hell's Kitchen might as well have been high prison walls with sharp, barbed wire on top as far as the kids were concerned. The urchins were not welcome in the respectable neighborhoods and business areas of Manhattan. If an urchin crossed over, he or she would be caught and sent back to be dealt with by the gangs to enforce those barriers.

The citizens and elected officials of New York felt sorry for the orphans, but fear was a greater motivator than sympathy. Containment of the urchins in their ghettos was always the most critical objective of the police and city officials.

In return the police did not harass the established gangs unless absolutely necessary. Occasionally, they provided favors, up to and including clubs, knives and other coveted weapons to strong leaders. They did draw the line at the distribution of guns. However, passing guns to gangs still occurred clandestinely by rogue policemen seeking illicit favors, usually of a sexual nature.

Each Christmas, when the police dispensed gifts or food from some well-intentioned philanthropist or organization, they passed the booty to the most powerful gangs for distribution.

The cops knew they were playing with fire. All knew these youth gangs bred future criminals who they would probably have to face someday. But it was such a seductive control mechanism because it made their job in and around Hell's Kitchen infinitely easier, so they found it irresistible. It was just the way things worked in Hell's Kitchen and few ever questioned it.

In 1884, the youth leader of the Bowery Boys was a fourteen-year-old adolescent named Christian Gunther. He was over six feet tall and broad at the shoulders. He was also lightning-quick, powerful and, unbefitting his first name, utterly ruthless. The Bowery Boys had adopted him and he quickly became a legend on the streets. He rose rapidly through the ranks and became the gang's leader by age 11. He looked and acted much older.

By age 14, he was a master at evoking respect and fear in the children and adults with whom he dealt. Word on the street was that he was responsible for more than one death and a bevy of lesser crimes. To those who did not know him, he appeared to be the epitome of violence and brutality. To his gang members, he was a generous, steady, smart and innovative leader who commanded their loyalty. But even inside his gang, no one considered him a close friend.

He had steely blue-gray eyes that never seemed to blink. When he stared at a person, whether a gang member, a policeman or a victim, his gaze could mesmerize. He seldom smiled, and when he did, it was more frightening than when he did not. He never raised his voice. He understood the advantage of listening over talking. He was seldom known to joke or rough-house with his comrades.

He had been in numerous street fights and had never lost. He never showed mercy to his opponents, hitting them with everything he had, even when they were down. This was particularly so for adults who attempted to take advantage of his gang. Two such instances had gained him his reputation as a killer. When he did speak publicly, it was generally for threat. His voice commanded respect. Only infrequently did he need to reinforce it with violence, but when he did, he left nothing to the imagination.

He was endowed with invaluable characteristics that worked flawlessly for the benefit of his gang. He was smart, insightful, fearless and totally oblivious to danger. He was a careful student of human nature, always interested in what made a particular person tick. When troubles occurred in Hell's Kitchen involving the Bowery Boys, he was not always visible, but there was never any doubt that he had pulled the strings. The police consulted with him regularly on peacekeeping matters in Hell's Kitchen.

He reported to an even more infamous figure in New York, a man named Chuck Connor, who was connected to prominent adult crime syndicates as well as to leaders of legitimate political organizations. Connor was a dashing, but harsh, character who had already become a Manhattan legend.

By late 1884, Christian seemed more withdrawn than usual to those who knew him. He had already served three years as the gang's leader, which was a long tenure, and he was anxious to move on to the next level. He knew he could succeed--lesser leaders had--but he had one major problem. He had no capable successor. His lieutenants who might have fit the bill had died in gang fighting during the last two years.

A leadership succession plan was a pre-requisite for Gunther's graduation to an adult gang. Christian had hesitantly recommended some of his lesser lieutenants to Connor, but all had been summarily rejected. Christian knew he needed to find a suitable replacement soon or his promotion could be in jeopardy. He fretted about Connor's pickiness and his seemingly cavalier attitude toward holding him back. But he was a good soldier and followed orders, even when he believed that they were not in his own best interest.

Christian's own considerable skills had worked against him. Connor and his adult associates had been spoiled by his leadership. His youth gang was widely considered the most effective (and most lucrative) on the streets. They knew he needed to move on, but they hated to lose what he brought to the table. He knew all this, and even understood it, but it was still deeply frustrating. He thought it fundamentally unfair and, in his most private moments, he began to question the very system that had brought him to power.

Actually, he thought that he had found a potential successor. He had kept his eye on the boy for over a year, but there was a problem. When asked to join the Bowery Boys the candidate had repeatedly refused. He had also declined to join every other street gang as well. Ultimately Christian's surprise at the boy's demurring turned into frustration. Time was passing. There would need to be training and the time to build acceptance in the gang and with the adult bosses. This boy was an outsider and little known.

He considered threatening the boy, but he had watched him closely and he suspected that threats wouldn't work. He even considered having him strong-armed by "unknown" thugs to inspire him to join the safety of the gang, but this boy was big and smart and a good fighter. Somebody was likely to get seriously hurt, probably the boy himself, but also some Christian's own people. That would not be well received by the bosses.

To make matters worse, Christian had talked personally with the boy more than once and liked him. He was surprised by that. He seldom liked anyone. For all those reasons, he hesitated to push him unless absolutely necessary.

Christian had assumed that he would eventually identify something the boy wanted or needed, or someone close to him that needed the gang's protection—anything with which to negotiate--but to date, he had found nothing. The boy seemed connected to no one. He came and went quietly, almost like a ghost. Christian had no clue where he slept at night and none of his gang had been able to find out. By late 1884, Christian was becoming increasingly impatient. The boy's time was running out.

Chapter 4

The girl's name was Anna Murphy. The Irish version of Anna was "Aine", which was the name given to her at birth. That was what she was called throughout her young years in her homeland, but her father changed it on the voyage to America, explaining that the name, Anna, would better fit the new land to which she was sailing.

She didn't like the change at first. She preferred Aine, which stood for "splendor and radiance" in her home country. Her father had told her the folktales of her original namesake, a famous Irish queen. He said she was "the best hearted woman who ever lived, lucky in love and money" and that Anna would be just like her. Anna liked that she had been named after a queen.

Now her name was all that was left for her and she no longer felt lucky. She had entered the streets with the clothes on her back, her name, a comb and a family photo she had taken with her to her mother's grave because it was the only one she had of her father and she wanted something of him to be there too. Her dress, now torn and filthy, would not last much longer, but she doubted that it would matter.

She had thought about changing her name back to Aine on the day she came to the streets, but her father had given it to her and she honored his memory by leaving it alone. Anyway, the name of a street orphan seemed of little matter. No one had asked; no one cared anymore who she was.

On the first day on the streets, she studied the photo closely. It was of the three of them together, her dad and she smiling as she sat on his lap, her mother sitting beside them on the arm of the chair, staring soberly at the camera. Apparently it was not proper for a woman to smile when her picture was taken, although Anna was never sure why. Perhaps her father shouldn't have smiled either, but she doubted that he would have been able to keep from doing so even if he had tried.

Late on the first day, without thinking, she absently took out the comb to brush her hair as she walked along a bustling street. It was snatched violently from her hand by a boy not even as tall as she, his dirty fingernails scratching her as he jerked it loose.

"Give it back!" she exclaimed, shocked by his boldness.

"Sell you this for a penny, bitch," he said as he held it just beyond her reach.

She reached for it and he jerked it back from her.

"Give it back, please. My mother gave it to me."

"Aw, really now? Ain't that nice. Give me the penny, and you git it back."

"I don't have any money. Please give it back to me. It's all I have from my family."

He paused, looking contrite. She thought he was sincere. "Oh, I'm so sorry. I didn't know! That makes all the difference, doesn't it?"

He stepped toward her gallantly, comb in hand. She reached out for it, but he jumped back, grinning, then held it out toward her again. She lunged at him but he sidestepped her and stuck out his foot, tripping her. She fell awkwardly into the mud. He cackled and ran away. She never saw him or the comb again.

From dusk to dawn the ghetto was an overwhelming, abrasive world of constant motion and loud sound to her. At night it became an eerie, frightening and deadly landscape of shadows. On her second night out, there was a heavy downpour, a cold rain that drenched her and sent raw sewage--including human and animal feces--floating freely along the streets. Garbage and filth were everywhere. Feral dogs and rats competed with her for the few food scraps she found in piled garbage.

Most people in Hell's Kitchen tried to rid themselves of litter by burning it along the edges of the streets. There was nowhere else to dispose it. These never-ending fires burned at all hours, day and night unless it rained. Then they smoldered, waiting to be fed again. The garbage and coal smoke combined to create perpetual, stinking smog that made her cough.

The buildings along the streets and alleyways of Hell's Kitchen were all of one color, a deep and dirty charcoal gray, but not by design. Perhaps once they had been brighter, but no matter what their original hue, they all had soon turned to that same drab gray from soot of the burning coal and trash. Architectural individuality was no longer valued in Hell's Kitchen.

The windows of the buildings had become so coated with soot that it was a losing effort to clean them; and anyway, the soot protected those inside from prying eyes. The only light that escaped most windows was through the obscene finger paintings of older children who fancied themselves budding artists.

Anna was already exhausted and dangerously malnourished by the time she entered the streets. Her condition quickly grew worse. Fed by depression, she no longer felt the urges of hunger, but she could not shut out the cold.

Wherever she went, she was accosted by street urchins, young and old. The youngest held out their arms and cried: "Help me! Me cold! Me thirsty! Me hungry! I scared!" At first she picked them up and held them. Some fell asleep within a few seconds in her arms; some, in their sleep, tried to nurse. But eventually, when they understood she too had nothing to offer, they squirmed until she set them down and they toddled off. She wept each time they left. Eventually, she refused to pick up a pleading child. In the cold light of one morning, she found a child she had held the day before, frozen and mutilated. She didn't know if the mutilation was from feral dogs or from violence.

The older children were not friendly to her. The only attention they gave was to harass her. Occasionally, she was pushed or shoved for sport until she slipped and fell to the dirty, wet or frozen ground. Her miserable clothing was thoroughly caked with mud. She tried to wash it off, but the only available water was from mud holes. That water dried and just made her clothes stiff and dirtier. Her long hair had become matted and tangled.

She kept her head down and tried to stay out of the way. She never looked anyone in the eye. She lost all meaningful human contact. She wandered the streets aimlessly by day and spent her nights lying on grates or leaning near broken windows to soak up what little heat escaped to the street. When she could not find that, or when threatened, she hid behind trash bins, or in tight alleyways, or anywhere that offered some protection from the elements and the violence.

Her gait became unsteady. She moved like a drunken person. She began mumbling to herself as she staggered along. The other children thought she had gone mad and were not at all shocked by it. They had seen it happen before.

Had she looked even partially healthy, she would have been snatched by some enterprising pimp and cleaned up for the sex trade, but her rapidly deteriorating condition, her filthy, torn dress and the mud caking her body masked her attractiveness. She had become a rail-thin, miserable specter with a look of death that was all too well known on the streets.

She drank water infrequently, finding it only occasionally by watching where the other children drank, including from mud holes. On rare occasions someone discarded a moldy piece of bread or a cracker in front of her. She picked it up and ate if she could get to it before the younger children, dogs or vermin. If they got to it before her, or snatched it from her hands, she didn't fight for it. If she smelled food in a trash container, she sometimes dug it out and ate it, but she did it out of habit, not from conscious desire. She was never really that hungry.

Each night, before fitful sleep, she prayed to the God who had abandoned her family. Her mother and father would not have liked her prayers. She asked God for a merciful death in the night. She wanted to go to her father and mother if that was truly what happened—to oblivion if not. She awoke disappointed each morning.

By the end of her second week on the streets, her condition had deteriorated so rapidly that each passing hour brought her closer to the answer to her prayers. On that evening, as the darkness settled, she was too weak and disoriented to remember to hide. She slumped over in the middle of a dead-end alleyway into which she had wandered, violating one of the most critical laws of the street that even the youngest child had learned. One had to find a hiding place as dusk approached. Little children, playing with seeming abandon in the daylight, whimpered as the shadows deepened, and ran for cover, fearing the real monsters that would soon be among them. Because the he nights belonged to the gangs.

The alley Anna had entered was not far from the entrance of the building that housed the Bowery Boys. As she half fell and half sat down, she slumped over slowly until her elbow hit the ground and held her up like a prop. Five members of the Bowery Boys came down the main street on their way to their dormitory, including Christian Gunther himself. One of the boys, Gunther's current lieutenant, Big Mike, spotted her not more than 30 feet into the alleyway. He pointed her out silently to the rest of the group.

At first they saw no movement and thought she might be dead, but since she was still partially sitting up, they decided to check her out. As they approached, Anna sighed and began to mumble incoherently. Then she moved her arm and her upper body listed all the way over exposing the calf of one of her legs.

"Will you look at that, now!" exclaimed Big Mike. "I think we got us one still kicking here."

Four of the boys moved up both sides of the alley, trying to detect a trap. It was highly unusual for a girl of this age to be out alone on the streets at night. Perhaps she had been beaten and left for dead.

Christian Gunther stayed at the opening of the alley. He wasn't going to stop his mates from their fun but he didn't feel like participating himself. Even from a distance, he could tell this girl was near done.

The four boys finished their scouting and came back to stand over her. They then realized Christian hadn't joined them. He would be given first dibs if he wanted it, so they waited; but still he didn't come. Big Mike finally called back to him. "You coming, or not?"

"Na, have your fun if that's what you need. I am not in the mood. I think I'll head on home. Just watch for traps. This all looks too easy. She's not a child. Be careful of a setup."

Mike responded impatiently. "We checked the alley. It's short and there ain't nobody in here 'cept her." But Christian's admonition made the boys nervous and hesitant to make their move on the girl. This could be entertaining diversion, but none of them wanted to take a lump for it. They scouted the alleyway again and came back to stand over her. It was obvious that she was not right. She was still mumbling and hadn't acknowledged their presence.

Big Mike, who carried a staff instead of a club, had hooked one end of the rod under the edge of her dress and slowly moved it up her leg. Anna finally recognized that she was not alone, and wearily opened her eyes. She didn't protest or try to move, but she understood what was happening. She had heard other children talk of it in whispers. It occurred to her that she should be frightened but she was just too tired. With the huge boy now leaning down directly over her, she closed her eyes and hoped it would all be over quickly.

The boys, still cautious, were surprised that she offered no resistance. Big Mike was disgusted. "She's nigh done in. Won't be much fun, but still…" He laughed and reached down, pulling her dress roughly up to her waist. She was so skinny and muddy that it repulsed him for a second, but he hadn't had much fun with a girl lately, and a dirty girl was better than no girl at all, even a starving rag doll.

He fumbled at the rope holding up his trousers. The other boys, anticipating their turn, also began to loosen the strings of their trousers, licking their lips and watching Big Mike as he got down on his knees between the girl's legs.

Christian had watched this little adventure long enough. He was tired and ready to get off the streets. He turned away to go on to their headquarters.

Chapter 5

Ben McDonald was named after his grandfather on his mother's side. He was the oldest child in a family of six that included a harried mother and a violently abusive alcoholic father. Emily, Ben's mother, spent most of her time and energy trying to protect her children from her husband's wrath--usually unsuccessfully. John was a mean drunk, a bully whose drinking enhanced his pleasure in causing pain to those around him, particularly to his family.

Ben was the intended target for much of the abuse. For as long as he could remember, and for reasons he did not understand, he was the special object of his father's hatred. It was always dangerous for him when John was drunk, which was most of the time, but still harrowing even in the rare times he was not, because John's hatred for Ben was always there, drunk or sober.

Ben's other three siblings, ages three, five and six, included two younger sisters, Julie and Alyssa, and a little brother, Matthew, who tagged after Ben wherever he could and wailed out when he could not.

John seemed to have a warm spot for Matthew and seldom struck or yelled at him. But Matt was old enough to understand John's wrath and he ran to his favorite corner for safety whenever John's tirades began, holding his ears and crying until it all stopped. Then he would try to make the hurt go away by repeatedly kissing and hugging whomever John had just finished beating. Surprisingly, John never seemed to pay much attention to Matthew's attempts to right his father's wrongs.

The family lived in a shabby, two-room apartment in a run-down tenement complex. It included a larger room for cooking and dining, and a bedroom for the parents. The furniture was sparse, a feeble table and five rickety chairs in the main room and a bed in the other. The apartment came with a small cooking stove that provided the only heat. Over time, John had sold all the family's remaining furniture to buy his drinks during their stay in Hell's Kitchen.

The family's shabby clothing resided in wooden crates along the edges of the walls in the bedroom and main room. The children slept on the floor in the main room on thin pallets in summer. They slept huddled together under those same pallets in winter when it was cold. John refused to allow the cook stove to be used for anything but cooking. He said that the coal was too expensive. There was no ventilation for the summer heat in the main room. The only window in the apartment was in the bedroom.

Both parents were well educated and both were native-born, unlike nearly everyone else in their tenement. John spoke flawless English and tolerated nothing less from his wife and children. He zealously corrected their grammar at every opportunity, punctuating his lessons with a slap of his hand when they misspoke. After the correction, John would repeatedly expound on why a particular word or phrase was objectionable, and always end his instruction with:

"We are not illiterates! We are not ignorant immigrants who can't speak English. They should not even be allowed into this country to compete with its true citizens. They will die as paupers in this God-forsaken ghetto. We are here temporarily until I get back on my feet. I do not want you to associate with them. You will never befriend them and remain under my roof."

Despite his elocution demands, John denied his children the

opportunity to attend the local public school. He did not want them associating with the "riff-raff" of the neighborhood. Matt was too young to go and, according to John, formal education wasn't necessary for the girls.

That left Ben. John took his greatest pleasure in denying Ben the opportunity for school, just because he knew Ben wanted to go so badly. Emily disagreed but John's vote was supreme. She pleaded with John on Ben's behalf until he told her that if she didn't stop hounding him, he would put the boy out the door. She feared he would make good on that threat, so she stopped harping about it and tried to teach Ben while John was away, but she had no materials or books to help in his education.

When Ben turned eight years old, John insisted that he begin working. He found Ben a job in a run-down garment factory where Ben could work six days a week. John had a drinking associate who was the foreman at the factory. The foreman turned Ben's weekly earnings over to John each Saturday afternoon just before the bars opened. As horrible and tiring as the job was, it came with one blessing. It temporarily removed Ben from John's reach.

One Sunday, after a particularly harsh beating for some mythical cause, Ben waited until John had left and then, with quivering lip, asked his mother a question that he had been mulling in his head for a long time. "Mother, what makes him hate me so?"

She didn't answer at first. She just looked away. But Ben persisted, staring at her, waiting for the answer. When she finally looked back at him, he saw a deep anguish on her face and tears in her eyes. She tried to speak but her voice faltered and she had to cough to clear it. "It's a long story, Ben; something that I did back home in Indiana a long time ago, before you were born. Maybe I can explain it to you someday, but not now; you aren't old enough yet."

She paused and sighed deeply. "All I can tell you now is that it isn't you that he truly hates. When he sees you, it reminds him of someone else. I know it doesn't help, but you are not really his target. You just represent something he thinks is a wrong that he can't change. I'm so sorry I brought this on you, Ben. It's my fault. I'd do anything to make it go away, but I don't know how. I promise you that it is nothing you ever did—or that you ever deserved."

Then she pulled him to her, holding him so tightly he almost couldn't breathe. Her tears fell wet on his neck. Ben patted her on the back, trying to comfort her. "It's okay, mother. I understand. It'll be okay."

But he didn't really understand. Nor did he think it would be okay. He felt powerless in the face of his father's hatred and remained confused about its underlying cause. She hadn't answered his question, but he now knew that she believed something she had done had caused John to hate him. "Someday," he thought, "I am going to find out what she means and I am going to stop him from hurting us!" With that thought, he fully realized for the first time that he hated his father. He knew that wasn't right, but he couldn't help it.

Emily was the stabilizing force in Ben's life. Their bond ran deep and he believed with all his heart that it would never die. At least he had that to help him through the bad times. She was smart and caring and beautiful, and she would always be there for him, no matter how bad it got with his father.

For her part, Emily held out no hope for herself. She knew she was being punished for past sins. But she did still hope for her children, particularly for Ben who, even in his earliest days, showed a high degree of intellect and curiosity. She continued to dream of school for him. She knew he dreamed of it as well—that he wanted it more than anything else. But John finally halted those dreams by beating her to the floor one day in Ben's presence when she slipped and brought it up again. He said that the boy was working now and that's all he was good for. He turned on Ben and beat him too, ordering him to stop pestering his mother for something that would never be granted. If he didn't, his mother would get what was coming to her again, only worse. Ben refused all lessons from her after that.

John despised Ben exactly as much as Emily loved him. He had determined long ago that it was this illegitimate, unwanted child who was responsible for ruining his life. From the day Ben could toddle out from his mother's protective arms, John had taken every opportunity to inflict pain without actually killing the boy. He thought it might break her down if he went too far with him. John still needed her around for his occasional sexual urges and to take care of the other children. He knew he couldn't afford prostitutes or housekeepers in his current financial state.

On the Saturday of Ben's eleventh birthday, Emily took a huge risk and planned a birthday celebration for him. He had never had one and she instinctively knew that her time with him was running out. For his gift, she purchased a new pocketknife with money she had squirreled away during the year from her housekeeping and laundry work. She didn't make much money because there wasn't much work to be had in Hell's kitchen, and she dared not leave the area to seek work in the better neighborhoods because of the danger to the children when John was at home. Pitiful as her earnings were, they were usually the only resource the family had for food.

John tracked her money like a hawk. When Ben's earnings weren't enough to support his drinking, he raided her money jar. Eventually, Emily started keeping a little of the money in her apron pocket to avoid him taking it all. The purchase of the gift and the baking supplies for the cake came from that pocket money. It was a great sacrifice to the family's food allowance, but she felt that Ben needed this one good thing to remember.

On that Saturday afternoon, the minute John left the apartment, Emily recovered the gift and baking supplies, along with a borrowed baking pan from an elderly neighbor woman. She quickly commenced baking, fearful that Ben would arrive before she was ready. As it baked, the children were inundated by the wonderful smell of the cake. They kept distracting her by asking to hold Ben's pocket knife. Emily allowed them that pleasure until nearly time for Ben to arrive, at which point she insisted that they wrap the gift. It was done with real wrapping paper with a bow on top. They had never seen anything like that before in their own house.

Ben arrived from work that day exhausted from another hard week. As he climbed up to the second floor and reached the apartment door, he smelled the cake and heard the excited chatter of his siblings through the thin apartment walls. He opened the door and they yelled, "Surprise!" as they ran to him, pulling him into the room and dancing around him.

When their mother said, "Let's sing!" they began singing happy birthday. They had practiced that song for days. Even little Matthew joined in at the top of his lungs, and what he lacked in words and tune, he made up for in enthusiasm.

Emily had practiced the song with them, all the while living in terror that one of them might slip and sing it around John. She needn't have worried. The children avoided him whenever possible and never spoke to him unless required. Singing around him, or any form of enjoyable activity, would never have crossed their minds.

The children adored Ben. He had been their protector all their lives. He acted as their true father and brother combined. As with the oldest child of most alcoholic families, Ben tried to be the glue that held his family together.

Unfortunately things did not go well for John as he made the rounds late that Saturday afternoon. When he arrived at the factory, it was already empty except for the foreman, who said the factory was closing immediately--something to do with poor fiscal management.

John sneered at the news. He had seen the filthy working conditions and constant turnover of the employees. The cloth from which the garments were made was shabby and cheap- looking. As he had picked up Ben's past wages, he had often thought that he could have made the place a financial success if he were managing it. He was sure the foreman was inept. He was not surprised in the least that the company had folded.

Nor was he particularly worried about the loss of Ben's job. There was other employment for a boy Ben's age if the parents were not too picky. The next job would probably pay even better than this one. He was pretty sure he could get Ben on at one of the meat processing or packing houses if he lied about his age. The only thing of any value about the boy was that he was tall and strong and looked older than his true age. He would take the boy out job hunting first thing Monday morning and get him relocated. The thought of Ben earning more money actually excited him and he cursed himself for not thinking of moving him sooner.

John spoke condescendingly to the foreman about the closing. "Doesn't surprise me in the least. It's obvious you didn't know how to run this place. I assume you have my son's money for me?"

John's attitude was the last straw in a very bad day for the foreman. He stared at John, realizing how much he disliked this miserable little man. He laughed bitterly and spoke sardonically, "Well, McDonald, if you run very fast, you might catch the owners of this dump on their way out of town and ask for your son's pay. I'm sure that, with your smooth manner and good looks, they will accommodate you. They weren't much interested in leaving wages with me, being the poor manager that I am to your trained eye. Nobody got paid today, including me, so just get the hell out of here and leave me be!"

John's face turned red and his anger flashed. He considered thrashing the foreman, but he was a big, tough old bird and John's good judgment prevailed. It might have been different if it had been a few hours later, but John was not yet drunk. He cursed the man violently as he left for the bars. He headed to a favorite bar that had once allowed him a few drinks on credit. He needed that credit again. When he got there he bellied up to the bar and said, "Give me a whiskey, Luke. I've had a rough day and I am parched."

The bartender knew John well, including where he got the money for his drinks. John had bragged about it often. "Gonna spend some of your boy's hard earned cash again tonight, are you, John?"

Normally John would have let that pass, even had a laugh about it, but he was already irritable. Tonight it rubbed him wrong. He raised his voice. "None of your damn business what money I spend tonight, Luke! Just give me the damn whiskey right now!"

The bartender loathed John. He was familiar with his type. He was an abusive loudmouth and a bully. Still, it wasn't his usual practice to ask John for his money in advance because he knew it might cause a scene. And Luke seldom had to. John almost always flashed his money around for all to see before his first drink. But tonight no money was flashed, and from John's reaction, Luke estimated that he might not have it. He set down a whiskey glass in front of John and held up a bottle, but didn't pour. "I'll need to see your money first, John; new policy here."

John's face went white, then his neck reddened, as he gave the bartender a vicious stare. It occurred to the bartender that this was an evil man who probably enjoyed hurting people when he had the chance, as he would have done now to him if he could. "When in hell was that new policy enacted, Luke? I am guessing that the board just met a second ago and passed it right there in your addled brain. You just took the initiative to make up that marvelous new policy all by your lonesome didn't you, Luke? I would complain to your chairman of the board, but I guess I'm looking at him; isn't that right? Now you give me that damn drink and stop your silly games or you will have reason to regret it!"

John had gotten louder. The noise in the bar became hushed but John didn't notice. Anger had replaced his reason. He would back this disrespectful bastard of a bartender down.

The bouncer, a big burly man, began to edge quietly toward the bar. The bartender smiled and tried to diffuse the situation. "Actually, John, I regret it already. Just show me a little cash and we'll all get back to our business here. That's not asking too much is it? You know we're a proprietary establishment. You're an educated gentleman aren't you, John? You know we can't just give our product away; that's not good business. You wouldn't accept that if you were in my shoes, would you? You usually show me your money. What's the big deal?"

John fumed a minute, embarrassed but not placated by the bartender's conciliatory language. "The big, damn deal is that the damn factory where my son worked closed today, so ask the foreman for his cash when he comes in here if you're going to ask me, or I might get the impression that you're discriminating, Luke! That's the big damn deal! Now pour that drink!"

Luke glanced over at the bouncer, who nodded. He was ready. Luke was tired of dealing with this loudmouth. "Well, sorry, John, but that chairman of the board you were talking about a minute ago just gave me another message that your credit's no good here anymore, so unless you produce some money, it'll be time for you to leave."

It was more than John could take--more, he believed, than any reasonable man could take. He lunged forward and swung at Luke across the bar. His arms were too short and he only landed a glancing blow, but it had a satisfying effect. Luke, backing away from Johns swing, slipped and fell backward, his elbow hitting the neatly stacked glasses on a shelf behind him. They crashed to the floor, shattering along the inner aisle.

John only had an instant to admire his handiwork. He saw a flash of movement in the mirror behind the bar and glanced up as the bouncer came at him. He turned to take a swing, but he was too late. The bouncer's fist, bolstered by iron knuckles he had slipped on his right hand, smashed into John's left cheek with a force that sent John sprawling to the floor.

The bouncer had very big hands; so large that he had to pay a local blacksmith to tailor-make those knuckles he now used so efficiently. The blacksmith had done a good job, deliberately leaving sharp edges on the front of the knuckles at the bouncer's specifications. The blow tore the left side of John's face wide open, ripping through flesh and muscle all the way to his cheekbone. His blood spurted bright red as he fell to the floor. The gash on his face extended from the corner of his mouth all the way up to the bottom of his left eye, which immediately blurred and began to close shut. As he tried to get up, the cut on his cheek gaped open exposing his inner mouth and the cheekbone. He was unable to recover quickly. As he rolled over unto his stomach on the floor, the bouncer kicked him violently in the stomach. John tried to crawl toward the barroom door, which pleased the bouncer. He didn't want to have to pick the bleeding slob up to throw him out. The bouncer kicked John again and again, each time propelling him a little closer to the door. John tried to help the process by crawling forward as fast as he could, but each kick took him off his hands and knees.

It took six such strategically-placed kicks before John half rolled, half crawled under the swinging doors. The last kick, applied from behind as he was nearing the swinging doors, was aimed just below his buttocks at his testicles. It launched him forward out onto the sidewalk in unspeakable pain. He began to vomit. He tried to get air back into his lungs, but couldn't. He lay in the middle of the sidewalk gagging, trying to catch his breath. The blood was still flowing freely from the face wound, pooling on the walkway. His vest and shirt were already a warm, gooey mess.

It was a busy night. The street was jammed with the weekend crowd. They walked around and over him on their way to their own activities. A big man shoved John's legs out of the way so a female companion could pass. Every movement caused John excruciating pain. He vomited again into the pool of blood near his head until there was nothing left in his stomach.

Then he passed out. As he lay there, unconscious, the bleeding slowly diminished. He finally came to and began to drag himself up by a lamp post. When he could, he staggered dizzily toward the only safe haven he knew, holding the torn skin on his face together with his left hand as he stumbled along.

He was still in intense pain when he reached the tenement but the bleeding had all but stopped. He continued to hold the two jagged flaps of skin and muscle on his face together. He could no longer see from his left eye. It was excruciating to climb up the two flights of stairs to his apartment, and it took him a while. He nearly passed a couple of times and had to halt his climb, clinging weakly to the flimsy stair rail, fearful that it might give way with his weight or that he might pass out. When he finally reached the landing to his apartment, he slouched down in the hallway. He remained there for a few minutes.

As he sat, he smelled the cake and wondered what fool in this wretched building had the money to waste on such luxuries. When he finally pulled himself up and staggered to his apartment, the smells became stronger. He finally realized that his own wife was that very fool! He leaned against the door, clearing his head and listening for noise inside. It sounded like a party in there! Despite the pain, his adrenaline began to flow. He had caught her in an act of pure sabotage! He waited in the hallway a little longer, nursing his wrath, building it to a delicious, sweet explosion.

She had obviously spent their money frivolously! Never again would she tell him she was saving the money for the family's survival. That was what she had always thrown into his face when he needed a little drinking money. She was spending it on luxuries when he wasn't around. She had destroyed his trust in her. She would never live this down as long as he lived. As he thought more on it, he concluded that this probably wasn't the first time she had wasted his money. He became more indignant. Her sins increased exponentially in his throbbing head.

To John, vengeance was a deeply satisfying thing. It had the taste of righteousness usually reserved to God Himself. In fact, John often justified his own actions by his interpretation of a vengeful Old Testament Jehovah, who meted out unmerciful justice to the unrighteous. Standing outside the apartment door, he channeled all the atrocities that had happened to him that day into the sweet justice he would deliver to his deceitful wife. He could barely contain himself. Even his l pain seemed to subside from the adrenaline now flowing through his body. He steadied himself and flung open the door.

Emily and the children were caught red-handed with the cake in their mouths. Their eyes reflected a terror that sent a shiver of delight down his spine. On his wife's miserable face was the most exquisite expression of guilt that he had seen since her shame in Indiana. His good eye took in the decorative wrapping of the small box on the table. It reminded him that she had, in passing, mentioned it was the boy's birthday before he had gone out that afternoon. But she had said nothing about a gift or a party.

The fury of his well-honed hatred, ignited by his afternoon of public humiliation and pain, came upon him in one great final surge. He moved more quickly than he even thought possible-- faster than his normal dexterity should have allowed. He reached Ben first, picking him up and flinging him across the room into the wall. The boy crumpled to the floor. Some of John's own blood stained the front of Ben's shirt.

John then turned on his traitorous wife. He landed a haymaker directly to her mouth and saw the delicious red blood spurt from the resulting split in her lip. It was a warming sight to him. He grabbed her collar and jerked her up off the floor, then slapped her across the face repeatedly with his left hand, forgetting all about his hideous, gaping cheek. He slammed his fist into her stomach. Air and saliva wooshed out of her mouth and she went limp. She would have fallen but he didn't choose to let her go just yet. This was just the beginning. He pushed her body against the wall with his left arm under her throat, cocking his right to smash his fist into her face again.

But just as he started to swing, he was stunned by a sharp blow between his shoulder blades. It was so powerful that it drove him forward into Emily. Righting himself, but still holding her up, he looked back to see what had hit him. What he saw was a chair in a demon's hands already flashing through the air at him again. At that instant that he realized his mistake by looking back instead of ducking out of the way. Had he done so, the blow intended for him might have smashed into Emily, and that would have been delightful justice. But it was already too late. A leg of the chair drove directly into his torn left cheek.

The pain that exploded through John's head this time was even more intense than from the initial brawl in the barroom. He howled as he sank to the floor, grabbing at his face. As he looked up in terror, he saw the chair rising again, and he saw an expression of fury on the boy's face that shook him to his core. At that second, he realized that the balance of power in his family had shifted and would never return to an equilibrium he could control. It also flashed across his mind that it might be a moot point since he might not even live to see the next day.

In terror, he pulled his hands up to cover his head and pleaded, "Please don't! Please don't". He lay cringing, awaiting a blow that never came. Eventually he raised his head to see the boy slowly lowering the chair. Ben was shaking violently now, and looked dazed. John realized this might be his only chance to get away. The pain in his face was horrendous as he crawled toward the bedroom, still fearing the attack to be renewed at any second. He dared not look back. He slithered through the bedroom doorway and pivoted his body back around to slam the door shut. He leaned against it heavily, gasping for breath. He became dizzy and passed out with his body still leaning against the door.

In the main room, air had finally returned to Emily's lungs. She lurched across to the bedroom door and grabbed the knob, holding it shut with every ounce of strength she had left. Ben's sisters and baby brother were paralyzed, cowering together in a corner of the room, their faces panic-stricken.

Emily knew that Ben had crossed a line of no return. He would not be alive tomorrow if he remained in the apartment. She screamed at him to come to her. He quickly came and kneeled beside her, thinking she was wounded. "You've got to get out of this apartment right now, Ben, before he comes back out! Get your clothes and run!"

He didn't move. He stood dazed, not understanding what she was saying. She reached up from the door and slapped him across the face. "You must get out of here right now! Do you understand me?!"

Finally, it registered to him what she meant. The full impact of what he had done came to him and he began to shake even more violently. His knees became weak. His mother still clinging to the bedroom door, reached up to pull him closer for a brief instant. She moaned and half whispered. "You leave now! You mustn't come back for a few days…maybe a week. Yes, a week! Take your clothes. Don't forget your coat. Oh, Ben, I am so sorry it's come to this! You were so brave!"

She began to wail, her voice at a high pitch. "I can't protect you anymore! You must go! I love you so much, but I can't protect you anymore! You must go right now and you must not come back for a while. Do you understand!?"

He did. He slowly and carefully removed her arm. He put his own arms around his mother's shoulders and hugged her tight as she pulled against the doorknob. He kissed the top of her head and turned away. He went to his brother and sisters and hugged each of them as they sobbed, their eyes pleading. "It'll be okay. I'll be back. I promise."

He got his coat but forgot to take his other shirt and pants. He picked up his gift in its open box and left the apartment, then the building, and into the night. He was immediately engulfed and swept along by a crowd of strangers. Despite the crowd, he felt frightened of the streets for the first time with no idea of what to do or where to go for a whole week.

John awoke an hour later and staggered into the main room, looking for the boy. Emily tried to keep him from leaving the apartment, so he knew that the boy was gone. Maybe he was still in the hallway. He shoved her to the floor and opened the door. The boy wasn't there. He'd gotten away.

A strange calm came over him. He turned back inside and jerked Emily toward him. To her surprise, he released her without hitting her. He awkwardly attempted to straighten her disheveled dress, an odd, totally foreign, gesture that confused and frightened her even more than being hit. He told her to go out and get some fresh water to bathe and bandage his wound. She did.

She finished cleaning his wound and wrapped a clean dishcloth around his face, which he held as he limped slowly back into the bedroom. He would deal with the situation tomorrow. The most intense pain had abated but his face and head still throbbed horribly. He wished he had a drink. He lay down on the bed. Sleep slowly came to dull his pain.

Emily and the children huddled together in the main room all night. The children wept themselves to sleep. Emily did not sleep at all. She was terrified of what might be happening to Ben. Her head told her that he was resourceful and safer there than here. Her heart had trouble with the logic.

John awoke late the next morning feeling slightly better despite his wounds. As he lay in bed, he began to think about what to do next and a brilliant plan came to him. Now was the right time to leave this God-forsaken hell-hole and take his family back to Indiana to claim what was rightfully his. New York held nothing for them now. All the jobs he had lost here were the result of miserable working conditions and unfair bosses who didn't realize true talent when they saw it. He was, after all, a well-trained and highly educated accountant.

But that no longer mattered. He would return to Indiana where he would demand his rightful inheritance from his parents instead of it going to that good-for-nothing bastard of a younger brother. The old man might be dead by now, and good riddance, but his mother would help him.

It was unbelievable to him that his old man would have passed over an elder son of John's caliber to give what was rightfully his to Jake. The business was probably in big trouble by now. It was John's birthright, and it had been stolen from him by his younger brother. But he would fix that now. Without his father in control, Jake could be handled; John could always handle his little brother. It would be easy to play on Jake's guilt; just as it had always been. He would even reveal the full truth if need be. He had been unfairly blamed for Jake's sins for far too long. There was a time when he still protected him, for reasons that even he couldn't understand, but he was wiser now and that time had long passed.

As he lay in his bed, still somewhat woozy from the loss of blood now caked on the bed cloth and his clothes, he vowed to moderate his drinking a bit and try to be a little nicer to the family; not that they deserved it, of course. The main source of his embarrassment was gone now and it would be better.

He wanted to act fast, before the prodigal son returned. He dragged himself out of bed and went into the main room. Emily and the children froze in place when they saw him. He walked over to Emily and took her hand. She flinched and tried to pull away, but he just laughed and held on until he could wrest the wedding ring off her finger. It wasn't much—he knew just how cheap it was—but every little bit would help.

He made her sew his cheek up with her needle and thread. It hurt, but it had to be done. Emily shaped a poor bandage and used string tied around his head to hold it in place. Then, he left the apartment without a word.

He walked to the nearest pawn shop and sold Emily's ring and his prized, expensive pocket watch, the last remaining gift from his father. He then headed for the train station to buy tickets. He would board his family on the first train bound for Indiana.

He was animated and almost friendly when he arrived back at the apartment, which terrified his family. He was gory looking with the deep facial wound still oozing around the bandage. He had to knock to get in because they had bolted the door from the inside after he left. He laughed at that.

At first Emily did not understand what had come over him, but she soon realized the reason for his good spirits as he instructed her to prepare the children immediately for a trip.

"John, I won't leave Ben alone in this city!"

He had anticipated that. He spoke quietly, almost gently.

"Oh yes you will, Emily. You see, I'm taking the children with me and no one will stop me. They're mine. They'll go with me—and so will you. Think about it. Do you really want them alone in my care? Will that be safe, Emily? Will our youngest survive without his mother?"

"Just think of it as a simple trade—his life for theirs. One for three. It's actually a good bargain, you see. On the other hand, stay if you will. I'll tell your family that you neglected the children. I'll tell them that our poor Benjamin suffered a terrible accident because you left him unsupervised as I worked; left him to his own whims to roam the streets. Tragically, he died violently by the hand of a youth gang. Your extreme guilt addled your mind and caused you to take up drinking despite my pleas for you to think of the rest of the children. You became a whore and refused to come home. It was all terribly sad. I'll weep as I tell them. I'll tell them other things as well, Emily. How you were an unfit mother for all the children. I can be convincing. You know that from personal experience, don't you?" He smiled at her.

She shuddered. She knew he would do exactly as he said. She knew he could take the children and would ultimately abandon them or, more likely, kill them. The stories he would tell about her didn't matter, but he would destroy her children. She was certain of it. "John, I promise I'll go back gladly with you if you will just wait a week."

He laughed sarcastically. "Oh, Emily! Emily! Do you really think I'm that stupid? I know the bastard will be back by then. We aren't waiting. The train leaves in two hours. That's all the time you have to decide."

"Come children, let's pack our things now." His voice was pleasant and enthusiastic—just another caring father taking his family on a trip back to the homeland.

The children remained frozen and helpless, looking at Emily. A large tear began to cascade down her face. The silence in the room was deafening. Finally, in a voice that sounded a hundred years old, she said, "Let's pack. We 're going home."

The packing took only a few minutes. She helped each child gather what little she or he had. When they were done, John told Emily to pick up the two crates of belongings as he walked out the door.

Emily told the children to follow. She pulled a small lead pencil from the pocket of her dress. In the corner on the floor, where the children slept, she scribbled one word in big letters. It was "Bloomington". She was afraid to write more. She yanked out a couple of strands of her hair and laid them across the writing.

Just as she finished and stood up, he came back into the doorway. "What are you doing!?"

She hid the pencil in her palm and turned toward him. "Just saying goodbye."

He smirked. "Good memories, huh?"

She walked out of the apartment behind him. He didn't notice the message she'd left for her son.

On the long train ride to Bloomington, John thought only once about the prodigal son. He regretted that he had not killed him by his own hand, but there was some justice in this way of doing it. The boy would suffer longer and would die through starvation or violence. He was sure of it. It happened all the time. The boy would get his just reward. He smiled at that thought and put Ben out of his mind. He looked out the window to the dawn of a new day for himself and his family.

Ben stayed on the streets for a week, just as his mother had requested. It felt like an eternity, full of fear and confusion. He was hungry, but that was not a new sensation. He was surprised to see an uncountable number of unsupervised, homeless children on the streets. He watched them forage through garbage bins in the early mornings for discarded food and play with seeming abandon during the day. Many of the children were as young as his little sisters and a few as young as his little brother. In his prior trips to and from work he had never really focused on these children. There were so many of them. He wondered how they survived. When night fell, they disappeared--except for older boys who roamed in groups.

He stayed in the shadows and watched the commotion. He hid behind boxes and under loading docks for shelter at night and slept fitfully. It was chilly, but the weather was not that much colder than in the family's apartment.

On the morning of the seventh day, Ben returned to the tenement, eager to get home, no matter what the nature of the confrontation with his father might be. He didn't really fear him anymore. If he was lucky, John wouldn't be there when he arrived. He dreaded the confrontation but it would be worth it to be back with his family.

He climbed the stairs to find the door slightly ajar. That puzzled him. He explored the apartment. Their clothing and the furniture was gone. There was nothing left. He searched both rooms but found nothing except a penciled word on the floor with strands of hair lying over it. By the length and color, he assumed they were his mother's.

The penciled word "Bloomington" was already shaded with dust. The name sounded familiar but he couldn't remember exactly why at that instant. He also couldn't figure out why she had written it on the floor—if she had. It looked like her handwriting and her hair, but maybe the hair had just blown there by accident. But that word had not been on the floor before. There was no other note, no explanation and no instruction—just that one word.

They were gone. They wouldn't have moved their clothing if they planned to come back. He found it impossible to believe that she'd just leave him. With a sickening feeling, it occurred to him that something terrible might have happened to her and his siblings. He knew that his father would not want him back again—had never wanted him--but she loved him and would not have left him voluntarily. He feared the worst for her.

He sat down in the empty apartment, immobilized. He had no idea what to do. As the hours passed, his fear and dread increased. He thought about having struck his father—knew a son shouldn't do that—but what else could he have done? He was trying to protect

57

his mother. That should count for something. His father had repeatedly told all the children that he owned them and it was within his right to treat them as he chose. He suspected no adult would ever come to his defense for what he did, except maybe for his mother.

He stayed there for a full day before the tenement manager came. "Where's your mom and pop, boy?"

He hesitated to answer.

"What's the matter, cat got your tongue?"

He shook his head.

"Well, then where are they?"

"I don't know."

"What do you mean, you don't know? Where are they? Did they take off without paying their rent? Damn them! It's the third time that's happened this week! Well if they're gone, you'd better go find them. You can't stay here. I'm locking the place up until I get the rent from your family or get new tenants. So get out and good riddance! If you find your sorry folks, tell them for me that I hope they rot in hell!"

Ben left the apartment and returned to the streets. He was really alone now. If he survived, it would be by his own will and nothing else. In the first days, full of loneliness and feelings of abandonment, he wasn't sure that he had the will or the ability to survive. But his instincts kicked in as the days passed. He was depressed but he did not give up.

He couldn't shake the sadness over the loss of his mother and siblings, and his confusion about what had happened to them. And gradually, something else crept into the recesses of his mind. It was a slowly growing fear of the unthinkable. Could it be possible that his mother had actually made the decision to leave him because of what he had done to his father? His head told him that wasn't possible; she would never have willingly done that. But during lonely nights in dirty alleys, or under loading docks infested with spiders and rats, his heart began to whisper something else.

Chapter 6

Ben became a quick study of his new environment. He saw that most kids joined a gang to survive. It was obvious why. Gang membership brought companionship and safety not otherwise available. Loyalty and affection among gang members was better than in many families—his for example. The first rule of any gang was that its members always supported one another, no matter what the cost.

Ben also considered joining and was tempted to do so numerous times, particularly when he was lonely, cold, hungry, or in danger. He understood how tempting it would be for orphans to make that choice. He didn't fault them. He just couldn't bring himself to do it. He had heard what was required of a new gang member at initiation and that he would routinely have to participate in or condone activities that were unacceptable to him. He decided that he would never join an organization that could be as abusive as his father had been to his family. So he remained a loner.

There were attempts to recruit him. He was petitioned by a number of gangs in Hell's Kitchen, including the Bowery Boys. For some reason, they were the most persistent. He declined them all but tried not to offend them in doing so.

One afternoon, as he was sitting on a crate, leaning back against the wall of a building, watching a group of children playing red rover, a large solidly built youth sat down beside him. He was shocked that he had allowed anyone to get that close without being aware of his presence. He was normally extremely cautious when anyone approached, but this boy had seemingly appeared out of nowhere.

His unexpected companion said nothing at first and they sat there, close together on the crate that wasn't more than four feet long, watching the children play for a time. Finally, the young man spoke, quietly, almost as if only to himself. "Funny, I never played that game. As long as I've been on the streets, you'd think I'd have played it once or twice."

Ben wasn't sure how to respond, so he remained silent.

After a brief silence, his companion spoke again. "Your name's Ben McDonald, right?"

"Yes, that's right."

The youth extended his arm sideways, without turning toward Ben. "I'm Christian Gunther."

Ben hesitated for just an instant when he heard the name, but then reached across his body and shook Gunther's hand. "Pleased to meet you, Christian. I've heard of you."

Christian smiled a little. "All bad, I'm sure."

"There was some bad and some good. The word I get is that you can be violent, but that you are the best there is at taking care of your gang." Neither of them had taken their eyes off the children's game and both spoke quietly.

"That's fair. I've been violent and it's my job to take care of my people. Sometimes that requires violence, but I've also been guilty of hurting people when I didn't need to. I don't know about being better at taking care of my people than any other gang leader, but I'll take that as a compliment. So, I have a question for you, McDonald. Some of my members have asked you to join us. You declined. As far as I know, you haven't joined any other youth gang either. Why not?"

Ben thought about the question, and then answered. "It's complicated for me. I'd like the companionship and I've heard that the Bowery Boys are the best gang in Hell's Kitchen. But I've also heard that new members have to prove themselves by hurting some other kid or some adult who is weak. I had enough violence in my own family before I lost them. I'm tired of it."

Christian paused. "Okay, I understand that." He paused, looking at the children playing and then resumed. "Believe it or not, sometimes I get tired of it too; more now, I guess, than earlier in my time on the streets. When I was younger, I didn't think about it so much, or I really didn't care is more factual, I guess. Now I tend to think about it too much and it's probably affecting how I lead. But it's been the rule of the gangs for a long time. It's a test to see how strong your loyalty is to the gang. It was in place long before me and it'll be here long after. Tell you what, though, you join us and I'll waive the initiation."

Ben looked over at Christian for the first time, surprised. Christian continued watching the game and didn't look back, but Ben could tell that he meant it. The word on the street was that Gunther never backed off his commitments. "If it's a tradition, why would you break the rule for me?"

Christian smiled. "I need you in my group. You're strong. You don't intimidate easy. Not many people would even sit here beside me and talk without fidgeting. You're either smart and comfortable in your own skin, or you are very stupid. I've watched you. You're not stupid. You could be influential in our team. We need people like you right now. And I also think you need us as much as we need you; maybe more. The survival rate isn't good on the streets when you're alone."

Ben reflected a minute and then responded. "But it's not just the initiation, Christian. Your gang is violent by nature. It preys on children and the weak. It takes what it wants whenever it wants and it doesn't care who gets hurt along the way. I've seen your gang do that. I can't help but wonder how I'd feel if my brother and sisters had been put on the street and your gang members got hold of them."

"I don't challenge your points, McDonald. But can you see any other way to survive on these streets? Nobody cares about any of us. They leave us all here to starve or make out the best way we can. We don't have families to take care of us. No other adults will come to our rescue. All we have is our friends in the gang. We can't leave. We can't even go into respectable neighborhoods outside the kitchen unless asked. We might as well be living inside prison walls. It's the same thing. We're nothing to society except trouble"

"Sometimes we do bad things. Sometimes it's to survive. Sometimes it's because we're bored or mad at the world and we take it out on each other. Some among us are pretty damaged, weird kids. I get tired of it too, but it's my job to take care of my people. I'm their leader. I'm the head of their family. I don't know another way to do it. I know I'm losing my stomach for this way of life, but I don't see a different way out as long as we are on these streets. Do you?"

Ben eventually shook his head. "No, I guess I don't. I avoid hurting people unless I'm defending myself, but that doesn't make me clean. I turn my head away when little children cry out for help. I know I can't really help them, so I just ignore them. I see some of them dead on the street the next day and it makes me sick, but I don't do anything about it."

"Maybe you could do more in the gang than out of it, McDonald. There are things we do that you don't know about. Think about it. We could use you." With that Christian got up and started walking away. As Ben watched him go, he couldn't help but notice how smoothly he moved for a big guy.

Before Christian had turned the corner, Ben called out. "Hey Christian!"

Gunther turned back.

"Thanks for the offer, and thanks for taking the time to talk to me. I don't get much chance for conversation anymore."

Christian paused, looking back at Ben. He smiled ever so briefly and nodded his head. He turned and disappeared.

Two months later, Christian appeared out of nowhere again to talk with Ben.

"So, McDonald, I must not be as good a salesman as I thought. You still haven't joined us."

Ben laughed. "Don't underestimate yourself, Gunther; you're an extremely good salesman. I am just a poor buyer. It was very tempting, and personally, I think I'd have felt good being under your leadership. But it's not right for me. Given what you told me, I'm not even sure it's right for you anymore. I know most of us can't get away from here, but I'd guess you have connections outside Hell's Kitchen. I don't know why you stay."

Christian didn't answer right away. From their prior conversation, Ben knew he chose his words carefully. Finally, he answered, "In part, I stay because I'm more like you than you think. I don't know anything else and my opportunities outside aren't any better than yours right now. If I do get to leave, it'll probably be to join an adult gang. I'd have a nicer place to live and I wouldn't be locked into these ghetto boundaries. That's tempting. And I probably wouldn't be responsible for anybody for a while, and that's even more tempting. But other than that, it wouldn't be much different. Being in an adult gang just means I'd be doing the same things we do here, but on a bigger scale. I've begun to sour on that some."

He paused, reflecting, then went on. "Despite what I just told you, you ought to join us. You need the safety and camaraderie of the gang. You need to belong—at least until you get older. After that, you can decide what you want to do. It won't be forever. You've got to be pretty miserable right now. I'd like to have you by my side. I think we could be friends. I don't have many and you don't have any. Why not give it a shot? If you can't tolerate it, I'll let you out. That's a special offer, Ben. No one has had that before. I won't talk to you again. If you don't come in, I'll not bother you again. But it'll be a mistake that you shouldn't make."

Ben nodded. "Thanks, Christian. I'd be lying if I said it wasn't tempting, and I'm grateful for what you offer. If I don't come in, it won't be because of you; it'll be in spite of how I see you. Under other circumstances, I think we could've been friends. It'll be a shame if I have to lose that opportunity." They parted on that note.

But despite the personal visits from Gunther, Ben didn't change his mind, even though he found himself constantly rehashing what Gunther had said. It surprised him that Gunther was so insightful and was fighting some of the same demons that plagued Ben. He knew he was flirting with trouble by not joining the Bowery Boys. Rejecting friendly invitations would eventually be seen as an insult. He became more cautious around the gangs, avoiding direct contact unless absolutely necessary. He was forced to fight with gang members on only two occasions, but the skirmishes were brief and he held his own.

Gunther never approached Ben again. Weeks passed and Ben remained alone. He increasingly detested what was happening to younger children on the streets. He realized that their fate could easily have happened to his sisters and little brother. Had they had been thrown onto the streets with him, for their protection, he would've had no choice but to enroll them and himself in a gang.

He saw hundreds of small children during his first year on the streets and he knew they had no real chance for survival. He watched them beg for help when none was available. He saw them die of starvation, cold and violence. Being on the streets was bad enough at his age. It was unthinkable what these small children must be experiencing.

He also saw some children die without any seeming reason. They didn't appear physically ill, nor did they look as though they had reached starvation levels. The weather wasn't cold. They simply grew lethargic and withdrew from life. They seemed to consciously choose to die. He wondered if children could die from sheer loneliness. Sometimes he, too, felt death would be better, even for himself. And sometimes, he saw some of the youngest children just disappear overnight, never to be seen again. There were lots of rumors as to why, but no one really seemed to know for sure.

In his early days on the street he had tried to comfort some of the young children who sought his help, but as soon as he did, more children appeared, pleading for assistance that he couldn't give. He ultimately withdrew and avoided direct contact with them, even yelling at them to drive them away. It sickened him to do this and to watch them suffer without trying to help.

He became that strange loner that many noticed but no one knew. He was tall and powerful-looking and carried himself with dignity. Even the police noticed him and wondered who he was and why he was there. He didn't seem to belong to a gang or be connected with any anyone else. That made them nervous. It was unnatural in Hell's Kitchen.

He didn't know that he was a frequent topic of the gangs, who were also uneasy about him. Some members bragged about what they'd do when they confronted him, but he never seemed to make that necessary, and no one seemed that excited about taking him on if he wasn't causing trouble.

And then there was that odd message from Christian Gunther regarding Ben. Why would the leader of the Bowery Boys declare "hands off" for a loner who had repeatedly refused to join them? It made no sense.

Ben turned 12 a year after entering the streets as an orphan. He was growing taller and stronger even with the scarcity of food. Being away from John was good for him despite his stark existence.

Occasionally, in passing, he thought about the contrast between himself and his father—not just the difference in values, but also the physical characteristics. John was a little man physically. Ben realized that he was already much taller than his father. It occurred to him that John would not have tolerated him under his roof for long even without that confrontation on his eleventh birthday. Ben would have become too much of a threat.

After the first year, the gangs noticed that he disappeared most nights only to reappear on the same streets the next day, as though he had just been in a nearby alley or under a warehouse dock. But they knew all those nighttime haunts and he hadn't gone there. They'd checked for his whereabouts repeatedly. Not knowing his habits worried them. But Ben had discovered a secret retreat that he was careful to protect from the prying eyes of other urchins.

He had grown tired of having to search for a safe place to sleep every night and he hated the unceasing noise and commotion of the streets, both day and night. His worry about being attacked by gang members caused him to change his sleeping location frequently. He never slept well; he was a light sleeper from his days with his father and that continued on the streets. He was frequently jolted awake during the night by the noises around him. He awoke each morning feeling as tired as when he had laid down to sleep. "There's got to be a better way," he thought, "but if there is, surely somebody else would have figured it out long ago."

On the other hand, he knew his situation was not typical, that most kids who had been on the streets for long would be resting under the protection that their gangs provided. "Maybe, just maybe, there aren't enough loners like me to have discovered a safe place." So he began to look for something that others might have missed.

He started by watching where other urchins slept who were not associated with the gangs. Many sought a quiet alley with nooks behind trash bins, sometimes even crawling inside when they became frightened enough. In cooler weather, any warm place was an attraction. Children would take chances if they found a heated grate or any other place emitting heat.

Some climbed down manholes and into underground sewers, but

when he tried that, the sewers he entered were so filthy, damp and full of rats that he rejected that option. Underneath warehouse docks, or on top of them behind stacked materials, were always popular places. Ben had often used these early in his time on the streets. Some urchins slept in coal chutes if they were left unlocked or if they could break into them, but these were unreliable, dirty and uncomfortable options.

Breaking into any building in Hell's Kitchen was always risky. Abandoned buildings housed gangs. Occupied buildings had bars on the windows and doors, or were often guarded by vicious dogs. In the case of retail stores, proprietors usually lived above the business. They were not hesitant to shoot at intruders first and ask questions later.

Ben changed his strategy and began to look for where gang members and other urchins didn't go at night. That was when he struck pay dirt. Almost no urchin, gang member or not, was comfortable in graveyards. If they went there, it was on a dare and not for long. The Urchins were a superstitious lot, generally uneducated, and readily believed in haunts and ghosts.

Further, they almost never hung out around churches. As a rule, they mistrusted and disliked church people, who pretended to be righteous but never offered real help. Church people were always trying to "save their souls" or place them in an orphanage. Orphanages meant starvation, brutality and the lack of freedom. Anyway, churches made it clear they didn't want urchins around. They put bars on their windows and some even used dogs at night, just like the business establishments.

Ben, on the other hand, had no fear of churches or graveyards. He knew he was too old to be a target for placement in an orphanage and he was skeptical about ghosts. He toyed with the idea of finding a nook somewhere on the grounds of a church building but had no luck when he tried. The churches of Hell's Kitchen had long since child-proofed their facilities and warehouses.

But graveyards were a different matter. They were easily accessible and never guarded. There were some that were so old that few people ever went there in the daytime, much less at night. In fact, they were among the few quiet, peaceful places left on Manhattan Island other than the new Central Park to the North, beyond Hell's Kitchen and out of reach.

One such cemetery was behind a recently constructed catholic church, called The Church of the Sacred Heart of Jesus, up toward the northern edge of Hell's Kitchen, just beyond 51st Street. It had initially adjoined property owned by a Baptist Church that had disbanded after more than a century of existence due to dwindling membership. The cemetery was bordered by two narrow alleyways running north and south, by the new church grounds on its southern edge, and by a fence with a line of tall trees and brush to the north.

Street urchins were not frequent visitors in that area. They seldom spent much time up toward the northern boundaries of Hell's Kitchen, which was a bit more residential and affluent than areas to the south.

Ben could see that the cemetery was not well-kept. Some of the headstones were leaning, the grass was tall and fallen limbs lay rotting under the trees. The gates of the Mausoleums hung askew on broken hinges. If one were superstitious and feared ghosts, this old cemetery would be a very scary place.

Ben found himself drawn to it for exactly the opposite reason. To him, it was peaceful and quiet. He came back time and again to view it, resting behind bushes along its bordering alleys. Initially, he chose not to enter it directly. He just observed it carefully. He saw that few adults ever visited the graveyard. Those who did were generally old and infirm. There were never many flowers on the graves, even in times of memorial, the grass was long, and there were always weeds at the cemetery's edges.

One day he arrived late in the afternoon and hung out until dusk. As usual, the cemetery was empty when he arrived. At sunset, it seemed particularly peaceful and quiet. He was weary and decided to sleep in the area that night. Nothing was going on at the church to the south so there was little risk he would be discovered.

In the late twilight, on a whim, he entered the cemetery. He walked among the gravestones, trying to read the dates. The most recent gravestones, down close to the new church, were all together and dated from 1860 to 1865. They were obviously from the civil war. The names on the gravestones were mostly men and the majority of the gravestones were uniform in size and style. They filled a whole section of the graveyard. It was the only area that was better manicured. The few visitors that came usually went there.

He left that area of the cemetery and moved to its north side to explore the mausoleums. The stones and mortar were faded and old. As the day's last light faded, he reached the largest mausoleum at the very back of the cemetery, against the tree line. The mausoleum's heavy Iron Gate hung half open and askew on its hinges. When he moved it, it made a loud screech that caused him to jump and duck to the shadows, prepared to run for cover, but no one came to investigate.

The tomb was large. He slid past the outer gate and made his way down two steps to reach the stone floor. With the little light that came through the outer gate, he could still make out dusty coffins on either side of chamber, stacked on low platforms. Spider webs were everywhere and he had to cut through them with his arms to keep them from his face. He worried about being bitten by a spider as he tore them away. He paced off three long steps to the back wall, reaching out to touch it since he could not see it in the dark. He sat down and leaned against the wall. He was weary and it occurred to him that it might be a good place to spend the night. The floor was relatively dry.

As he leaned back, he became aware of a protrusion pushing into one of his shoulder blades. He tried to ignore it at first, but then became curious as to what it was. He shifted around and touched it with his hand. It felt like a rusty handle. He ran his hands along the wall on either side of it. The surface felt different than stone, more like metal. He traced the edges of the metal with his fingers. Maybe it was a mural built into the wall. It seemed to be about 3 feet square. He felt for raised or indented letters or pictures, but found none. If the protrusion was a handle, this must be some sort of door to the outside, but why would there need to be another exit from the mausoleum?

He took hold of the protrusion and tried to move it. It didn't budge. He pulled it toward him, thinking it might have a spring release mechanism, but again, it didn't move. After fiddling with it for a while, he decided to give it up, assuming that, if it was a handle, it had frozen with rust. But as a final try, he stepped up and balanced a foot onto the handle, leaning against the wall for leverage. He placed his full weight on the protrusion, but there was still no movement.

He leaned his body further into the wall and bounced on the protrusion a little more. He thought he felt a slight give. He bounced again, this time with more force. It moved downward an inch or so. Through repetition, the protrusion began to angle down, until suddenly his foot slipped off, banging his ankle and causing him to curse in pain. He rubbed the ankle until it felt better. He began to work the protrusion up and down with his hands, loosening it a little more each time. He began to sweat from the exertion. Finally, the handle, if that is what it was, turned all the way down and he heard a click. He pulled and some sort of trap door swung open with a screeching noise.

He cautiously stuck his arm into the space beyond the door to see if the opening was to the outside of the mausoleum. He did not encounter brush or feel the outside air. Instead, his hand felt even more spider webs and empty space. He pulled his hand back and leaned his head and upper body through the opening. As he did so, he reached out and down to see if he could feel the ground or some sort of floor. His hand touched stone far quicker than he had expected. This was some type of floor, but significantly higher than in the main chamber, only a foot or so below the bottom of the metal trap door. He backed off, and holding the upper edge of the metal door, lifted his body up and slid through the opening, feet first, into the space beyond. At first he could see nothing.

He lay still on his back, and reached up. His hands touched nothing. He got onto his knees and reached overhead. His fingertips barely touched some sort of ceiling. He would not be able to stand without bending over, but he could sit or kneel comfortably. Although it was dark, as his eyes adjusted, there seemed to be weak light entering an area high up on what must be an outer wall in front of him.

He reached left, then right. He touched nothing. He scooted left, reached out again, then scooted left some more. This time he easily touched a wall. He repeated the process to the right and found the wall on that side. He judged the width of this back chamber to be the same as the larger, outer chamber. He moved forward on his knees until he could touch the far back wall. It was a short distance, maybe six feet or less.

As he reached that wall, he was now sure that there was some source of faint light entering the compartment. He stood in a crouch, raising his head carefully toward the ceiling to avoid cracking it. There, just below the ceiling, was a narrow opening. He felt fresh air flowing in from the draft created by the narrow window and the open trap door behind him.

The window was about a hand width and maybe as long as the distance from his finger tips to his elbow. He could see that it was protected by some sort of metal grill or heavy screen. As his eyes adjusted to the dim light, he could see that the mausoleum's outer roof line extended beyond this wall about a foot or so. Someone had gone to some trouble to build that narrow window and still protect it from the elements. He guessed no one would see it from the outside unless they walked directly behind the mausoleum, and he could see that the brush on the edge of the cemetery had nearly closed off the space behind it. Someone would have to push through the brush to get to the back of the mausoleum.

He moved about the small chamber, expecting to feel a coffin, but he felt nothing. He explored the floor and traced the large flat stones by their grouted connections. The stones were cool, but not damp like that of the outer chamber. It all seemed very odd.

As his fingers moved across the stones, he felt indentions that might be carving, first on one side of the room, then on the other. The indentions seemed evenly spaced on each side of the chamber. He wondered if someone was buried beneath the stone. That could explain the higher floor. He could detect nothing else in the dark. The next time he visited, he would bring matches and a candle stub for a little light to explore the chamber better.

He finished cleaning away the spider webs in the inner chamber and closed the trap door. The room quickly warmed and was wonderfully quiet. There was a handle of the same design on the inside of the trap door. He tested it. It moved at the same time and direction as the outer handle. They were obviously connected. He lay down on the floor of the inner chamber and drifted off to a sound sleep. It was the most peaceful slumber he had yet experienced since coming to the streets.

It was daylight when he awoke. He could see the light filtering through the little window. At first he was confused by the quiet of his surroundings, but then quickly remembered where he was. As his eyes adjusted, he surveyed the inner chamber more carefully.

Its floor had a thick coat of dust. Remnants of the cobwebs that he had torn away hung from the side walls. The chamber's dimensions were about six by eight feet. He estimated the ceiling to be between four and five feet high. He guessed that the inner chamber's floor was at least 24 inches higher than the outer chamber, maybe more.

He could not clearly see the letters and numbers of the inscriptions on the floor, but he was confident that it was what they were. They were indeed equally spaced and parallel to each other on both sides of the room. He would have to wait for better light to decipher them.

He remained in the chamber all day. He heard nothing in the outer chamber or the cemetery beyond. It was wonderfully quiet and peaceful. He had water in a small stone jar he carried, a biscuit in his coat pocket and beans in a dented can, so he did not get thirsty or hungry.

At darkness, he exited the inner chamber after spitting on the hinges of the metal door to lubricate them. He re-entered the outer chamber and surveyed the graveyard through the gate. No one was in sight. He left the mausoleum and returned to the streets to forage for food and to refill his water jug. He also looked for discarded oil or grease can with a few drops to lubricate the hinges to the inner chamber's door and handle. His wish list included candle stubs so he could decipher the writing on the floor. He decided that, over time, he would create a cache of slow-perishing food and find larger containers to hold water.

He was excited about the mausoleum and its inner chamber. If he cleaned it up and found bedding, and if he was careful in his coming and going, it could be the safe haven he had been seeking.

In the coming weeks, he stocked the inner chamber with jugs that he filled with water from a cistern he found at the back of the church grounds. He confiscated food from the trash of area restaurants. He found stray boards at construction sites and shaped a base for his bed. He stole a bale of straw and blankets for bedding. He found a slab of cedar board slightly wider and longer than the chamber's little window and hinged it with wire so it would cover the window to avoid light escaping when he wanted to use his candles.

The mausoleum was definitely old. Its inscriptions dated to the mid-1700s and listed the name of the family. It must have been one of the first burial sites in the cemetery. He suspected it had been built by a lost generation since he never saw or heard any cemetery visitor approach it. It was at the very back of the cemetery. The tree line was within a couple of feet and bushes brushed against its back wall. Someone might get around the mausoleum from the outside, but they would be scratched by limbs in doing so.

Once he had cleaned the floor of the inner chamber and had candles, he could read the inscriptions in the inner chamber. There were two names, both of girls. According to the dates, both had died within a week of one another and both before their first birthday. He was sharing this room with little children. He felt close to them and offered his thanks for allowing him to use their resting place.

Each day before daylight, he left the mausoleum and made his way south to familiar haunts. On rare days, when he overslept and saw daylight through his window as he awoke, he didn't leave the chamber until the darkness of the next evening. When he returned to the area, he never entered the cemetery until after dark. He varied his routes to and from the graveyard, always fearing that he might be observed or followed.

And so his reputation as a loner who mysteriously disappeared at night and reappeared during the day continued to grow.

Chapter 7

It was in late November of his third year that Ben McDonald saw the girl appear on the streets, looking frail and wretched. He watched her but did not approach. Even from a distance it was obvious that she was in very bad shape. He doubted that she would last a week. He could tell that she had already given up on life. He seldom saw her forage for food. For some strange reason, it bothered him that she did not, but he wasn't sure why. It didn't really matter. Soon, she wouldn't need to.

Late one afternoon, about a week after he had first spotted her, he saw her again. Her gait was becoming unsteady and she seemed to be mumbling to someone, but no one was near her. It was easy to see that her time was drawing to an end.

At first, he thought that would be a good thing for her. She was obviously suffering. But as he watched this sad, haunted figure, a frustration that he could not explain began to build in him. Underneath her filthy, torn clothing and matted hair, he sensed that this had once been a beautiful girl. It should have mattered to someone she was starving to death. She might have been a future artist, a dancer, a nurse, a teacher or a mother if she hadn't been consigned to these streets. But none of those futures awaited her now.

And then an illogical thought captured him. What if he took her off the streets tonight? What if he fed her and nursed her back to health? What if he helped her learn to survive? Could he personally save her?

Even as those thoughts flashed through his mind, he rejected them as gibberish. Why was this girl any different to him than any other vulnerable child on the streets? He had tried helping before and it always turned out badly. So why was he even thinking this? He couldn't save anybody! He could barely survive himself! It would be too risky and complicated. He could never afford to get attached to anyone and try to keep them alive inside Hell's Kitchen. And it would be too costly for him to fail. He couldn't live with getting close to someone and then abandoning that person, like his family had abandoned him.

He watched the girl a few more minutes. He knew he should leave. He had delayed too long already. He should be near the cemetery right now. Night was on him. He saw her turn into a dead end alley with no good cover. Then he saw her sink to the ground in the middle of the street. So this was it for her then? What a horrible place to die. He slid back in the shadows to see if she might get up again, but she didn't.

He was torn. He could at least go get her out of the street and put her in some safer spot before he left so that she could die in peace. He had just about decided to do that when he saw the group of boys coming down the street. He recognized one of them. He was impossible to miss. It was Gunther himself.

Ben hoped they would pass by and not see her. He held his breath as they neared the opening of the alley. His chest felt tight. He had seen children being attacked by gang members before. If they saw her, this girl would likely be brutalized before she died.

They were almost past the alleyway. He released his breath in relief--but too soon. One of the gang, a very portly boy who was as tall, or taller, than Gunther, stopped and stared into the alley. Had they seen her? Obviously they had. Four of them, including the portly gang member, entered and headed toward her.

For some reason, Gunther had stayed at the entrance, watching the rest of his gang as they went in. The other boys walked the length of the alley and came back to stand over the girl. The heavyset boy yelled back at Gunther, who apparently wasn't going in. They walked the alley again. They were obviously nervous about finding her like this, out in the open. They came back and stood over her. The big boy dropped his pants and bent down to the girl. The other boys untied their belts, waiting their turns. They would gang rape her as she lay there dying.

A great rage came over Ben. He wished that he had acted earlier instead of hiding and procrastinating. He wished she had already died. But he had not acted when he could. Now, her last conscious memories would be of horror. Dying on the streets was one thing. Being raped when she was lying helpless and near death was another.

Big Mike had dropped his pants around his ankles and knelt down over her. He used his knees to spread the girl's legs. He thought, in passing, that her legs were long and would probably have been shapely had she not been skin and bones. He wasn't sure how old she was, but she was certainly not a child. This might be more enjoyable than he had anticipated. He ran his hand up her leg, which was still warm.

He became aroused and distracted—caught up in his own little erotic fantasy. He paid no attention to the three other boys standing over him. He vaguely heard a cracking sound from the entrance to the alley, followed quickly by a duller thud. Those sounds would normally have raised his hackles and caused extreme caution, but now he was oblivious to anything but the girl below him.

Christian, who had watched the beginning of the action in the alley, shook his head and turned away for home. In that instant he sensed, even before he saw, the flash of movement to his left. He lifted his left arm instinctively to fend off the blow that he knew was already on its way. That action probably saved his life.

A heavy object smashed into him with a force that ripped through the flesh of his forearm and shattered the bones midway between his wrist and elbow with a sharp cracking sound. He saw his left arm drop at an awkward angle and knew that could not be good. He felt no pain yet, but he knew it would come in a second. He started to yell to his mates. But the object was flashing again. He tried to turn out of its path, but he was too late. He felt a powerful blow to the back of his neck, sending him forward to the ground, losing consciousness as he fell.

The sounds from the main street did register with three of the boys standing around Big Mike and the girl. They looked back and turned toward the sound just in time to see a large dark figure already on them. They fumbled frantically to fasten their pants but it was too late. A swift demon was among them.

They saw glimpses of a large club as it struck them. Two went down immediately, both with blows to the head. As that happened, the third did get his pants up and fastened, and had reached for his club that he had carelessly dropped on the ground as he watched Big Mike on the girl. He retrieved it and sprang back up, turning in the direction of the attacker only to have a powerful blow hit him full in the face. He fell into an awkward heap, moaning.

Big Mike's pants were still in a knot around his ankles. By now he was aware of the attack. All his erotic notions had been replaced by a sickening sense of fear for his safety. He was in big trouble and he knew it. In only seconds he had seen his comrades immobilized and down on the ground. It was incredulous to him that they all went down so fast.

In the brief seconds that it took for him to realize that no one else was left standing, he realized his own predicament and tried to spring to his feet. He had always been awkward. Now that awkwardness put him at extreme disadvantage. He tripped on his pants as he tried to get up and sprawled down beside the girl. He cursed and rolled over unto his back, reaching for his staff. His clutching fingers missed it. He saw the attacker towering over him with a club. It was already in striking position with the club moving downward. He rolled to the right because the girl blocked his way to the left, but that was the wrong direction. He had moved into a perfect intersection with the flashing club.

The blow smashed squarely against his temple, reversing his roll and snapping his head back around, toward the girl. He felt the bones in his skull give way. It didn't really hurt. It just felt very odd. In his last seconds, he saw the girl's face right in front of him. She seemed to be asleep. With that fleeting thought, his world faded into oblivion.

Ben spun around looking for more gang members, still fueled by a massive surge of adrenalin. No one was standing. He crouched, still expecting a counterattack. He counted the bodies on the ground. His mind was racing. In the intensity of the moment, he couldn't remember if there had been more than four gang members in the alley. He looked back toward entrance of the alley. He wasn't sure where Gunther was, or whether he was still down. Having stopped, and finding no one left standing, adrenaline drained from his body as quickly as it had come. He lowered the club and started to shake.

For the first time, he felt intense pain in his hands from the deep splinters from the rough 2 x 4 oak board in his hands. He looked at the board, surprised. He had no idea where it had come from. He didn't remember picking it up. It was now cracked and broken, hanging at an angle. His shaking receded, but was quickly replaced with nausea. Through the board, he had felt the skull of the last boy give way and had heard the crunching sound. He saw how he now lay on the ground, unmoving and twisted in a heap. He suspected he had killed that boy and maybe some of the others as well. It made him sick to his stomach. Then he heard moaning sounds from two of the fallen gang members nearby. A final silent body lay at an odd angle a little further off, unmoving. Ben felt faint and wished he could sit down, but he knew he was out of time.

His own movements during the attack had felt eerie to him. The attack had happened in mere seconds, but it didn't really seem that fast to him. His movements felt like a slow motion dream--his own little violent ballet. He had felt no personal fear during the attack. Actually, he hadn't really felt much of anything but rage about what was happening to the girl. It was odd to him that the people he had attacked had all just seemed to be frozen in place, unable to put up any real resistance.

The board in his hand must still be green. It now felt heavy and awkward, but he hadn't felt its weight during the attack. It had swung so easily. Now, he looked at it as though it was a foreign object. He dropped it to the ground.

He looked over at the girl, lying silent and unmoving, her eyes closed, as if in sleep. He wasn't sure what to do next, but realized that he had to get himself and her away as soon as possible. He couldn't just leave her lying here. The rest of the gang might arrive at any minute if someone had heard the commotion, or if a gang member he hadn't seen had already summoned them. If he left her here, they would find her surrounded by their downed comrades and would either kill her immediately, or would torture her to find out what had happened. She wouldn't know but that didn't matter. They wouldn't care.

It was a cool night but he felt perspiration trickling down his forehead and back. He stood there a few more seconds, recovering control of his body. Then, he reached down and lifted the girl. He had expected her to be light—he had seen how thin she was in daylight—but he was shocked by her lack of weight. She was at least as light as his sisters. She must be just skin and bone. He balanced her body across his shoulder and turned toward the main street.

As he neared the entrance, he saw Gunther, leaning at an odd angle against the sidewalk. Gunther called his name. He set the girl down in case he still needed to fight. Gunther didn't try to get up. Ben moved closer to him and picked up Christian's club.

"Hello, McDonald." The voice was calm but labored and slow. "So it's you...Not many boys on the streets as tall as you and me, are there?" You've done a really stupid thing, haven't you? You realize that you just signed your death warrant, right?....I'll have to find you, no matter where you go now....I hope she was worth it ....Who is she anyway?"

"I don't know her, Gunther. I never met her before."

Christian snorted. "You've got to be kidding me, McDonald!" He paused for breath. "Are you totally daff! What do you think you were doing, saving some fair damsel? There are hundreds like her on the street. She was just a dirty starving girl who would have been dead by morning, even if my boys didn't touch her. She probably wouldn't even have known what was happening. I thought you were smarter than that."

"I don't know why I did it, Gunther. I know it makes no sense to you. You can call the action stupid if you like."

"Really stupid, yea, but I'm not surprised. You'd have broken one time or another. He moved his arm slightly and groaned involuntarily. "Your only chance was to join us and become something that made all this tolerable. I understand what drove you tonight, but it doesn't matter now. You'll still have to die for it. And it'll have to be by my hand. It's a shame. You could have been a force if you'd joined us." Christian's breath was coming harder now and he coughed. It was all he could do to keep from passing out.

Ben moved to hover over Christian. "What makes you think you are going to live to do that, Christian?" He started to raise Christian's club.

For a split second, Christian was surprised. Then he laughed. The laughter had a tinge of bitterness in it. "Well, you got me there, don't you, McDonald. I don't have any fight left in me right now. If you have the guts to do it, I'm an easy target. I guess you're finally coming back to your senses."

Ben raised the club higher. Christian prepared himself for the blow. He lifted his head and looked straight up at Ben's face in the dim light to await his fate. There was nothing else to say. He wouldn't beg, like some dog. He would die like he'd lived. He would do it with dignity if he could. He had lived better than most orphans and had left his mark. A few would remember him. So be it. Strangely, he felt an odd sense of relief to be done.

Towering above, Ben prepared to swing. He would finish this with one lethal blow to the side of the head. He assumed Christian wouldn't feel much. Ben had likely already killed people tonight. One more wouldn't matter and it could buy time.

He saw Christian's head come up and his shoulders straighten. As he watched this boy prepare for his fate, and realized that Christian wouldn't plead or beg, he realized that he couldn't deliver the blow. The thought disgusted him. It would be justice to kill Gunther for all the children his gang had robbed, tortured and killed, or left to die. He deserved it. Christian had lived long enough on the streets to understand how this worked. He might be the only one left who could identify Ben and the girl. The gang might figure it out eventually, or they might not. They'd have a hard time believing one person did all this.

He held the club high for a few more seconds and then slowly brought it down. He dropped it beside Christian and started to walk away. Christian's eyes followed him, puzzled. He called after Ben. "You might have lived if you finished the job, Ben. You know I would have done it. You're not a coward. I've seen you fight. You probably killed at least one of my boys tonight, maybe more. So, what is it McDonald? Can't kill someone who can't fight back? That's a weakness that you can't afford. You should come back and do what you intended, you know."

Ben stopped and turned back to Christian, anger rising in his voice. "Damn you, Gunther, don't press your luck. If you want to die that bad, kill yourself. Kids die every night on these streets without anyone caring. I just added to that list, and as you said, probably for no good reason. I doubt if I can get her out and she'll probably die anyway. We're all killing each other, or watching each other die, and no one gives a damn. We just turn away because we're too cowardly to do anything about it. Today is my day to take a stand, I guess. You think you'll ever have one?" He walked over to the girl, picked her up and started walking south.

Christian watched him go. He knew that it would take him a while to drag himself back to his gang. Then he would send the rest of the boys for their comrades. McDonald would get away for now, but not for long. He wouldn't make it through Five Points, if that was really where he was going. Christian doubted it. He had no allies there.

Hell's Kitchen wasn't big enough to hide them. His boys would find them and then, unlike McDonald, Christian wouldn't hesitate to do his job. The code required it. He would have to kill them and do it with witnesses. But he already realized that he would regret it. McDonald's words stuck uncomfortably in his head.

Once out of Christian's sight, Ben turned west two blocks and then quickly entered an alley heading north. He picked up the pace. Carrying the girl was awkward but he couldn't slow down. He didn't know how long it would take for Christian to reach the rest of the gang, but as tough as Christian was, it'd probably be sooner, not later. Then the search would begin in earnest. Gunther was right. Eventually the gang would flush them out.

He would have to find a way to get out of their reach or he and the girl had no chance. Figuring that out could wait; right now he needed to concentrate on getting the girl to his shelter to see if she could be revived.

Chapter 8

The trip north felt like it was taking forever. It was dark in the alleys, thankfully, with little moonlight that night, but it wasn't yet that late and some people were still on the streets. He stuck to the deep shadows and stayed in the darker alleys as much as possible. He still had to cross the larger east-west numbered streets, and even in side alleys, he knew there would be prying eyes watching from hidden locations.

He didn't go directly to the cemetery. He went west toward the Hudson River, then north up a side alley, then back east. He took that indirect route in hopes of making it tougher on the Bowery Boys when they questioned witnesses about where he had gone. Word of his route would travel quickly through the urchin community the next morning, even if he was lucky enough to avoid the gang members tonight.

He knew he would be seen when crossing the main streets, so he just plodded slowly across with the girl on his shoulder, not trying to hide. Passersby glanced at him suspiciously but didn't challenge him. People minded their own business in Hell's Kitchen. He assumed they would think he was taking some drunken girl home. Both his and the girl's size helped. They could easily pass as adults in the dim light. As long as he didn't run into a gang member, he might just make it.

The cemetery was only ten blocks north of the attack point. It normally took him less than 20 minutes to get there, even using his circuitous routes to divert watchful eyes. With the girl on his shoulder, and with his meandering route, it would take much longer. He had to be patient. He expected to be challenged at every step. On the side streets, he stopped often to listen for approaching footsteps behind him. He moved slowly from shadow to shadow, always listening.

He finally crossed 51st street, but decided to keep going to take suspicion away from that area. It worried him to take that risk. The likelihood of being challenged by a policeman increased dramatically beyond 54th street. The gang would expect him to try to escape from Hell's Kitchen, either south or north. They'd figure out that he hadn't gone south through sources on the street, and they would definitely talk to people who saw him go north. He might as well play the ruse out to its full measure.

He finally reached 59th Street. Central Park was just across that street. He was well beyond the northern edge of Hell's Kitchen now and definitely in taboo territory for urchins. His energy was waning and the girl hadn't moaned or moved at all since he picked her up. It worried him that she was still unconscious, but he was pretty certain that she was still alive. When he touched her arm, her skin was still warm. He had to get her to shelter as soon as possible and see if he could revive her.

He crossed 59th Street after watching quietly from the shadows until there was a complete lull in pedestrian and carriage traffic. He was at least five blocks north of the Kitchen now. He didn't believe that he could cross the streets openly anymore without being challenged.

The buildings along the street were more modern and well-kept. To his relief, they were all business establishments and closed for the night. He still worried that some night watchman might be staring out of one of the darkened windows as they crossed.

He had never been as far as 59th Street before. For all he knew, cops patrolled the area regularly at night. The risks he was taking were growing dramatically now, but he felt that he needed to do this to throw the gang off his trail.

Immediately beyond 59th Street he entered manicured woodland that he assumed must be Central Park. He turned west onto a walking path angling slightly away and then roughly parallel to 59th Street. After a hundred feet or so, he ducked into the shadows of bushes and overhanging trees. He laid the girl down and checked her pulse. Her heart was still beating.

He waited for what he estimated to be a half hour or so. No one had followed him. He then picked her up again. This time he did not return to the walking path. He made his way through the trees, angling toward 59th Street. As he worked his way along, he was estimating how far he would need to go to be approximately due north of the cemetery. After a few minutes, he guessed that he had gone far enough.

He stopped behind bushes where he could view the street. The windows in the buildings were all still dark and the traffic was infrequent. He picked his time when he could see no foot or carriage traffic and made his move.

He re-crossed to the south side of 59th Street at a jog. As soon as he was across, he found the nearest alley going south and hurried down it. Nothing about him being there and carrying a girl over his shoulder would be acceptable in this geography. He had to get back into Hell's Kitchen as quickly as possible.

He was now roughly seven blocks north of the cemetery. He continued to walk briskly south until he reached 54th Street and then turned a little west until he found one of the alleys that he believed bordered the cemetery. He was now less than three blocks from his sanctuary. He walked more rapidly now, crossing 52nd Street, and continuing down the same alley.

Just as he thought he was in the clear, someone yelled from behind him, "Hey you, what are you doing with that woman?!" He looked back but could see no one in the dark. He jogged down the side street, running rapidly on the balls of his feet to keep from bouncing her too violently, listening for sounds of pursuit behind him. It had been a deep male voice. It might have been a policeman but he doubted it. He would already have been caught if it was.

He entered the cemetery and ran even faster, jouncing the girl on his shoulder. He reached the mausoleum, praying he had had not been seen. He slipped through the outer gate, bumping it and making it squeak. He set the girl down in the main chamber and bent over at his waist, panting for breath. When he had recovered a little, he opened the iron door to the inner chamber. His nerves were on edge. He was grateful that at least the inner door didn't squeak, thanks to the lubrication he had administered to its hinges.

Now he had a problem. How would he get the girl through the narrow opening without injuring her even more? He decided his best choice was to lay her on the mausoleum floor with her head next the inner chamber door, climb over her into the chamber and then reach back out to pull her through the opening. It was better than trying to shove her through from the outer chamber.

He moved quickly. If he had been followed, or if that anonymous voice had alerted the authorities, he had little time to get her inside before being discovered. Otherwise, he might have dismantled his bed and used one of its boards to make a ramp, but he didn't want to risk the time and noise, or leave her alone in the main chamber. He now hoped that she would remain unconscious just a little longer. It worried him to think that, at this critical moment, she might wake up and scream as he was stuffing her into a crypt.

He positioned her under the door and climbed over into the inner chamber. He reached down and placed his arms under her upper torso to pull her up to the opening. It put him at an awkward angle and, despite her light weight, it was a strain. He got her head and shoulders through the opening, but her body was now contorted into a strange limbo position. She was dead weight. If he simply pulled her in now, he would scrape her lower body on the sharp stone edges of the opening.

Leaning her head and shoulders on his chest, he reached down to her thighs. It was embarrassing and he hoped she never found out. With some effort, he lifted her up and pulled her into the chamber. Even so, he heard her lower legs scraping the edge of the door sill. She moaned a little and he knew it must have hurt. She would probably have scratches, but it was the best he could do.

On his knees, he moved her over to the straw bed, then came back hurriedly and closed the trap door, bracing a board under the inner handle to block anyone from turning it from the outer chamber. Then he collapsed to the floor.

After a few minutes he felt for his water jug and the battered tin cup to take drink. Then he decided to try to see if she could drink. He only had one cup. If she lived, he would need another container. He poured her a drink.

He had no idea whether, or how, an unconscious person could drink. He cupped his left hand behind her neck and lifted her head and shoulders. He put the cup to her mouth and tried to tip it properly so a little water would flow into her mouth. She coughed. He paused until she stopped and tried again, reducing the flow. He feared that she might not be able to swallow, and that the water would enter her lungs. To his surprise, she gulped the water down.

It took a while because he was afraid to give her much at a time, but eventually she took a full cup.

As he administered the water, he listened for noises outside, but heard nothing. He thought about trying to feed her. He had a can of peaches with syrup that might do her good, but he was still worried about choking her. When she finished drinking, he covered her with his blanket and placed his coat on top. He suspected she was feverish; her skin seemed almost hot to the touch. While she remained unconscious, he could hear her breathing and it didn't seem labored.

The pain in his right hand was becoming intolerable. It had gotten worse as he had carried her. The largest splinter in the fleshy portion between his thumb and forefinger felt like a spear stuck in his hand, but he could also feel the smaller splinters in his palm and fingers. He tackled the largest splinter with the point of his knife, finally pulling it out. The smaller splinters would have to wait for more light until he could either pull them or cut them out. He lay down on the stone floor near her and passed into a troubled asleep.

He awoke from nightmares a few hours later and could not go back to sleep. He began to fret over the situation. "What have I gotten myself into? I don't know how to care for this girl. If she dies inside this crypt, what will I do, dump her body back on the streets or leave her here?" He decided that he would have to remove and hide her somewhere, making the gang think she had died on the way out of Hell's Kitchen. "If she lives, will she recover quickly enough for us to get out? We won't have much time till the gang closes in. Hopefully they'll believe I took her across Central Park, but they may eventually find out that I didn't from whoever saw me up north. Then they'll come looking, and they'll find a way to flush us out. I'll have to leave here when the food and water run out. If they kill me while I'm out foraging, what happens to her?

If she goes out unprotected, she won't last a day."

The longer he fretted, the more he worried. "Why on earth was I so stupid!? I had no right to interfere. Gunther was right. It'll still end badly for her, and now I'm doomed as well. Maybe we'll be able to run, but to where? I can't swim. There are only two bridges off this island. I can't get south to the Brooklyn Bridge through Five Points territory. The only other bridge is supposed to be at the far north end of the island, up past Central Park. People will stop us long before we get there. I could try to give us up to the police, but they'd deliver us back to the gang to keep harmony. Gunther has to make an example of me. If he doesn't, he loses too much face."

No matter what alternative he explored, he could think of no good outcome. He and the girl were in deep trouble, and he knew it. If there was another way out of Hell's Kitchen, he had to figure it out, and fast.

He didn't sleep at all that night, mulling repeatedly over untenable escape options. Morning finally came, and with it a little light for the chamber. He had learned to tell whether it was sunny or cloudy by subtle differences in the light filtering through the inner chamber window. Today would be sunny.

He could now make out her facial features more clearly. Her cheeks were sunken and hollow and her face was dirty. He took a rag and poured a little water on it to wipe away some of the grime. Her skin still seemed far too warm. He bunched more straw under her head for a pillow.

He decided he had to feed her something, so he opened the can of peaches and used a bent spoon that he had scavenged to feed her some of the syrup. To his relief, she swallowed it without choking.

He wondered if she would eat the peaches if he crushed them. He pushed them against the sides of the can until they were squishy and then spooned a small quantity into her mouth. Again, she swallowed. He opened a can of beans and did the same. It took over an hour to feed her. Then he waited. He had no idea how long it would take her to revive, or even if she would. But she did seem to be resting peacefully. After a few hours he lay down to nap, knowing it would be a good idea to rest while he could.

He awoke with a start. He didn't know how long he had been asleep but something had stirred him. He glanced at a shadow against the wall and was surprised to find her sitting up, staring at him like a frightened animal. She had pulled the blanket up to her neck. He was careful not to move.

"Hello. So you are finally awake, huh?"

She didn't answer.

"Have you been awake long?"

Again, no answer.

"My name is Ben McDonald. You needn't be scared of me. I won't hurt you."

She spoke for the first time. "Where is this place?"

"Well, it's a little complicated. Let me just start with how you got here. Last night, I saw you being attacked by a gang of boys. I got you away and carried you here. This is the place where I come at night for safety. Do you remember anything about last night?"

She shook her head no.

"I know this is all confusing, but you're safe here. What's your name?"

She paused, surprised. No one had asked her name since her parents died. "Anna Murphy."

"Well, Anna Murphy, I am glad you're awake. You had me scared there for a while. Are you thirsty or hungry?"

"Thirsty."

"Well, we have two drinking cans now but yours still has a little peach juice left in it. That should be okay. It might even make the water taste a little better."

He cut the lid out of the can and ran his knife handle around the inside to make sure there were no jagged edges. She watched him and the knife warily as he worked on the can, not moving from her position. He poured water from the jug and leaned toward her to offer the can. She shrank back.

"Sorry, Anna. I understand why you're still a bit gun shy, but I promise, it's okay." She cautiously reached out and took the can. She brought it to her lips. She gulped the water greedily and then looked embarrassed. Some of the water trickled off her chin and she wiped it with her sleeve.

"Would you like more?"

She nodded and held out the cup. He filled it, and again, she gulped it down. She took a third, and then leaned back against the wall.

"Food?"

She hesitated, but shook her head no.

"When's the last time you ate?" He knew the answer but wanted to see what she would say.

She finally mumbled, "I'm not sure, but I am not hungry."

"I know, but here's the problem. You're very weak. If you and I have to run, you won't be able to go very fast and that spells trouble for both of us, so I'd really appreciate it if you would try."

She didn't answer at first. Her eyes misted. "I'm not sure I want to."

"Why not?"

She didn't respond.

"Why not, Anna?"

She sighed. "I don't really see any reason to get better."

He paused, thinking about what that meant and how best to respond. He continued to look at her as he contemplated until she became embarrassed and looked away. Finally he said, "Well, I may understand that more than you think, but here's the problem. The guys attacking you were part of the Bowery Boys gang. One of them was the leader of the gang, a guy named Christian Gunther."

He paused. "I probably hurt them pretty bad. I may have killed one, or even two of them. I'm not sure. They'll be looking hard for us and we'll need to leave here soon. I won't be able to carry you and we'll both be in danger if you are still weak."

She waited for him to continue, but he didn't. Finally she said, "How many of them were there?"

"You mean how many attacked you? Five."

"You took me away from five Bowery Boys?"

He nodded. "Yes."

"How did you do that?"

"They were distracted."

"Distracted by what?"

He didn't answer at first. She asked again. "Distracted by what?"

He glanced down, and then looked at her "You."

He saw her body stiffen. She said nothing more for a while. Then he thought to say. "I don't know for sure, but I don't think they had time to do anything to you."

There was longer silence.

Finally she spoke again. "Ben, right? You said your name is Ben?"

"Right."

"Why did you do it, Ben? I'd be gone by now if you hadn't." She lifted her hands to her face. He saw tears slide through her fingers.

He slid over and leaned against the wall beside her. When she dropped a hand from her face, he took it. Surprisingly, she didn't resist. Eventually the tears stopped, but still she didn't take her hand away. They sat like that, saying nothing. He found himself, foolishly, not wanting to let go of her hand. She continued to lean against the wall, her eyes closed.

Finally, he released her hand and crawled to the other side of the room to find a jar of green beans. It had mold at the top—otherwise it wouldn't have been trashed—but he knew from experience that the beans underneath were still good. He ran his knife around the top of the rusty lid and unscrewed it. He siphoned off an inch or so of the moldy beans into his waste container. He tasted one of the remaining beans, waited, and then tasted another. They seemed okay.

He got the spoon and her tin can. He placed some of the beans in it and handed it to her.
She looked at the tin with distaste, then glanced at him, sighed and began to nibble on a bean. He tried not to stare as she ate, but he was pleased.

He took a few of the beans into his own tin cup and began to spear them one at a time with his knife. He paused with a bean midway to his mouth, remembering another item that she might like. He scooted over to his pile of goods and unwrapped something from a newspaper. He scooted back to her with a piece of bread. He inspected it closely. The bread was rock hard, but would melt with the saliva in her mouth. She took it and alternated tearing small pieces off to eat, then taking a bean. She ultimately ate all he gave her.

When she finished, he said, "Thank you."

She looked surprised and then laughed a little. "You're welcome. Thanks for the food."

"No problem. Let's do this again sometime." He grinned at her.

She laughed despite herself. She began to survey the chamber with greater interest. She saw the writing on the floor but couldn't make out what it said. Finally she said, "Where are we!?"

He laughed nervously. "Okay, now promise me you won't scream. We can't afford the noise. We're in a small hidden chamber in the back of a large mausoleum in a cemetery on the northern side of Hell's Kitchen. The writing on the floor that you see is for a couple of little children who died—probably twins. The light in here is from that narrow window on the wall over there. It's hidden behind an overhang below the outside roof. You can't see it if you're outside because of the trees and brush. I have no idea why the window was put in here. Maybe it was intended as some kind of light for the children. Maybe they were scared of the dark. Anyway, I'm talking quietly because I don't know if there are people outside who might hear us. They might think we were ghosts; or worse still, that we're alive and hiding here. We'll have to keep pretty quiet when the light is in that window."

She sat silently for a minute, reflecting, and then said, "Then we're very lucky to share this place with these children."

He was relieved. She hadn't quivered or made a scene about being inside someone's tomb. She didn't act afraid. She sat quietly a little longer and then spoke, this time hesitantly. "I'm a little tired and would like to lie down if you don't mind. I hate to take your bed but it is wonderfully soft." "And…." she paused, obviously embarrassed, "I need to relieve myself first."

"Oh sure, I understand! The problem is that we can't really go outside the mausoleum until it's dark. The gang is likely looking for us all over Hell's Kitchen and they have lots of spies. Why don't I go out to the main chamber and check it out. If it's clear, you can go there. I will close this door. Over in the far corner on the right, the stone has cracked and it is a good place to relieve yourself. Is that all you need to do now?"

She nodded.

"Good, I'll check it out. If you need to do more, we will go outside much later in the night if that's okay with you?"

He opened the inner door and slid through. He looked outside through the gate and could see most of the cemetery. He saw no one. He slipped back into the inner chamber. "Just tap on the door when you are ready to come back in. Please don't go outside, and stay away from the gate if you can. Stay around the edges of the chamber so you're less likely to be seen.

She nodded and awkwardly slid through the opening into the main area. He pulled the door shut and waited. He reopened it when she tapped.

"Thank you." She sounded relieved.

"No problem. Get some rest. You'll need it."

She lay down. He could tell by her rhythmic breathing that she had dropped off to sleep almost immediately. He stayed awake for a while, leaning against the wall until it was fully dark in the chamber, listening for outside noises and to her breathing.

Much later, he slipped outside to relieve himself and to see if anyone was searching in the night. He heard nothing. He returned to the mausoleum and crawled back into the chamber to lie down. As he started to drift off, the thought struck him. "She was worth it!" He smiled at that and drifted off to sleep.

Chapter 9

On the night of the attack, after Ben and the girl were gone, Christian Gunther had a hard time making it back to his headquarters. Every time he tried to get up his stomach lurched. He felt dizzy and unbalanced. He had a violent headache. His arm hung at an unnatural angle and the pain was intense. Even in the dim light he could see the torn skin and the bone below it. Surprisingly, there wasn't much bleeding from the wound.

It took him a half-hour to navigate the two blocks to home. He had no idea how the boys in the alley had fared, but since they had not come out by the time he left, he assumed they were badly hurt or worse. As he staggered along, he became confused and couldn't remember how many gang members had been with him, or which ones they were. He was pretty sure Big Mike was one of them, but the memory of who else was in the group was blurred. He still remembered that they had been attacked by McDonald but he couldn't quite remember why. He remembered that there was a girl involved somehow, but the rest was hazy.

He knew he needed to get home and send the gang back for the others, so he concentrated on that. McDonald had hit him hard and he assumed that he had probably done the same to the others. Why hadn't they fought back? He didn't remember that McDonald had any allies, but perhaps he had. If so, he had no idea who they would be. All these thoughts kept bouncing around in his head and he was having great difficulty sorting them out. He felt as though he was in a heavy haze.

As he crossed the threshold into his headquarters, he vomited and collapsed into unconsciousness. His gang members there were shocked and unsure what to do. They mulled around him and finally decided to lift him and carry him to his cot. They sent someone for an old doctor who lived nearby, who was a perpetual drunk. They had used him when they had to, although they didn't like him much. Beyond that, the gang wasn't sure what to do. Finally one of them asked, "Who's missing?" They took a survey. Big Mike and three others had not come in yet.

Wasn't Mike with Christian today? Were the others with him too? They weren't sure. Who could have taken down Big Mike and Christian together? That seemed incomprehensible to them. No one had ever bested Gunther, and while Big Mike was slowed by his weight, it definitely made it hard to bring him down. Were the Bowery Boys being attacked by another gang? Were there rogue adults on the loose in Hell's Kitchen that they didn't know about? None of this made sense to them.

After a useless debate that wasted time, one of the members said, "We should try to find Mike and the others." As soon as he said it, they all knew it was the right action. They decided to leave five members with Christian in case the gang's headquarters came under attack. The rest decided to go in groups of four after agreeing on a signal so they could reconnoiter quickly if any group was attacked.
But just as they exited the building, two of the boys who had been with Gunther staggered in. Both were in a lot of pain, but were able to communicate where Big Mike and their remaining comrade lay.

Gang members grabbed their weapons and headed to the scene. They were shocked by what they found. Big Mike lay sprawled and still with his pants still down between his ankles. His skin was already cool to the touch. They tried to shake him, but he was completely unresponsive and, they assumed, dead. The other boy was breathing but unconscious. His face was smashed in. They carried both back to headquarters. Big Mike was extremely heavy and smelled of feces and death. It took four boys to carry him. The other boy was smaller and easier to handle. As they made the trek back to headquarters, all of them were wondering who could have been powerful enough to take out five older members of their gang? The two boys who were conscious hadn't known whether it was just one person or more. They just knew that whoever did it was very quick and powerful. It was deeply unsettling to the group to think that there were enemies on the loose bold enough to attack a group of five Bowery Boys.

By the time they made it back to the gang's den, the old doctor, obviously drunk, was administering to Christian. He staggered around and gave grandiose orders, most of which made little sense. He finally made it clear that he needed soap and hot water and some clean rags. He tried to reset the broken bones in the arm before he wrapped it, causing Christian to scream in pain, even in his delirious state. No member had ever heard him do that before. I t was scary. They knew the pain must be horrible.

On inspection of the body, the old quack declared that Big Mike was definitely dead, but that the other boy would probably regain consciousness, although he said he might be retarded from the blow to his head. He said he probably deserved what he got. That angered some gang members, but others told them to forget it; the drink was talking and they needed him right now. The old man had no medicine to give the boys, or any further advice, so they sent him, unceremoniously, to the street. He hung around the front of the headquarters yelling loudly for his fee for the house call. One of the boys finally gave him a quarter to shut him up. He staggered away, cursing them all.

Christian moved in and out of consciousness throughout that night. Gang members took turns at his bedside in case he might wake up and tell them more about what happened. When he did awake the next morning, his headache was less intense and his mind was a little clearer. He asked about Big Mike and the other boys. They told him what they had found. He cursed with the news, and then told them what he knew of the attack. He and his comrades had been heading for home. Some of the boys got distracted by a girl lying in the alley. While they were fooling with her, they were attacked by Ben McDonald.

One of the gang asked incredulously, "Just McDonald? Just one guy did this to all of you?"

"Yea, I think so. I am not sure how he did it. It was dark and he had some kind of heavy club. He hit me first and I went down. I heard noises after that but couldn't tell what he did to the others. When he came out of the alley, he was carrying the girl and was alone. He talked to me before he left. He could have killed me, but he didn't."

"Why not?"

Christian paused, "Not sure. He said something about too many kids dying already, but I really can't say. He considered it, but he didn't follow through."

The boys averted their eyes. It made them anxious that McDonald had bested Christian. They were relieved he was still alive but incredulous that he had been so easily disabled. They had always assumed that no one would ever catch Christian Gunther unprepared.

Christian was through talking about it. "I want you guys to get busy and start tracking where he went. I want him and the girl found, assuming she's still alive. I saw him go south but he's cagey. I doubt if that was his real direction. He wouldn't have gone far that way until he hit Five Points territory and he'd have no friends there. Just in case, though, Joe, you still have a few connections down there. Ask around about McDonald and the girl without saying why."

Joe nodded. "What's the girl's name?"

"I don't know. I don't think she'd been on the streets long. I doubt she was connected to anybody. She was older and in bad shape. Ask around. Somebody may know something about her."

"Aaron, Sam, Seth and Johnnie, you each take some guys and spread out. Ask around about who saw McDonald or the girl that night and where. Go all over Hell's Kitchen. Throw some weight around and scare a few people. Also let them know there'll be a reward in it for good information. Let's assume he's actually going north since he wanted me to think that he headed south. I want to know where he is by this time tomorrow, you understand?"

They all nodded. Sam asked, "If we find him and the girl, do we kill them?"

Christian smiled and shook his head. "No, you don't. You find out where he is, pin him down if you can and come get me. Even if you can't pin him down and he starts running, track him and send somebody back to get me. You all got that?"

They did. They scattered immediately and began the search. They knew that McDonald had a big head start, but if he was still in Hell's Kitchen, they'd find him.

By nightfall, the groups had returned with clues, but those clues were inconsistent and confusing. Aaron and Johnnie were in an animated debate as they entered Christian's room. Aaron reported first.

"I tell you, some of those kids are just lying or making stuff up to get our attention. One kid says McDonald is carrying the girl over by the Hudson River and another kid says he spotted them in an alley a good five blocks east. Somebody sees him going west a couple of blocks south of the alley where we found Big Mike. Then another says he sees McDonald carry her across 49th street, to the north. We got spottings of McDonald with the girl all over Hell's Kitchen. That can't be right!"

Johnnie's group added to the confusion by sharing reports from kids who claimed they had seen McDonald just trudging along all the way up north near 51st. Nothing pointed to a clear direction. From all indications, McDonald had the girl over his shoulder but did not seem to be in a big hurry.

Christian remained silent during the reports. When they had finished, and after they had argued themselves out, he spoke. "He headed north. Those east-west jogs were just to throw us off. The one thing that is clear from what you got is multiple sightings north of the attack point. He was just trying to distract us by going south or in east-west directions. Joe, did your contacts down South see him down that way at all?"

Joe shook his head. "Nope, they didn't see hide nor hair of him down toward Five Points."

"Okay then, the furthest north your witnesses saw him was 51st. Let's start there tomorrow. He may have tried to get up to Central Park, or even past it. We need to check witnesses from 51st to 59th."

The noose was tightening. Ben might have gotten off the island, but Christian doubted it. He would have been seen by too many suspicious adults and reported to the police. Christian had already gotten word through his police informants to have the authorities be on the alert for a couple of runaways from Hell's Kitchen. He had told them McDonald had killed a gang member and his return was a high priority for the Bowery Boys. So far, the police hadn't indicated any sightings. Either McDonald had outside help to disappear quickly outside the Kitchen, or he was still hiding somewhere close. Christian guessed the latter. If McDonald had help, he would've left long ago.

On the third day after the attack, the gang began to query their contacts on the northern edges of Hell's Kitchen. None had personally seen anything. The trail went cold beyond 54th. However, on the following day a source reported that a man or large boy with what could have been a body across his shoulder had crossed 59th and entered Central Park late on the night of the attack. Another source, a homeless man with an alcohol problem, looked them up and said he had some information he could give for money. They gave him a half-dollar and he proudly indicated that a man or large boy had been seen carrying what looked like a female across 52nd Street headed south. He had yelled at him, but had not followed.

That information from the homeless man was contradictory, and considering the source, was not considered reliable. That night, as they reviewed the tips, most were ready to discard the 52nd street sighting. Upon rehashing all their information, most gang members came to the conclusion that Ben McDonald had somehow gotten up to and through Central Park. He was a smart bird and had either made it off the island with the girl, or was hiding out in northern Manhattan, outside the boundaries of Hell's Kitchen. Other than alerting having alerted the authorities, they believed there was little else that could be done but wait.

Satisfied with their conclusion, they reported to Christian, expecting him to agree and call off the search. He sat silently for long minutes, staring at the group with that intensity that always made them squirm. Finally he said, "We'll keep looking for him and the girl in Hell's Kitchen."

Sam, one of the boys hopeful of taking Big Mike's place, immediately spoke up. "Why would we do that, Christian? It's taking a lot of time and you said yourself his true direction was north. We've got a sighting that says he entered Central Park. We ain't got no sightings after that unless you count that homeless drunk who thinks he saw em going back across 52nd. It makes no sense that he'd reach the Park and then turn around and come back into our territory. We've lost him. Mike's gone. The other guys will recover. We should get on about business. We're out of good leads."

Christian didn't answer immediately, seeming distracted. When he responded, he looked directly at Sam. "I know that old drunk. He is usually accurate in what he sees, drunk or sober. McDonald probably did go up to Central Park, but I'm guessing he did that for our benefit--or maybe he just got cold feet when he got that far north. Either way, I think he doubled back into the Kitchen. If he'd gone on into or beyond Central Park, I think the police would know that by now. We told them he could be dangerous and it was a priority for us to get him back. They've been watching and we've not heard from them."

"And where would he go if he left Hell's Kitchen? Who would have taken him in? If he and the girl were on the streets up there, they would be noticed scrounging for food or shelter, or the girl would have been visible because she is so sick. None of us could go north and stay there three days without being spotted. He doesn't know that territory and I'm guessing that he doesn't have help up there—otherwise he would have left here a long time ago. I am sure of that from talking with him. He snapped the other night. It wasn't planned or thought out. He hates the Kitchen more than most. From what he told me about the girl, he probably didn't know her before he attacked us. Think about it. He's been disappearing every night for more than a year and we don't have a clue where he goes. But then he was right back with us in daylight. A smart guy doesn't give up a place that good to head into territory he doesn't know without thinking it through first. For all he knew, we were on his tail within an hour after he attacked us. He doesn't know that I was out for a while. I talked to him, so he knows that I know who he is. I think he tried to throw us off and then went back to wherever he's been hiding at night."

"I'm guessing his hideout is somewhere between 51st and 54th. Most kids outside a gang don't regularly go that far north for shelter. They just duck to the nearest place they can for protection. McDonald is smart. He's figured out that north of 51st is a kind of no-man's land—still in Hell's Kitchen but far enough north to be near respectable areas where kids could get in trouble with the authorities if they loiter." If he was spotted crossing back over 52nd that could mean his hideout may be somewhere south of there. Since nobody saw him again much further south, he was probably pretty near his hideout when he was spotted. It could be below 51st, but not by much or we'd have heard."

"Tomorrow, we'll narrow the search. We'll look from the Hudson all the way to Sixth Avenue between 45th and 52nd. It could be anywhere and it could be anything—above ground, below ground, in a building or not. But it must give him shelter and protection. If he's got a hideout around there, we'll find him if we look hard enough. If we don't, then we'll know for sure he is out of the Kitchen and we'll wait on the police. Get some rest. You'll be busy the next few nights."

Chapter 10

Ben's estimate about the food was overly optimistic. It did not last a week--more like five days--but they were good days. Anna was getting stronger. She now ate everything he gave her without question and she drank a lot of water from Ben's jugs. He gave her as much of both as she would take. Her energy returned and with that came more curiosity about this boy who had risked everything to save her.

They became nocturnal. During the day they seldom spoke for fear of being overheard, and when they did, very quietly. Instead, they slept as much as possible or played rudimentary games that Ben or she remembered. He had previously found a discarded slate with a large crack in it and chalk rock for drawing. On it, she taught him the game of tic tac toe. He was amused to find that she was a fierce competitor who greatly enjoyed beating him. It made her so excited that he had to "shush" her occasionally. He laughed and considered his losses well worth it, even if she was a girl.

Ben had also found an old, abandoned game board for "fox and geese", probably thrown away because of missing pegs. It was easy for him to replace them by carving a crude "fox" from a darker walnut sapling and the "geese" from lighter wood. It was a more complicated game offering greater opportunity to match their competitive skills. She had never played it, even though it had probably originated in her native land. After she learned the rules, she held her own against him and enjoyed it more than the easier tic tac toe. They also played jackstraws using a few stiff pieces of straw from the bed. He also had found a checkerboard and some wooden checkers. He had become very good at the game and she could never best him. All these games had the benefits of passing the time quietly and teaching them something about each other's personality.

Then, late at night or in the wee hours of the morning, they slipped out of the Mausoleum, with Ben leading and Anna following silently behind. They always exited the graveyard as quickly as they could, seeking the shadows of the bushes along the alleyways. Hidden by bushes, they sat or stretched out on grassy areas sometimes for hours at a time, until near dawn.

Back in their chamber early in the mornings, in the hour or so before the light filtered through their window, when it was highly unlikely that anyone had entered the graveyard, they spent precious time talking, pausing occasionally to listen for outside noises.

In the predawn of the fourth day Anna's curiosity overcame her and she asked, "Did your mother and father die? Is that why you wound up on the streets?" Ben was slow to answer that. She ultimately became uncomfortable, worrying that she had offended him. "I'm sorry, Ben. I shouldn't have asked."

"No, no, it's okay. I probably need to talk about it to somebody. No, my mother and father didn't die. They left me here in Hell's Kitchen about three years ago. I still don't know why—actually him, I do know why--but her, I don't. I thought my mother loved me and I would never have imagined she would abandon me—but she did."

"My father always hated me and beat me at every chance he got. He beat my mother, too, when she tried to protect me. My mother told me once it was because of something she had done back in Indiana, but she didn't tell me what it was."

Anna was so shocked that she didn't know how to respond appropriately. The idea of a parent beating or even speaking ill to his own child was foreign to her. All she could think to say was,

"I'm so sorry, Ben".

He shrugged it off and said it was okay. "So what happened to your family?"

That question might have sent her in a tailspin earlier, but after hearing Ben's story, hers seemed less bad. "My dad and mom died within a few weeks of each other--him in a work accident and her to illness. I had no one else to take me in so I was turned out to the streets. It wasn't very long ago, actually, but it seems like forever now. My dad was wonderful, and my mom too. We would have been on a farm somewhere soon if he had lived. We almost had enough money saved to leave."

"I wish you all had made it, Anna. They sounded like great parents."

Her eyes misted and she smiled sadly. "They were. You would have really liked them and they would have liked you. I guess I was lucky to have them, although I hadn't thought about it in that way before. I just miss them so much." It was the first time she had talked to anyone about her parents and it made her feel better, although she wasn't exactly sure why.

On that fourth day, Ben's anxiety increased by the hour. He knew their time was running out. He continued to mull over their options. He would have to scavenge more food if they stayed, which under normal circumstances wouldn't have been difficult. But now he was sure the gang was looking for him and there would be prying eyes everywhere. If he were caught he would not make it back. At some point, hunger and thirst would drive her out too and she would have no chance for survival. He could take her with him to forage for food, but that just doubled the chances that they'd be caught.

They could try to make a run for it. He knew they couldn't go south to the big Brooklyn Bridge, even though he assumed it was a lot closer than the older northernmost bridge off the island. To get to that northern bridge, they would have to cross Central Park and the land beyond. He had no idea how far that might be, nor how heavily it was populated. Hijacking a boat to cross the Hudson or East River might be a possibility, but they could easily get caught and he knew he wasn't familiar or comfortable with the currents and other dangers of the rivers.

He kept mulling these ideas over in his head. He didn't want to frighten Anna, so he had avoided talking to her about it for as long as he could. They were able to replenish their water from the Church's cistern each night and she seemed not to have noticed the dwindling food supplies.

When she finally asked about it late on that fourth day, he lied and said they had enough food for a week. It might have been the truth had he restricted the amount he gave her, but he hadn't done that. He had told himself she needed to eat everything she could for what was to come. He secretly rationed himself severely during the four days.

He still couldn't think of a clear option for escape. He would have to talk to her soon. He decided to do so after they returned from their nightly outing. She had a right to understand what they faced and to be in on the decision.

Chapter 11

Per Christian's instructions, the gang concentrated their search north of 45th street. During the day, all the members were out. At night, they took shifts, about half of the gang roaming the streets in groups of four or five while the others slept until an early morning shift change.

Christian's arm was still swollen and feverish, with an aching pain that did not get better, but he was careful not to let those around him know. He suspected the old quack hadn't set the bones properly, but he had no other medical person to gauge how bad it really was. He thought the pain should've subsided by the third day, but the throbbing and swelling was at least as bad on day three as on the first day, and maybe worse.

Early on the third day, he was summoned to a meeting by Chuck Connor. Christian assumed it would not be pleasant. He was right. When he walked into Connor's office there were no casual greetings—just rapid fire questions. "So, how the hell did you lose big Mike and get the others hurt so badly?" Christian, in his usual style, stared back at Connor and was silent a few seconds before responding. Connor waited, trying to stare him down. He had never succeeded doing that with this kid.

"It was coming night. We were headed home. The boys saw this girl slumped in the middle of a dead end alley and decided to have some fun. I didn't feel like it so I didn't enter the alley. The boys walked the alley before they began. They walked it twice. I decided to leave for headquarters. The last I saw of them, they were standing over her with their trousers loose. Mike was probably already on top of her. I was hit first. You can see the results. I started to fall and was hit again and passed out. I don't know what happened after that. I suspect they were distracted by the girl when they were attacked."

Connor nodded. "How many of them attacked you?"

"Just one, I think."

Connor's sources had already told him this, but he acted as though it was surprising news. "Just one? You and your best got taken down by just one guy? He must have been a monster. Who was he and who does he affiliate with?"

"Ben McDonald and as far as I know, he's connected to nobody. He's a loner. I tried to recruit him. If he'd joined, he'd probably be your next gang leader—but he wouldn't, no matter what I offered. We saw him fight a few times. He's big and fast. In darkness, with the element of surprise, and if he were riled to a maddened state, what he did wasn't that surprising."

Connor glared at Gunther. Secretly, he deeply admired this boy. Christian had never pulled punches or groveled, and he obviously wasn't going to start now. "So why was he riled? What was the girl to him?"
"Nothing as far as we know. He'd been on the street a good while; she only recently. They probably had not met before that night. I came awake as he was carrying her out of the alley. I asked him why he did it. He said that he didn't really know her. He was just tired of the violence to innocent kids and that it had to stop somewhere."

"You believe him?"

"Yea, I do. He doesn't brag or tell stories. He always shot straight when I talked to him. He was talented. I wish I could have brought him in."

"Well, if he was tired of violence, he sure did a lot of it himself, didn't he?

Christian nodded. "Funny, isn't it? But I'll tell you, I don't think he knew what he was doing when he did it. It was dark and he was attacking a bunch of guys who would have taken him out if they could. He knew that. McDonald is smart and very cagey, but I don't think he planned it out that night. He just snapped and reacted when he saw the girl was going to be raped. What he did after that had no logic to it. It probably wasn't just about that girl. It was everything he had seen on the streets. Every once in a while, we all get sick of it."

Connor was a little surprised by Christian's frankness. His face softened just a touch and he paused again, but this time not for effect. "You all live in hell, that's for sure. Sometimes I don't know how you do it. Someday it might not be like this, but that day isn't now. What do you plan to do to fix your problem?"

"We're looking for him and the girl. If they're in the Kitchen, we'll find them. I don't think they've left yet. He had a hideout that we never found before the attack. I think they're hold up there. I think it's somewhere on the north side, around 51st or 52nd Street."

Connor paused. He almost hated to say what he had to say next. "You'd better, Christian. If you don't get him and the girl and make a public example of them, your reputation is ruined. If they already got away and are never found, you're tainted. I tell you frankly, I'd hate to see that. You're good at what you do. But if you don't fix this, you can forget about any advancement in the ranks. You understand?"

Christian didn't blink, and he hesitated only a second, staring at Connor. "Yea, I got it. I'd expect nothing different." He got up and walked out of the room without a goodbye.

Chapter 12

On the fourth day, despite the throbbing pain in his arm, Christian personally joined the hunt. His lieutenants had reported no success during the first three days and he felt the need to take charge. By that time, enthusiasm for the search was severely lagging among the gang members. Most believed that McDonald had somehow made it off the island.

Big Mike had not had many real friends in the gang and was not greatly missed. He was sneaky, abusive and manipulative. He lied often, even to his friends, and was a braggart. Only his age and massive size, and the death of better lieutenants before him, had allowed him to rise to his rank in the gang.

Christian knew that he needed to infuse some energy into the search or it was doomed to fail. McDonald was not likely to make a stupid mistake. He still believed that McDonald was somewhere along the northern edges of Hell's Kitchen.

Christian and other gang members searched throughout the day from 45th to 54th street, from the Hudson to Seventh Avenue, but they found no trace of McDonald and the girl. Christian organized the night shifts and went back to headquarters to sleep a little before coming back out, but the throbbing ache in his arm had increased to the point that he could never get comfortable. He finally gave it up and got back to the streets to rendezvous with the gangs covering the early night shift.

They searched until midnight, when they were scheduled to head back home to be replaced by the next shifts. Immediately before the shift change, Christian and his group were in an alleyway just north of 51st street. His arm was killing him. He wasn't sure he could even make it back to headquarters. He pulled one of the boys aside. "Joe, I'm going to stay up here until the next group arrives. Tell Johnnie and his group to meet me at this spot when they get up this way."

Joe hesitated, then whispered. "You shouldn't be up here alone in your condition. Why not come back with us and get some rest?"

"Couldn't if I tried. I'll be fine. Nobody out now but us. I'll just sit down behind the bushes here and rest a bit. Tell them to come up this alley and give the usual signal. If you guys are right about him being gone, I won't be in danger anyway. Besides, he's already spared me once. He's not likely to reverse that on the off chance that I spot him before the boys get back."

"Okay, I'll get them back up here soon as they can." With that, Joe and his group headed south.

Christian moved up the alley a little further to make sure he wasn't visible from 51st Street. He was now north of a new Catholic Church and just east of an old cemetery. He slid back into a cluster of tall grass and sat down to wait. He wasn't worried about his safety. There was a moon out and his night vision was good. He sat for a while and then lay back with his head resting on a cluster of grass. Despite the pain, exhaustion set in and he drifted off.

It took a full hour for Johnnie and his group to be rousted from sleep, dress and get up to 51st Street. They quietly made their way up the alley where Christian was supposed to be, but didn't find him. They whistled lightly—the rendezvous signal—but still nothing. They knew better than to yell for him—he would punish them for that—so they went all the way to the end of the alley, then back to 51st Street, and then up the next alley west of the cemetery, just in case Joe had gotten mixed up; but still no sign of

Gunther.

Johnnie surmised that, if he had been there, he would have joined them. He motioned for his boys to follow him. Maybe Joe had been confused about the rendezvous spot; or maybe for some reason, Christian had moved on, either continuing the search alone, or becoming tired and headed back to home, missing them on the way. It made him nervous, but he decided to push north to check out more territory along the Hudson, around 54th Street. He was sure it was all futile, but as long as Christian said to search, they would have to go on.

Ben and Anna didn't leave the mausoleum until after 2:00 AM that night. Ben had awakened at midnight, as usual, but Anna was still asleep and he didn't want to disturb her. It didn't matter when they went out. In fact, the later into the night they left the mausoleum, the better, particularly with the full moon, as he knew it would be tonight. He might have to wake her at some point, but for now there was still time for her to sleep.

She awoke later on her own and they were soon through the chamber door and into the main part of the mausoleum. Looking through the bars of the gate, the stones in the cemetery reflected brightly in the moonlight, creating eerie shadows. It worried him that it was so light out. They would have to get through the cemetery quickly to the protection of the bushes and tall grass. He also decided not to stay out too long before returning to the protection of the mausoleum.

They slipped through the door and, in a crouching run, made their way quickly east until they crossed the alleyway and reached shadows on the other side. Once there, they separated briefly to relieve themselves and then returned to a cluster of bushes that was their rendezvous point. They sat down on a small, grassy knoll for a few minutes to relax and smell the fresh earth and vegetation. The night was beautiful. It was mild with no wind.

Anna sighed and to Ben's great surprise, reached over and took his hand. It sent a tingling sensation through his body. Her hand was warm and soft to the touch. He was hesitant to move for fear of breaking the spell. They sat that way for what must have been at least half an hour. Then he reluctantly squeezed her hand and stood, still holding on to her hand. A small twig snapped under his boot. It sounded like a cannon to him but he knew it really wasn't much noise. Still, they hesitated a few seconds in the shadows, holding hands, watching the alley and church to try to detect any possible movement. When there was none, they made their way back across the alley and into the cemetery, hand-in-hand.

Christian Gunther's resting place was no more than 30 feet from where Anna and Ben had been sitting. He had awakened just before they rose to go back to the mausoleum, but they were hidden by the bushes and tall grass, so he had no idea anyone was near. He remained silent by habit as he regained his bearings and realized he had been in a deep sleep; how long, he did not know. If he had been out a while, it was possible that his gang had passed on by. He looked at the moon and estimated it had been far more than an hour. He became irritated with himself.

He was just about to rise when he heard the twig snap somewhere to his left. He froze in position and waited, listening for more noise. At first he heard nothing, but Christian was a good hunter and patient. He knew the twig didn't break by itself on a calm night. Something alive had done that and he wanted to know who or what it was before he revealed his position. He heard stealthy movement to his left. As Ben and Anna crossed the alley and entered the cemetery, they crossed his line of sight. He knew instantly that it was McDonald and the girl. He waited until they were well into the cemetery before he got up and began to follow at a distance.

They moved in and out of the shadows in the cemetery. He lost sight briefly, but then saw them again moving near a large mausoleum at the back of the cemetery. They disappeared in the shadows around it. He followed cautiously, quietly approaching the structure and keeping it between him and the western side of the cemetery, where he assumed they had crossed. He stayed in its shadow as he carefully moved to its opposite side to pick up sight of Ben and the girl as they crossed the rest of the cemetery. He had believed what he told his gang about McDonald being unlikely to attack him, but he couldn't be certain what Ben would do if cornered.

He paused at the west corner of the mausoleum, assuming he would easily pick up sight of the figures moving across the far side of the cemetery, but he didn't. He left the shadows of the mausoleum, increasing his pace a bit, but still didn't see them. That was odd. They weren't that far ahead of him and their movement across the west side of the cemetery should have been clearly visible in the moonlight. They seemed to have vanished into thin air.

He backtracked to the mausoleum where he had last seen them. He stood outside and listened but heard nothing. He inspected the mausoleum's outer gate. It hung half open and looked like it hadn't been used in a while. He tested it, moving it only a little way to accommodate his entry without having it hit his left arm. It squeaked, just as he assumed it would.

He slipped inside. The entrance did not directly face the moon, so the interior was mostly dark. He could not see the back of the chamber. He moved around slowly from side to side. He found nothing out of the ordinary. He felt his way to the back of the mausoleum holding his right hand up at face level to avoid bumping into the wall with his broken arm. He touched stone.

He turned and made his way back through the gate. Despite his caution, he bumped his broken arm on the way out, shooting pain up his shoulder. He staggered a little and his body hit the gate again. It squeaked louder this time. He looked around, but saw no one in the cemetery. He decided to cross the cemetery and move up the west alleyway. He would find them. His hunch had been right. They were somewhere nearby, but where?

Inside the inner chamber, Ben and Anna held their collective breath. They had entered the inner chamber and closed its iron door only a minute or two ahead of the squeaking gate. It might have been rats, but Ben doubted it. Something bigger had come inside the tomb. Ben placed his hand on Anna's shoulder for silence but she had heard the noise and didn't need the admonition. Her heart was beating faster. She didn't make a sound.

Then they heard the squeak of the outer gate again. Ben was now sure that it wasn't a small animal. Someone had been in the mausoleum. Perhaps someone was still there. She and Ben waited a few minutes before Ben spoke in a whisper. "Anna, I think someone followed us into the mausoleum. They are probably gone by now. Maybe they didn't discover the door to our chamber, but if they saw us coming in, or even through the cemetery, they will be back to search when it's light. We're going to have to move quickly, and that's going to be dangerous." He paused, his voice grave, "And I don't know where we can go."

"We can't go south. By this time they are looking for us everywhere and we would be seen by too many eyes if we tried to go back through Hell's kitchen. We could try to get to the Hudson or the East river--the Hudson is closer--but I can't swim and both rivers are wide. We could try to steal a boat, but I have no idea where one is and I am afraid we'd be caught trying. If we do, we'll be handed over to the Bowery Boys and that will be the end." He didn't tell her that she would probably be raped and brutalized before they killed her. "They say there's a bridge off the island somewhere north of Central Park. I have no idea how far it is and what lies between it and us. That may be our best choice, but I'm not sure. Can you swim?"

She shook her head. "No, not well enough to get across a river. Plus it's cold. The water would be freezing now. We probably wouldn't last even if we could swim."

He nodded. "Yea, you're right. So what do you think about trying to get across Central Park and going north to try to find that bridge? I have to warn you, even if we get across, if the police pick us up, they'll probably take us back to the Bowery Boys. I've seen that before. The police don't like kids leaving Hell's Kitchen and entering other neighborhoods. They usually just take kids back and hand them over to a gang for punishment. Most of those kids just vanish."

She shuddered. "We don't have much chance do we?"

He didn't want to answer but he thought he should. "Maybe not, but it's worth a try. We probably should wait a few more minutes to let whoever came in here get further away. Somebody might still be watching. But when we move, we'll have to move quickly and we can't stop for anything."

"I understand. I'm ready when you say."

"Okay, then, we will wait a little more. He paused. "This would

127

have happened soon anyway. I'd be afraid to leave you here alone to go after more food. We'll go together and see what comes of it."

She took his hand again. They sat waiting, hoping that a little time might clear the way for their escape.

Chapter 13

After Christian exited the Mausoleum, he walked quickly across the cemetery, trying to figure out where they had gone, assuming he would eventually run into one of his groups if he didn't spot Ben and the girl first. He would backtrack with his gang and concentrate the search west of the cemetery. As soon as he reached the shadows of the alleyway, he slowed and moved more cautiously.

Moving from shadow to shadow, his mind kept returning to the two ghost-like figures he had seen crossing the cemetery and the mausoleum he had just searched. His instincts told him that he had missed something, but he couldn't put his finger on it. As he contemplated that, he subconsciously slowed his pace until he ultimately came to a full stop under a tree no more than two blocks past the northern edge of the cemetery.

Something hadn't been right with the mausoleum, but what was it? He had inspected it; it was empty. The spaces where the coffins were stored on each side of the mausoleum were not wide enough for a person to slide in and hide. What was he missing? He stood still, thinking hard. What wasn't right?

Finally, in a flash, it hit him. He cursed and immediately turned back toward the cemetery. No spider webs inside! That's what had bothered him! Someone had been entering that mausoleum recently. Someone had been all around the inside. He had not encountered one spider web in there.

It could have been visitors, but the mausoleum didn't give the appearance of being visited much or kept up. He supposed someone could be keeping it clean, but if so, no one had bothered to fix the gate or close it. What had he missed inside? There didn't seem to be anywhere to hide, but he needed to check it more thoroughly this time.

He reached the cemetery quickly and crossed to the mausoleum. He stopped in the shadow of the wall near the outer gate and looked around, listening carefully before entering. Even in the dim light of the moon, he could see the unkempt nature of this end of the cemetery. Some tombstones were at odd angles or had fallen completely over. The grass was tall and weedy. Limbs that had blown down from the trees had not been removed. This was an old cemetery, or it was certainly an older, unkempt section of the cemetery. And in the moonlight, this mausoleum looked worn with long age. There were weeds along its sides.

He moved to the front of the mausoleum and then inside, this time being careful not to touch the gate. He looked around and then silently sat down in the middle of the chamber. He waited for his eyes to adjust to the darkness, concentrating on the back wall.

After a minute or two, as his eyes adjusted, he could make out a few more features of the interior. When he looked left and right, he could clearly see the outline of the coffins. There definitely would not be enough space behind or at the ends of them to hide. He stared at the floor. He could make out some of the grouting in the stone floor most of the way back. Nothing seemed unusual. If there was a trap door in the floor, it wasn't obvious.

He turned his focus again to the back wall and inched slowly in that direction, ever so quietly along the floor, feeling it for unusual indentions as he went. He touched the back wall and immediately became puzzled. It didn't seem to him to be as far back as it should have been and what he was touching now did not feel like stone. He moved the fingers of his good hand slowly along the wall, certain now that he was no longer touching stone. He pulled his hand away and sat quietly, listening carefully. He remained immobile for a number of minutes, listening for any sound around him.

Anna and Ben were listening just as carefully, but they hadn't heard Christian enter the Mausoleum again and didn't know that he sat just on the other side of the iron door. Ben decided it was time for them to move and he began to talk to Anna quietly. If the gang had already discovered them, silence was no longer going to protect them; they would not make it beyond the gate of the mausoleum.

"We'll leave in a minute, Anna. I don't know what's out there. We may not get 20 feet or we may get further. Once we start moving we won't talk. Stay behind me or beside me but never in front."

She nodded and squeezed his hand.

"Before we go, there's something else I want to tell you. You asked me why I attacked the gang. I told you I wasn't sure why I did it. Now I think I know. I saw you shortly after you came on the streets. I watched you getting sicker and I knew you wouldn't survive. And I saw you on that night in the alley before the gang got to you. I could tell that would be your last night. I am ashamed of it now, but I decided not to help you. I just watched, hoping you would die in peace. There was something different about you, but I didn't know what exactly, and I wasn't going to try to find out. To do that meant I had to get involved and I was too big a coward to do that." He paused.

"But then they came along and I knew what they would do and I just lost my senses. They wouldn't just let you die quietly. Now that I really know you, I can't even imagine why I didn't help you earlier—why it took what they were going to do to cause me to act. I don't know if I am more angry with them or myself. They were following their instincts; I was rejecting mine. I thought I was better than them, but I wasn't. I was just selfish. I thought that I wouldn't survive if I helped you."

"I saw lots of kids die during the three years I've been on the streets and I didn't do one damn thing about it. That's the hard part—to know that I just watched horrible things happen and turned away. Those kids died cold and lonely, never understanding why nobody cared enough to help, probably feeling that they must have done something terrible or had something so wrong with them that it made it okay for them to die like they did."

"Now that I know you, and know how nice you are, I can't imagine what I was thinking that night when I was just standing by and watching you suffer. You ought to be able to grow up…to have a life…to have a family…to have somebody who cares about you. That's what you deserve…what every kid deserves…even what somebody like Christian Gunther deserved. A guy with his skills could have really amounted to something if he'd had a chance."

"So, I just want you to know that saving you was the most important thing that I have ever done, or probably ever will. No matter what happens out there, I could never stay in Hell's Kitchen again and watch kids die and do nothing about it. That's what being with you has taught me. I'm proud that I did one right thing just once while I was here."

She scooted over and put her arms around him and held him tight, her head leaning on his chest. "You are such a special person, Ben McDonald. I hope I never lose you."

On the other side of the door, Christian Gunther heard every word. He swallowed hard. He wished McDonald hadn't spoken. He swore quietly, "Damn you, McDonald! You are such a pain in the ass!" He knocked on the iron door and addressed them quietly, "McDonald, I know you're in there with the girl. I am alone right now. You two come out. Let's talk."

Ben and Anna froze. Anna gasped. Ben tried to think what to do. They were trapped with no escape! He would not be able to protect her. He didn't really care about himself anymore, but he was deathly afraid for her. He quickly calculated a last desperate move. He whispered to her fiercely as he pushed her back from the door, "I am going out. You stay here till I call for you! Don't come out until I tell you to!"

She gasped. "No Ben, don't go out there!"

He kept pushing her back from the door toward the back wall. "I'm going out. If you try to come, it'll be worse for me. Please do what I tell you and stay here! Put the wooden block under the handle as soon as I leave. If I don't call for you, don't let anyone in, no matter what. Stay in here until daylight if you can and then yell as loud as you can. Keep yelling till some adult comes!"

"No! I'm going with you!"

"No you're not! I know what I'm doing and I don't want you in the way. Stay here. Block the door like I told you. Keep quiet till daylight, then yell loud and long. Please, do as I say! I can't protect you and me both out there, do you understand?"

She sobbed, "No, you can't go!"

But he just kept pushing her until her back struck against the wall.

Before she could move, he whirled around, grabbed his club, jerked the door open and dived through. He rolled into an awkward somersault in the outer chamber, then scooted backward and pushed the door shut behind him. He was so accustomed to stealth that the noise of the door slamming against stone sounded horrendous. But he knew that noise didn't matter anymore.

He had assumed he would be attacked as soon as he entered the main chamber. He would fight and try to get to Gunther if he could. He would negotiate for the girl. He would let the gang take him and make him an example in any way they chose if Gunther would promise to let the girl go. He would stop fighting and cooperate if only Gunther would promise. He had to take the chance on Gunther keeping his word.

If he could overcome those inside the mausoleum, the others would have to come through him. If they tried, he would do some damage. Outside, he would stand less chance. If he could hold his own inside, maybe they would bargain and save themselves some grief. It was all he had.

But nothing happened.

Christian had expected Ben to come out fast. Before the trap door opened he had backed up to the iron gate. He chuckled when Ben flipped awkwardly through the door and hit the floor. "Really dramatic exit, McDonald! But kind'a loud. I'm hoping my boys were too far away to hear it; otherwise we'll have a problem. Hope you didn't break any bones. I can tell you from recent experience, that doesn't feel good."

Ben ignored Gunther for the moment. He looked around frantically, trying to see how many of the gang members were in the mausoleum. He saw no one but Gunther, but he still couldn't believe that Gunther would be inside alone. There had to be others.

But still no attack. He jumped to his feet. On the other side of the wall, he heard Anna push the board under the handle. Good! She'd done as he told her.

Gunther spoke again. "So, here we are, Ben; just you and me, about to have a little chat. I heard the stuff you said to the girl. It was touching, actually. It finally all makes sense to me. Sadly, I now realize that you are a hopeless do-gooder. Maybe we'll have room for people like you in Hell's Kitchen someday and that will change things, but right now, there's just not much of a market for your kind. You don't belong here anymore—probably never did. I should have known that by watching you more closely."

"I know another guy who thinks just about like you. I'm going to try to get you and the girl out to him, crazy as that sounds. I'm going to give you this one chance to break free. But if I get you out, and if you wander back onto to Hell's Kitchen for any reason, or even if you're brought back by the authorities, I'll personally gut you in public and hang your carcass from the nearest lamppost for everybody to see."

Ben still didn't buy it. He was sure it was a setup to get Anna out in the open. "I don't believe you, Gunther, and I'm not bringing her out to you and your boys without a fight. The way I see it, I don't have much to lose. I can take some of you down with me if that's what you have in mind. But, I'm willing to deal. I'll give myself up to you without a fight if you give me your word that you'll get the girl safely out of Hell's Kitchen. That way, none of your guys get hurt. I'll take whatever justice you want to mete out. You can say she's dead already. I won't resist. You give me your word and I'll bring her out."

Christian smiled. "That's a tempting deal, McDonald, and one I should take you up on; but being the fool that I am on this particular night, I'm declining. I'm serious about getting both of you out of Hell's Kitchen, and we don't have time for your theatrics. So come over here and take a look outside to assure yourself that I don't have my boys lined up to jump you as soon as she comes out. Then get her out here and let's get moving before one of my groups wanders back this way. If they find us together, my offer is off."

"Don't screw around with this. It's better than you deserve and you know it. It wouldn't take much for me to change my mind. You've already caused me no end of grief and it's just beginning. So come take a look and make up your mind. I'm a cripple right now. You know I can't hurt you. If you refuse and I have to walk away from here without you, then you're both on your own when I get back with my boys. There'll be no deals at that point."

Ben still hesitated for a second, thinking fast. He knew Christian Gunther to be many things, but dishonesty was not his style. He got up and walked over to the gate. The cemetery looked empty. Gunther could have his boys waiting in the shadows across the alleys, but why would he bother? He held all the cards. He didn't need to hide his gang. They could have smoked him and Anna out—literally.

He found it unbelievable that Gunther would actually take them to safety, but what were his choices? At least he and Anna would be in the open. He could best Gunther in his current condition and then they could run if they smelled a trap.

"Ok, Christian, I'll get her." He called to her. "Anna, come out. It's ok for now."

She opened the door immediately and slipped through. She stood up in the mausoleum. She saw no one other than Ben. Gunther was waiting outside the gate. She and Ben walked out to meet him.

"Christian, this is Anna."

"Hello, Anna. You are a lot of trouble. I guess you realize that by now?"

She nodded and said nothing.

"Okay, here's how this is going to happen. I'm taking you northeast to 59th Street. There's a warehouse there. The manager is a man named Bill Chambers. He was an orphan once. Now he's a do-gooder who takes kids off the streets and sends them away somewhere to families who take them in. He'll probably help you."

"We're going to be passing through territory my gang is searching, so you two walk just a little behind me. We won't talk on the way. If I see the Boys, I'll motion you back. You'll need to find a hiding place quick. I'll send them somewhere and we'll go on. You understand?"

Ben nodded, still doubtful that Christian would do what he said, but grateful to be in the open. Christian looked at Anna. She nodded as well. He led them quickly across the cemetery to its northeast corner, then up the alleyway. He moved slower after that, moving from shadow to shadow, often stopping to listen. Ben and Anna followed anxiously, wary of attack at any minute.

They crossed 54th Street. It was still hours before morning light;

no one was on the street. They hit another alley going north, keeping to the shadows. They had walked three blocks when they heard voices ahead. Christian stopped abruptly and pushed his hand back toward Ben and Anna, alerting them to hide. They stepped to the side of the alley behind some bushes. After a brief pause, Christian moved forward toward the voices, whistling softly as he went.

Ben took Anna's hand and prepared to pull her away and run. As they had followed Gunther, Ben had been trying to guess what he was up to. It had occurred to him that it was possible that Christian had been the only one who saw them return to the cemetery. That would mean he had no backup, which meant that he needed to lure them to the other gang members. His injury would have made it impossible to take Ben and Anna alone. If that was what had happened, they would soon be surrounded.

But why wouldn't he just have summoned his gang and surrounded the mausoleum? Perhaps he had heard them talking about leaving and was afraid they would get away before he could get the gang. In any case, Ben had just about decided to try to escape when he heard Christian speak to his gang—a little louder than normal, perhaps for their benefit.

"So why didn't you guys connect with me where I told you to, back south in the alley and what the hell are you doing all the way up here?" His question was harsh and had an accusatory ring to it that startled Johnny.

"We did! We looked for you up and down the alleys by that cemetery. We couldn't find you."

Christian sounded skeptical. "Well, that's really strange isn't it, since I was there all the time."

Johnny was whining now. "I swear! We looked all over for you. I don't know what happened but we were there where you said."

Christian's replied, faking disgust. "Well, we'll talk more about this later, but right now you boys haul your miserable asses back down to the area around 51st and comb every inch of it from the Hudson to Sixth Avenue. And you keep looking in that area until I tell you otherwise. You hear?"

Johnnie was angry and offended that Christian didn't believe him. Worse yet Christian had called him down in front of the group. He had never done that before and Johnny didn't like how it felt. He spat in defiance and started to leave.

Christian stopped him. "Who else is up here?"

"Nobody as far as I know."

"Well, if you see any more of the boys, tell them I said to help you out down near 51st. I still think they've been hiding out somewhere around there. If we don't find them by morning, I'm calling it off. I'm going to go look for our other groups after I take a short break here and if I find them, I'll send them back your way."

That last bit of information helped Johnny a little. Gunther was just irritable because he was going to have to admit he was wrong and there would be hell to pay. "Sure, we'll look a little longer." With that, Johnny and his group turned south.

Ben and Anna heard all of the conversation. They hid in the shadows as the gang passed no more than 15 feet away. A few seconds later, Christian whistled softly and they caught up with him. He started walking north again without looking back. Ben wanted to thank him but he knew Gunther wouldn't appreciate the noise.

It took them only a few more minutes to reach 59th and turn east. They neared the East River and stopped in front of a massive brick building with large windows in three of its floors. Christian leaned down and picked up a pebble. He tossed it up to a third floor window directly above the building's main entrance. Then he backed them into the shadows and they waited. Within a couple of minutes they heard a window opening.

Christian stepped into the light. "I've brought you a couple of kids. They're different than usual."

There was silence for a second; then a man's voice responded from above, "Ok, I'll be down in a minute."

Christian turned to Ben and Anna, still standing behind him. "Bill will do what he can for you. You can trust him. You'll like him. Remember what I said earlier. I never want to see you in Hell's Kitchen again. You'll be dead in an hour if you come back and it'll have to be by my hand, assuming I still have one."

"Why, Gunther?"

"Why, what?"

"You know what. Why did you bring us out? This can't be good for you."

Christian smiled a little. "You're a persuasive man, McDonald. We may not be quite as different as you think. But you're right. You getting away will not be good for me. If you come back, it'll be even worse for me. So you damn well better stay away and make something out of this. If you're going to be a do-gooder, you'd better become a damn good one." He turned to Anna. "Same with you, lady. Someday I'd like to know the price I'll pay was worth it."

Just then the main door of the warehouse opened. A tall, lean figure stepped down to street level. The man looked at Ben and Anna. "What are you doing, Christian? These kids are far too old for me to help. You know that."

"You'll have to do your best, Chambers. They're dead if they come back to Hell's Kitchen. You'll figure something out."

Bill looked at Christian for a second, incredulous, then turned to Ben and Anna. "Sorry about my rudeness. You're just a lot older than the children Christian usually brings. I'm Bill Chambers." He stuck out his hand to Ben first, then to Anna. They shook it. He turned back around to speak to Christian, but he had already disappeared into the shadows.

Ben also turned in the direction Christian must have gone, trying to fathom why the toughest urchin in Hell's Kitchen had just saved their lives. Finally he murmured, "Thanks, Gunther, if you can still hear me. We'll try not to disappoint you." But he didn't figure that Christian was close enough to hear. He suspected that he wasn't a person inclined to wait around for words.

Chapter 14

Bill Chambers took Ben and Anna up to his third floor apartment. He set two bowls and spoons in front of them and got out some cereal and milk from his ice box while he began to make coffee. He also retrieved six eggs and some bacon. Soon luscious smells spread throughout the apartment, causing Ben's stomach to grumble violently and Anna to feel a little dizzy. It had been a long time since either had experienced those smells.

"Take off your coats, sit down at the table and eat some of that cereal for starters. The rest of the meal will be finished shortly."

When they removed their outer garments, Bill was shocked that Anna's clothing was so filthy and torn that it hardly held to her body. Ben's was more typical of the clothing of a street urchin. Bill was familiar with what kids faced on the streets. He knew from the looks of her clothing and her extremely thin features that she had fared badly. Both Ben and Anna began to eat the cereal eagerly.

"Have either of you ever had coffee?"

They indicated they had not.

"Well, it is sort of an acquired taste, but I think you'll feel better if you sip a little." He poured coffee into two mugs and set them on the table. "Just take small sips. It's hot. It'll warm you up inside and give you some energy. Since it's so early, I doubt that you had a lot of sleep last night."

They didn't tell him that they had been on a different sleep cycle.

He turned back to a small counter and cracked the eggs, spilling their contents into a bowl. He had already placed a half dozen pieces of thick bacon into a frying pan. The bacon began to sizzle as he stirred the eggs and then poured them into another skillet. "The eggs and bacon will be done in a few minutes." He also retrieved some biscuits from a container for the meal and set out jelly and butter. By the time Ben and Anna had finished their cereal, Bill had placed three plates on the table, each with heaping scoops of scrambled eggs, as well as the bacon. He placed a large biscuit on each plate.

"So, eat before it gets cold."

He didn't have to ask twice. Over the next half hour, Ben McDonald partook of the best meal he had ever experienced in his life. Anna's family had once provided good meals for her, but she had almost forgotten what it was like to eat so well. During the meal, Bill peppered them with questions about their families and how they wound up on the streets. By the end of the meal, he had learned both of their stories. He listened with interest and treated them with empathy and respect, putting them at ease.

Toward the end of the meal, Bill asked, "So how do you know Christian Gunther? Were you members of the Bowery Boys gang?" Bill already suspected that Anna probably wasn't, but Ben could certainly have been. He was intrigued with why Christian had chosen these two children—actually these two teenagers—to bring to him. This was a highly unusual situation.

Ben replied. "No, neither of us was in his gang. I only met Christian a few times over the last three years and Anna probably never met him at all before tonight." Then he told the remarkable story to Bill with a little commentary from Anna.

After hearing it, Bill was incredulous. "So, Ben, you were on the streets for over three years and you never joined a gang?"

"No, I never did. It was tempting, but I didn't agree with some of the things they did."

"And when you saved Anna, you fought five of the gang alone?"

Ben could tell that Bill found that hard to believe. "Yea, but it was dark and they were distracted. They weren't in good position to defend theirselves."

"I heard there had been an attack on some of the Bowery Boys, including Christian, and that he'd been injured. I didn't know why or who did it. Most of us outside the Kitchen assumed it was inter-gang rivalry. Your story is incredible! If Christian hadn't brought you here himself, I wouldn't have believed it. Since you attacked him and his gang, why did he bring you out?"

Ben and Anna sat silently, mulling the question. Ben finally tried to answer. "I really don't know. He'll take a lot of heat for letting us get away. I guess it could even ruin him. What he did doesn't make any sense."

A slow smile crossed Bill's face. "Well, sometimes people aren't always what they seem. He's done other good things that very few know about—certainly no one in Hell's Kitchen—but never anything quite like this. Frankly, it worries me a little. I don't know how he'll explain it to his bosses."

Ben nodded. "I know it'll give him trouble. I regret that, but if all this hadn't come down the way it did, Anna wouldn't be with us. Whatever it took to keep her alive is what had to be done."

Anna blushed. She reached over and took Ben's hand. Bill

noticed that she didn't let it go quickly.

Bill Chambers was the manager of the largest warehouse operation on the East River, headquartered in the building in which Ben and Anna now sat. Although still young, he had risen quickly through the ranks to his current position. It was also the most efficient warehouse system in Manhattan. He had a sterling reputation with everyone who did business with him or worked under his supervision. He worked hard and seemed to have no personal life. He lived alone—he had never married—and his only avocation was working with groups interested in changing the plight of orphaned children in New York City.

As Christian had told them, Bill had been an urchin himself for five long years before taking an entry-level job at the warehouse. The Reverend Charles Loring Brace had gotten him out of Hell's Kitchen. Brace had met Bill as he negotiated with the youth gangs there. At that time Bill was a member of the Bowery Boys, rising to the rank of lieutenant, but no further. He did not to have the stomach for what was required to rise to the top. But he was well-liked by his fellow gang members, who knew that he was very smart and a great communicator. Despite never rising to the head of the gang, he had become its spokesperson, and that's how he met Brace.

Brace wanted Chambers to help him with negotiations with all the gangs, not just the Bowery Boys. To do that, he had to get him out of Hell's Kitchen. He appealed to a philanthropic friend who owned the warehouse operation to arrange the job. Then Brace talked to the leader of the Bowery Boys and laid out his proposal. He wanted to take the youngest of the children off the streets and needed the gangs to help. That required an intermediary who spoke their language. He thought Bill was the one for that job.

To his surprise, the leader agreed, since he knew that Chambers didn't really cotton to some of the gang's more nefarious activities and he was always a little nervous that Chambers, who was charismatic, would give him competition if he ever chose to do so. Sending him with Brace would remove that threat and do some good at the same time. The leader called Bill in and told him what Brace was proposing. He said he'd support it and cooperate with Brace in the future if Bill chose to join his cause. Bill was at the warehouse within a few hours of that discussion.

Bill's apartment was one of the few luxuries in his life. It was large and spacious. It had a sitting room, a kitchen with running water that operated through the same piping system that served the warehouse, two spacious bedrooms and a real bathroom. It had all the modern technologies of its day. The bathroom contained a Victorian tub, a real flush toilet powered by the gravity of a water tank hanging on the wall over it, and a good-sized vanity with a large mirror on the wall above it.

It was past 6:00 a.m. when Bill, Ben and Anna finished their breakfast and conversation. Bill could tell that the kids were tired, and he needed to get to his office. He took Anna into the bathroom and showed her how to draw the running water. He put a large kettle of water on the stove in the kitchen to warm and told Ben to take it into the bathroom after it heated so Anna could mix it with the cold water.

He provided a shirt and trousers for Anna to use after bathing, indicating that they would find something better before the day was out. He provided a change of clothing for Ben as well. He told Ben to use his bedroom that day and assigned Anna the guest bedroom.

"I've got to get to work in a few minutes, but I'll check on you at noon and be back as soon as I can this evening. I think you have everything you need here. Please don't leave the apartment today. We'll make plans for you in the next few days. There's food in the ice box if you get hungry before I get back. I'll return at noon and get you some lunch. For now, clean up, relax and get some rest."

Ben and Anna offered their grateful thanks and Bill left for work. When the kettle was hot, Ben carried it into the bathroom for Anna and mixed it with the cold water from the faucet. After he left, she closed the bathroom door, shed her filthy rags and climbed into the tub. She imagined that the sensations associated with that bath were something like going to heaven. There was soap at the edge of the tub and she used it liberally. There was shampoo for her hair. She lay back in the tub and soaked for a full hour. Before she got out of the tub, she rinsed herself with water flowing directly from the tub's faucet. It was cold, but invigorating, and oh so clean! She couldn't help but giggle as she did it. She had never had access to water simply by turning a handle.

There was a huge dirty ring circling the tub when she got out. She was embarrassed and cleaned it since Ben would be taking a bath next. She slipped into the shirt and trousers Bill had provided. They were far too large for her slim body. She had to roll up the sleeves and pant legs numerous turns. The pants had a belt but there weren't enough holes for her to buckle it. Luckily, Bill had anticipated this and also provided a piece of cord she could tie around her waist. She left the shirt tail out and it came halfway down her legs, almost like a dress. She was worried about having no undergarments beneath the shirt, but there was nothing she could do about that.

She spent another half-hour combing out her tangled hair. It bothered her that she was hogging the bathroom so long, but it felt so good to get clean. Finally, she put her dirty clothing in a bag

Bill had provided for her to discard them, and timidly made her way back to the sitting room.

Ben was sitting in a chair, looking at a magazine when she came in. He glanced up at her and then did a double-take. Clean and with her hair combed, even in Bill's baggy clothing, she was the most beautiful girl he had ever seen. He gaped till her face turned red. He realized what he was doing and blushed. "I'm sorry to stare, Anna, but I'm really just seeing you for the first time. You are really pretty."

She blushed again. "Thanks. But I think it's just because you have finally seen me clean."

"Maybe", he said. But he knew it wasn't so. He had never seen anyone as pretty as she, including his own mother.
Ben had already heated his water. He took a shorter bath than Anna but enjoyed it almost as much. Bill's clothes were a close fit for Ben's size. When he came out Anna made a point not to stare, but from side glances, she determined that he was at least as handsome as her father. It was the highest compliment she knew. His hair was still long and shaggy, but even that wore well on him.

They took catnaps until it was time for Bill to come back at noon. When he walked in the door they were in the sitting room. He saw them and immediately whistled. "Wow, you two cleaned up really nicely!" They laughed. The three of them ate a hearty meal. During lunch, Bill told them, "I'm having a lady come over from our church with some clothes and shoes later this afternoon. Her name is Mrs. Bonham. I tried to guess your sizes and hope I came close. These are gifts from the church. We do this all the time, so don't worry about the cost. You will need the clothes for whatever next steps we take to get you out of here."

Mrs. Bonham arrived about 3:00 p.m. that afternoon. She was a portly lady and carried a large suitcase, which she set down in the middle of the floor and then fanned herself with her hands while catching her breath. As soon as she could, she began talking. "My, my, you two! Bill told me you were good looking kids, but he understated the case. Your names are Anna and Ben, right?" She continued even before they nodded. "Well, Anna, you're a little taller even than he said, but I think we have that covered." She flipped the catches and opened the big suitcase.

Anna gasped. There were all kinds of new clothes in there! She had assumed the clothes would be hand-me-downs but these still had the store tags on them. On the very top of the pile was a beautiful blue and gold calico dress with a matching bonnet. Under it was a yellow dress nearly as pretty.

Mrs. Bonham laughed heartily at Anna's reaction. "Okay, young lady, take the blue one and go into the bedroom and try it on. I just hope it's long enough. Oh! And here are a few things you will also need." With that, she pulled out nice cotton underwear and a petticoat, passing them to Anna, who stood staring at the clothes in her hands, dumbfounded.

"Go on, go on! Try them on. Let's see how they fit." She gave Anna a gentle push toward the guest bedroom. Obviously she had been in Bill's apartment before. Anna snapped out of her stupor and headed to the bedroom.

While Anna was gone Mrs. Bonham turned to Ben. "Now, young man, let's trim off some of that hair! She pulled out a pair of hand clippers and scissors. "Pull a chair over here." Ben hesitated and she laughed. "I've done this many times with my own kids, Ben. I'll not butcher you too badly." He smiled and pulled up the chair.

Once she finished with his hair, she pulled out two pairs of pants, two shirts, underwear, socks and a pair of shoes and handed the whole bundle to Ben. "You go into Bill's bedroom and try these on. Bill said you are almost identical in size to him except taller. We'll see how well he guessed. I'll clean up all this hair on the floor."

Ben was even more surprised than Anna. He had never had new clothes. "Are you sure these are for me?"

She laughed and exclaimed, "Of course they are for you, dear! You see anybody else in this apartment right now that could fit in those big shirts?"

He went into Bill's bedroom to change. The clothes looked so fine that he was almost afraid to put them on. He finished dressing quickly and was back before Anna and came into the sitting room. The clothes and shoes were a perfect fit. "Well, I see Bill guessed right after all. What a handsome young man you are, Ben!" He blushed and smiled. Unconsciously he kept rubbing the shirt and pants with his hands. He had never experienced such fine clothes.

Finally Anna came out of the guest bedroom in the blue and gold dress. Ben had the presence of mind not to gape, but he couldn't believe how beautiful she was in those clothes! Mrs. Bonham, who never hesitated to say whatever she thought, exclaimed, "My goodness, child! I don't think I have ever seen a girl any prettier than you, even if you are way too thin! That dress will fit a bit better when Bill gets some food in you. I thought it might be a little short in the hemline, but it looks just about the right length. Turn around for me."

Anna did a pirouette.

"Why yes, we've done very well today haven't we. Both of you are the right size for what I brought. I am so pleased with myself! Bill may not even recognize you when he gets back. Anna, we still ought to do a little something with your hair, but that can come later. In the meantime, here's a comb and brush and some ribbons that will be more appropriate than what Bill has to offer."

"Oh, I almost forgot! We're not done. I have a couple of coats in here. They're what made the suitcase so heavy." She pulled out two attractive wool coats. Both were of good quality and looked wonderfully warm. "Get over here, you two, and try these on. Then you can take the rest of these clothes in the suitcase and put them in your bedrooms."

The coats fit perfectly and they were so warm that both Ben and Anna began to perspire, but still hesitated to take them off. Finally, Mrs. Bonham laughed and insisted that they do so when she saw beads of sweat popping out on Ben's forehead.

They carried their respective bundles into the bedrooms and came back to Mrs. Bonham. "It is so wonderful meeting you young people! Bill finds such nice children to help, although I must say, I've never seen any of your age come through here before. This is kind of fun! Well, I must be off. Hope you enjoy the clothes!"

They thanked her repeatedly as she left. When she had gone, Ben and Anna looked at each other incredulously, and then started laughing. "Can you believe this, Ben? This must be a dream. I'm afraid I'll wake up and find it's not true and have to cry."

He laughed. "Yea, I know what you mean, but I guess you won't have to cry. I just can't believe there are people who would help us like this without knowing us."

She nodded. For the rest of the afternoon, they tried on their new clothes, modeling for each other, napping and enjoying the wonderful warmth of the apartment.

Chapter 15

Bill had not been entirely truthful about the clothes. The cost of a few of them had actually come from the church, but the price of most of the clothing from Mrs. Bonham's shop was paid by a single philanthropic individual.

When Mrs. Bonham left the children, she went down to Bill's office. "Charge this to your usual account, Bill?"

"Yes, and thanks for bringing the clothes over. Did they ask any more questions about where they came from?"

"No, no. They believed what you told them. What would the Reverend Brace say about your falsehoods, Mr. Chambers!" She laughed. "It's all for the right reasons, isn't it. I get the feeling they have seldom had new clothes before. They were pretty much speechless; but oh, how nice they both looked! They seem like such good children. You pick them well, Bill Chambers, but as much money you spend on clothes for all the children coming through here, you're going to go broke!"

He laughed. "It's not really that much, Mrs. Bonham. I don't have many other things to spend my money on. Most kids coming through here don't ever remember having decent clothes. It changes their perspective."

"Well, just so, Bill, I think you are the nicest man I ever met! And that's not just because you buy the clothes from my shop. If we had a few more like you around, I think there wouldn't be any kids left out on the streets. It's a horrible shame they're there. You and Reverend Brace are doing such important work. I just wish I could help more."

Bill smiled. "You do just fine, Mrs. Bonham. Despite your sneakiness, I know you have never charged me more than wholesale for any of the clothes I buy from you." He came over and hugged her, kissing her on the cheek. She felt faint and blushed. He was such a handsome man! For one of the rare times in her life, she was too flustered to say anything. Her eyes misted and she hugged him again before bustling out of his office.

Bill walked over to the large window facing 59th Street. It was beginning to rain. He regretted that Mrs. Bonham would get wet lugging the suitcase back to her shop. The sound of the rain held him at the window. It would turn very cold and wet on the streets tonight. He stared down at the street and wondered, as he always did, how the children of Hell's Kitchen would fare.

He was always depressed when it rained, particularly in the cold months. Not only did it bring back painful personal memories, but it reminded him that he, Brace and the others in the Children's Aid Society weren't moving fast enough. More kids would die tonight in Hell's Kitchen.

Bill had never married, although he had attracted the attention of numerous New York socialites. Every time he thought about having a family, he drew back. He was afraid to commit to a relationship that would result in children. He rationalized that it would interfere with his passion for the urchins of Hell's Kitchen, but the real truth was tied to the loss of his own parents. It was illogical, he knew. They had been nurturing and supportive, but when they died in a cholera epidemic, no one was there to save him from the streets. What if he sired children and then something happened to him and his spouse? He knew he was in stronger position financially and better connected than his parents. He could make contingency plans and leave money to assure that his own children would be protected. Brace would take care of them if need be. But life was so uncertain, and a child's loss of a parent left too many unhealed scars. He feared risking it.

And then, there was the depression that haunted him. He assumed it was from his past troubles, but he wasn't sure. It intruded on his life at such odd times, seemingly with no triggering events. It was most debilitating for him on dark, cold and wet winter days, draining him of all his energy. It was all he could do to mask it from his coworkers and friends. He wasn't sure what it would do to a family.

Perhaps that would all change in time. He hoped so. He hungered for the companionship of a good spouse. He loved children and knew he'd enjoy being a father. But for now, he would dedicate his energy and skills to the children clinging to life by a thin thread on the streets of Hell's Kitchen.

He had great allies at the Children's Aid Society—friends and colleagues as close as family. Most important, he had the unconditional support of the Reverend Brace himself. But lately, he worried that Brace was showing his age from his significant health problems. Bill wasn't sure how long Brace could continue his pace as head of the Society. It could be devastating to lose him at the wrong time.

Bill knew that he had to talk to Brace about Ben and Anna--and soon. He couldn't keep Anna in his apartment long. It would be viewed as unseemly. He already knew what Brace was going to say and he dreaded it. He could think of no other options for her except placement in the West, but she was far older than anyone they had ever taken on the trains. As Christian had said, he had to think of something; he realized already that she was too exceptional to be discarded to fate. Charles Brace would help him think of something.

By 1884, the Reverend Charles Loring Brace was an icon in the state of New York and for that matter, across much of America, well known as a fearless champion for orphaned children. He conversed with mayors, governors and even Presidents. He testified to Congressional Committees. He had earned the right to confront the powers that be about abandoned children because of he had become one of America's foremost experts on the subject. He was considered a benevolent god in the liberal circles of New York Society.

Brace was born to a well-educated family in Litchfield Connecticut in 1826. He had lost his own mother to disease when he was 14 years old. She was his life's light and he had great difficulty recovering from her death. His father, a history teacher, understood his pain and continued to provide a caring environment for him. He also had his faith, immersed by his parents in the tradition of Calvinism. As a result, he developed an undying inclination for reform.

In 1846, at the age of 20, he graduated from Yale University, but stayed on a while longer to study divinity and theology. He ultimately decided to transfer to the Union Theological Seminary, where he graduated in 1849. He found his calling in New York, the center of American Protestantism and the place where his brilliant and close friend, Frederick Olmsted, lived.

By 1852, at age 26, he was serving as a minister to the poor on Blackwell's Island, a two-mile slip of land in the East River of New York City between Manhattan and Queens (now called Roosevelt Island). It was the site of a large penitentiary for inmates with misdemeanor offenses including debtors and those of the chronic drunken and disorderly kind. The total facility housed nearly a thousand inmates. All were required to perform some daily labor, the tasks varying according to inmate skills and strengths. Many of the inmates became permanent residents, although that had not been the intent of the city when the penitentiary was created.

Brace ultimately became disillusioned with his work there. He felt most of the prisoners were beyond reform and that his efforts were making little to no difference. He wasn't sure whether this was his failing—he believed, accurately, that he was not a dynamic preacher—or simply the fact that it was just too late to change the inmates on Blackwell's Island.

In his spare time, he worked in the Five Points area with newly homeless children, and in that role, he came in contact with the urchins of Hell's Kitchen. He was aghast at their living conditions and couldn't understand why no one was making a serious effort to remedy the situation.

He had his life-changing epiphany in 1852. He decided to leave his ministry at Blackwell's and concentrate solely on the children of Hell's Kitchen. In 1853, he formed the New York Children's Aid Society, dedicated to improving the lives of children of the city, particularly abused and abandoned orphans.

In August 1854 he met the love of his life, Leticia Neill, on a trip to Belfast, Ireland and promptly married her. She would provide lifelong support for her husband's child reform efforts. Charles had chosen well. Reform was in Leticia's blood, too. Her father, Robert Neill, was an avid abolitionist who opened his home to some of the world's most famous anti-slavery leaders, including Frederick Douglass.

Brace was heavily influenced by the writings of Edward Livingstone, a prison reform pioneer who believe that the only real way to stop crime and poverty was to prevent it before it happened. Brace started by focusing on finding jobs and training for poor and destitute children so they could help themselves. He supported free kindergartens, dental clinics, job placement, training programs, reading rooms and lodging houses for boys. He and Leticia even created a summer retreat for children so they could have a break and breathe fresh ocean air.

From the children on the streets, particularly Bill Chambers, Brace learned to loathe orphanages. At best, they provided meager food and shelter. At their worst—and most were—they were cesspools of death and despair.

He had an idealized vision of rural families and decided that younger orphaned children could best be helped by being placed on farms, first in upper New York, then in all the North Atlantic States and New England, and ultimately to the "West", a geographic definition that included Michigan, Illinois, Indiana, Iowa, Missouri and Kansas. Despite his Calvinistic leanings, Brace believed that a family's heredity did not predetermine the moral outcome of a child. To him, a wholesome rural environment trumped family genes.

By 1865, the Children's Aid Society was sending nearly a 1,000 children per year out of the City toward the rural areas of America. Later, it would be multiple times that. Brace's "Emigration Plan" quickly became widely characterized as the *Orphan Train Program*. He once wrote. *"In every American community, especially in a western one, there are many spare places at the table of life…They have enough for themselves and a stranger too."*

Passenger trains transported children, the younger the better, from New York City lodging houses, orphanages, private homes or the streets to rural towns where local organizers promoted family placements. These organizers would post notices in town newspapers and post offices, informing locals when the next shipment of children would arrive at a chosen viewing location. Children arrived in groups ranging from three to thirty-five, along with two adults for supervision.

Brace did not, however, support the theory of indenture. He was an outspoken abolitionist and did not want to promote slavery of any kind. He saw himself as placing children as true members of warm and loving families. He asked selecting families to agree that if the child did not like his or her placement, she or he could leave. It was a good theory that failed to mesh with the reality of a young child in a foreign environment having any real choice about whether or not he could leave, except perhaps by running away. Even if a child decided to appeal his placement, to whom would he petition? There was very little follow-up on the families who took the children.

Brace's vision was embraced by New York socialites in very high places. His efforts were widely supported financially. The first check the Children's Aid Society received for the effort was from Mrs. John Astor herself, for $50, in 1853.

Brace served as the executive secretary for the Children's Aid Society for 37 years prior to his death in 1890 from Bright's disease (kidney problems).

In 1870, while trying to reach out to gang leaders in Five Points and Hell's Kitchen, Brace had met 14-year-old Bill Chambers. The boy had already been on the streets for years. He was bright, inquisitive and articulate. He was also very charismatic. That got Brace to thinking.

Chambers was a member in one of the most notorious youth gangs of Hell's Kitchen, the Bowery Boys. When Brace asked for an appointment with the leader of the Bowery Boys, his invitation was scorned. Brace, not one to give up easily, hounded the gang for a meeting. Finally, in exasperation, the gang's leader sent Bill Chambers, the most articulate among them, to meet with Brace.

At that time, Bill had no respect for ministers. They were never interested in dealing with real world issues, like food and shelter, or kids dying on the streets. They seemed only interested in "saving souls". To Bill, they were all hypocrites. He whined about having to go to the meeting with Brace but his leader just laughed him off. Bill finally swore loudly and exclaimed, "He's not going to like me and I'm sure as hell not gonna like him!"

But Bill was wrong. Brace wasn't like other preachers. He wasn't pretentious; his clothes were worn and looked like he had slept in them. He never once said anything about "saving souls". He treated Bill as an equal. He got right to the point as soon as they were introduced. "Mr. Chambers, I need your gang's help. My colleagues and I are trying to get young children out of orphanages and off the streets before they starve to death, freeze or get killed."

Bill acted disinterested. "So what's your scheme, preacher, and why are you bothering us with it?"

Brace became animated in his speech, trying to sell his idea. "It's simple. You bring the youngest of the children to us. We clean them up, make sure they're well-fed, clothed and healthy, and then we'll take them to rural areas in the northern or western states and find them a good home. They get placed with loving families where they're cared for in healthy environments. We don't place them in orphanages and if they don't like where they're placed, they can ask to be moved."

"Frankly, it would be good public relations for the gang and you will be doing the right thing. I know some of your guys will think these young kids might become future gang members, but most will know better if they think it through. The vast majority of young kids thrown out onto the streets won't live long enough to be in your gang and you can't afford to take them in when they are that young. It's too much of a burden because they can't contribute except by begging or stealing, and most are good at neither. The people of Hell's Kitchen ignore and avoid them. You get almost nothing from them. Eight out of ten will die before they are old enough to be worthwhile to your gang."

"If I were going after your older kids, I'd understand your gripe, but families out west don't want older kids. They want young kids who can grow up as part of their family. This would be good for everybody. If you help, I'll give your gang lots of credit for what you are doing with local authorities. If you don't want the credit, I'll work with you quietly."

"We'll spend every cent we have cleaning kids up and getting them off the streets, but if you guys think you have to have a bounty for the children you bring in, I'll find the money somehow. But I hope you'll do it because you know this is right and smart. You'll always have enough older kids coming to the streets to feed your system. You're smart enough to understand the public relations value of this to the powers that be."

Bill acted nonchalant but was actually impressed by the logic. He had no negative comeback. He sat silently for a few seconds before responding. "Well, preacher, I give you this. You've got balls making this proposal. Let us think about it and get back to you."

"Fine," said Brace. "Don't take too long, Mr. Chambers. Every day we don't work together more young children are going to die for no good reason. I think we could form a partnership here to stop that."

"We'll see," countered Chambers. "It's not my decision. We'll let you know."

As Bill headed back to the gang's headquarters, he thought about what Brace had said. He, himself, had come on the streets when he was a bit older. Even then, he was scared to death during his first year there. He had seen a lot of young kids die in many bad ways, some of them friends he had played with when he was younger. If he hadn't been smart and quick on his feet, he probably would have too.

He used to dream about a family who would take him in and care for him. But after a while, he knew there was no one for him but the gang. Now Brace was offering something else for young kids. If he was shooting straight, it could be a good thing.

He reported to the other gang leaders. He surprised them by indicating that he thought that Brace seemed different. He explained Brace's scheme. Some of the members swore and said it was just more bullshit. No one really cared about any of them. Some said a kid that survived on the street from a young age was going to be a good recruit and those that didn't, they wouldn't have wanted anyway.

Bill didn't try to sell them; he was too smart for that. He listened and they kept talking. He knew that, even as some of them cursed the idea, in the back of their minds, they were thinking about what that could have meant for them if they'd had such a chance.

The leader, after hearing all the babble, finally turned back to Bill. "So, Chambers, you told us what he said, but you haven't said what you think."

Everybody looked at him. He thought for a second about how to answer. "If he's for real, I think the preacher's scheme is not bad. We all know that most kids who come on the streets that young don't make it. We also know that there are plenty of kids coming on the streets when they're older. He's right about us getting most of our recruits from kids of older ages. We don't take in real young kids to babysit 'em. We don't feed 'em. We don't protect 'em. They can't fight. Sometimes we teach the boldest of them how to pick pockets, but it's true that they're not very good at it and get caught a lot. They can't be expected to make much begging on these streets. Nobody in Hell's Kitchen has anything to beg for. This could have value for us if the preacher really is connected with hotshot politicians. They can all put in good words with the cops and city workers and give us more breaks when we need 'em. I don't see much to lose and maybe some to gain."

"We could control who goes to him. We could send the weakest and keep the strongest. And frankly it would be the right thing to give some of these kids a chance instead of just standing around watching them die. It's too late for us, but may not be for some of them. I think we should test it, to see if the preacher can deliver. If he doesn't, then it's no skin off our nose. If he does—well, it might be a good thing all the way around."

The room was silent. The leader finally said, "Okay, I've heard you all out. Let me think about it and talk to some people." Then he dismissed them.

Bill heard nothing more for two weeks. Then the leader called him in. "I used your points with the bosses, Chambers, and they like the idea. I've sent a message to Brace. You're going to talk to him again. Tell him we'll test his little system. If we help and he gets us some appreciation for it, we might play more. If he doesn't, we dump the scheme and he'd better not show his face around here again."

Bill nodded. "I'll talk to him."

And talk they did. Brace was ecstatic and didn't hide it. "Thanks, Mr. Chambers! I suspect I owe you a great deal. Your boys don't have to do much. Just bring us a few kids, the younger the better. We will do the rest. Here's where you bring them". He handed Bill a slip of paper with an address. Let me know when you're coming and I will make sure my friends in the police department are aware that you are bringing them. You'll have no problems, even if the kids squall."

"But one more thing, Bill; they have to be orphans. If they tell us you took them from their families, your help won't be well received and the police will be very unhappy. If you participate, you'll get our grateful support. Does your gang want a bounty?"

Bill shook his head. "Not asking for it. If you're straight, we'll help. If you're not, don't come talking to us again. You won't be well received. Agreed?"

"Agreed! And Bill, we appreciate what you did. I suspect you had to do some selling on this."

Bill smiled and shook his head. "Not my decision."

Braced laughed. "Just the same, thanks. You just may have just saved a lot of kids." Bill didn't respond. He just turned and walked away. But he had a very good feeling about himself for the first time in his life.

During the next two years, the Bowery boys sent over 100 young children to Brace and his people, always arranged through Bill. He and Brace got to know each other well. They even had dinner together a few times. It took some prodding, but Brace got Bill's personal story. Every kid in Hell's Kitchen had a story, but seldom did any adult care to hear it.

Over time, it became apparent to Charles Brace that Bill Chambers was an exceptionally talented boy. At the end of the second year, Brace went to Bill's leader with the proposition to move Bill out of the Kitchen. And that's why Bill Chambers started his work at the warehouse and how he became one of the best friends Charles and Leticia Brace ever had.

Bill's new work with the gangs was tricky at first—not with the Bowery Boys—but with the rival gangs who were hesitant to collaborate with a former Bowery Boy. But positive word of the effort got around and Bill always treated every gang with the same respect.

In time, the youth gangs of New York, who were bitter rivals in all other ways, set aside their differences to participate in Charles Brace's effort to get the youngest children off the streets. That would have never have happened without the persuasion and trust of the former urchin, Bill Chambers. By 1884, thousands of young children had been removed because of Bill's work with the gangs of New York. He moved freely among them and they all treated him as though he was one of their own. They respected his work. He was a straight shooter who never broke their trust. And just like Chambers, most came to feel good about what they were doing for the young children.

Young children still died in Hell's Kitchen. But many were saved; taken quietly to the Children's Aid Society and then sent for placement across the American Midwest.

Chapter 16

Ben and Anna experienced two wonderful days at Bill's apartment. Bill joined them for lunch each day and cooked a delicious meal each night. On the second evening, he took them to dinner at a nice restaurant overlooking Central Park and then to a concert of the New York Philharmonic Symphony. The music was so beautiful that it nearly overwhelmed Anna.

The warmth of the apartment, the healthy food and the good companionship worked wonders for her. Color returned to her skin and she began to develop a healthy glow. As her energy returned, she became more animated, articulate and witty. Both Bill and Ben were shocked at how funny she could be and how well she could sing.

On the third morning, as they were having breakfast, Bill suggested that Anna and Ben take a picnic lunch and go to Central Park to spend the day. He could see from the look on their faces that they were surprised and anxious about the suggestion. "I know that might sound a little scary for you, but cleaned up and in your new clothes, I seriously doubt that anyone who ever knew you before would recognize you now. You will fit in well with the crowd there. Both of you look older than you are and could easily pass as young adults. You won't meet gang members inside the park. They're strictly forbidden this far north. I'll go with you and show you a few of my favorite places. Central Park is such a great place and I think the fresh air will do you good."

Ben saw that the proposition was tempting to Anna and he knew why. She would be remembering the promises of her father. He became less anxious. Bill further reassured them. "In case you get questioned by the authorities at the Park, I'll write you a note indicating you are my relatives here for a visit. They know me.

I'll put it on company stationery. All of them are aware of the company."

They agreed and their anxiety quickly turned to excitement. Even on the streets, they had heard about some of the wonders of Central Park. By the time they had finished breakfast and packed a picnic lunch, both were almost giddy in anticipation.

If Wall Street is the engine of Manhattan, Central Park is its heart. The park had been completed only eleven years before Anna and Ben visited it, and it was already spectacular. Ultimately comprised of a little more than 800 acres in the very heart of Manhattan, it was a perfect rectangle of nature and serenity on an island that had become one of the most highly populated and congested places on earth.

The length of the park, running south to north, stretched fifty blocks, all the way up to 110th Street. The width, limited in part by the narrowness of Manhattan Island, was about a half-mile wide. It was bounded by Fifth Avenue on the east and 8th avenue on the west. It had already become the most visited urban park in America and served as the inspiration for many other urban parks being constructed across the country.

It was designed for the look of a pristine natural setting with only a few glorious manmade nuances. It had been difficult to get that look. The land on which the park was built was poor with scant topsoil that could not have supported the trees and shrubbery envisioned by Olmsted and Vaux, the Central Park designers. Over 18,000 cubic yards of prime New Jersey topsoil were brought in to overcome that problem. Interspersed throughout the park were seven bodies of water, all manmade, but many looking as though they were a creation of nature. The largest was *the Reservoir*, which encompassed over 100 acres and held a billion gallons of water. Other bodies included *The Pond* on the south side, just beyond 59th Street, the *Harlem Lake* all the way up near 110th Street, and *The Lake*, a beautiful, body of water sitting near the middle of the park on its west side, meandering the length of five blocks between 72nd through 79th Streets.

The whole park was intricately laced with walking paths, carriage roads, horse paths and other avenues to allow easy access to every attraction in the park. A major commercial thru fare allowed traffic flow across the Park, but was carefully obscured by sunken roads, trees and shrubs to protect the pristine environs of the rest of the park.

There were birds and numerous other small animals there, as well as a large flock of sheep that lived in *The Meadows*, reinforcing the illusion that the visitor was in a pastoral setting instead of one of the busiest cities in the world.

It took only a few minutes for Bill, Anna and Ben to make their way west on 59th Street to the edge of Central Park. They entered at Scholars Gate and then took a pedestrian path that ran northwest. They quickly came to *The Pond*, which was beautiful on this late autumn morning. Bill gave them a map of Central Park and pointed out some of his favorite areas. After a while, he left them there, heading back to work after telling them to enjoy the day and see as much of the park as possible.

Anna and Ben were awed by the beauty of *The Pond* and found it difficult to tear themselves away to explore other areas. But everywhere they went, they saw something even more beautiful than before. They wandered slowly, taking it all in, each pointing excitedly to something new that attracted them every few hundred feet. They walked past a building called the *Children's Cottage* and its Summer Playground.

By ten that morning they had walked under *The Archway* and crossed a main thoroughfare to view a series of exquisite sculptures, including those of Shakespeare, Sir Walter Scott and The Hunter. They saw the beautiful *Bethesda Fountain* with its Angel and walked through the spectacular *Bethesda Promenade*.

They stopped at noon at Cherry Hill to share the picnic lunch Bill had prepared for them on a grassy knoll overlooking *The Lake*. It was the most beautiful landscape either of them had ever seen. They were so captured by that scene that they remained there long after lunch. A great sense of peace came over them, something Ben had never experienced and Anna had lost with the death of her parents. The day was uncommonly warm with plentiful sunshine. They lay back on the knoll and drifted off to sleep.

When they awoke, they realized it was already late afternoon. Bill had told them that they must get back to the apartment well before sunset, so they reluctantly turned south and made their way back toward 59th Street. From the map Bill had provided, they knew they had seen less than half of Central Park. They decided to ask him if they could return the next day. There were still so many things to see and the bliss of walking casually among such beauty and not being cold, hungry or scared was an elixir to their souls.

When they arrived back at the apartment that evening they told Bill about all they had seen. They were so animated that they kept finishing each other's sentences. He smiled at their enthusiasm and shared additional details about the park's construction when they identified a particular area they especially liked. He also thought their idea of exploring the rest of the park the following day was a good one.

Ben and Anna had never experienced such a day in their young lives. Bill knew they would probably remember it as long as they lived. And watching them tell their story of the great day, seeing their mutual excitement, he became acutely aware of what he had already sensed. These two people had formed a special bond with one another that was powerful and rare. It was pleasant to see, but it also gave him a sinking feeling. That bond would be severely tested soon and might have to be broken. He dreaded the day that would have to happen.

Chapter 17

After leaving Ben and Anna with Bill, Christian Gunther trudged home, fully aware that he had just derailed the future he had been working toward for most of his young life. But he wasn't sure he cared anymore. He knew he had acted impulsively in taking them out of Hell's Kitchen and he detested impulsivity; but upon reflection, he still believed he had made the right decision, even if he couldn't yet explain why. But he was still torn by his decision. Ben had killed one of his gang and crippled others, including himself. No matter how sleazy Big Mike had been, Christian had taken an oath to protect him, or to take revenge if he could not. Yet he had just thrown away his own future to protect the very guy who had done that to him and his gang.

He doubted that he could ever rehabilitate his reputation with his bosses. He knew for certain that he had no chance to do so if they, or any of his gang members, found out that he had personally orchestrated McDonald's escape. It would be treason in their eyes, and frankly, that was a truthful assessment. He'd be lucky to remain alive.

Now he would have to call off the search and pretend that McDonald and the girl had gotten out of Hell's Kitchen on their own. He would have to admit that he had been wrong while knowing that it wasn't true. But even as he thought all this, he felt no guilt or disappointment.

Why not? He should at least be anxious. It was his future he had just pissed away. What if he got kicked out of the gang and received no offer to go to the Bigs? What would he do then? Go rogue? Leave Hell's Kitchen? Chambers would probably help, but to do what? He sure couldn't help Bill get kids out of Hell's

Kitchen. He'd be lucky if they even let him walk the streets without attacking him.

His feet were heavy. His arm was killing him. He wished he had a place to go for a few days to think things over, but that wasn't going to happen. He still had responsibilities. The gang was still out searching. He needed to call them off. Then he'd have to go see Connor. That would be a nasty meeting.

He came across his group near 51st Street. He sent most of them home with a remainder to find the other groups to call off the search. "Go get some sleep. McDonald isn't in Hell's Kitchen anymore. We're wasting our time." Then he trudged home and lay down on his bed; but he didn't sleep. When he and the other gang members got together later that day, no one said a word about McDonald, but they also avoided eye contact with him and acted subdued. The doubting had begun.

The meeting with Chuck Connor was brutal. It wasn't a private meeting. To make his point, Connor had invited five of his colleagues, all crime syndicate and political associates. They sat together behind a table. They left Christian standing in front with no chair to sit on. His arm was still aching and his head hurt, but he stood straight and was as impassive as always. Connor spoke for the group. "So, Christian, we hear you called off the search for this McDonald guy. Why?"

Christian didn't flinch. "Because McDonald and the girl aren't in Hell's Kitchen anymore."

"And how do you know that?"

"We searched the place. If they were still here, we'd have found them."

"But you're the guy who was convinced a few days ago that they hadn't left Hell's Kitchen?"

"Yes."

"So you're telling me now that you were wrong all along."

"I'm telling you they're not in the Kitchen anymore."

Connor paused, still staring at Gunther, who refused to blink or look away. Connor was amazed at his chutzpah. "You've botched this one badly, Christian. You let your boys get attacked and one get killed. You let the guy who did all this get out of your grasp."

Christian shrugged and said nothing.

"You're set back, Christian. Way back. You're not much use to us now and I hear your boys are uneasy with you. That's trouble. You might hold it together for a while, but you've got a lot going against you. I'm not going to replace you right now. Even crippled, you're probably better than my other choices. But you're on a very short leash, boy, and I don't have much use for losers. We'll talk again in a couple of weeks after I think this over some more."

"In the meantime, here's the name of a doctor you're going to go see. That arm isn't doing you or anyone else any good if it doesn't heal. It needs to get fixed by somebody who knows what he's doing. Mr. Price here is going that way now and will take you over to the doctor's office. The doc is going to reset that arm. I've told him not to be gentle. I told him you're a tough guy. I guess we'll find out whether I'm right or not."

With that, Connor got up and walked out of the room followed by the rest of the group except for the guy who must have been Price. He motioned for Christian to follow and they headed to the doctor's office. Christian wondered why Connor bothered to get another doctor on his behalf. He wondered if Connor still thought there might be some sort of role for him.

The doctor, a crusty old man who didn't bother with niceties, inspected the arm, which was still badly swollen and an angry bluish-red. "You could lose this arm pretty quick, boy. I'm not sure but what it's already too late. We're going to have to re-set the bones."

Christian nodded. He had anticipated the news.

"I'm going to give you something to make the operation painless. I know what Mr. Connor was proposing, but I'm a doctor, not a torturer. He can torture you himself if he wants to. I suspect he will. He seems to like that sort of thing. You okay with me putting you to sleep? It could kill you, but it rarely does, and it makes my job a lot easier."

Christian nodded. "Thanks."

"Okay then. Go in that room and take off your shirt and shoes and lie down on that table. Here's a sheet. I keep it cold in there to fight germs while I'm operating. I'm going to scrub up. Then I'll be in with the gas."

Christian did what he was told. The doc washed up and put on an apron and mask. When he came into the room, he was holding a bottle and cloth. He poured a little clear liquid from the bottle onto the cloth and said, "What's your name, boy, in case I need to write it on your death certificate?"

"Christian Gunther."

"Who do I notify if something goes wrong?"

"Connor."

"Anybody else?"

Christian shook his head.

The doc shook his head also, and said. "Well, ok, Mr. Gunther. So here we go." The cloth came down over Christian's mouth and nose. Within seconds, he was transported to a temporary nirvana where all his pain and doubts vanished. He awakened several hours later on the same table. Although the room was still cold, he felt warmer now, with blankets covering his body. He was slightly nauseated and groggy, but when he looked down at his arm, there was a new plaster cast on it and he no longer felt much pain—just a dull ache.

In a few minutes, the doc stuck his head in. "Well, I see you didn't die on me. How does the arm feel?"

"Better."

"Good. I think we saved it, but it'll be a little crooked and you'll probably have a knot on it for life. Otherwise, I think it should heal alright. We'll see. You rest there another few hours and then we'll get you up. I'd keep you here, but I need the table for other work, so you're going to have to go someplace else to lie down. I assume you have someplace?"

Christian nodded.

"Well good; take a couple of hours to get clearheaded, then you can leave. I want you back here in two weeks, or sooner if the arm starts hurting more than it is now. There's a sling over in the chair. Keep that arm in it for six weeks. Then you can test it. No lifting and as little moving it as possible till then. Give that bone time to mend or we'll be using a saw next. You got that?"

"Yea, I got it….and doc…thanks for doing this and for putting me out."

The doctor's expression softened a little and he smiled. "You're welcome son. And don't worry, I'm telling Connor you were conscious the whole time. The bastard doesn't need to know anything else."

Christian smiled a little. His life was way off track, but at least his arm was fixed. He'd find a new way to get where he wanted to go. He drifted off to a peaceful sleep.

Chapter 18

While Anna and Ben spent their second day exploring the rest of Central Park, Bill Chambers paid a visit to the Reverend Brace at his office to talk about what to do with the two young people. Bill had briefly described their situation to Brace earlier, but they had not had time to talk about it in detail.

After the usual greetings, Bill began. "These are a couple of very exceptional kids. Anna is a very attractive girl with a sparkling personality; she'll soon be a beautiful woman. Ben is one of the most mature teenagers I've ever met. He'll make something of himself if he's given half a chance."

"The problem is that they've formed a strong bond toward each other—partly because of what they've gone through together and more because they're cut from the same quality of cloth. Ben saved Anna's life on the streets by taking out five members of the Bowery Boys. From what I hear, he may have killed one of them, so he's dead if he returns to Hell's Kitchen. It's risky even keeping them at the warehouse right now. I wouldn't have done it except Christian Gunther personally brought them to me."

That shocked Brace. He interrupted, "Wait a minute! That can't be right. Gunther wouldn't bring this boy out of Hell's Kitchen if he had killed a Bowery Boy. If your information is accurate, he would've destroyed them. I know Gunther has cooperated with us on young children, but that's politics for him and he has the blessing of Connor to do it. Gunther has a brutal reputation. He would follow the street code to the letter. Your boy wouldn't be alive if he had attacked the Bowery Boys."

Bill nodded. "Yea, I know this makes no sense, but the word about the gang being attacked and a Bowery lieutenant being killed has been all over the streets for over a week. It's all the kids are talking about. And they all believe McDonald did it and took Anna out of Hell's Kitchen. What they don't know is that Ben didn't leave the Kitchen. He hid in a mausoleum in that graveyard just north of the 51st Street catholic church. Apparently Gunther found them himself, but for some reason he didn't call his gang and instead brought them to me. He didn't hang around long enough for me to ask him why."

"Actually, I'm worried about him. I know Christian. I don't believe he's the guy he's made out to be. But I guarantee you that he'll lose a lot of face over this. I'll be surprised if he's allowed to stay in his position much longer. I don't think they know where Ben and Anna went and how they got here, but it won't matter. Christian didn't catch and punish them, so his reputation is shot."

Brace looked puzzled. "This is really strange! I'm not sure what's accurate in all these stories but Gunther obviously brought them to you, so there's more to it than meets the eye. But he knows we have no ability to place older children. Both Ben and Anna are far too old to find a home out west. Moreover, there's absolutely no chance that I'd place them together, even if I could. If they're as close as you say they are, that would be inviting trouble and lots of potential negative attention to our work. I'm sorry, Bill, but I don't think we can help them."

"Yea, I know, but I can't keep the kids in my apartment much longer either—for some of the same reasons. I sure as hell can't send them back to Hell's Kitchen. If Ben and Anna wound up back in the Kitchen, not only would they die, but Gunther would probably be lost too, if he isn't already. People would find out how they escaped. Something really unique has happened here and I can't help but think there's a reason.

Brace reflected, "Can you send them off somewhere? You and I could probably raise a little money between us."

"I've been thinking about that, but to where? They're too young to be together as a couple but they don't want to go their separate ways. No orphanage would take them at their age. Frankly, I'd like to take a chance on keeping Ben at the warehouse and give him a job. He's 14 but looks and acts a lot older. He'd be a trusted worker. But that doesn't work for Anna. She needs schooling and opportunity for advancement of a different kind. She still needs the support of a family. I've been wracking my brain thinking about who might take her in and I'm getting nowhere. If I were married, I'd even take her in myself."

"We've just not faced this kind of problem before and we don't have anything designed for it. And these kids are sitting near the edge of Hell's Kitchen and they're marked. Gunther obviously won't come after them, but others might if they find out where they are. If the gangs know I harbored fugitives, my chances of working with them in the future won't be high. The word on the street right now is that they somehow left Manhattan. If the truth becomes known, we might not be able to protect them."

"If I can get Anna out of here, I'll go talk to Connor. He owes me a favor. Ben should be okay, but I can't keep Ben and Anna together. That would be playing with fire. We have to decide what to do and act soon or the consequences could be bad."

Bill went silent and Brace contemplated. He hadn't fully comprehended the gravity of the situation. He was particularly concerned with Bill's comment that this situation could easily derail the tenuous relationship of the Children's Aid Society with the youth gangs. "Where are the kids now? In your apartment, I assume?"

Bill hesitated. "No, they're touring Central Park."

"What!! You let them go alone to Central Park!?"

"Calm down, Charles! That may be the safest place for them right now. They wouldn't be recognizable to anyone who had seen them before. No gang member is allowed to go into the Park or even past 54th Street unless it's a leader. They're not known by people outside Hell's Kitchen. Both look older than they are and could easily pass for a young married couple. I admit there is a little risk, but not much right now. Remember, these kids evaded the Bowery Boys for almost a week, even though the gang was combing Hell's Kitchen. Frankly, I was more nervous about them just sitting around the apartment, unsupervised, and waiting for whatever is to come. Central Park is one of the wonders of the world. These kids know that something has to change soon. They deserved to see it together before whatever next happens to them."

Brace released a little tension from his posture and leaned back in his chair. "Ok, I see your point. And you're right, of course, this has to be resolved quickly. Give me a little time to think. Come back later this afternoon and we'll talk again. Maybe I can figure something out."

Bill smiled. "You always do, Charles. That's what I admire about you."

Brace laughed. "Oh, get out of here and stop brown-nosing an old man! I'll see you later."

Late that afternoon, Bill returned to Brace's office. "So what's the answer, oh Wise One?"

Brace frowned a little. "You aren't going to like this very much, but it's the best we could come up with. Emma Mason is taking the next group of orphans west—leaving tomorrow afternoon. We're having a difficult time finding another sponsor to go with her. Janet Hasten just came down sick and can't accompany Emma. I am willing to take a chance and send Anna as Emma's assistant to supervise the younger children if you can get Anna to agree and be ready to go. The difference will be that she can also be considered for placement, just like the younger children."

"Now, I must tell you, I think that there is very little chance that she'll be placed; but even if she isn't, she'll be out of harm's way for a while and it'll give us time to think about other alternatives. We'll buy her a round trip ticket. If she doesn't get placed, she comes back with Emma. If, by some miracle, she gets placed, well then, that part of the problem will be solved. What do you think? Can you get her to participate?"

Bill frowned. "Frankly, I don't know. All she has left in the world now is her connection to Ben. She might consider it if she knew that she would be returning, or that he could come to where she is, but we can't assure that. I don't know. I'll just have to talk to them."

"Well, it's really the only sure choice we have for now. And I doubt that the choices will get any better. I believe you when you say the girl is exceptional, but we just don't have any reputable families in this area willing to take a chance on a 13-year-old girl out of Hell's Kitchen. Do the best you can to convince her. Unfortunately, you don't have much time."

"Yea, I understand. I'll see what I can do. I assume it's out of the question to send Ben along with them for potential placement?" Bill felt he had to ask, but he knew it was a futile request.

Brace smiled a little. "Getting soft in your old age, Bill? You know I couldn't do that. I already admitted to you that Anna has very little chance of getting placed. I can tell you with certainty that a 14-year-old boy who has lived on the streets, and is as big as you say Ben is physically, has absolutely no chance at all."

Bill countered, "I know, but if she gets placed, maybe Ben would choose to stay in that area and look for work or something?" But as he said it, he knew it would only make things worse. He answered his own query. "No, I guess that wouldn't be good for him or her, would it? His being connected with her would probably guarantee her failure in a placement. Sorry, I am grasping at straws. Let me go do what I can." Bill headed back to his apartment. That sickening feeling he had in the pit of his stomach before was now back full force.

Ben and Anna had already returned from Central Park when he arrived. They looked gloriously happy and it caused him to hate what he had to tell them even more. He thought he should tell Ben first, so he asked him to come to his office briefly while Anna began to prepare supper. The request surprised Ben a little but Bill seemed troubled, so Ben agreed, glancing at Anna as he did. She gave him a nod and a smile and told them she might have supper ready by the time they returned.

Bill and Ben headed downstairs. When they arrived, Bill told Ben to have a seat. "I talked to Reverend Brace about Anna."

Ben's chest tightened.

"He wants to visit with Anna. He has a trainload of orphans leaving for the West tomorrow afternoon with a chaperone named Emma Mason. The second chaperone got sick and Reverend

Brace always sends two adults with the children. He's willing to send Anna to help Miss Mason. Bill paused, "And maybe to give her a chance to get placed with a family out west."

Ben didn't respond. Bill let the message sink in. He knew that Ben had already begun to fantasize a life with Anna.

"Ben, I know this is hard. I understand how very special Anna has become to you. But she's a 13-year-old girl and you're only 14. I realize the two of you have lived through events that make you a lot more mature than most young people your age, but the rest of the world won't understand or acknowledge that. You'll be considered too young to enter into a permanent relationship now. Even if that were possible, I don't know how you'd support yourselves. I have a job for you here at the warehouse, but it doesn't pay enough for both of you. Because of appearances, I can't keep you and Anna here together. It'd be frowned upon and could reflect badly on the Children's Aid Society. People watch what we do and some of them take every possible opportunity to criticize us. I can't afford to jeopardize our efforts by the two of you remaining here together."

He paused again and then asked, "What could she do here if she stays, Ben? We could try to enroll her in school, but there are none near here and we don't know anyone who could take her in safely. She could try to get a job, but those available to young girls are not good ones. She couldn't just sit here. That would be unfair to her. She also can't stay with you and me in my apartment much longer."

"If we try to keep her near here in a separate apartment, it could easily become known. If you and she tried to live together, it's sure to become noticed. I am worried about your safety too, but you're more capable of taking care of yourself. She would be at great risk all the time. She needs a better chance than you or I can give her right now. She needs to be able to finish her schooling someplace safe. She's an exceptional girl. She'll make something of herself. We need to give her that chance if we can."

He paused again and then continued, regret apparent in his voice. "I tried to get Reverend Brace to take you too, but he won't allow it. He knows of your affection for Anna. It will make him vulnerable to a lot of criticism. And even if you went, there's little chance that another family in the same town where Anna is placed would take you in. Even if you got placed somewhere else, and frankly, that is highly unlikely, she'd be living in one area of the country and you in another."

"I know this is hard news, but I have to give it too you straight. If you two want to try to make it together, I'll help every way I can, but I don't think it's the right thing for Anna now, or for you either at this point in your life. Maybe someday...."

Ben stared at the wooden planks in the floor until they blurred. He quickly pushed his hand across his eyes. He still couldn't speak with the lump that had formed in his throat. Bill let him sit in silence.

Ben finally responded with the voice of an old man. "If the Reverend can take her to the West, she should have that chance. She'd do well there, or anywhere she had half a chance. Anyone who sees her will want to take her in. He paused and took a deep breath. "When does she need to see the Reverend?"

"Tomorrow morning. The train leaves tomorrow afternoon at 3:00 p.m. Do you want me to tell her?"

Ben shook his head. "I should be the one who talks to her." He left the office and walked wearily up the stairs to the apartment. Bill stayed in his office to let them talk. When Ben entered Anna was cooking. She smiled at him brightly. It killed him to see it. She saw his face and her smile froze. "What's wrong!?"

Ben broke the news as gently as he could. She listened without saying a word until he finished. She began shaking her head, slowly at first and then furiously. "I won't go. I won't do that, Ben! We can find a place…or we can go back to the streets. I don't care where we live. We can go anywhere. I'm not leaving you, Ben. You're all I have left!" Her eyes were pleading and tears were already forming. It sickened him, but he knew he had to convince her to leave.

"You have to go, Anna. There is nothing here for you, and we're too young to live together. We won't survive on the streets. I want you to have a chance to…to have a good life and make a difference for other people. I can't give you that. This is our only chance. We can't stay with Bill. People will talk. School is too dangerous for you here. So is work. We have no choice. This is all there is for you." His own eyes misted. His voice caught in his throat and his chest heaved in a deep sigh.

She saw it and said no more. It was obvious that this was as painful for him as for her. She wouldn't make it worse. She ran to him, throwing her arms around him. It would tear out both their hearts, but there seemed to be nothing they could do. Even the people who cared about them had decided they couldn't stay together. She felt his tears running down the back of her neck. They stood frozen, holding each other, too sad to let go.

Finally she spoke again, this time in a whisper. "When will I have to leave?"

"You will meet with Reverend Brace in the morning and leave tomorrow afternoon if he lets you go."

That was too much for her. She released him and ran to the bedroom. She threw herself across the bed and began to sob.

Ben remained in the kitchen. He ached all over as though he had been beaten within an inch of his life. He barely had the strength to stand. His throat was painfully constricted and he had trouble breathing. He sighed repeatedly. There was a terrible tightness in his chest and the feeling of a knife twisting in his stomach. He didn't know how to stop the pain, but he knew he had to stay strong for Anna. Bill came back and tried to talk to Ben but he couldn't respond. Bill respected his feelings and didn't push him.

Neither Anna nor Ben slept at all that night. When Bill awoke the next morning, they were staring out the window of the sitting room, holding hands. Bill had no idea how long they had been there. No one wanted breakfast. No one talked more than necessary as they prepared to meet the Reverend. They walked to his office in silence.

After formal greetings, Brace asked Bill and Ben to wait in the vestibule while he visited with Anna. A half-hour later the Reverend came out as she waited in the office. Ben had gone for a short walk. He could no longer sit still. Brace's face was somber, even sad. "You're right about Anna, Bill. She strikes me as exceptional, with great potential. But she is the saddest girl I have ever met!"

Bill nodded. "She and Ben shared something very special. It is killing them both to separate. They're all each other have right now."

"Ah yes, young love," smiled Brace sadly, deep sympathy in his voice. He sighed, "Well, this is her best option. They're too young to marry, and the Lord knows we don't need more children in this world from parents who can't care for them. They'll recover, Bill, and they'll thank us all for the chances they received someday."

"I hope you're right, Charles," answered Bill, "but I am not so sure. I guess time will tell." He believed the affection between Ben and Anna was deeper than Brace realized. Had Ben and Anna been a bit older, he suspected that they would have made a powerful, enduring couple.

"So you invited Anna to join Emma Mason on the train and she accepted?"

Brace nodded. "Yes. She's resigned to it and I think she'll be fine once she gets out of this city and meets western families."

"Okay. I'll get them to the station early this afternoon to help with the children."

They arrived at the railroad station in early afternoon. As usual, the train was running late. They met the group of children who would ride with Emma Mason and Anna. They ranged in ages from three to eight years old, a total of twelve boys and six girls. All would board the train with hopes for a new life in the West, wherever that was—all but the oldest member among them. She would ride this train hoping all the time that it would bring her back to Ben, no matter how dangerous Manhattan might be. She had lost her mother and father and she didn't think she could stand to lose Ben as well. It all felt like a cruel joke. She clung desperately to the fragile hope that her time away would give Bill and Reverend Brace opportunity to think of something that would allow her and Ben to stay together, or at least be near each other until they were older.

Emma Mason was an energetic widow in her forties who had no children of her own. She had dedicated her life to helping the homeless orphans of New York and considered them her family. She had already escorted more than twenty groups of children to the West. She was a brilliant strategist and charismatic. She could have sold ice to Eskimos. Brace may have developed the vision, but it was Bill Chambers and Emma Watson who were the operative architects of the success of the Children's Aid Society. Both were pragmatic and would work with anyone if it furthered the orphan cause.

She introduced herself to Anna and emphasized how very grateful she was to have her along to help with the children. She said, with a little too much assurance, that she was sure there were families out West who would be delighted to take in a girl as nice as Anna, even at her age. She spoke as though trying to convince herself as much as them.

Anna tried to pay attention to Mrs. Mason's words but her concentration and energy had abandoned her, so she could only nod respectfully. Bill, sensing her pain, asked Emma if Ben and Anna could be excused for awhile before the trip began. Emma was a little taken aback but agreed. She knew Bill must have good reason for his suggestion. Emma Mason worshiped the ground on which Bill Chambers trod. She admired him more than any other man she had ever met.

Bill led Anna and Ben to seats as far from the commotion as possible and left them there. They didn't talk. Anna took Ben's hand in both of hers and held it tightly. Mrs. Mason occasionally glanced their way, wondering if the good Reverend really had given her any tangible help for the children as they ran around the station screaming and yelling. But Bill stayed to help, and together they easily kept the situation in hand.

After almost an hour of silence, Anna exclaimed, "I never taught you to read better!"

"What?" said Ben, startled by her words.

"You asked me to help you with your reading when we were in the mausoleum, and I promised I would, but I never got the chance." Great tears were forming in her eyes and beginning to roll down her cheeks.

"It's okay," said Ben, "I guess that it just wasn't meant to be." She leaned her head on his shoulder and he put his arm around her. They sat in silence until they heard the whistle of a train. It startled and agitated her.

"I want you to go now Ben. I can't bear to have you see me leave!" She was weeping openly now, tears streaming down her cheeks. He looked into her face, trying to memorize every feature, to hold that picture forever in his mind. His vision became blurred and he had to look away.

They stood slowly, her breath coming in gasps. He took her into his arms. They rocked back and forth, each not wanting to let go. The train wailed again and drew closer. She squeezed him tightly, then released him and abruptly turned away, hurrying toward Mrs. Mason and the children. He watched her until she had rejoined the group, then slowly turned toward the exit and disappeared.

Mrs. Mason was trying to round up and count the children. Bill was busy helping and didn't see Ben leave. Anna stood in a zombie-like daze in the middle of the station as children encircled her. Now Ben was gone from her too.

The train, an imposter, came to the station and stopped on an opposite track. It held cattle, not people. Exasperated, Mrs. Mason asked the station attendant when their train was coming. He answered nonchalantly that it was late out of Boston and would arrive "when it gets here."

"When it got there" was nearly two hours later, giving Mrs. Mason more than ample time to reintroduce Anna to the children and provide her with instructions. Bill stayed to help. He asked Anna where Ben had gone but she shook her head and didn't answer.

When the train finally arrived, and before she climbed the steps into her passenger berth, Bill hugged her and leaned down to kiss her on the forehead. "You go make something of yourself, Anna, for yourself and for Ben's sake. He has great faith in you. We both believe you have very special talents. It was a hard thing for him to let you go. He only did it because he knew it was best for you right now." She nodded, but said nothing. She could not bring herself to speak.

Anxious passengers pushed past her and on up the steps of the compartment. She finally boarded and sat down on a seat near the back. The other children had moved to seats ahead of her, except for two of the smallest children who ran back and crowded in around her.

The train whistle screeched twice. Pistons pumped and wheels began to turn. She stared vacantly out the train window toward the station. She saw a flicker of movement by a building across from the terminal and for a fleeting second she thought she saw his figure in the shadows. But it must have been a trick of her imagination, because she could not pinpoint him again.

And then the full weight of her loss hit her. Ben was gone, maybe forever. Her mother and father lay in the cold ground. She was leaving all of them. She was alone. Her heart felt as though it was tearing apart. She turned and closed her eyes tightly, trying to push out the world, trying to learn how to breathe in this alien environment—not sure that she really wanted to.

Chapter 19

The train rumbled through the darkness, reaching Philadelphia to stop for passengers. After a few minutes, it continued on its way. The orphan children didn't get off in Philadelphia. They would leave the train in Chicago and points farther west. Each stop at way stations in the smaller towns took about 15 minutes. By midnight, only Anna and Sally, a precocious eight year-old, were still awake. Even Mrs. Mason was catnapping in the far back seat where she had stationed herself so she could watch all the children.

Anna sat in the middle of the four-year-old Stewart twins, a boy and a girl, clinging to her on either side, their heads in her lap, sleeping fitfully. Even in their sleep, they fidgeted and whimpered as the train clattered along its uneven tracks. Gravity pushed each child toward or away from her as the car rounded winding curves. The child on the outside clung to her leg, little fingernails digging into her skin. On an opposite curve, the other twin did the same.

She didn't try to push them away. The twins were terribly frightened of the train. She knew her presence was their only comfort. In their frightened little minds, she reminded them of someone they had known before, but couldn't quite remember who. Anna's back was aching and her legs were cramped. She absently stroked the little heads in her lap without realizing what she was doing. Her eyes stared vacantly into the darkness beyond the windows, seeing nothing in particular. It was impossible for her to sleep.

Daylight comes more subtly on a train headed west, but it does come. Anna, still awake, was startled to realize she was now looking at a dimly lit landscape instead of blackness. She had lost her sense of time and perspective, accepting darkness as a permanent condition. That day was going to be cloudy and gloomy. She thought it appropriate to the circumstances.

The twins finally stirred. She allowed them to wake slowly and then took them to the car that housed the toilets. She and Mrs. Mason unpacked some breakfast snacks. Some of the children devoured theirs quickly, while others refused to eat due to their motion sickness. Anna didn't eat due to sickness of a different kind. The train continued westward late into the day, stopping frequently at smaller towns along the way. It would reach Chicago sometime that night, where they would have a two-hour layover and a change of trains.

Anna continued her caretaking duties, shepherding the youngest children. They found solace in her kind attention. She found the work helpful in gradually shaking her from her numbness. Anna's group included Zachary Simmons, a five-year-old boy with a shriveled body and a gray, pinched face. Zachary had already wet his pants twice in the first 12 hours of the train ride.

Her group also included five-year-old Melissa Stone, a quiet, pretty little girl with beautiful blond hair and natural curls. Melissa watched events around her through large, alarmed blue eyes and tried hard not to cause trouble for anyone. Anna was grateful to have her because she could count on Melissa to do anything she asked without being told more than once.

To everyone's surprise they arrived in Chicago on time. They would get to stop for a while there and get off the wearisome train. Mrs. Mason decided to hold the supper meal until they all exited into the station and promised the children candy if they would all stay close together and behave themselves. They were happy to take her up on that bargain. Candy was an extremely rare treat for them.

Mrs. Mason had never attempted to arrange a placement meeting in Chicago for any of the urchin children because that city had its own orphan problems. Reverend Brace and his colleagues did not want to exacerbate them and draw that sort of criticism to their work. He might not have done it even if Chicago didn't have its own problems. Brace was convinced that children were far better cared for, and experienced healthier lifestyles, in small towns and rural settings where they could breathe fresh air. His theory, particularly correct for young boys, was that orphaned children would be more highly valued in agrarian communities.

Reverend Brace and his associates did not monitor the children after placement, or even keep good records documenting their placements. That fact was not lost to his critics. He did receive wonderful anecdotes from some of the children through the years, but it was a biased sample. He was less likely to receive stories from children abandoned by families, or abused, or from children who were treated like indentured servants.

From later research, a large percentage of the children did fare well, certainly compared to their potential fate in Hell's Kitchen. Many grew up in loving and humane families. But there were a few cases of tragedy, where children *were* worked like slaves, fed poorly and abused. Some were shuffled from family to family, with little stability in their lives.

In a few instances those children fought back. Their stories were sensationalized in local town newspapers as examples of why New York urchins, dumped on well-meaning Midwestern families, were an insult foisted on rural America by callous urbanites unable to solve their own problems. Some of the most severely abused children ran away, becoming homeless again, but this time in unfamiliar lands without the support of a youth gang.

Brace never attempted to refute or deny the fact that some of his orphan train children were harmed by their placements, nor that some committed criminal acts. He never tried to paint a rosy picture of his strategy. He firmly believed that these few bad outcomes were outweighed by the good, and the criticism never detracted him from his goals. He and his colleagues knew from personal observation and experience the fate of the children left on the streets of Hell's Kitchen.

Brace was not an eloquent speaker. In fact, by his own estimation, he was not even a good one. He was, however, a man possessed with a deep and unbending faith in the amazing resiliency of a child given half a chance, and he had a passion for offering unwanted children the opportunity to have that chance in rural settings where they might be more valued. Although some of his lambs were lost to the wolves, he was convinced that the majority would thrive. He gladly traded the loss of a few for the good of the many. His orphan train strategy, which he had copied from an earlier, less ambitious, program in Boston, ultimately resulted in more than 150,000 children being shipped to rural communities in the Midwest from the mid-19th century into the early years of 20th century. The placements continued long after his death. He reshaped the histories of thousands of children from Hell's Kitchen, and that of the Midwestern communities to which they migrated.

It was 8:00 p.m. by the time Anna's group switched to another train at Chicago. In the darkness, and with the rhythmic sounds of the wheels on the tracks, most of the children quickly dropped off to sleep. They were now experienced passengers, lulled by the rocking of the passenger compartment. As they moved further west, the train was not so crowded, allowing some of the children to stretch out in the seats. The Stewart twins, however, took their usual position beside Anna and she was forced to continue sitting in an uncomfortable upright position. By now, she was past exhaustion.

In the wee hours of the night, they had arrived in Springfield, Illinois, their first overnight stop in the West. In 1884, anything beyond Chicago was "the West". Anna and the rest of the tired party finally exited the train for an overnight rest and their first placement event scheduled on the following day. They were taken by wagon on a cold ride to the church where they bedded down on pallets. This same church had previously housed hundreds of Brace's little wanderers, and before that, it had secretly housed African refugees as they traveled the Underground Railroad on the northward journey to their freedom.

None of the group, save Mrs. Mason, knew much about what awaited them the next day. She thought it best not to raise their anxieties earlier than necessary. Tomorrow would offer time enough to get them ready for the first meeting. They lay down on pallets on the church floor and slept in small clusters, many of the children sucking their thumbs and whimpering fitfully through the night. Anna finally got to lie down too, with her little charges all around, scrunching as close to her as they could. She was so exhausted that she finally fell asleep.

At 7:00 a.m. Mrs. Mason, excited and energized, woke Anna and took her aside out of earshot of the children. "Anna, today begins a special process for the children. We'll freshen them up as best we can—you must work hard at this with your little group, dear— and we will tell them what to do when the people come to inspect them this afternoon. Families from all around Springfield will come to look at the children. If they like a child, they will adopt him or her."

Mrs. Mason's instruction was inaccurate in one regard. The orphan train children were not formally adopted by the families who selected them. They were just taken away. A few were adopted later. Most were not. They were treated as foster children by the families who took them. Even then, there was no formal application process, no parent training and no supervision of a child's situation with the family.

Mrs. Mason continued with Anna's placement instructions, emphasizing the critical points. "Now Anna, how the children present themselves is very important if we are to find homes for them. You must explain to each child how to behave when the families come to look at them. They must smile and not be too bashful. However, they should be polite, and never rambunctious. They must not shy away when a man or woman wants to feel their bones, look at their hair for lice, inspect their ears or has them open their mouths to look at their teeth."

"The smaller children should climb into the laps of any woman inspecting them if she allows it. They should indicate they would always be very good if they are allowed to go home with the family. They must do everything possible to present themselves in their best light. Do you think you can instruct your children properly?"

Anna indicated that she understood the importance of the children's looks and presentation. Mrs. Mason gauged Anna's response and was satisfied. Anna quickly fathomed the marketing process, although she was somewhat shocked by its commercialism. It never occurred to her or Mrs. Mason to think about how she should present herself.

Anna went over to her children, gathering them around her and passing on the instructions. "Today will be a special day for some of you. Some families are coming this afternoon to see you, and they may want to take you home to live with them. They will become your new mommies and daddies, and some of you may have new brothers and sisters," she said as positively as she could and with as much confidence as she could muster.

They nodded their little heads. Some looked sober and frightened as Anna proceeded with the instructions, but not Zachary Simmons. He was ecstatic at the thought that he would have a new mommy and daddy by nightfall. It was something he never remembered having because he had been left at the doorstep of an orphanage shortly after birth, but it was something about which he had often dreamed.

Other kids at the orphanage, who once had mommies and daddies, had told him how wonderful it had been. Children at orphanages always talked about how great it was, or would be, to have a real family to live with; one that fed you well and took care of you, held you, loved you, played with you and brought you candy and presents. He was ready to be adopted by one of those families at the earliest possible moment!

He kept pestering Anna about how soon his new mommy and daddy would arrive, and could hardly contain his excitement. His gray, pinched little face took on an almost normal color. After listening to Anna's instructions, he tried to straighten his little humped shoulders so he could look his best for his new family, whom he was sure would be coming shortly.

The Stewart twins were another story. They were frightened at the thought of leaving Anna, with whom they had bonded at a speed that only deprived orphan children can when they receive kindness for the first time. They cried and told Anna they didn't want to go. They clung to her legs until she had to physically pry them loose. No matter how hard she tried, she couldn't convince them that the coming events would have a happy ending for them. Sadly, at least in the short term, their assessment was to prove more accurate than hers.

At 2:00 p.m. twenty families from all around the Springfield area came to view the children. Actually they had come an hour earlier, wanting to be the first there to get the best pick of the litter. They were initially thwarted in that strategy. Before they could inspect the children in any detail, the local minister insisted on "preparing them for this blessed event in their lives" by preaching a long sermon on the Biblical virtues of showing kindness to orphans and widows. He would not begin until he was sure all had arrived. The preacher was never one to waste the opportunity of a captive audience. While there were no widows there to be helped, he felt it improper to separate the Biblical citation, so he preached on the virtues of both, assuming that they would be inspired to help widows at some future point.

He rounded out his sermon by extolling the importance of strict family discipline, which he thought particularly important to the occasion. Some of the families who would be selecting the orphans did not yet have children of their own and likely had little experience in keeping children in line. He anticipated future problems in his worship services if proper discipline was not applied immediately.

At last, after the preacher was winded, the families were free to inspect the children—which they did with shocking boldness. They started by talking to the children about general topics, then quickly proceeded to questions they had practiced beforehand to give them some insight into the soundness of a child's mind. Then they thoroughly inspected them physically, as though they were buying horses or cattle.

The older children did their best to present themselves as desirable candidates, but were not to be successful in Springfield that day. The competition was too stiff from their younger peers. Only one child of age 8 was placed in Springfield. Most families in this semi-urban community were looking for healthy *younger* children, and that made Anna's little group the main attraction.

Zachary went boldly from family to family introducing himself, asking if they would like to take him home. His enthusiasm and marketing strategies were admirable, but the merchandise he was selling was seen as inferior to that of his competitors. To his great chagrin, he was not selected by any of the Springfield families. Later that night he would cry himself to sleep on Anna's lap over the rejection.

The Stewart twins, trying desperately not to be noticed, hid behind Anna's legs, which of course, made them infinitely more noticeable to the families. To their terror many of the families inspected them closely. In the end, little Samuel Stewart was taken by a nice farm family. Since the family already had a girl of their own, and had already determined that they did not need another one, Samuel and his sister were separated that day and would not see each other again until they were adults beyond forty years of age.

Samuel had to be torn physically, first from Anna, and then from his sister, and carried from the church screaming. In all her remaining life, Anna would never forget that scene. Samantha joined Zachary on Anna's lap that night to cry herself to sleep over the loss of her brother.

Six of the children were chosen by their new families, which pleased Mrs. Mason greatly. She told Anna enthusiastically, "We seldom have this much success at our first stop!"

The next morning the remaining party boarded a 9:00 a.m. train to

St. Louis, Missouri, a name that meant nothing to most of the children. Anna had seen it on a map of the states that her father had used for geography lessons. They arrived in St. Louis in only three hours. They stopped to eat and change trains yet again, this time headed for Jefferson City, Missouri's capital. There another placement meeting would bring more families to inspect the children.

The train made a brief stop for passengers, water and coal in Herman, Missouri, a small, picturesque town founded along the Missouri River by industrious Germans. There was no planned placement meeting at that stop. But when it arrived, to the surprise and irritation of the conductor and the utter amazement of Mrs. Mason, five families boarded the train without tickets. The conductor insisted they must buy tickets if they planned to ride the train. They informed him that they didn't plan to ride it and that tickets were unnecessary for what they had in mind.

The conductor, a rather proper gentleman who believed that rules were made to be followed, was certainly not going to leave Herman until these obnoxious Hermanites got off his train. They, just as intent on their goals, told him they were not going to get off his train until they had seen the orphan children, no matter what his threats. There was a constable of the town but he was drunk and unavailable. Train personnel and the shopping families were obviously at an impasse.

The five families had heard of the Jefferson City Placement through a local priest who had attended a mass at the Jefferson City diocese three weeks earlier. They knew that the train routinely stopped in Herman to take on water and fuel, so they staged their own little train robbery. Jefferson City was fifty miles away and they did not want to travel that far. Jesse James, a native of their state, would have been proud of their gall.

Their boldness was facilitated both by the opportunity to select a free child and, just as important, by the thrill of beating snooty Jefferson City residents to the punch. They decided they wanted these children, needed these children, to help work their farms and assist with their growing grape vineyards. They weren't too picky about the looks of the kids, as long as they were sound. Older or younger children would do. It was a winner-take-all mentality and these families were not to be denied. Five of the children had new families within 20 minutes, as the increasingly huffy conductor kept trying to shoo them off his train.

Mrs. Mason was torn between indignation and elation. She wasn't sure which of her emotions should take precedent. The prospecting German families were incredibly pushy, but they were also responding to a seller's market! They were presumptuous and overbearing and some didn't even speak proper English. But five of her children would have new homes. So she lectured the families soundly for not playing by the rules and attending the placement meeting in Jefferson City, as she deemed they should have. They took this as a compliment. She then blessed them for opening their hearts and homes to the wonderful children they were taking. They acknowledged her appreciation and got off the train, pleased with their good fortune and their acquisitions. The conductor, furious at the delay, pulled an extra-long blast on the whistle and got the hell out of town as fast as he could, vowing never to stop there again when he had orphan children on board.

Zachary was not one of the children selected at Herman. His little shoulders drooped lower and his pinched face became even more drawn, but this time he did not cry.

The delay at Herman presented a new problem for Mrs. Mason and Anna. The placement meeting in Jefferson City was to occur at

5:00 p.m. and due to the unexpected delay, they would probably not arrive by that hour. Mrs. Mason fretted that people would leave, or that they would not have adequate time to prepare the children. But thanks to the angry conductor, who poured on the coal, they actually arrived only fifteen minutes late. Mrs. Mason rushed the children to the Methodist Church, which was within walking distance of Lohman's Landing, where the Jefferson City train depot sat.

They had hoped to wash the children's faces and comb their hair before the families arrived, but of course, the families had already begun arriving as early as 3:00 p.m. and were anxious to see the children. All they could do was to take off the children's coats and display them. There were a number of families looking in Jefferson City that day and a goodly number of them left with what they wanted. All the remaining children were placed—except two.

Little Samantha was one of the first to be taken by a kind family named Bax. She was terror-stricken, but Mrs. Bax was gentle and didn't rush her. More important, Mrs. Bax was tall and slim and attractive, somewhat like an older version of Anna. By the time Samantha went out the church door, she had her arms around Mrs. Bax' neck and was smiling. It would be a good home for her and a good selection for them. She would reward the Bax family and her little community of Rich Fountain by becoming the family's first college graduate and full-fledged nurse. She would serve the area for many years.

Zachary was not taken by any family, nor was Anna, but Mrs. Mason was again delighted at the Jefferson City outcome, and she said so to Anna in the presence of Zachary. According to her, the trip had been "eminently successful." In her heart, Mrs. Mason thought Anna too old to be adopted and Zachary too deformed.

She suspected they would make the journey with her back to New York City, but then one never knew. Mrs. Mason was an optimist and accustomed to small miracles on such trips. They had one more stop in a town sixty miles south of Jefferson City, called Rolla. Perhaps there someone would take the boy since they would have no one else with whom to compare. In her wishful thinking, she forgot that Anna was also available for the taking.

Chapter 20

Jess and Bessie Lough, pronounced like the word low, was a family of Irish or Scottish ancestry with a mix of Cherokee blood. They lived on their farm in the small community of Jadwin, located nine miles south of Salem, which was 22 miles south of Rolla. Jadwin was primarily comprised of a couple of rural churches, one Baptist and other a Church of Christ, a country store with an attached rural post office and a one-room schoolhouse. It was typical of many small rural outposts in Missouri at the time.

Rolla was the "urban hub" of the surrounding area, and as such it was where Jess and Bessie traded two or three times a year for larger farm equipment and their Sunday clothing. It was the home of a young, but already prominent, engineering school that provided academic training for the men and women who would serve as engineers in Eastern Missouri's massive lead mines.

The Lough farm consisted of 80 acres, with a nice little farmhouse whose sandstone walls had been cut and laid by Jess himself. He was good with his hands: a fair carpenter and a better stonemason.

By November 1884 Jess and Bessie had already been blessed with four children, all stair-stepped between the ages of two and seven. Both Jess and Bessie were caring, kind parents. But Jess had one little character flaw: he was a man with the soul of a wanderer. He managed this wanderlust as best he could by making it an asset for the family's financial support whenever possible.

In the summer of each year he traveled for six or eight weeks with a crew through western Missouri and Kansas to help put up hay, making a little cash to tide the family over another year. In the fall he hired himself out as a logger in Shannon County where oak, walnut, cedar and bull pine were tall and plentiful. He felt perpetually guilty about leaving Bessie with the kids during these long treks, but so far, she seemed to have taken it in stride.

Local merchants also knew of Jess's little flaw and used it to their advantage. They would hire him to take a wagonload of goods to Rolla or, on rare occasions, even to St. Louis or Kansas City. He accepted every possible opportunity to travel. Since he was honest and trustworthy, these opportunities were frequent. He was also a talker and talented negotiator and he often got better deals for the local merchants than they could get for themselves. Many of them knew it and were grateful. He was liked by everyone and he seemed never to meet a stranger.

While his travels served him well, they left Bessie alone with their growing crop of children. When she glanced into a mirror, she fretted that she was beginning to look tired and worn before her time. But it was not in her nature to complain. Jess was a reasonably good provider, a good husband, father and all around good man. She had seen the plight of some other wives in the community, who had married drunks or lazy good-for-nothings. She knew she had it better than them. So she tolerated the loneliness and fear on that somewhat isolated farm while her man worked out his wanderlust.

Bessie thanked God every day for her family. She was a deeply religious woman, who assumed that all good things came directly from God and bad things were simply His tests of her strength, just like He had done to that man Job, one of her favorite Old Testament characters.

On the day after Thanksgiving in1884, Jess got itchy. He decided he needed a new plow for spring planting and he reasoned that it would be best to get it now before the hard winter set in so he could be prepared for plowing early. He also figured a plow would be cheaper now than in March. Plus, he wanted to get Bessie and the kids some Christmas presents—not much, mind you—Lord knew they couldn't afford much, but he had seen some pretty gold and brown material in a store in Rolla that he wanted to get Bessie. Besides, he was confident that he could get a better deal on a plow in Rolla than that old pirate Sullins would give him in Salem. So his rationalization went on that day to justify a two-day jaunt away from the farm. It inspired family action.

He told Bessie of his sound logic and suggested that she pack snacks and put the kids into their warm clothes and under the travelin' blankets while he hooked old Jim and Prince, his powerful black work horses. In no more than an hour after breakfast, they were hell bound for Rolla! It was another adventure for the kids that even the youngest loved. Their dad always kept them guessing what he would do next and they reveled in the thrill of it.

Jess and Bessie laughed a lot and sang gospel songs—and some not-so-gospel songs—and told stories all the way to Rolla. It was a seven-hour trip if the roads were good, counting pee stops in the woods. Bessie drew the line at peeing over the edge of the wagon, although Jess could definitely see the logic of it for the boys, but hadn't quite figured out a reasonable strategy for the girls, although he had contemplated a sliding door in the bottom of the wagon once. Bessie had vetoed that as a health hazard.

They arrived in Rolla, did some shopping, and eventually wound up at the house of a cousin named Sam Kofahl to board down for the night. After catching up on the news and touring the lumber company where Sam was head man, they settled into Sam's parlor. During the ensuing conversation, Jess wondered to Sam whether there was anything going on in town that evening that Bessie might like.

"There's a pie supper at the Community Center," replied Sam. "Martha and me had talked a little about goin. Sally could watch the kids. What would you say to you, me, Bessie and Martha takin it in?"

Sally, Sam's thirteen-year-old daughter and oldest child, who heard them talking, certainly knew what she would have said, had she been asked. She was not smitten with the idea of taking care of all the brats. She had planned on going to the pie supper herself; but as usual, nobody bothered to ask her opinion on the matter. So she sat on the sideline of the conversation, pouting and emitting fatal sighs to signify her displeasure. Jess, no more cognizant of poor Sally's tragic condition than her clueless father, reckoned that Bessie would like that just fine. So they went.

It was a great pie supper, with young ladies displaying their baking skills and the young man of each young lady's fancy trying to out-bid everyone else for her pie and other related favors. Of course, Jess and Sam had to bid on a few pies just to run up the price and make the boys from Sam's church a little more miserable while Bessie and Martha fussed at them to stop, laughing all the while. Their mirthful admonitions only egged on their husbands' delinquent behaviors.

Jess and Sam were cautious not to bid up the price if they thought that the young man couldn't afford it. They just bid a little if they knew the boy's financial backing, something that had happened to them a few times in their youth. Their advancing age played tricks on their memories. They had forgotten how very "un-funny" they had considered such tactics in their own days as beaus.

They did, however, actually buy a tasty-looking pie baked by a homely girl who did not get any bidders, and, true to tradition, they shared it with her afterwards. She was grateful for not being embarrassed by having her pie go unsold, but not nearly as grateful as they, because her apple pie was the best they had ever eaten. Bessie and Martha asked the girl for her recipe, which made her blush with pride. They also assured her that she would definitely find a man when the word got out that she could cook like that if, after viewing the poor examples of their husbands, she really wanted one.

Jess walked outside to the outhouse midway through the festivities to pee. On his return he loitered at the entrance to read the posters and announcements on the Center's bulletin board. His eye caught a strange poster featuring a picture of a train with a group of children standing on the station platform. The poster told about New York orphans and a "placement meeting" the next day in Rolla. The poster said children could be "interviewed and inspected" at 11:00 a.m. at the Community Center.

As he read this, he wondered how these children must feel coming to a strange land to be inspected by people they had never met before. And then he wondered how different New York children would be from his own.

When he got back to the table, he asked Sam what the orphan train was all about. Sam explained it to him. Sam and Martha knew about it because their church had sponsored other children who had come on trains before, even boarding some of them overnight prior to placement inspections.

It was an intriguing thought to Jess to be able to go and just pick out children and take them home with you. He wondered what kind of families did that. That night, as he lay in bed, he wondered about all this out loud to Bessie. "Oh, I don't know, Jess," she reflected, sleepily. She was tired from riding the rough wagon and staying up too late. She had already said their prayers and was ready to drift off. "I guess there are quite a few couples who are barren, or who just have enough love in their hearts for another child."

He stayed awake thinking about it after she had dropped off to sleep. He thought what she said was probably true and he wondered what kind of children would be offered tomorrow at the Community Center—not that he wanted another one, of course. He and Bessie obviously had plenty of their own; but he still couldn't stop wondering what these children from a place like New York City would be like.

The next morning after breakfast he said to Bessie, "You know, that Community Center is right directly on our way back to Salem Road. Why don't we stop by there and watch that placement inspection on the way home?"

She gave him one of those looks.

"Aw now, Bessie, I'm not trying to find you another young'un to take care of," he laughed. "I would just like to see how it all works. We could tell some of the people in Jadwin about it. A few of the young couples in our church who don't have kids might consider it someday."

And so they planned their departure to fit the time of the placement event to see for themselves just how it all worked. But they were slow getting away from Sam's, and then in picking up the used plow they had purchased, which had needed a little work before it was ready. When they finally got to the Community Center it was already 11:30 a.m.

As they walked to the door, families were walking out, looking a little disgruntled. He heard a man say to his crestfallen wife, "The pickins was slim this year, Mary. Maybe we should travel up to Jefferson City next time, before all the good kids have been taken." He, Bessie and the four kids made their way through the door as the last family was coming out. They didn't seem to be fawning over any new acquisitions.

Inside, they were warmly greeted by Mrs. Mason, who was surprised to see them coming so late. She saw Jess and Bessie as the last faint hope for Zachary. She bustled them over to where Anna stood, holding Zachary. He was sucking his thumb and staring at the wall, his curly-haired little head lying across her shoulder. He had lost all hope for a family. Mrs. Mason tried to introduce them to Zachary, but he wouldn't respond. As an afterthought she introduced them to Anna and indicated that she was also available for placement.

Bessie and Jess were both struck by the beauty of the tall, stately girl who held the little boy. The boy was clearly as unattractive as she was pretty. They politely told Anna their names and the names of their children. The girl smiled in return and greeted each of them as she shifted Zachary's weight from one hip to the other. The little boy remained silent and did not acknowledge their presence.

As they were passing conversation with Mrs. Mason about the orphan train process, a thought struck Jess. As it always was when self-perceived brilliant ideas came to mind, he became agitated and started to fidget. He asked Mrs. Mason if she would watch his children while he talked to his wife outside. Mrs. Mason said she was more than happy to do so. She had been sure this was only a "looking" family and had not expected anything to come of it, but now she had a ray of hope that she would not have to drag Zachary all the way back to New York.

Bessie was too surprised to resist, so she and Jess exited the Community Center to the graveled front yard. As Jess pulled Bessie aside, he said excitedly, "Bessie, let's take that girl with us!"

Bessie did not voice her first thought, which was "Have you entirely lost your senses, you fool!?" Being a diplomatic wife, familiar with his occasional flawed thinking and fully aware of her role as the anchor of the family, she usually tried to let him down gently when he got a wild hair. "Well, Jess, that would be a kind act, but the girl is a teenager and we don't know much about her. It will be far too late to shape her in good Christian ways if she isn't already so, and she could have a bad influence on the children."

She read his face and then added quickly, "but it was a kind thought on your part, Jess." She reached up and touched the side of his face as she always did to let him know that any temporary insanity he might experience would always be forgiven and that she would always love him anyway.

"But Bessie," Jess countered undeterred, "Her age is just the reason I want us to take her! I am gone so much and you are left to take care of the kids by yourself and keep up the chores to boot. Frankly, I worry sometimes that it will send you to an early grave. You aren't looking any younger you know."

He realized immediately that his last statement may not have bolstered his argument, and he would probably have to "clarify" it a few times in the future. He decided the best strategy now was just to plow ahead full steam. "This girl could be a lot of help to you. And she has kind eyes, Bessie, like your eyes"— compliments would be necessary now to obscure his earlier blunder—"And did you see how that little deformed boy clings to her? I bet she is great with kids. I'd feel a lot better if you had some help raising our young'uns. God knows we have enough

213

food for a girl as thin as her. I'd really think we should consider this." He stopped, out of breath, trying to think of more good arguments to bolster his case. He was generally of the philosophy that the quantity of the argument was just as important as the quality in winning her over.

Bessie stood silently for a minute, holding his arm, thinking about what he had said. He had surprised her. Amazingly, there actually was a tiny bit of sense in his arguments. She could use the help and she truly did like the appearance of that beautiful, sad-looking girl. On top of that, it would be the Godly thing to do. But she still worried about what this girl was like and whether she had Christian ways.

In her long reflection, Jess realized that she wasn't going to reject the idea outright, which amazed him even more than the idea itself. He tried to think of new arguments to drive the proposal home, but before he could even think of anything more, she shocked him by laughing and saying, "Oh, alright, Jess Lough. Seein' as how you are only thinking of me and the kids; let's go in and see what this girl is like. But mind you, if she doesn't measure up, we are not going to be taking her, and I will only do this if I have final say!" The threat in her voice, coupled with that firm look she gave him, suggested that he shouldn't put up any resistance to her veto authority or say anymore.

"Absolutely, Bessie, you know I'd not want the girl to come live with us if it didn't please you." They went back inside to talk to Anna. On the way, he secretly reveled in just how easy a victory that was! He knew Bessie was a pushover for people who needed help, and this girl qualified big time. But his victories were rare with her.

"Anna," said Jess, in his most persuasive tone, "we was a wonderin

214

if you would tell us a little about yourself?" His question shocked both Mrs. Mason and Anna to the point that their mouths dropped open simultaneously. They had assumed that he and Bessie had been trying to decide on Zachary.

Anna didn't know what to say. She stood staring at them in shock. Neither she nor Emma Mason had ever seriously considered this possibility, and no family had ever questioned her before. Mrs. Mason recovered more quickly than Anna, but only to evolve to an immediate state of suspicion. She wasn't sure this was all up-and-up, even though they looked like a normal couple. "Mr. Lough, may I inquire of the nature of your intentions?"

Jess was a little confused by the question, but then assumed that this might be a prerequisite to taking an orphan child. He wasn't sure what the right answer was but he knew there must be one and that this lady would only agree if he got it right.

While he was thinking this through, Bessie responded for him, "Well, Mrs. Mason, my husband travels a lot in his work and I am left alone with the children. We were thinking that Anna might be of help in that regard. I assure you that we are faithful members of the Church of Christ over at Jadwin, where we live, and our intentions are sincere in thinking that we might be able to give Anna a good home with meaningful responsibility."

That relieved some of Emma's anxiety about Jess' intentions. She had heard that there had been Mormons in Missouri and it had occurred to her that this man might be looking for another wife. But Mrs. Mason knew about the Church of Christ. They were not associated with the Latter Day Saints, and were, in fact, quite prejudiced against that religion, as they were with most denominations other than their own. "Oh, then you are not Mormon, right?"

"Why no." said Jess, puzzled at why she would think that and wondering if that was a prerequisite to taking the girl home. "Why would you think we're Mormon, Mrs. Mason?" But even as he asked her, it hit him what she was thinking. His face went deep red. Bessie, who had not yet figured it all out, was still puzzled.

Jess said a little hotly, "I am not looking for another wife, Mrs. Mason. I travel a lot and Bessie is home alone with the kids. I think Anna here could be of great assistance to her." He hastened to add, "And we have a good home that I think Anna would like, in a good community of nice people. It's just a family we are offering her and nothing more!" His voice had risen to a higher pitch and was a little too loud. Bessie was now squeezing his arm to contain him.

"I do apologize, Mr. Lough," said Mrs. Mason politely, but a bit coolly, "but I do have to ask these questions you know. After all, these children are our wards until placed, and we are their responsible representative."

By then all parties understood each other a bit better and Jess' temper had cooled slightly. "I'm not taking offense, Mrs. Mason. I just don't want you to think that we have any ill motives toward Anna."

Everyone now turned attention back to Anna who, gratefully, had been given time to think as the verbal sparring was occurring. She wanted to go back to New York and find Ben again. She had ridden the orphan train; she was exhausted and all she wanted to do now was to get back on a train headed east. She had ached for him every day since she left the city. This man and woman seemed very kind and would probably be acceptable to live with, but it would be an unhappy life without Ben.

Zachary stirred and changed thumbs as he leaned his head on her other shoulder. She became aware of his presence, small and frail, his little arm around her neck, abandoned of all hope. She knew that feeling all too well and thought that no child should have to experience it.

"Mr. and Mrs. Lough, you are so kind to consider taking me in, and I will always remember and appreciate your gesture. But I ask you to reconsider and take Zachary here instead of me," she pleaded. "He has been hoping and praying for a real family all his life, and he has never had one. He is such a good little boy, and he could look a lot healthier if properly taken care of by a family like you. He could eventually be a big help to you. I'm sure he could."

Her eyes darted back and forth to Bessie and Jess, hoping to convince them. All Jess could think was that she was rejecting them. He looked a bit confused and crestfallen. But Bessie was thinking something entirely different. She looked carefully into this girl's eyes. Eyes always told Bessie a lot about a person. She liked these eyes. She saw this beautiful girl pleading for her little deformed friend and she fell in love with her right then and there. She would love Anna Murphy from that moment for the rest of her life.

She tugged at Jess' arm and dragged him outside. Their children, watching all this with growing interest, not sure whether to go or stay. So they stayed and stared at Anna and Zachary, wondering if their mother and father were going to "buy" one of them, getting more excited with the prospects by the minute. Mrs. Mason, terribly proud of Anna's sacrificial offer, assumed they were going outside to discuss Zachary again. She was partially correct. "Jess, I want to take them both!" exclaimed Bessie as soon as she had gotten out of earshot.

"You what! Why Bessie, that little boy has some big health problems and we've got plenty of small children to take care of now without adding a sick one." He became fearful that his brilliant victory was getting far more complicated than necessary.

"Jess Lough, if ever a child needed a good home, it's that little boy," she lectured. "And did you see what that girl did? You were absolutely right about her. She is special and she could be a great comfort and companion to me. I want them both." And with that she turned her back on him and marched toward the door, disappearing inside before he could say another word. He followed her, wondering just how much he had lost.

"Anna," said Bessie, in the gentlest of voices, "If you will come live with us, we would be honored to take Zachary too."

Anna was floored. Her mind raced. Would they take Zachary if she didn't go? She tried to think of some other argument but none came. Finally, she looked at Bessie and said, "Would you take Zachary if I couldn't stay?"

Bessie, who prided herself on honesty, even to the point of it causing pain, shook her head no.

Zachary had finally tuned in to the conversation and was looking back and forth from Anna to Jess to Bessie with increasing awareness that something special might be happening. Anna saw a small glint of hope flicker in his eyes. She knew it would crush him if she refused to go and they chose not to take him.

The thought of not returning to New York City to find Ben almost overwhelmed her and she felt faint. A tear spilled down her cheek. Bessie, assuming the tear was the result of their offer, moved to

Anna and took her in her arms with Zachary squeezed in the middle. Zachary closed the deal by reaching out and putting his arm around Bessie's neck as Anna, now weeping openly, continued to hold him while being squeezed by Bessie.

"We'll go with you and thank you for being so kind," Anna sobbed. Mrs. Mason was also weeping, sincerely touched by the scene. Even Jess had a tear in his eye, which he quickly wiped away when he was sure no one was looking. The Lough children, who couldn't believe their luck, danced around Bessie, Anna and Zachary chanting, "We're buying you both! We're buying you both!"

So Anna Murphy and Zachary Simmons climbed up into the wagon with the Lough family and headed toward Jadwin, Missouri on that crisp late-November day in 1884. Their lives, and the lives of their new family, were forever changed by a man who liked to wander, a poster at a pie supper, and a woman with all the gold of Fort Knox tucked right down there in her own heart.

Chapter 21

On that sad day that she had told him to leave the train station, Ben crossed the street and stood in the shadow of a nearby building. He had wanted to catch one last glimpse of her as she boarded the train. As he watched, the first train came to a halt on tracks not connected to the passenger platform and he realized it was not hers. There might still time to see her before she boarded. He started to return to the depot, but then hesitated. His departure had been almost unbearably painful for them both. He wasn't sure that going back and putting her through that experience again was the right thing to do in the little time left before the arrival of her train, which would surely come soon. He leaned back against the building to think about it and ultimately decided to wait where he was a little longer.

But the train did not come soon. Minutes dragged by. As he waited his anxiety grew. At least three times he started to go back into the depot, but each time he hesitated again. Finally he decided it was too late. If he went back now, she would not understand why he had waited so long.

The torture of this indecision and the knowledge that she was still there, just across the street, made him even more miserable. His torment was finally interrupted by the distant wail of another train, and this time it was hers. He saw her preparing to board with the group of children and the middle-aged lady. He saw Bill give her a goodbye hug, and he saw her disappear from sight into the passenger car.

It was all he could do to keep himself from sprinting to the car and pulling her away. He stood frozen in place, his mind screaming for him to act before it was too late, but remembering what Bill had said about this being her best chance. His heart told him that going anywhere with her, no matter how destitute, would be better than losing her, but he knew in his head that it was not true. Anna had almost died. If they were separated again he feared she would, and he could not allow that to happen. He was immobilized by his better judgment.

He moved out of the shadows of the building to see if he could determine where she was sitting on the train for just one last glance, but he couldn't find her. He shrank back into the shadows. He knew her chances for a better life were somewhere away from Hell's Kitchen and he wanted her to have it.

Hopefully she would find a place with people who would care about her nearly as much as he did. She would be safe. That was what was important. She would get past her sorrow. They had really known each other only briefly. They had bonded through extreme danger and adversity. Maybe that wasn't the way it should happen.

The train pulled away slowly from the station. A deep sense of depression enveloped him. This time it seemed even worse than when he had been abandoned by his mother. The whistle wailed one last time and the train departed. She was gone.

He saw Bill look around on the station platform, re-enter the depot, and then leave. He should go after Bill and thank him for all he had done, but somehow he couldn't bear to talk to anyone now. He turned and exited down an alleyway--to where, he didn't know or care at that moment. He just knew that he had to be alone.

He decided to go to Central Park where they had their happiest time. He found shelter under a tree by The Pond. He didn't try to sleep. He eventually became chilled and got out of the wind into the shelter of bushes. As he hunched down, he thought, in passing,

"She never got the chance to help me improve my reading, but maybe she'll help somebody else. I bet she'd be a great teacher if she had an opportunity someday."

He thought of all Bill had done. Tomorrow he would go thank him and then figure out what to do next. He had no idea what that would be. In his sorrow, he'd forgotten Bill's offer for a job. He felt the hopelessness settle in. His family was gone. She was gone. No one who ever really mattered to him remained for long in his life.

The darkness finally gave way to a gray dawn. The air hung heavy with the threat of rain or snow. As the full light came, he made his way back to the warehouse. It was a weekday and men were already arriving to work. He walked into the building and climbed the stairs to Bill's second floor office. Bill was already there. He looked up, saw Ben, and motioned vigorously for him to come in. "Where in Hell did you go yesterday, Ben!? I expected to see you back at the apartment when I got home." Bill's voice betrayed exasperation and concern that surprised Ben.

"Sorry, Bill. I went to Central Park to be alone. I didn't mean to worry you."

Bill saw Ben's expression and didn't press. "That wasn't her train, when you left. It didn't come until later."

"I know. I watched from across the street."

"Why in the world didn't you come back to the depot?"

"I thought it would've been too hard on her, having to say goodbye twice." He looked away.

222

Bill fell silent for a minute. "You were probably right about that. That was thoughtful of you…and, I suspect, very hard."

Ben didn't respond; he just continued looking away.

"So what are you going to do now?"

Ben shrugged, "I don't know. Guess I'll try to find a job somewhere."
"Well, I told you I wanted to talk to you about that. I have an entry level position available. It's the same job I started out with a few years back. I want you to take it if you will. I'm not supposed to hire you till you're 16, but you'll pass for that now and I doubt if anyone will challenge me. It'd be a favor to me. I need someone I can trust."

Ben finally remembered the offer and was shocked that Bill had been serious. He had assumed it was just a courtesy when Bill said it. Nothing that good ever happened to him that easily.

"Mind you, it doesn't pay much," continued Bill, "but it's a start. And if you're willing, I'd like you to stay in my apartment until you can save up enough for your own. Frankly, I could use the company. It gets lonesome for me at times. Having you and Anna there these last few days was very good for me."

Ben didn't know whether Bill was being honest or just nice. Either way, he appreciated the gesture. "Thanks, Bill. That's awfully kind of you."

"Nonsense," Bill responded. "Kindness doesn't have anything to do with it. Smart workers that I can trust are hard to find. You definitely fill that bill. Come with me and let me introduce you to some people." He put his arm around Ben's shoulder and escorted him out of his office and down to the main floor of the warehouse. The people at the warehouse were friendly and treated Ben with respect. Despite the terrible ache in his heart, a tiny glimmer of hope crept into his head.

Days came and went. They turned into weeks and months. Ben heard the generalities of Anna's placement through Bill. So it was done. She was safe. Not a day passed that he didn't think of her, even though he often chided himself for doing so. She was gone to a new life now.

He fantasized that she was adopted by some wealthy family with a fine house, good food and nice clothes. He believed that she would be well received. She would bring out the best in people and she would do well, wherever she was. At times the pain of remembering was too much. On those occasions he would try to put her out of his head for good, but he never succeeded.

He was a serious, dedicated worker and totally loyal to Bill. He quickly learned the operation of the warehouse and excelled at every task Bill gave him. Bill called in his favor to Connor regarding Ben's safety. Connor indicated that no one in his organization really cared anymore about Ben McDonald, and he was glad to repay Bill for past favors Bill had done for him.

After months had passed, Bill began to send Ben up and down 59th street as a courier, often carrying important papers and contracts. Ben's math skills increased as Bill gradually showed him more about handling money. Ben was intensely proud of Bill's trust and frequently wished his reading skills were better so he could be more useful. It was apparent that the ability to read and write was prerequisite to any career beyond the most menial labor.

Once he asked Bill how he had learned to read so well, knowing

Bill had spent much of his young life on the streets. Bill laughed and said he learned the hard way with a little help from his boss, but that he was still pretty uncomfortable with serious reading. What he knew he had picked up by necessity through his work, but he still struggled at serious reading. Ben remembered seeing him puzzling over documents at night. He developed a new appreciation for Bill's dedication to his work, realizing how difficult it must have been for him in his early days as his leadership role at the warehouse grew, and how far Bill had obviously come.

"Anna was going to teach me how to read better, but we never got the chance," he reflected wistfully, one evening as they sat in the apartment. Bill, who was pouring over his paperwork from the day, paused and looked up. Ben had not mentioned her name in a while and Bill had assumed that he had begun to put her out of his mind. He saw the haunted look on his young friend's face and realized that the wound was still there.

"Oh, well, that's too bad. I suspect she'd have been a good teacher for you," Bill mused.

"I think so," said Ben. "She had schooling before her father died. He had insisted that she go. He apparently spent a lot of time with her on her books as well. She told me that she loved to read about faraway places and do math and other studies." He said no more about Anna that night and Bill didn't return to the subject, but it was obvious that Ben still had Anna on his mind.

Ben was well liked by his co-workers, who often remarked to Bill how mature he was, but that he seemed so serious all of the time. Bill just told them he had recently lost his family and no one said more about it.

Bill thought about tutoring Ben in reading himself, but he was uncomfortable with his own reading skills and wasn't quite sure how to go about it. He decided he would ask Brace to help, but they were so busy that he kept forgetting to raise the subject. He was also increasingly worried about Brace's health and didn't want to add to his stress. Time slipped by.

More than a year had passed since Anna's departure. Ben saved every dollar he made except for buying his clothing and paying his share of the food. He never went out with his coworkers, even though they pestered him to do so. Eventually Bill allowed Ben to clean out a storage room on the third floor of the warehouse that he could call his own, but Ben still usually ate with Bill. He was grateful for his own private space and glad that he was not imposing on Bill all the time.

In 1886, on the occasion of his sixteenth birthday, Bill took Ben to dinner and a musical concert to celebrate. It was a fabulous evening of good food and great music like Ben had heard only once before. Late that night, as he lay on his cot, he thought about how much Anna would have liked it. He wondered if she had occasion to hear music like that where she was.

He no longer experienced that intense, stomach-sinking ache when he thought of her, but he thought of her no less frequently. And she was still in his dreams every night, to the point that he began to dread them. Some of the dreams were pleasant, but most were frightening. She was falling and he couldn't catch her. She was being chased by wild animals and he couldn't get to her, his movements maddeningly slow in his dream. She was being attacked by evil men, but he couldn't stop them. Each time he saw her face, her eyes pleading to him for help that he couldn't give.

And then there were other kinds of dreams. In one, she had met another man and told Ben that she wasn't interested in him anymore. On the morning after those particularly bad nightmares, he woke up in a sweat.

He was a young man now, with a young man's urges, and not unaware of the attention of some of the young ladies that he met; but he never seemed to get around to returning their interest. When he was attracted to a young lady he always caught himself comparing her to Anna.

He wondered what she must be like now. She would be fifteen, probably beautiful, and courted by all the young men around her. That was an unhappy thought that he tried to put out of his mind.

Bill called him into his office on that Monday morning after his birthday. "You've done well for yourself here, Ben. I'm proud of you."

Ben blushed and said, "Thank you," always appreciative of Bill's compliments. Pleasing Bill and honoring his trust was now Ben's main mission in life.

Bill continued, "I think it's time you take on more responsibility. One of the supervisors quit last week on the warehouse floor and I'd like to offer you the job. The work is hard but the pay is better. The job is yours if you'll have it. The only catch is that you'll have to find another place to live. I can't play favorites by letting you stay here once you become a supervisor. There's a good boarding house a few blocks away. I spoke to the lady who owns it and she has a room if you're interested. And by the way, sometime after the first of the year, when things get lighter around here, I was wondering if you would like to hit the books with Reverend Brace a little?"

Ben was elated. "I'd really appreciate the opportunity, Bill, thanks! And learning from Reverend Brace would be a special privilege." The boarding house idea pleased him as well. He said he'd check into it on the weekend. He began his new work responsibilities that day.

On Sunday, he went to Mrs. Sullivan's boarding house and took a room. It had a window with a nice view, a bed and washstand with a pitcher, a small chest of drawers and a chair. It seemed like such luxury that this could actually be his private space. Mrs. Sullivan was friendly but direct, making sure he understood the house rules: no drinking or smoking and no women guests. He assured her that was not a problem and she exclaimed, "Well then, you and me will get along just fine!"

His boarding fee was three dollars a week and that included breakfast and dinner. Breakfast was at 6:00 a.m. sharp, and dinner at 6:00 p.m. She said he would do well to be on time if he wanted his share; he assured her that he did and he would.

Bill was right, the supervisory work was harder; but Ben liked it and assumed his new duties with enthusiasm. He had already worked on the floor on many previous occasions filling in for absent workers. The people he supervised liked him and didn't seem to mind that he was younger than them.

Except for his troubled thoughts of Anna and worrying about the whereabouts and well-being of his mother and siblings, it was a very good time for Ben McDonald. He and Bill remained close, still spending much time together outside of work. The only small disappointment was that Brace's physical problems acted up and he didn't yet have the energy to spend time with Ben on his reading skills.

Bill had become like a brother to Ben, who came to love him as such. He marveled at Bill's talents and his work with the Reverend Brace to help orphan children. He decided he would like to figure a way to help in that effort if he could be of meaningful assistance.

One Saturday evening at Bill's apartment, in the late autumn of that year, Ben indicated that he was thinking about going back to see the apartment in Hell's Kitchen where his family had lived. Bill expressed grave concern about the risks and tried to talk him out of it. "Do you really think it's worth it, taking that kind of risk, Ben? You have a new life now. You don't need to do that. If the Bowery Boys got wind of you being there, you might not make it back out."

"Yea, I know. But it haunts me how my family left. I need to find out whatever I can. I keep wondering what the landlord might know. He might talk to me now. Besides, I don't think many of the gang would know me anymore. I'm taller than I was and filled out more thanks to yours and Mrs. Sullivan's cooking." He grinned a little. "Anyway, I'm an old story in Hell's Kitchen."

"Maybe, but you were a big story, Ben. I can't stop you. You're a man now and have a right to your own decisions. But think about it carefully. You may be throwing away everything you've worked for since you got out of the Kitchen. I'd be glad to go with you if you decide to take the risk"

Ben reflected. "I'll think about it, Bill, but I don't think you should be seen with me under any circumstance. It could risk your work with the gangs. If I go, I'll pick the right time and be careful."

Bill nodded. "Okay. This is your call, but I strongly recommend against it."

Ben thought about it for a couple of weeks. He respected Bill's advice but ultimately decided to go. If the landlord at the old apartment knew anything about why his family left and where they went, he wanted to learn what it was. He picked a Sunday morning and left a little before dawn, when he guessed that gang members would still be sleeping. He was soon walking down past the cemetery where he and Anna had hidden. He stopped and looked at the mausoleum, giving thanks again to his little friends in their quiet resting place. It took him less than an hour to reach the street of the run-down tenement house where his family had resided.

As he entered the area, walking south and then west, he gained new perspective on the ugliness and squalor of Hell's Kitchen and the deterioration of its streets and buildings. As full daylight came and more children came out to the streets, he paused on the sidelines to watch them, now feeling very much of an outsider to their world.

The people of Hell's Kitchen seemed different to him now, even though it hadn't been that long ago that he was one of them. They were pinched and worn-looking and far more ragged than he had remembered. Their faces were unfriendly. No adult smiled or gave greetings of any kind. They were always glancing around, as if wary of attack at any moment. Only the raucous children gave loud greetings to each other, often laced with obscenities.

A few people warily glanced his way but none seemed to recognize him as anything but an out-of-place stranger. His clothes betrayed that he was not one of them. The younger children were watching him and he knew they were trying to decide whether or not to approach him to solicit money.

He realized how truly foreign and ugly this place was, and how much he must have changed to see it that way now. He felt like an alien in a foreign land. Maybe Christian was right, maybe he had never really belonged. Oddly, that brought a tinge of sadness for some reason, but also relief that he no longer felt bound to this morbid place.

When he reached his family's apartment building, it was abandoned. The entry door to the building was charred and broken, with only a single hinge holding it to its frame. Every window in the building was broken out, with fragments of the remaining glass splintered and blackened. The building gave off an acrid sulphur smell.

He stood across the street, watching to see if anyone came in or out of the building. No one did. He eventually crossed over and carefully made his way up the front steps to the main entrance. The stairs to the second floor, where his family's old apartment was located, were still standing but didn't look trustworthy. They too were blackened and sagged dangerously. He tested them, staying close to the wall, hoping they were strong enough to hold his weight.

He reached the second floor hallway and moved cautiously down it toward his family's apartment, testing each step as he went. He wanted to see the apartment one more time, the last place he had seen his mother and siblings. He entered it. There had been a lot of smoke damage and the walls were charred. Some of the floor had burned through, leaving gaping holes that he had to work his way around. He realized that one of those holes had been where the word on the floor had been written, the last message from his mother.

The dingy rooms brought a flood of painful memories. He

searched the outer room, but found nothing. He looked through the opening of what had been the bedroom where his mother and father had slept. That door had been removed and was no longer in the apartment. There was a larger hole in the middle of the bedroom floor, charred around the edges, giving a clear view of the burnt-out apartment below. He dared not enter. He saw rats scurrying below him across the lower floor. The building was obviously a hollow, burned-out shell.

He made his way out of the apartment and back down the steps to the outside. He sat down on the edge of the front steps, not sure what to do next. It irked him that he had gained nothing from this trip. He had just about decided to head home when a group of urchins appeared from around a corner, halting in front of the steps when they saw him. They looked to be about seven or eight years old—four boys and two girls. They requested money from him, a solicitation tinged with intimidation. He caught himself smiling and struggled to keep from laughing outright. The leader of the little mob saw Ben's smile and was affronted.

"What're you grinning at, you big monkey? You think we're funny? He pulled out a short homemade knife from his pocket and held it up. You think this is funny too, mister? We mean business. We'll cut you like a stuck hog if you don't give us your money."

Ben's smile faded. "Tell you what, ladies and gentlemen. I will give each of you a nickel if you can answer a few questions for me."

They stared at him mistrustfully. The boy with the knife said, "Let's see the money."

Ben laughed. "I'm not that stupid. You'll answer my questions first, if you can, and then you'll see the money, depending on what

I think about your answers."

The boy gave Ben a hateful stare and spat into the street, but said nothing more. The others in the group had not moved. After a few seconds, Ben said, "Okay, first question, did any of you know the landlord of this building?"

Knife boy spat on the street again. "Yea, I knowed him. So did Sean, here. We snuck into this rat hole a few times after most people were gone to see if we could find anything left behind. The bastard tried to catch us once, but we got away. I cut him on the arm as I got out and he yelled. He was a mean son of bitch. I'd a killed him if I could."

"Is he still around?"

The boy laughed derisively. "Na. He got drunk and started the fire that took out the building. I hear that the owners weren't too happy with him. Word is he died of natural causes. Probably because his head just caved in naturally or he developed air holes through his body."

Ben nodded. His memory of the landlord matched the boy's assessment.

"That it, mister? We answered. Give us our money."

"Not quite yet. Second question, is Christian Gunther still leader of the Bowery Boys?"

They looked surprised by the question and stared at Ben more closely. "Na, mister, he been gone for well over a year now."

"Where'd he go?"

"You don't keep up, do you? He got kicked out'a the gang. He let somebody get away who hadn't ought'a. It wasn't 'preciated. The bosses moved him. He's lucky they didn't kill him. He's doing low work down at the Haymarket, on 30th."

Ben paused for a few seconds. "Ok, one last question. Who is the leader of the Bowery Boys now?"

"Joey Drescher. He ain't much, though. He's the second since Gunther left. Ain't nobody as good as Gunther was."

"Okay, you've earned your money. Ben reached into his pocket and pulled out thirty cents. It was in three dimes, but that was their problem. He flipped the coins over the kid's heads and out into the street. All but one turned instinctively and ran toward the rolling coins. The boy with the knife didn't.

"I ought'a cut you for that mister."

Ben's face turned hard and he stared at the boy, speaking with a cold edge to his voice. "Well, you little punk, there's 30 cents out there and five of them are yours. You can try to cut me, but you won't get it done, and meantime, you might lose your share. Why don't we declare truce and you get on with whatever you were doing? Take your friends and move on."

The boy hesitated, looking a little cowed. "Who are you, mister?"

"Nobody important."

"Why'd you want to know about Gunther?"

"I knew him once. Just wondered how he was doing."

"You live hereabouts?"

"Not anymore.

The boy looked at him suspiciously. He knew there was more to the story but he wasn't going to get it. He shrugged and walked away to where the rest of the group stood, counting the money. They left as quickly as they had come. Ben headed south. Why hadn't Bill told him about Gunther? Bill surely knew. Maybe he didn't want Ben to feel guilty.

Ben remembered passing by the front of the Haymarket clubhouse during his time in Hell's Kitchen on one of the few times he had gone that far south. He was pretty sure it was near Sixth Avenue. He walked east, trying to get out of the Kitchen quickly, trying not to call too much attention to himself, hoping not to run into someone who would remember him. He would travel down Sixth Avenue to get to the Haymarket. That would keep him just outside the eastern edge of Hell's Kitchen as he walked south.

The Haymarket was situated near the southeastern edge of Hell's Kitchen and Five Points so that it could be reached in relative safety by the respectable citizens of Manhattan looking to dally in the dark side. It was one of the wildest places in Manhattan. It had started as a legitimate theater, but then the owner decided he could make more money by converting it to a nightclub catering to the rich and powerful who wanted more risqué shows that featured scantily clad dancing girls, many of whom were also prostitutes. By 1884 it was well on its way to becoming the most notorious night spot in the city.

Ben walked south in leisurely fashion and paused frequently, leaning against a building to survey the activity around him. It was late morning when he reached 30th Street. He walked west nearly a block until he saw the sign above the entrance to the Haymarket. He paused a few minutes to survey the area. It was quiet on the street; as he had assumed it would be on a Sunday. He crossed to the opposite side the street and entered a small café with a view of the Haymarket entrance. He ordered coffee and waited. He suspected the Haymarket would not be open on Sunday, or at least not until evening, but he hoped he might spot someone leaving the nightclub. He would try to talk to them to see if he could get some news about Gunther. This side trip would probably be as futile as his visit to the apartment.

After 20 minutes of nursing his coffee, he decided he wasn't going to have any luck. The Haymarket still looked dark and lifeless. He picked up his bill and walked to the counter to pay. He glanced over at the Haymarket as the cashier took his money and saw a woman exit from the building's front door. He started to make his way to the door of the café only to find that the woman was crossing the street and heading to the café herself. He opened the door for her. She was young and pretty and smiled at him as she entered. He stood at the door until she sat down and then doubled back to her table. "Mind if I bother you a minute?"

She looked up at him and smiled somewhat tiredly. "I'm really not in the mood for company today. Sorry."

Ben smiled back. "I understand, but I just have a quick question. I'm looking for a guy named Christian Gunther who is supposed to be working at the Haymarket now. I saw you come out of the club and hoped you might tell me how I can find him."

She looked relieved. "Oh, sure; I know Christian. He does work for the Haymarket. He's over there now. He actually lives there." She paused, looking a little anxious. "How do you know him and

236

what do you want to find him for?"

"Actually, I don't know him well. I only talked with him a few times. But he saved my life once at considerable risk to himself. I'm just interested in knowing how he's doing."

She stared at him for a couple of seconds and then motioned to an empty chair at her table. "I actually think I believe you." That seemed to surprise her. "Sit down a few minutes and let me order some soup. When I'm done, I'll take you to Christian."

Ben sat down. "Thanks." He didn't say anything more until she had ordered. She kept staring at him in a direct way that made him uncomfortable. She laughed a little and said, "You're a big, good looking guy. At first I thought you were older and were trying to hook up with me, but you're just a kid yet, aren't you?

Ben blushed. "I'm over 16, ma'am."

She laughed. "Yea, just like I thought. You're still a kid." His face turned red and she laughed again. "Oh, don't be so embarrassed! It was a compliment. You could pass for a lot older unless somebody's up close to you. You seem nice enough and I'm just saying that you act more mature than your age."

Ben smiled. "Thanks, I guess. I've seen some tough times. That can age you a bit."

She stopped smiling. "Yea, tell me about it. Actually I'm not that much older than you, but sometimes I feel twice my age. I heard Christian grew up on the streets. Is that where you met him?"

Ben nodded.

She waited for him to share more, but he didn't. "Okay, well, I bet that was hard. I didn't have a great life as a kid either. I had an Alcoholic father who liked to play games with his daughters that he shouldn't have, but I guess even with that, it was worse on the streets."

"Sorry to hear about your dad. That wouldn't be easy."

She shrugged, and a somber look flashed across her face. Then, just a quickly, she switched back to her "devil may care" attitude. "Well, I'm not the only one. It happens more than most people know." She went back to eating.

Ben thought about his sisters and felt his stomach turn.

She dabbed her napkin to her mouth. She had eaten very little of the soup. "Well, I'm done. I'll pay and we can go see Christian."

"If you don't mind, I'll pay for your soup and drink. I didn't expect it to be so easy to find Christian. I appreciate your help."

She smiled, a bit surprised, and said, "Well thank you. I'm Sadie Smith—not really, actually—but that's the name I use nowadays. I guess it's as good as any."

Ben smiled and said, "Hi, Sadie, I'm Ben McDonald. It's the only name I've used so far. Let me have your bill and I'll be right back."

She handed it to him and touched his hand as she passed it over. He blushed again. Her gesture was obviously deliberate. She grinned. "Oh, sorry Ben. It's just habit. Didn't mean to embarrass you again."

He grinned and went to pay the bill.

They walked across the street to the entrance of the Haymarket. She took a key out of her purse and unlocked the door. After she and Ben entered, she locked the door behind them. They were standing in a lavishly decorated entryway. "Hey Christian!" she yelled. "You've got a visitor."

In a minute, Gunther appeared through an archway on their left. He had a broom in his hand and wore an apron. He glanced at Sadie and then at Ben. "McDonald? What the hell are you doing here? You shouldn't be anywhere around these parts."

Ben laughed. "That's what everybody keeps telling me, Gunther. I was in the neighborhood, so I thought I'd drop by."

Gunther snorted. "Just in the neighborhood, huh? You never change, do you, McDonald? You're still the fool you always were. So, how's the girl?"
Ben's smile diminished. "Fine, I hope. She's gone west. I haven't seen her in a long time."

"Well, now that you're here, let's visit a bit. Thanks for bringing him in, Sadie. I won't ask you how you hooked up with him."

She laughed. "Nothing like that, Christian. I was getting lunch across the street and he came up and asked me if I knew you. He seemed harmless and said you saved his life once. He looked on the up and up, so I brought him over. I hope it's okay?"

Christian chortled. "Harmless? Why, this guy is a killer, Sadie! But as for the up and up part, you're probably right about that. He can't help it. It's one of his biggest character flaws. You did fine. Thanks."

She looked from Christian to Ben, obviously interested in knowing more, but neither offered. She shrugged and said, "Nice to meet you, Killer. If he was talking about your looks, I'd agree, but knowing Christian, I doubt if that's what he means. You boys have a good time. And Ben, she lowered her eyelids and gave him a seductive smile, "if I can help you out in any other way, Christian can tell you where to find me."

Ben smiled back. "Well, Sadie, you've helped me a lot already. And thanks for your offer. I suspect that I'll keep it in mind."

She laughed and came over and kissed him on the cheek, brushing her body lightly against his as she reached up to his face, sending a shock wave through him. "You do that, honey. I can be really, really helpful." She took her hand off his arm, turned and sashayed over to the door, glancing back over her shoulder to make sure they were still looking. They were. She giggled, unlocked the door and left, locking it behind her.

Christian grinned at Ben. "She's after you, McDonald! You could do a lot worse. Underneath all that acting, she's a good person." He motioned to the side room. "Follow me. Let's find some chairs."

Once they had settled in, Gunther said, "So what really brought you all the way down here through gang territory? It must be important to take that kind of risk."

Ben laughed. "You sound like Bill Chambers. I just needed to talk to the landlord of the tenement house where my family lived for a while. They disappeared after I had a fight with my father and was sent away by my mother until things cooled down. When I returned, they were gone. The only clue left was the word

'Bloomington' that I think my mother had scribbled on the floor. That was all before I came to the streets."

He paused longer than necessary and then spoke again. "My dad was a violent drunk who beat me and my mother a lot. I am the oldest child in my family. He particularly hated me. I think he took them away against their will, but I could be fooling myself. They may have just taken the opportunity to get away from me. I can live with that, I guess, but I can't get it out of my head that he may have harmed them to get them to go. I thought the landlord might know something."

"Did you see him?"

"No, he's dead and there was nothing in the apartment. The place almost burned down."

"Dead end then. So where is the building?"

"46th street."

Christian frowned. "So you came down to 46th street, taking the chance that someone would see you and remember who you were. That wasn't smart, McDonald." He paused and looked reflective. "We all wonder about our families sometimes, I guess. What was your mother like with you?"

"She was wonderful. She protected me every way she could and usually paid a heavy price for it."

"You said she sent you away after the fight with your father?"

"Yea, she was desperate that I get away, and she was right. I'd gone too far. I hit my dad and knocked him down for beating up on my mother. She knew he'd kill me if he could. The last time I saw her, she was hanging onto the door of their bedroom where he had crawled to nurse his wounds, trying to keep him from coming back after me."

"How old were you?"

"Eleven"

Christian laughed. "You started beating people up early, didn't you McDonald!"

Ben grinned sheepishly. "I usually don't make a habit of it. I just pick on the bad guys."

Christian laughed again and then turned serious. "You're right, I think; your mother doesn't sound like somebody who would leave you willingly. I suspect your father threatened her with something that she was more afraid of than leaving you. What could that have been?"

Ben hesitated, thinking, "I don't know."

"You think he threatened to kill her?"

"He did that all the time. That wouldn't have changed her mind."

"Maybe he threatened to kill you when you came back and she thought she couldn't protect you any longer?"

"Maybe. She would've believed that. She knew I crossed the line."

"You said you have sisters and a brother. You're the oldest, right?

You said he didn't beat them as much. How much younger are they?"

"Quite a bit. My little brother was still a toddler. He followed me around wherever he could. My dad didn't like that, but he didn't beat him."

"So, if your old man threatened them or told your mom he would take them away from her if she didn't leave with him, what would she have done?"

Ben's face froze and then turned ashen. He spoke as though he had been shocked, "I don't know for sure, but I think she would've had to go. She couldn't let him take them. They would've died for sure."

"So she might have had to trade three for one then? From what you've told me about your old man, if I were thinking like him, and if I wanted to scare her into leaving you behind, that would have been how I would've laid it out to her."

Ben grimaced. Why hadn't he thought of that? Gunther had just given him a scenario that finally made some sense. He began to nod slowly and then, almost in a whisper, said. "If I were him, it's what I'd have done too. That's how he thought."

Christian didn't say any more. He left Ben to his thoughts and got up to find a couple of coffee mugs. He brought the coffee back and handed a cup to Ben. "Here, drink this. It's nice and strong. One of the few vices I can afford nowadays since it's on the house."

"So, I can see what brought you to 46th street, but now how do you explain coming all the way on down to 30th?"

Ben laughed. "Once you start acting stupid, it's hard to stop, I guess."

Christian grinned. "Yea, that's true. But how did you know to come down here? Bill tell you?"

"No, he didn't. If he knows you're here, he never told me. He has to know you left the gang, so I suspect he knows where you went. He values you a lot. I guess he didn't tell me because he didn't want me to feel guilty."

"Why would you feel guilty?"

"You know why. I caused your problems. I'm the reason you got thrown out."

Christian laughed. "Good. I like that. Guilt is a good punishment for you. I ought to just leave it at that, but you're being a little naive, as usual, McDonald. I made those choices. You didn't put a knife to my throat. You have your stupid moments. I have mine. So if Bill didn't tell you where I was, how did you find out?"

Ben grinned. "At the tenement, I was 'solicited' by a group of younger orphans. I traded them some money for information. That's how I know the landlord is dead. I asked them about you and they told me. Seems they don't really like your successors very much. I don't know if they were members of the Bowery Boys or not. Doesn't matter, I guess."

"So you decided to just waltz on down and pay me a visit?"

"Something like that. I was just interested in how you are doing."

"Well, let's see. I didn't graduate to the Bigs and I also lost my position with the gang. In fact, I got kicked out of the gang entirely. But the big boys didn't have me killed. They actually saw to it that my arm got fixed and they gave me this job, if you can call it a job. Not exactly the career path I had in mind, but I guess it could be worse."

Ben nodded. "So, what do you do here?"

"Everything from washing dishes, to night guard, to bouncer. I have a little room upstairs where I stay. I will say that the view is good. The girls are pretty and they run around semi-naked most of the time. The average Joe would think that's a great side benefit." He laughed. "But I am learning a lot about the business and they are beginning to trust me again. I'll probably own the place in ten years if they're not careful."

"That wouldn't surprise me one bit. In fact, I'd bank on it if I had the money. So, I've got another question for you."

"Ok, McDonald. Since we've become such good pals and all, what is it?"

"Can you tell me more about what motivated you to take Anna and me out of the Kitchen instead of making an example of us to save your own skin?"

Christian hesitated and then answered, "Well, that's complicated. I should've killed you for what you did. A year previous, I would've in the blink of an eye. But I was in a different place in my head when you attacked us. I was getting weary of my position. The Bigs were stalling about moving me up for no reason other than I was good for them where I was, and because I hadn't found the right successor to replace me." He smiled mischievously at Ben. "By the way, that's why I kept pressuring you to join. I had this fantasy that you could replace me. Funny isn't it, how far off base I can be sometimes. Anyway, I guess I just lost my enthusiasm for the whole bit."

"Chambers had been bugging me about coming off the streets—even offered me a job. Like you, I was getting sick of seeing kids starve or be killed for sport, or being sold off to some pervert to be abused. That's why we helped Chambers get the youngest kids to his orphan train program."

"That night, when my boys saw the girl, I was tired and needed to get some rest. They wanted to have some fun with her, even if she was almost dead. For some reason, that struck me as disgusting. I don't really know why, except that she was in terrible shape and all they could think about was pulling down their pants. I understood it. At an earlier time, I might have been thinking that too, but not that night. It just seemed to be more of the same sick thing."

He paused, reflecting, and then resumed. "Of course, I wasn't going to stop them. They wouldn't have understood why if I did. But I didn't feel good about it, so I took the easy way out and decided to go on home, leaving them to their little orgy. I suspected they would kill the girl; but then, she looked like she would have been dead by morning anyway. I decided that, at least they would put her out of her misery."

"Then you came along—the great white knight! You killed Big Mike, by the way, and banged us all up pretty good. And the weird thing about that was that I didn't really care. Mike was always a pain in the ass to the gang. But, not caring about a gang member that gets taken out, that's when I knew I was really screwed up in the head."

"Then, of course, I had to come after you. The weird thing was, I liked your style before and for some weird reason, I didn't like you less after you attacked us. But I had to kill you or my reputation was screwed. So I ordered an all-out search. I would have killed you both if the boys had been with me when I found you. But they weren't."

"Funny circumstance; I found you during a shift change when I was too tired and miserable to go back to headquarters. Strange how things happened, isn't it? I could have waited till they came by, but I heard you and the girl talking. I decided then to get you out. Not, by the way, because I suddenly saw the light on the Damascus Road or anything of that nature. You just became a symbol of a bigger battle I was having with myself."

"So, truth be told, I took you out of Hell's Kitchen for my own sake, not yours. The choice I made was about where I was in my head, not what you did or didn't do. It was personal. I hate to bust your little balloon like this if you were thinking I was a good guy in disguise, but it really wasn't about that."

Ben mulled that over. "Well, Gunther, let's agree to disagree on the good guy question. You made a choice. Maybe you made it from a different place than me, but it pretty much had the same end, didn't it?"

Christian smiled. "Maybe."

Ben continued. "So, why are you still here at this place, doing what you do now? If Bill offered you a job, why didn't you take him up on it?"

"Ah, an even better question, McDonald! I've thought hard about that. I like Chambers. He's the best I've met. But I was guilty of violating a code that I had lived by and believed in, even helped create, you see, and deep down, I felt I deserved to pay a price for breaking it. The big boys chose this as my purgatory. They could have killed me instead. I still don't know why they didn't. But since they didn't, I figure I owe them something. I don't know how much or for how long, but I guess I'll know it when the debt's paid. Sounds pretty lame doesn't it?"

Ben laughed. "Not really. "I'd personally consider it warped logic, but it fits your sense of loyalty, I guess."

Christian thought about that a minute and said, "Well, yea, I guess. I don't expect it to much sense to most people. So how is it to work with Chambers?"

"It's the best thing that ever happened to me except for meeting Anna. He's definitely the best guy I ever met. If you ever get that debt paid off, you should take him up on that job. Maybe we'd be working together. I'd like that."

Christian laughed. "Best buds, huh. Well there could be worse things, even if you aren't the brightest star in the heavens. You still miss the girl then?"

Ben's face told the story even before he answered. "Yea, I do. That is really stupid, isn't it? I didn't know Anna that long, but she has invaded my mind and won't leave. I can't stop thinking about her, day or night, and its going damn near on two years now. It's not fun. She's gone. I should get past her, but I can't."

Gunther's nodded. "Well, that doesn't sound like fun. Personally, I've never been much attached to anybody, but I can see how it could happen. Truth is, McDonald, it might be nice to have some of that kind of pain, those kinds of memories. Would you forget her today if you could?"

Ben was startled by the question. Well, no, I wouldn't. Not at all. I never looked at it that way."

Gunther grinned. "I'm just here to serve. Most of us don't like pain, so we can't see its true value; but pain is not always a bad thing."

It was getting late and darkness came early that time of year. Ben got up and handed his coffee mug to Christian. "I guess I'd better get back up north. It was good seeing you. I know what you said about why you got Anna and me out, but I still want you to know that I'll always be in your debt. If I can ever help you in any way, all you have to do is ask."

Christian laughed. "Well, thanks, McDonald. Any time I need a social worker to save me, you'll be the first guy I look up." Then he got serious. "My instincts about you were right, I think. You were worth saving. I don't know enough about the girl, but from what you tell me, she was too."

"Now, if you'll just wait a few more minutes, some of the other staff will be here and I'll go with you up to 59th. It'd be kind of a waste for me to have made that valiant sacrifice for you only to have you taken out trying to get back through Hell's Kitchen. You don't look the same, but there are people on the streets who might remember you."

Christian laughed. "That's kind of you, Christian, but even I am not that stupid. I'm not going back up through the Kitchen. I'll walk over to Sixth, or maybe even Fifth Avenue and go north that way. I doubt if I'll be stopped, but if I am, the authorities know Bill and I'll just tell them I work for him. That'll give me the pass I need. If that doesn't work, I'll tell them I know you. I'm sure that'll solve the problem, right off.

Christian laughed again. "Absolutely! No doubt about it. My influence is everywhere. But I forgot, you've become legit, haven't you McDonald? You've done well for yourself."

Christian escorted Ben out of the Haymarket and walked with him over to Fifth Avenue. He stuck out his hand as they were parting. Ben took it quickly. "Hope to see you soon, Christian. I was serious. I'd like to work with you and I know Bill would too. You'd be good up there and it's hard to find good people."

Gunther laughed. "You trying to make me legit too, McDonald? Well, I'll think about it. In the meantime, keep your powder dry, and do me a favor, will you. Don't come down through Hell's Kitchen again. Your magic can run out, you know."

Ben laughed. "You got it, Gunther. I'll try to stay away. But you know, that girl I met today….."

Christian just laughed and shoved him up the street.

Chapter 22

Ben's trip to Hell's Kitchen worked wonders for him. Christian's comments had lifted a load off his shoulders by opening doors in his thinking that he hadn't accessed before. He still hadn't resolved his feelings for Anna, but he knew he'd have to figure that out on his own; although the conversation with Gunther had even helped with that too. It was true that he wouldn't have traded knowing her for anything in the world, including the pain of her loss that he couldn't shake.

It would just have been nice to know that she was okay. He had tried to get in touch with her, beginning only a few days after she left. He had talked to Bill, who offered to try to find out where she had been placed and get her mailing address. Ben was enthusiastic about it so Bill asked for the information from Emma Mason.

Unfortunately, she didn't have much to go on. Of course, she remembered Anna's placement as one of the most unusual that she had ever supervised. She remembered that it was with a couple named "Lowe" and that they had four or five children of their own. She assumed they lived somewhere near Rolla, Missouri but she also remembered that they talked about attending a church that had another name. She just couldn't remember it. Bill showed Ben where Rolla was on the map. At least now he had some idea of her general location.

Bill offered to help Ben draft Anna a letter and Ben agreed eagerly. They sat down and wrote it out that night.

Dear Anna:

I hope you are in good health and happy. I am working for Bill now at the warehouse and I like it a lot. I am able to save most of the money I have earned. I was wondering if I might take the train to visit you when I get time off from work. I would like to know more about where you live and who you are with.

If you get this letter please write me in care of Bill Chambers at the Simmons Warehouse, 417 east 59th Street, New York, New York. Tell me about all that you are doing and I will write back. I miss you and would like to hear from you soon.

Ben

He asked Bill how long it would take for the letter to get to her. Bill speculated that it would only take a week or two by train. They sent it in care of Mr. and Mrs. Jess Lowe, Rolla, Missouri, assuming that the post office might know the family.

Emma said she would also write a letter to the sponsoring pastor at Rolla, although she wasn't certain it would be of much help. The pastor had already left before the Lowe family came into the building that day and Mrs. Mason remembered that he had said he was moving to a pastoral assignment in another state. Despite the ambiguity, Bill put on an optimistic front for Ben. He said that if Rolla was not too big a town, the postal workers would probably know the family. If so, Ben might hear back from her in a month.

Unfortunately, that was not to be the case. Surprisingly, the letter did make it to Rolla, but the postmaster there had never heard of a married couple named Lowe. He decided to send it to a Rolla resident named John Lowe, whom he knew, on the off chance that it was someone in his family. But John brought it back to the post office some time later and said he had no relatives in the area and had never heard of that family. So the Postmaster stamped the letter, RETURN TO SENDER and sent it back to New York. Bill received it a few weeks later. Ben was devastated. Bill tried to console him, indicating that people came from miles around to orphan placement meetings. The Lowes must not live in Rolla.

Ben was even more mystified as to why Anna had not written to him to tell him that she was okay. She knew where he was, or at least knew where Bill was, and she should have assumed that Bill would forward the correspondence to Ben, even if he had already moved on.

Maybe she had decided to put her bad New York experiences behind her. Or maybe she had been injured in some way or had become ill and couldn't write. Maybe the family wouldn't let her write. Maybe she was dead! Maybe.....the maybes kept piling up in Ben's head and all of them were confusing and full of anxiety. The pain of not knowing paralyzed him. He didn't ask to write again, and the months passed. He finally gave it up as a lost cause.

Chapter 23

On Christmas Eve in 1886, Bill Chambers decided to give his courier the afternoon off. As a result, he personally took the week's revenues to the bank for deposit. He had concluded his transactions at the teller's window and was wishing the bank staff happy holidays when three armed men burst into the bank and declared a hold-up.

They had decided to rob the bank on a whim; they were not strategic thinkers. They assumed security might be light on Christmas Eve. They had never heard of a bank robbery at that time of the year, so they assumed that they had struck upon a novel strategy. Why they thought there would be lots of money at the bank on a holiday was later used by their defense attorneys as an indication of their limited cognitive skills. In keeping with the appropriate holiday spirit, they all wore Santa suits and masks as disguises.

Bill and the other customers complied fully with the robbers' requests as the tellers anxiously shoveled what little cash they had on hand into sacks provided by the robbers. By their movements, Bill could tell that the thieves were novices, and he knew that made this situation more dangerous.

Disappointed with the amount of cash that the tellers gave them, the robbers huddled and debated what else to do. It came to them that the customers actually might have money on them, so they demanded that each customer fork over their cash and other valuables. They went from customer to customer to rake in the booty.

One of the young men came over to Bill and demanded his money. Bill complied. As he did so, the robber tried to intimidate him, pushing him a around a little. The cheap string on the robber's mask broke and his disguise fell to the floor. Bill recognized the man instantly. He was an orphan named Jamie Rollins, whom Bill had tried to help by getting him a job at a local mercantile only a year ago. The boy was shifty and intellectually slow. He was gullible and easily mislead by the wrong crowd. Jamie had been unable to handle responsibility or criticism at his job and was fired. He begged for more help and Bill reluctantly found another job for him, with the same result. Bill did not help him a third time and Jamie resented it. He fell in with a group of young hoods who Bill also knew. Bill assumed that some of them probably comprised the other two bandits.

Despite his resentments, Jamie respected Bill. He didn't really want to take his money, but had thought that if he acted tough it would raise his image with the group. He panicked when he lost his disguise. Now Bill knew who he was. He said, "I'm sorry Bill. It's okay; you can keep your money."

Bill shook his head once to signal him to finish his business and not talk to him. Unfortunately, the leader of the gang heard what Jamie had said and hurried over. He had been angry that Jamie had been included in the group's plans in the first place. He thought he wasn't smart enough to be trusted. He had warned his comrades that Jamie would screw something up and that they would all take the fall if he did. Other members of the gang liked Jamie just fine and refused to do the hold-up if Jamie wasn't included. The leader leveled his shotgun on Jamie's stomach. "You know him don't you!"

"N-No I don't," Jamie stuttered, lifting his hands up in front of him. "He don't know me. I never see'd him before in my life."

The robber didn't buy it. Bill saw the finger tighten on the trigger.

He yelled for him to stop, but it was too late. The blast of the shotgun tore Jamie's stomach open. He screamed as he fell. Bill lunged for the leader, who turned the gun quickly toward Bill. Bill ducked, but too late. He felt the powerful punch high in his chest even before he heard the blast. It knocked him back against the counter and then to the floor beside Jamie, who was clutching his stomach, crying and trying to stop the flow of blood gushing from the wound.

Bill felt nothing, but was still conscious. He knew his wounds were severe. He became light headed and realized that he was passing out. Jamie looked over at him crying hysterically, "I'm sorry, Bill. I didn't mean for anybody to get hurt and sure not you! Bill nodded and slowly reached over to take Jamie's hand. Jamie stopped squirming. Bill tried to smile at him. Everything went black and he died a few seconds later.

The other two robbers dropped their money sacks and ran out of the bank. Jamie lived long enough for the police to arrive and to finger the other two before he died. A city-wide dragnet quickly netted them. They had a speedy trial and would face the gallows within months.

The city had loved Bill Chambers more than it had realized while he was alive. It would avenge his death with a righteous zeal, all the while lamenting the terrible underclass children of Hell's Kitchen who grew up to kill the good people most intent on helping them. The fact that Bill had also been an urchin was not publicly discussed.

With all the publicity, Bill's funeral was attended by more than ten thousand people—far too many to fit inside the Church where his body rested. The majority had to stand outside to pay their respects and honor what Bill had done and what he stood for.

Those who were closest to him, like Ben, Emma Mason and Charles Brace, were totally stricken and nearly paralyzed by their grief at his illogical loss.

He was eloquently eulogized by all those who spoke at the funeral ceremony. The Mayor called him a kind, generous and charismatic friend of the poor, who had come from nothing and had risen to high leadership by using his talents for the good of mankind. They lamented that he had been taken too soon by a senseless act of street hooligans who would pay dearly for what they had done. They marveled at what Bill might have become in the future had he lived longer. They regretted that God's plan had not allowed it, but were sure Bill had been called to God's right hand in Heaven.

The Reverend Brace did not speak at the funeral. He was too stricken with grief. He wept for days after Bill's death and commented repeatedly how dreary the work would be without him.

Among the mourners standing outside the church were many former street urchins who were the only ones who truly understood what Bill Chambers had done. Among them was Christian Gunther, who had not told anyone that he was coming to the funeral.

Ben McDonald was beyond grief. Upon hearing of Bill's death, he had refused to believe it. When he finally accepted that Bill was indeed gone, he felt an unspeakable rage that morphed into a deep depression. The man who was his brother had been snatched away by a senseless, silly act, a horrid, useless folly. People told him it was God's will, but no god worth believing in would have allowed that. And down in the darkest recesses of his mind, he harbored still another unspeakable fear. Would no one for whom he really cared ever be allowed to remain in his life?

He also internalized an irrational guilt that he could have stopped the events of that Christmas Eve had he just kept his first job at the warehouse. It would have been him making the trip to the bank, not Bill. He wouldn't have known the robbers and he personally never carried much money on him, so it would have just been a silly robbery. Even if he had been hurt or killed, that would have been nothing compared to the loss of a man like Bill Chambers. But all the wishing in the world didn't change anything.

Christian Gunther was as shocked as Ben, but he didn't show it openly. On Christmas morning, the story of the robbery and murder, and the identification of those responsible, was major headline news all over New York City. Christian had known Jamie Rollins on the streets. Jamie was weak and slow, and often abused. Bill Chambers had thought he would do better outside Hell's Kitchen. He had not.

Christian immediately guessed who the other two young hoods were. They were loudmouths that Jamie had recently started hanging out with. On rare occasions, when they had enough money, they came to the Haymarket. Christian had thrown them out a couple of times when they got too loud.

As soon as he heard of the events at the bank, he vowed to hunt them all down and kill them. He asked around and found out where they lived. He was on the way to find them when he heard that they had just been arrested. Otherwise, he would have brought them "gifts" on Christmas Day that would have been their last. Now that they were caught and, reading the sentiments of the city in the papers, he assumed that they would see the gallows quickly, so he dropped his own crusade.

Christian anticipated that Ben would have trouble handling Bill's death, so he stayed after the funeral to spend time with him. In the life of two young men who had already experienced many dark holidays, none was ever darker than the festive season of 1886.

Chapter 24

Jess Lough and his family, including its two newest members, arrived home from Rolla long after dark that late November day in 1884. Jess took the horses to their stalls and cared for them while Bessie and Anna herded the children into the house.

The Lough house overlooked a meandering valley that lay below the peninsula on which the house sat. No more than 50 feet beyond the fenced back yard, the peninsula ended and the ridge dropped off steeply to that valley, where the sandy lowland fields were perfect for raising the big watermelons for which Jess had become locally famous. The rock house Jess had built stood like a little castle overlooking this scenic panorama. There was not another farmhouse or building in the whole range of sight. Jess particularly liked that.

Even by moonlight, Anna noticed the quaint beauty of the little home, sitting out on the farthest point of that peninsula, with the world dropping off to the dim scenes below. When they entered the house, it looked spotless, although well worn, and it was easy to tell that an active family with young children lived here. There were homemade dolls on the beds and old family pictures on the walls. There were children's drawings everywhere representing various skill levels. All of the little artists seemed to be inspired by one of two themes; there were lots of pictures of a mother and father and children holding hands and nearly as many pictures of the farm animals, particularly dogs.

Bessie started the stove and within minutes the house was toasty. They ate an abbreviated meal, after which Bessie hurried the children to bed. Sleep captured them quickly as the warm blankets were snuggled around them and the heat moved up the staircase to the open attic.

The house was about 25 feet wide and 40 feet long. It had a main floor and an attic loft. The north side of the main floor included a living room on the east and a parlor on the west. A doorway off the living room allowed access to a homey kitchen located on the southeast side of the house. Through the back door of the kitchen Anna could see a screened porch that extended across the entire back of the house.

Jess' and Bessie's bedroom was off of a small hallway leading out of the kitchen. The hallway also housed the stairway leading to the second floor attic, divided evenly by the stair rails. The girls slept on the north side over the parent's bedroom and kitchen while the boys' area was over the living room and parlor. Bessie knew that it would have been too noisy for her and Jess if the boys slept directly above them.

Bessie arranged new pallets for Zachary on the boys' side of the attic and for Anna on the girls' side. "Jess'll need to be making two more beds as soon as he can get to it. I think we can squeeze them in here," she said, laughing. "I'm afraid there's not much privacy in this house, Anna." Anna smiled and said that was not a problem. Compared to the streets, this was luxury. Bessie, remembering where Anna had come from, stopped fretting about their crowded conditions.

Anna was amazed at the ease with which she and Zachary had been accepted into this family. Now, without any complaint or second thoughts, room was being arranged for them in this comfortable little house. The Lough children seemed to think the overnight addition of a new sister and brother was just another exciting family adventure.

When they finished putting the children to bed, Bessie turned to Anna, "Come downstairs and let's have some hot chocolate." They descended the steep attic steps to the kitchen. It had a big, wood-burning cook stove and a long homemade table with benches on each side and two store-bought chairs at either end. Against the wall was a tall cabinet, standing from floor to ceiling where Bessie kept her plates, bowls, cookware and other pantry items.

The chairs were for Jess and Bessie. Anna slid onto the east bench as Jess came in from taking care of the animals. He went to the stove, rubbing his hands and holding them close. "It's getting colder out there. I bet tomorrow'll freeze the pond!"

Anna would later learn that this was his pet phrase for predicting the cold fronts that cascaded down from the Northwest, beginning in early November and continuing on through March. Bessie handed out large cups of hot chocolate, first to Jess, then to Anna. She poured the final one for herself. Jess took off his coat and sat down at the head of the table, blowing softly into the hot cup of chocolate, soaking up the warmth that transferred to his hands and face.

"Anna, tell us more about how you came to be on that train," inquired Bessie.

Anna didn't really know where to begin, so she started with the story of her father and mother, of their migration to America and of her father's plans for them in the future. When she described her father's death, Bessie and Jess sat silently, but Bessie's eyes were already misting. Bessie was a toucher. She believed the power of touch was far more soothing than words. At various points in the story that were particularly sad, she reached out and took Anna's hand.

When Anna told of her eviction to the streets after he mother's death, both Jess and Bessie were astonished. They found it impossible to understand why a neighbor had not volunteered to take Anna in. They had no comprehension of the isolation of an urban ghetto or its impact on people's generosity. As they listened, it hardened their hearts against urban dwellers in general and New Yorkers in particular. They knew that if they died unexpectedly, relatives or friends would take their children in without question, as would they if called on in a similar situation. It was the only proper thing to do.

Anna described the horrors of Hell's Kitchen and her rescue by Ben McDonald. From her description of Ben, Bessie learned two things. First, that boy was a hero beyond compare, and second, Anna Murphy loved him more than anyone else in the world.

By the time Anna had finished it was 2 a.m. Bessie, startled by the time, rushed Anna up to her pallet to get some rest.

In her bed that night, as Bessie held Jess, she prayed silently. "Lord, I thank Thee for bringing this amazing girl and this sad little boy into our lives. I know Thou hast a plan and a purpose for all this and I am grateful to be part of it." She usually prayed out loud for the both of them to assure that her wayward husband wouldn't forget. But this time it was just her prayer. Jess was snoring the minute his head hit the pillow.

This was not an empty prayer uttered thoughtlessly. She really was truly grateful. She already believed Anna was the most amazing girl she had ever met and that it was God's providence that had guided to her their home.

She ended her prayer with a footnote of thanks for that brave boy who saved Anna's life and an admonition to God to protect him, wherever he was. She asked God to allow them to meet him some day to thank him personally. Ben would have appreciated that prayer had he been aware of its utterance, and he would have appreciated even more what this good woman had done that day for Anna Murphy.

Bessie lay awake long after Jess had fallen asleep. It wasn't because of Jess' snoring. That was tolerable because it meant he was home. She often found it harder to sleep when he wasn't. She never let him know, but she was always fearful when she was alone on their isolated farm. If someone wanted to do harm to her and the children, no one would know about it for days.

But in this early morning, while everyone else slept, she was thinking about Christmas presents for her new children. Finding a way to provide a good Christmas for her family each year was of premier concern to Bessie that took most of her spare time and attention between the first of October and December 24th. Thank goodness she had already prepared the gifts for the other children!

She vowed to make this the happiest Christmas of all for Anna and Zachary. That would be easier than she knew for Zachary, because he had never yet experienced a real Christmas. And Christmas dinner at the Lough farm was always something amazing to behold! Bessie vowed this one would bring shame to all previous. At last, after 3:00 a.m., she drifted off to sleep for a short rest before beginning another busy day of service to her family, both old and new.

Chapter 25

The first year with the Loughs was a healing experience for both Zachary and Anna, but particularly for the little boy that nobody wanted. In short order, he found his place in the family as the witty, mischievous clown. His starving ego fed on the laughter of his new parents and siblings. His body responded just as dramatically. His cheeks filled out and his face lost its ashen color. His shoulders became ramrod straight. It soon became apparent to Bessie and Jess that what had been wrong with Zachary was not so much a sickness of the body as a starvation of the soul.

By spring 1885 Zachary was a rapidly growing, normal-looking boy only slightly smaller than average for his age, but much larger in spirit and intelligence than most. He morphed into an exceptionally fast runner who could outrace any of the Lough children, younger or older. He particularly took to Jess, who was flattered by the boy's adulation. Zach was always underfoot, constantly asking difficult-to-answer questions and eager to learn every detail of how things worked around the farm.

He loved the name "Lough" and wondered how a person got that name. Jess said it was a very old name, coming from Scotland or Ireland, and that it meant "a body of water". Without telling Zachary, Jess went to see the County officials. For his sixth birthday, on the fourth of July--a date they all made up since no one knew his real one--Jess gave Zachary an official looking piece of paper, framed in fine oak by Jess himself. It declared to all who could read that he was now a real Lough.

He hung it proudly on the wall beside his bed. During the months of July and August, he went up to look at it every few hours, just to make sure it was hanging straight. Any visitor to the Lough homestead during that time would be required to make that trek up the steep attic stairs to view this declaration of his family association.

Jess told him he had to go to school in September to learn to read exactly what that paper said, as well as all the other books he was always thumbing through around the house. He was elated. His education would eventually be of great benefit to his adopted family, as well as to the state of Missouri, because Zachary Lough was one of the most gifted minds to come out of southern Missouri in the late 19th century. After reaching manhood and obtaining his law degree, that adoption paper, still in its same homemade frame, would prominently be displayed in a stately law office in Rolla, and later in a State Senate office in Missouri's new Capital building that had replaced its predecessor in 1911.

Watching him flourish that first year gave Anna great pride in her decision to stay with the Loughs, despite her loss of Ben. Every day, he validated the value of her sacrifice. And, although it wasn't as obvious, she blossomed as well. She made peace with her losses and didn't let them show.

It was impossible to be morose in the Lough household. Some of the children would occasionally try their best to pout when things didn't go their way, but they were quickly teased out of it. It was a family characterized by boisterous children, laughter, continuous joke-playing and other forms of wholesome revelry.

The Lough children were wild and free spirits in a good way. Their parents encouraged adventure and play, and the telling of tall tales. Anna, who had never been around such a rambunctious group, was taken aback at first, but quickly determined that it was too much fun to sit on the sidelines. She caught herself laughing frequently and found it a worthy challenge to figure out how to persuade rowdy children to do what they should without crushing their spirits.

Bessie was only 27 years old when Anna arrived. She and Anna became more like sisters than mother and daughter. They talked as they worked together, sharing their most intimate hopes and dreams. Anna learned of Jess' inclination toward wandering and how Bessie controlled it. Bessie learned more about every detail Anna knew about Ben and just how special he was to her.

As Anna became more familiar with the Jadwin Community and its farm families, her admiration for them grew. They were considered a simple lot in the eyes of most outsiders, some living a life of subsistence nearly as severe as the immigrants in Hell's Kitchen. But it was a different kind of poor.

A large portion of the Jadwinites lived on modest farms where they considered a year successful if they could raise enough food for their families, clothe themselves respectably, put something in the collection plate at church each Sunday and purchase or make a present for each of their children for Christmas and birthdays.

Outwardly they seldom took personal notice of their poverty, and they certainly never judged one another by the amount of possessions they owned. They understood the value of family and community and cherished both. On that scale, most considered themselves well blessed.

Neighbor helped neighbor in hard times without being asked. If a man was too ill to plant his crops, others did it for him. If a family's house burned down, the community was there the next day to help build a new one. All they had was each other and Anna realized, more quickly than most, that this was the greatest gift of all.

And they had their unshakable faith in their God. The songs of the Jadwin church spoke of a worldly poverty that would be offset someday by spiritual riches. It soon became clear to Anna that there was a direct connection with the community's perception of its limited wealth, its poor medical care and how that resulting suffering would someday be offset by their faith in God.

They sang songs every Sunday about an everlasting life devoid of suffering and death, where they would have unimaginable wealth and live in the great mansions of Heaven situated on streets paved with gold. There, they would be reunited with their loved ones and friends who had gone on before and they would personally be in the eternal presence of God, Jesus, the Holy Spirit and the angels. These were the repeated themes of most of their songs:

An Empty Mansion

Here I labor and toil as I look for a home,'
Just an humble abode among men,
But there's a mansion in Heaven just waiting for me,
And a gentle voice pleading, "come in".

There's a mansion now empty just waiting for me.
At the end of life's troublesome way.
Many friends and dear loved ones will welcome me there,
At the door of that mansion someday.

Sweet By and By

There's a land that is fairer than day,
And by faith we can see it afar;
For the Father waits over the way,
To prepare us a dwelling place there.
In the sweet, by and by,

We shall meet on that beautiful shore.
In the sweet by and by,
We shall meet on that beautiful shore.

And then there was Bessie's favorite, sung at all the funerals:

Never Grow Old

I have heard of a land,
On a far away strand,
Tis the beautiful home of the soul.
Built by Jesus on high,
Where we never shall die,
Tis the land where we'll never grow old.
Never grow old, never grow old,
Tis the land where we'll never grow old.

But in their present world, she watched them struggle with life and death every day. Medical care in backwoods Missouri was weak to non-existent. Miscarriages and stillbirth were common and children often died in early infancy from any of numerous diseases that rampaged across the land.

And there just seemed to be no end to their hardships. So many family members and friends were taken away so swiftly that they all came to consider life a fleeting thing. Struggle and pain was their constant companion.

Anna saw the depth of their faith and wished she had it. She needed something to explain, or at least ameliorate, the loss of her own family and Ben, as well as to the horrors she had seen on the streets of Hell's Kitchen. But she could not find their peace. The words of one of their songs particularly haunted her.

All By and By

Farther along, you'll know all about it.
Farther along, you'll understand why.
Wake up my brother, live in the sunshine,
You'll understand it, all by and by.

It was hard for her to sing that song. She didn't understand it and
she doubted that she ever would. The loss of her mother and father
had been terrible. The loss of Ben had multiplied her pain. She
told no one how she really felt, not even Bessie. She knew that if
she did, they would just say, "Put your faith in God and you will
find your peace." She didn't know what that meant, either in her
head or her heart.

Anna quickly garnered a reputation as the prettiest girl in the
Jadwin community. She turned the heads of every young man she
met, but she never acknowledged or furthered their attention.
Flirtatious behavior was not part of her personality. She was
friendly and warm with everyone, but for reasons that few knew,
no young man in Jadwin or the surrounding area ever broke
through her guard.

Chapter 26

On the day after she arrived, Anna made a wonderful discovery about the Lough household. It contained books, and lots of them! True, most of the books were old and had been obtained by Bessie at auctions and second-hand shops, but they were books just the same. Some of them were actually classics, while others were of lesser literary value. There were children's books and primers for teaching English, mathematics, science, and other school subjects. There were also novels for adults. Prominent among the lot was a multiplicity of religiously-oriented books. Anna treated them all like gold. She seemed to be carrying a book around wherever she went. When she finished Bessie's books, she borrowed others from her new friends at church.

Bessie watched Anna read every book she could get her hands on. It was a great delight to her to see that. Bessie loved books and considered them the doorways to knowledge and understanding. "Why, Anna," said Bessie one day as she watched her open a particularly difficult-looking book she had borrowed from the Jadwin teacher, "I do believe you are a scholar!"

Anna laughed. "I do love to read, Bessie. It was one of the things that I missed most after my parents died."

"How much schooling did you have?"

"I went through grade six. My dad said a good education was better than money and he always kept me in school right up until his passing." Her voice trailed off to the bittersweet tone she used every time she talked to Bessie about her parents.

All day Bessie thought about Anna's comment. That night she mounted an aggressive campaign against her unsuspecting husband, using a tone of voice that put him on the defensive immediately. He knew that she saved that tone for special discussions. Maybe she did read his moods like the back of her hand, but he was no slouch at hers either. When she wanted something that she thought he might not like, her communication style was somewhat like a good lawyer making a case before a slow jury. He braced for the assault. He had seen that look in her eyes and heard that tone of voice too often not to recognize the seriousness of the conversation they were about to have.

"Jess, we need to send Anna to school this fall and I want Brad Fletcher to test her to see how she should be placed." Brad Fletcher was the local Jadwin school teacher, a young man who attended the same church as the Loughs, and one who was still single and who had not failed to notice Anna's beauty.

Jess thought to himself, "*Well if that's all this is about it may not be so bad.*" So he said, "Well, Bessie, I guess it won't do no harm." Bessie cringed at his double negatives. He didn't notice, or at least didn't pay attention to the look she gave him. "I guess she could walk Rachael and Zach to school and escort them home. Probly a good idea."

"Yes, she could if she needs some more schooling up to the eighth grade level, but if she tests as well as I think she will, Jess, she may be ready for high school, and that means Salem."

It was then that Jess realized the size of this particular storm and suddenly felt the strong wind blowing. Salem was the only high school for miles around and it was too far for Anna to go back and forth daily. She would have to board there during the week. That would cost money, not to mention the travel time back and forth to get her when she came home. She would also need tuition, books, clothing, and God knows what else! Bessie had that look about her that told him her mind was already made up, but sending Anna to high school in Salem was a bigger mouthful than he thought he should have to bite off. He braced himself and pushed back against that wind.

"Now, Bessie, we brought Anna here to help you when I'm gone. You know I work over at the mill in Viburnum in the fall, and I'll be gone at least two months. She won't be any help if she's boarding in Salem, will she? And have you forgotten that it's expensive to send a kid to high school? I'm not even sure we can afford it when our own boys are old enough, let alone a girl we have just taken into our home…."

He realized immediately that he shouldn't have said that last part. They had previously been in delicate conversations about the value of education for girls as well as boys, and he had not failed to notice how close Bessie and Anna had become. Bessie no longer considered her "a girl we have taken in". He started to apologize, but he could already see it was too late from the look in Bessie's eyes.

"Anna is our child too now, Jess Lough, and it is no matter that she happens to be a girl! I know we will have to sacrifice a little more to do it, and I know she'll be gone during your precious sawing season when you waltz off to play with your buddies in Shannon County, but I'll make do. I always have. And she will still be here six months out of the year, which is six months more than I had before."

She had barely paused for breath. Speed of the argument was important when dealing with Jess because his mind didn't always work as fast as hers and she knew it. "I watch her, Jess, with the kids and all, and she's a natural teacher. And you know she reads everything she can get her hands on. If she can test out above the eighth grade level, she could get her teaching certificate in just a few years. She could do a lot of good for all of us by furthering her education. But that's not the really important thing. The important thing is that we have no right to stand in the way of her talents. We made a commitment to both Anna and Zachary when we took them in. We gave our word, and we'll honor it!"

She continued, he thought, without any pause for breath. He caught himself wondering how she could do that as he stood before her, his face red, like a child who had been caught with his hand in the cookie jar. Bessie carried on. "I'll tell her that if we send her, she has to pay us back someday. She can get a job in Salem while she's in school. She'll make something of herself. You know she will! She's special. Everybody knows that. We owe her this and we're going to do it!"

Jess' pride was hurting, but it was apparent that she was putting her foot down. He wasn't sure how they could afford it, but Bessie was, after all, the center of his universe and Lord knows she didn't ask much of him. He had seen that fire in her eyes a few times before. He knew full well that overruling her might afford him a brief temporary victory, but assure him painful long-term losses that he could not afford. So he chose the path he always took with Bessie when he needed to accommodate her. He grinned a little and threw his hands to the heavens in mock exasperation. It was then that she knew she had him.

"Well, Bessie, it's going to cost us and arm and a leg if she goes to Salem, but I can see it's going to cost me more if she doesn't!" He reached over and pinched her on the behind to emphasize the cost he feared most. The fire in her eyes gave way to a twinkle and her lips edged up a little despite her best efforts to hold her countenance until she was sure the battle had been won. She moved over to him and slid her arms around his big chest and

squeezed. "You are a smart man when you have to be, Jess
Lough." With that she released him and went to find Anna,
leaving him standing there shaking his head in mock disgust.

Anna was in the attic putting the children to bed. Bessie, in a
formal manner, asked her to come down for a little talk when she
was finished. Anna, worrying that she must have done something
wrong, hurried the children into their beds without the usual stories
and came downstairs to see what Bessie wanted. By this time Jess
had joined Bessie at the table and Anna, seeing that, was sure she
was in trouble.

"Sit down, Anna," said Jess. Now that he had run up the white
flag, he was going to reassert his authority and control this
discussion. He might as well get some of the credit for their
generosity. Anna slid onto the bench nearest Bessie at the table,
expecting the worst, trying to think of what she might have done.
From the looks on their faces this was serious.

"Anna," said Bessie, "Jess and I have noticed how much you love
to read and pursue your learning. We'd like for you to be tested by
Brad Fletcher to see what grade level you're at. We think you
ought to finish your schooling and we want to support you in that
effort." She paused, waiting for Anna's reaction.

Anna had not anticipated this at all and was stunned. She didn't
understand the full implications of "finish your schooling," but the
idea of going back to school almost took her breath away.

Bessie saw her confusion and continued. "I don't mean to put
pressure on you, but if you're as smart as we think you are, you
may be ready for high school. That would mean you would need
to go Salem in the fall and stay there till spring." She quickly
added, "Of course, you would be home on Thanksgiving and

Christmas. If you study real hard, I think you can finish high school studies quicker than most. You might become eligible for a teaching certificate. I've seen how you like to teach the kids and I think you would be an excellent teacher. I know this is kind of sprung on you, and it may not be what you want. If it's not, we'll be just as happy for you to go on just the way you are, but we wanted you to know how capable we think you are and to give you this choice." Bessie looked anxiously at Anna, awaiting a response.

Anna looked at Bessie, then at Jess. "I guess I just never imagined I'd have the opportunity to go to school again," she said, her mind racing, her heart beating faster, "so I had put it out of my mind. I loved school and missed it terribly when I had to stop attending." She paused, then exclaimed, "But I wouldn't be able to help you with the children! And school costs money, which I don't have."

"Well," said Jess, surprising Bessie with the interruption, "we've thought about that. Bessie has got on okay before with the kids and she can do it again. You'll be here to help her at least six months out of the year, which is more than she has ever had before."

The thought crossed Bessie's mind that Jess could always become a parrot if he didn't work out as a human. He ignored the somewhat incredulous glance she sent his way and plowed right on. "And as for the costs, we can help out some. We know a person in Salem who can provide a good safe place for you to stay at cheap rates. We can cover your tuition and books and you can get a job of some kind for your food and necessities. Bessie sews real good, and she can show you how to make the clothes you'll need that you don't have now." He finished with a flourish. "Someday when you're making good money teaching, or in some other profession, you can repay the tuition and book money we give you if you want to. If not, it doesn't matter. You're family now and this is what families do."

Bessie wasn't sure whether to hit him up the side of his head or kiss him. He had obviously learned his lines well, but he was saying them as though they were all his creation. But his reward, whatever it would be, could wait till the conversation was over and they were alone.

Tears welled up in Anna's eyes. She didn't know what to say. Their offer was far beyond anything she ever expected from these people she had known for such a short time. "I would love to go to school and I promise I'll pay back every cent it costs you! And I'll work hard and finish as quickly as I can."

And they had no doubt at all that she would.

So it was settled. There were hugs all around; including an especially tight one for Jess from Bessie that made him think he might get even more lucky that night! Bessie said they'd go that very next day and look up Brad Fletcher to see when the testing could be arranged.

Early the next morning Bessie and Anna set out. After some searching, they found Brad at the Jadwin store helping straighten out some financial records. Teacher's salaries were modest in the Jadwin area--about $30 per month--and a teacher often had to take on extra work in the summers to survive. Bessie explained what they wanted and Brad seemed more than happy to oblige. He asked all kinds of questions about Anna's past schooling, her grades, what she had studied and the like.

He already knew the part of her history that related to being an orphan. Everyone in Jadwin did. It was a small community and there was little about new residents left unknown. If that was not the case, the new person might not be trusted. At its worst, community gossip could be hurtful, but at its best, it was a vehicle for sharing vital information that allowed the community to understand, trust and help each other in short order.

When he was satisfied that he knew her past educational history, he said, "Anna, I'll order the proper tests from Salem. They'll arrive in a couple of weeks. The testing will likely take all day. Bessie, you and the kids are welcome to come up on testing day too. I'll prepare some fun studies for them to do." It was important for Brad to include Bessie and the kids in the day's activities. He was a cautious man. Spending the day alone with a beautiful girl like Anna might lead to talk. His and Anna's reputations were too important to risk to idle speculation. Bessie pleased him by saying she would be delighted to come and that she'd bring a picnic lunch.

On the day of the test, Anna was a bundle of nerves. She couldn't eat breakfast, a fact that fretted Bessie since she was sure Anna would need her strength to be sharp for the day. Farm people valued food above all else as a sign of good care for their children, and Bessie thought Anna particularly needed nourishment on one of the more important days of her young life.

Bessie, Anna and three of the children, including Zachary, walked the half-mile distance to the school. It was a pretty lane from their house to the school, rutted by the frequent passage of their horses and wagon. It meandered in and out of the woods along the edge of the ridge and peninsula that ultimately dropped off steeply into a wet-weather stream bed below the house. Their cattle grazed along the bone of that ridge in a field rising gently south of the house. The lane ran parallel to that field and then about a quarter mile or so through a wooded area that ended at the county road that ran west to the Jadwin Church of Christ and east to the Gladden community.

The school building sat on the corner of the Lough lane and that county road. Its location pleased Jess immensely. It wasn't many men that had a school right on the edge of his property! He almost felt as though he owned the building. In fact, he had dedicated the land for it ten years earlier. It guaranteed a convenient half-mile walk for his children to and from school.

The school itself was a simple one-room building with a high front porch and lots of windows along its sides. Its entrance faced due west, which could be a problem on bright, sunny days because of the glare of the sunlight coming through the door.

They arrived at 8:40 a.m. sharp since Brad had suggested that they start the testing at 9:00 a.m. That complied with Bessie's 20-minute rule. If an appointed time for church, a community meeting or a family visit was set, Bessie always had her family there 20 minutes early as a sign of courtesy, "so as to not make a commotion by entering late like some people did."

After greetings all around, Brad took Bessie aside to give her the materials for the children's "studies" that day. Bessie took them out under the big tree in front of the school so as not to disturb Anna's testing, and spread a large blanket for them to sit on. It was a beautiful summer day, not too hot, and the children were excited with this little adventure that was a nice diversion from their daily chore routines—including no weeding in the garden!

Each came around to hug Anna and wish her good luck before charging outside to play. They had already decided to start their "special" studies with a long recess—something they thought would be a good idea for regular school next year as well. They made a point of suggesting that to Brad. He smiled and said he would certainly take that into consideration.

Then the testing began. It covered five separate sixty-minute sections of reading comprehension, English grammar, math, science and geography. The reading and English were easy for Anna. She thought she had done well with them as she finished those sections relatively quickly. Geography had also been okay. She and her father had spent many a night playing geography games when she was young

After the first three sections they took a lunch break. Brad and Anna came outside to the blanket under the tree where Bessie had spread fried chicken, potato salad, tomatoes, homemade bread, and sliced cucumbers from a jar filled with a vinegar and sugar mix that was one of Brad's favorite dishes. The picnic would be topped off with a large apple pie, one of three Bessie and Anna had made the night before.

"Bessie, you'll spoil me with such a good meal!" exclaimed Brad, who knew of her reputation as one of the best cooks in the community.

"It's just simple food," she blushed. "I don't know how to cook fancy." She was a little intimidated and excited at the same time over the idea of cooking for this educated man from the city.

He smiled. "This is just as fancy as they cook anywhere, Bessie. It's not how fancy it looks that makes a meal great, it's how good it tastes." This pleased her and she responded, as any decent farm woman would, by pushing more food in his direction, which he gladly obliged.

Now that her nerves had settled, Anna was famished. She said she still wasn't so sure about the afternoon sessions. Math and science were more difficult for her, and she knew she had lost some opportunities to learn when she had to leave school in New York. She had studied every math and science book she could get her hands on in preparation for the test, but she didn't know how up-to-date those books were and s fretted about how well she'd do.

After the meal Anna helped clean the plates and pack the dishes and then went back for the remaining sessions. She was right; the afternoon was much harder than the morning. She took the full time allotted for each one, thinking and rethinking her answers. When the tests were completed, Brad put all her test papers in order and promised that he would personally take them to Salem the next day to make sure they weren't lost in the mail.

Chapter 27

Brad's offer to personally take Anna's test papers to Salem was a good strategy because Jadwin's postmaster was Billy Scruggs, who was a harmless little man with a very heavy drinking problem.

Billy came from a good family and was a faithful member of the Church of Christ, which he attended with regularity, whether sober or drunk. He and his family were there every time the doors opened—Sunday morning, Sunday evening and Wednesday night—and sat on the same pew every time. They sat near the back because his wife was often embarrassed that he sang too loudly when tipsy and did not always follow the same beat as the rest of the congregation.

Billy tried hard to be a good man. About once every three months he'd see the light and swear off drinking. That would always come on a Sunday and he'd make his commitment public by responding dramatically to the preacher's invitation at the end of the sermon for sinners to come forward to confess and repent their sins in front of the brothers and sisters of the congregation.

After Billy had repented for the fourth or fifth time, the minister became a little gun shy about his invitations. He would warily watch Billy as he was issuing the invitation for sinners to come forth, and he'd try to speed up his invitation if he saw Billy was about to make his move. In such cases he'd try desperately to get the song leader to begin the closing song before Billy made it to the front of the church; but it was a small building and the preacher was seldom successful in his strategy.

Some of the members initially thought that was kind of tacky of the preacher. After all, if a man didn't have the right to repent his sins in church, what good was the invitation in the first place?

However, after about the fifth confession by Billy, it became such a joke that some of them came around to the preacher's way of thinking. As Billy would begin to move up the aisle, some of the men actually tried to intercept him, but Billy, in righteous zeal, could seldom be waylaid.

The community knew that Billy was actually a kind little soul who would give any neighbor the shirt off his back if needed. He had grown up in the community. They all liked him. They just didn't like his drinking and the effect it had on his work, because, unfortunately, when he was drinking, Billy was known to lose mail. The Jadwin community found this maddening since one of their main means of communication to the outside world was through him.

Billy was the brother-in-law of the Postmaster in Rolla and his appointment was secure no matter what the frequency of complaints from Jadwin residents. The Rolla Postmaster had not appointed Billy to his post because he liked him. He appointed Billy there because it was as far away as Billy could be placed and still be awarded a job in the Postmaster's district. Generally the postmaster only had to see him twice a year on holidays, at which time Billy was always drunk. So the Postmaster knew the Jadwin community had a legitimate beef. Billy was a great embarrassment to him. He would never have given him a job at all except that his wife kept nagging him about it. And frankly speaking, he didn't care one whit about what the backwoods hicks of Jadwin thought.

Citizens of the community did complain to him, and regularly, but to no effect. Their main avenue of complaint was through letters, which of course, could be a self-defeating proposition. They couldn't prove that Billy deliberately sabotaged them. They knew he was proud of his job and considered his role vital to the community. Normally he would never even think about diverting any piece of mail....unless perhaps he thought it was a personal critique of his work. On those occasions, when the letters were going to his brother-in-law, his heavy workload might cause him to be "a bit careless".

Those complaining knew that the chances of their letters getting through to the Rolla Postmaster without being lost were about the same as their ability to predict Missouri's weather. Some got so offended that they would seek the Postmaster out personally on the occasions they went to Rolla, but he didn't treat them respectfully or offer any real remedy.

Citizens of the community would occasionally find bundles of letters dropped alongside the road or floating down the Current River. Billy loved to fish and did so whenever the whim hit him. It hit him more frequently when he was drunk. They often found parcels addressed to neighbors that had been placed into their mailboxes by mistake. They were always faithful to deliver that mail to the appropriate party themselves.

One more prominent Jadwin family had received extremely sporadic deliveries for months and they knew something had to be wrong. When confronted, Billy swore he had delivered mail to that particular household almost every day, including the seed and other mail order catalogues the family had been waiting for so patiently. Out of frustration the family placed hidden sentries near their mailbox for a week around the time Billy usually delivered.

Sure enough, Billy did come by and he did have mail for them. Unfortunately, on two of the days, he was so drunk that he had a very hard time sitting up straight on his wagon. He stopped within a few feet of their large, very prominent, bright-white mailbox which was store-bought, and which they had carefully attached to a post at chest height exactly as specified in the post office's written instructions. But the mailbox was also located close to a massive old oak tree at the head of their lane. The tree was hollow and had a large round opening about six feet off the ground, the edges of which were slick and shiny from frequent use by squirrels. One of Billy's stops that week quickly revealed what had been happening to their mail.

In fairness to Billy, the hole was only a little smaller than the opening of the mail box and it *was* shiny. And to further support the sincerity of his mistake, he had to work much harder to get the mail up into that hole than if he had placed it in the mailbox.

As a matter of fact, it had occurred to Billy on many an occasion, in his drunken state, that this family had not followed the prescribed height specifications for the opening. He could only get the mail in by reaching way up from his wagon, whereas at most other boxes, he reached down. He even remembered this potential problem when he was sober and went out more than once to measure the height of that box. Each time he did so, he found it to be exactly at specifications. This was a great mystery to him.

The family quickly solved the problem by cutting down the tree. When they did, they found mail dating back over two years (about the time Billy began his duties as postmaster). The letters were in relatively good shape, but the squirrels had seemed to take a particular liking to the shiny pictures in the catalogues and had shredded most of the pages for their nests. The squirrels glared down from another tree and chattered angrily as the family felled their home, not at all happy with this pragmatic solution. They, too, had fallen victim to the Jadwin community's dysfunctional postmaster.

Billy never knew of the fix because the family never told him. They realized that it would just humiliate him if he was sober and mean nothing to him if he was drunk. And they actually did begin to receive their mail more regularly with rarer mishaps.

The other advantage of Brad's personal delivery of Anna's test papers to Salem was that he hoped he could convince school officials to grade them quickly if he waited and thus get feedback to Anna as soon as possible. He decided he would stay in Salem overnight for that purpose. If she had done as well as he and Bessie predicted, he would also be able to pick up her enrollment papers from the high school principle for the next semester. Brad was infatuated by this pretty girl and was quite willing to support Bessie's effort to further her education. Furthermore, Jess was the chair of the Jadwin School Board that year. Brad knew the extra effort would not go unnoticed.

Waiting for the test results was sheer torture for Anna. She was distracted in her work around the house and could think of nothing else. To manage her anxiety, she took long walks up the lane along the meadow ridge toward the school whenever she had the chance. The meadow just north of the Lough orchard was her favorite place on the farm.

On Saturday, only five days after Anna had tested, Brad rode down the ridge lane to the Lough home. Anna was in a valley field helping Jess and had to be called by Bessie. She climbed the steep hill so quickly that she was completely winded as she entered the kitchen. Brad was sitting at the table, talking to Bessie and drinking a cup of coffee when Anna rushed in. Jess, who remained in the field to finish the work, would not hear the news till later.

Brad looked appraisingly at Anna before he began speaking. For a few seconds, she feared that she had failed. "Well, Anna, I will get right to it to cut out some of this suspense." Then he smiled broadly and gave her the news. "You tested at the 12th grade level of high school studies, which I must say is amazing for no more formal education than you have received. Your reading on your own certainly paid off. You earned some of the highest scores ever recorded in Missouri in reading comprehension, grammar and geography. You also did fine in math and science, although not quite as well as in the other subjects. You may need a remedial class in math to catch up, but you'll have no trouble doing that. Frankly, you could probably pass any high school examination right now, but that is not allowed in Missouri. You'll have to take at least two semesters of courses to qualify for graduation as a regular student."

Anna released a long sigh of relief and Bessie yelled and raised her hands to the heavens, bursting with pride. "I knew it! I knew it! Anna, you are a scholar and you're going back to school!" She jumped up from her chair and came around and hugged Anna, who was now laughing at Bessie's outburst. Laughing or not, she had tears in her eyes.

The kids, who had watched the suspense build and then saw it climax on a high note with both of their heroines happy, danced around the table yelling, "Anna is a scholar, Anna is a scholar!" Brad sat smiling. He was rewarded with a huge piece of pie and fresh morning milk. They thanked him profusely, repeating at least forty times their appreciation to him for making the trip personally to Salem and returning so quickly with the good news. Both Anna and Bessie kissed him on the cheek as part of his reward. The right cheek where Anna kissed him felt different than the one Bessie had kissed. He went on his way, satisfied by his efforts and the outcome, finding it hard not to think about this beautiful girl who would soon finish her high school education in Salem.

Chapter 28

The rest of the summer flew by; there was so much to do. Bessie insisted that Anna have at least three dresses--two for weekday wear and one for Sundays and special occasions. So the family made a trip to Salem the next Saturday, where they bought material for dresses and bonnets, another pair of shoes, the books and school materials Anna would need, as well as various other miscellaneous necessities as determined by Bessie.

Jess did not have the money readily at hand for Anna's tuition and supplies so he went to his uncle, Jim Medlock, a more established farmer who lived a few miles away. Jim always had cash available for a good cause. Jess borrowed thirty dollars, promising to pay it off with ten wagon loads of wood for Jim throughout the winter. It was a good bargain for Jim. Anna never knew this. If she had she would surely have resisted, so Bessie and Jess thought it appropriate not to tell her.

In Salem, they visited the home of Mrs. Doris Steelman, a widower, who lived in a large, immaculate corner-street house. She was a member of the Salem Baptist Church and a relative on Bessie's side of the family. She had grown up in Jadwin. Mrs. Steelman indicated she would be delighted to provide room and board for Anna during the school year.

She would willingly have done it for nothing but the family insisted on paying her. Mrs. Steelman, who took to Anna immediately, said she really didn't need or want the money. Anna's company would be far better payment. They finally settled on three dollars a month, a tiny sum considering the beautiful bedroom assigned to Anna and the wonderful meals she would receive while boarding there, but it made Jess and Bessie feel better to know they had paid their way. Mr. Steelman, who had passed away a few years earlier, had managed the Salem bank and had been well connected in the community.

Anna mentioned that she would probably come back a week before school started to find a job if Mrs. Steelman didn't mind. Mrs. Steelman was delighted. "Why no dear. That will be wonderful. I will look forward to having you as soon as possible." It was obvious that she meant it. She was quite lonely in her large house since her husband's death. She immediately began to calculate which of her husband's friends might benefit from the work of a capable girl like this. Something immediately came to mind, but she didn't mention it yet because she didn't want to get Anna's hopes up until the possibility was confirmed.

The ride home from Salem was a happy one. Along the way, in a moment of reflection, Anna thought how nice it would be if Ben knew of the opportunities she was receiving. He had made that possible for her. She still thought of him every day and wished she could share what was happening in her life and know what he was doing.

In fact, Anna had been trying to tell Ben what was happening in her life. At least once a week, after arriving at the Loughs, she wrote him a letter. It was a fact known only by Bessie, Jess and, of course, Billy, the Jadwin Postmaster. She had started writing the day after arriving at Jadwin. But there were problems with the delivery of her letters. Try as hard as she might, Anna could not remember Bill's address, other than that it was on 59th street near the Scholar's Entrance to Central Park. Nor could she remember how to get in touch with Emma Mason or Reverend Brace. She did remember the name of the warehouse that Bill managed. She hoped that someone in the New York postal service would recognize the warehouse and deliver the letters.

She addressed the letters to:

Ben McDonald
In care of Bill Chambers,
Foreman
Simmons Warehouse,
59th Street near the Central Park Scholar's Entrance
New York, New York."

She knew that if she could get the letters to Bill, he would get them to Ben.

She wrote long letters describing the Lough family and life in Jadwin. When the opportunity for school came, she described her excitement, thanking him again for saving her life and giving her this chance, which she promised she would not squander. When Mrs. Steelman helped her get a job at the Salem newspaper office, she described her delight about working at a job where reading and writing were so important.

She tried to strike a delicate balance between letting Ben know what she was feeling without sounding too "mushy" or embarrassing him if Bill or someone else had to help him with the letters. She wished a thousand times that she had been able to teach Ben to read better. She knew that it would not have taken long. Then her letters could have been more private.

Unfortunately, the letters never made it to Ben. To his credit, Billy didn't lose them. He sent them on to the Salem Branch office. He was particularly fond of Anna and tried to pay special attention to her letters, even when he was drinking. From the Salem post office, the letters went to the regional office in Rolla and finally on by train to St. Louis, where they should have been sorted and packaged for New York.

But the St. Louis Postal Service was operated under the harsh direction of a Postmaster who took great pride in his work and considered his authority a gift from God. He was one of the early sticklers for accurate addresses in the US Postal System. He passed an iron-clad policy along to his workers with written instructions including the following admonition:

If the people in these little out-state rural, hick postal communities cannot appropriately address their letters and packages, they should not expect the United States Postal Service to play detective for them. **THEREFORE,** *it is my order that if a letter is not explicitly addressed, with the full name of the recipient and a proper street number and address in an appropriately matching city, it will be marked* **RETURN TO SENDER, INSUFFICIENT INFORMATION FOR DELIVERY**, *and will be sent back to its rural post office for correction--* **NO EXCEPTIONS***!*

The Postmaster had specified "rural" because he believed that most of the address problems originated from such locales. As a further punishment, the return process was deliberately slowed, taking about two months for each inappropriately labeled package or letter to be returned.

So Anna Murphy's letters, which did not have the specific street address, and instead indicated "near Central Park" were halted in St. Louis and returned to Rolla. There each letter sat until making its way back through Rolla to Salem and finally to the Jadwin post office.

It was then that Billy Scruggs *did* fall down on his job, despite his best intentions toward Anna. It was tough enough for him to handle normal mail. To require him to process a letter with a large angry-looking stamp across the front marked "**RETURN TO SENDER, INSUFFICIENT INFORMATION FOR DELIVERY**" was just too much. He did not even bother to look at the return address of the sender; he just saw the shameful admonition of the St. Louis office and threw all such letters into a holding bin to be reprocessed later. He planned to review that bin at least once a month to get the letters back to the original senders but he didn't like conflict, so the letters piled up for months. The larger the pile, the more intimidating it was to him, and the longer he took to clear the bin. Anna's weren't the only letters that met this fate but, over time, hers comprised the majority of the pile.

Billy was personally embarrassed by these letters. He felt it was an indictment of the literacy of his community. Jadwin residents really did have problems writing their addresses and his admonition to them to make sure letters were properly labeled fell on deaf ears. Jadwinites assumed that postal workers would know all the families they served, just like in Salem or Jadwin, and would know where to deliver a letter sent to a family, even if it wasn't labeled exactly right.

Billy knew better. He had personally attended a training session in St. Louis. The Post Master, a man of considerable repute, who had been appointed directly by the President of the United States of America, had espoused his philosophy. It certainly made sense to Billy. He was particularly embarrassed at the Postmaster's allegation that most such errors were created by illiterate rural people, but in his heart, he feared that was mostly right. He vowed that he would chastise anyone in Jadwin guilty of this offense. It never occurred to him that one of his primary offenders would be Anna Murphy.

Unfortunately, with his increased drinking, it took 18 months for him to pull Anna's letters out of the bottom of the reject box and realize what had happened. He handed them over to Jess later that month, telling him that he was somewhat disappointed in Anna, and that she needed to be more careful how she addressed her mail.

Jess was furious. Had he been a violent man, he would have decked Billy right then and there. He took the letters home to Bessie and they discussed the situation. They hesitated to tell Anna that none of her letters had reached their destination. They didn't know whether that **"Return To Sender"** stamp had been placed on the letters by New York authorities who didn't know where the Warehouse was located, or whether the letters had been diverted before they reached New York. Jess suspected they had been stopped in St. Louis, not New York, because if they had reached there, he speculated that any respectable postman would know all the businesses in his town. They certainly would have in Salem or Rolla!

After fretting about it for a week and praying on it, Bessie finally sat down and wrote a note to Anna about the situation, hoping that the bad news would not disrupt her studies and asking what she wanted to do. On the evening Bessie's letter arrived in Salem, when Mrs. Steelman told Anna she had received a letter, Anna's heart jumped and she took it quickly. She saw it was from Bessie, but hoped it contained a letter inside from Ben. She knew Bessie probably wouldn't write otherwise, since they generally saw each other every couple of weeks. When she read the real news, she went to her bedroom and wept.

Until then, Anna could only assume that her letters were reaching New York, and for some reason, Ben had not responded. The fact that she had not heard back from him was troubling to her because she feared that something might have happened to him. Yet if that were true, she also could not understand why Bill Chambers hadn't let her know.

After more than a year of no return correspondence, she had written less frequently and began to give up hope of ever hearing from Ben again. Not hearing back from him was disconcerting to her. She could not imagine Ben ignoring her letters, no matter how much he might have changed.

She had continued to write while in Salem, but marked the return addresses to the Lough home because she was hesitant to impose on Mrs. Steelman with her mail. She did indicate in her letters to Ben that, if he wrote, the Loughs would let her know as soon as possible while she was away at school.

And they would have done just that! They would have hopped on their wagon as soon as they got a letter, come rain or shine, to bring it to her. They would have been more reliable than any mailman because they knew how important communication from Ben was to her. They were almost as anxious to see a letter from him as she, and were just as confused as to why Ben or Bill Chambers had not contacted Anna.

Now aware of the truth, Anna was devastated. Ben had never heard from her at all. He must think she didn't care. Even worse, she had no idea how to let him know what had happened or where she was. Somehow she had to find a way to get word to him. After a day of misery, she decided to try to write to Mrs. Mason or Reverend Brace. They might know Bill's proper address. The problem was that she did not know how to reach them either, and it was now apparent to her that she must have an accurate address.

She wrote Bessie and asked her if she knew how to contact Mrs. Mason or Reverend Brace. Bessie wrote back that she did not have an address, but that perhaps Sam Kofahl, Jess' cousin in Rolla, might get the information through the church. On that same day, Bessie wrote a letter to Sam, explaining the situation in detail.

But this time, fate played its hand and Billy lost Bessie's letter, a fact that she did not find out for two weeks as she waited anxiously for Sam or Martha's response. Frustrated that they hadn't answered, she finally wrote Sam and Martha again, asking them not to take offense at her second inquiry, apologizing if she sounded pushy, but emphasizing that she had hoped Sam could get the information for Anna as soon as possible from his church, since it was so important to her.

Sam and Martha responded quickly, indicating that they never received her first letter, asking her to tell them what it said. Jess, now even more furious with Billy, cut through all the red tape and went to Salem to send Sam a telegraph. Sam rushed over to talk to the preacher and telegraphed back. The preacher, unfortunately, didn't know Reverend Brace's address personally, but he was sure he could find out. Jess told Anna about Sam's response before he left Salem and they all waited again. Every day increased Anna's anxiety.

The preacher did find Brace's address by writing to one of his associates in New York. He provided the information about two weeks later. Finally, Sam was able to telegraph the information directly to Anna. Anna immediately wrote the Reverend, reminding him of who she was. She said she needed to contact Bill Chambers as soon as possible and asked for his address. Regretfully, she did not think to ask Reverend Brace directly about Ben's status. It was late January 1887 when her letter reached the Reverend. He remembered her well, and wrote her back immediately.

Dear Anna:

I was very glad to hear from you and hope you are well.

I am terribly sorry to have to tell you that Bill Chambers, your friend, and the friend of all who knew him, died in a terrible mishap last Christmas Eve. He was the victim of a bank holdup, in which one of our other orphans was involved. The orphan was also killed. He was a troubled young man who fell in with the wrong crowd. Bill happened to be at the bank on business as the robbery occurred. His death seemed so meaningless to all of us. Only God knows why. Your friend, Ben McDonald, has taken his death particularly hard. If I can ever help you in any other way, please let me know.

Sincerely,
Charles Brace

When Anna received the letter she was shocked and deeply saddened. Bill Chambers had been so helpful and kind. She wept for his loss. Once over her initial reaction, she became even more frustrated that she could not reach Ben or help console him. At least Reverend Brace's letter had mentioned him, so he must know where Ben was now living. She immediately wrote back to the Reverend.

Dear Reverend Brace:

Thank you for your letter. It was terribly shocking to hear of Bill Chamber's passing. He touched so many lives, including mine and Ben's, that it is almost inconceivable that he could be gone. I have been trying to reach Ben through Bill for nearly two years, but I did not have Bill's address and the letters were rejected by the postal service before reaching their destination.

I do not know how to reach Ben now that Bill is gone. If you have his mailing address, I would very much appreciate receiving it as soon as conveniently possible. If you see him, would you please tell him I have been trying to correspond with him?

Thank you in advance for any assistance you might give and thank you for your life's work that has saved me and so many others. We will be forever in your debt.

Sincerely,
Anna Murphy

P.S. Please tell Mrs. Mason that Zachary is thriving and has become a healthy, vibrant and brilliant boy.

The Reverend wrote her back the very day he received her letter and it reached her only two weeks later.

Dear Anna:

I received your correspondence and am sorry to hear of your difficulties in communicating with Ben. I know you and he were very close. Ben remained with Bill and worked at the warehouse until recently. He was an exemplary worker and received multiple promotions, ultimately rising to a supervisory position. After staying directly with Bill for a while, he boarded at the home of a Mrs. Sullivan, a wonderful lady both Bill and I knew.

As I mentioned in my last letter, Bill's death was particularly hard for Ben. My sense is that he and Bill had become as close as brothers.

Unfortunately, I must tell you that Ben and Christian Gunther left New York only a month ago, headed to Bloomington, Indiana, to find Ben's family if they could. I do not know how to reach him. I am not even sure he will find his family there. I am afraid I'm at a dead end. I'm terribly sorry.

I hope that Ben will write me or send a message through a local minister when he reaches his destination. Bill thought that Ben might be an important contributor to our cause someday. If he does contact me, I will let him know you are trying to reach him and will contact you immediately. In the interim, I wish you good health and peace, and await any instruction if I can be of further assistance.

By the way, Mrs. Mason will be delighted with your news of Zachary. I wanted to respond quickly and she is now out of town. I know she would want me to have expressed her fondest greeting and good wishes to you both.

Sincerely,
Charles Brace

When Anna received that letter she wept bitterly and chastised herself for not asking Brace about Ben immediately. He had probably long since given up on her, having not heard from her for over two years. He would not know how to reach her by mail. He would now have to be relegated to a special place in her memory. Reconciling herself to that was extremely painful. She decided that all she could do now was to redouble her efforts to achieve her educational goals and dedicate her work to honor Bill and Ben for all they had done for her. Perhaps someday, when she had the money, she would try to find Ben again and let him know what he had meant to her.

It was a fierce and determined dedication. By the end of the spring semester in 1887 she finished her coursework for high school graduation. She walked through the Salem High School graduation line in May 1887, less than three years after leaving Hell's Kitchen. Bessie and Jess were as proud as any parents could ever be. They knew what she had accomplished and how much tragedy and loss she had overcome to do so. She was just sixteen years old when she graduated.

Late that spring she applied for her Missouri teacher's examination. She took the teacher's examination and passed with flying colors. She was now a certified teacher in the state of Missouri! All she needed was a place to teach. Temporarily, she returned to the farm to help Bessie while applying to area school districts for a position in the fall. She received inquiries of interest from a number of them and sent her credentials to each one. Unfortunately, most were talking about a position for fall of 1888, since positions had already been filled for the coming year. She had hoped for a more immediate placement but was not really surprised by the information. Jess had warned her that placements were very unusual on such short notice.

Bessie told her to be patient, that God had a plan for her. He wouldn't have brought her this far otherwise. Bessie always turned to her faith in times of uncertainty. Anna didn't have Bessie's faith, but did feel the pull of fate. Little else could explain how a dying orphan girl from New York could have come this far this fast. She waited.

That summer Brad Fletcher, the Jadwin teacher who had originally tested Anna, was smitten by a young lady in Columbia, Missouri whom he had met over the summer as he was continuing his education. It was a whirlwind affair. They married in August and he was immediately given a lucrative position in her father's business. He notified the Jadwin School Board, regretting such short notice and suggesting that Anna Murphy might be able to fill in admirably. Jess still sat on the Dent County R-VII School

Board. To Brad's relief, the Board indicated that releasing him from his contract would not be a problem and thanked him for his recommendation of Anna. They sincerely appreciated his good work and wished him well in his new profession.

Apparently God did have a plan!

The Board, by consensus, voted to ask Anna Murphy to become their teacher. She was overjoyed with the opportunity, as were all the school-aged Lough children, especially a young man named Zachary Lough.

Before the first day of school Bessie gave stern admonition to all the Lough children that they must address Anna by her last name—Miss Murphy—to show their respect for her as their new teacher. They stood there in front of Bessie, with wide and innocent eyes, and promised solemnly they would do so. And then, immediately upon arriving at school on the first day of the fall, they promptly forgot that solemn promise. Anna had to call them aside at the first recess to remind them gently to call her Miss Murphy after all three bragged to their classmates that their sister Anna would be the best teacher the school ever had!

So Anna Murphy's life had all the outward appearances of phenomenal happiness and success. It was, by all accounts, an amazing and wonderful story to that point, even with her losses.

Her remaining unresolved loss was Ben McDonald. She had reconciled the death of her parents as acts of God. But Ben was still alive and she would have communicated with him in a heartbeat if she just knew how to do so. Even if he had moved on in his life, it would have helped her to stay in touch with him.

At night she often lay awake, a lonely, beautiful young woman who was sought after by nearly every eligible bachelor for miles around. But her thoughts in that way were still reserved for him alone and she was having trouble shaking that feeling. She knew that was unhealthy but she could not "will" herself beyond her belief that she was meant to be with him.

At least the Reverend Brace's communication let her know what had happened to him after she left. With Bill's assistance, he had thrived. She wondered if he still thought of her, or if she was now just a girl in his memory.

She loved the teaching and the children loved her. Even the older farm boys, who generally hated school and lived to torture teachers, took a shine to "Miss Murphy". It didn't hurt that she was so attractive and nice. Her greatest problem with the boys was that a different one seemed to become infatuated with her every week, sometimes causing friction among the other young males. She never demeaned them for their affection and, of course, never encouraged them. She treated them fairly and tried to channel their infatuation into pleasing her with good performance in their schoolwork. She was usually successful in this strategy.

The Board was exceptionally pleased with her work. At the end of her probationary period, they gave her their highest commendation and a modest salary increase. Anna Murphy was already a star teacher and they knew how lucky they were to have her. She was a positive influence in the lives of the children and in their community. They were, to a man, as proud as if she were their own daughter.

Chapter 29

Ben stayed with his job for two weeks after Bill's death, until he could stand it no more. Every time he walked through the warehouse or past Bill's apartment or office, it tore him apart.

He walked down to the Haymarket on a Sunday afternoon to talk to Christian. "I've got to get out of the warehouse. They want me to stay—said I could have Bill's position in a couple of years—but I can't. Every day I go to work, it's like a knife in my chest. I need to move on. I thought about looking for work outside of Manhattan, but I'm not sure what I'd like to do. I feel stuck. I can't seem to get past Bill's death, or the feeling that I'm destined to lose everyone I really care about. "

Christian nodded, but then admonished Ben. "You know, of course, that Bill wouldn't have wanted this to set you back so much."

"Yea, I know, but I can't help it. Next to my mother, Bill was the closest thing I ever had to family who cared about me."

Christian sat silently for a few minutes, thinking. Ben leaned back and sighed.

"I assume you've heard nothing from your mother?"

Ben shook his head. "Not a word. I don't think that's ever going to happen. She would have no idea how to reach me, even if she's still alive."

"Why don't we go find out?"

Ben was thinking and hadn't fully grasped what Christian said.

"Find out what?"

"I said, why don't we go find out if she's still alive? She left you a hint with that word on the floor. Brace can help us figure out where that is and how to get there. I'm bored here and I finally decided that I've paid my dues. Ironic isn't it. I've resolved that and now I don't have Bill around to give me a legitimate job anymore. I could use a change of scenery too. Let's go find out what happened to your family."

"Are you serious!? You'd just pick up and go with me?"

"Sure. Why the hell not? Both of us have a little money. What's holding us here? Let's go find out. We both need a change of pace and an adventure."

"What do you think the chances are we'd find them? I think Bloomington is a town somewhere in Indiana, but we don't know how big it is. If it's large, given how my father lived, no one will probably know anything about them. They would be in a dive somewhere, most likely."

"He drinks."

"Yea, so?"

"I'd guess there aren't that many bars in Bloomington. Somebody will know something about him."

"Ben thought about that. "You'd really go with me?"

Christian laughed. "Yep, you'll need at least one person with brains in the group."

Ben grinned. "Think pretty highly of yourself, don't you. Well ok, wise ass, why not? When can you leave?"

"Give me a week and I'll be ready. Why don't I come up a week from today and let's go talk to Brace. If he doesn't know anything about Bloomington, maybe some of his people do. They may have gone that way with orphan kids."

"Okay, then! See you in a week!"

Ben could hardly wait for the week to pass. Despite Bill's loss, he felt better as he walked back up Fifth Avenue toward his boarding room. "I might find out what happened to them! We might even find them!" All that time, wondering…at least now he was taking action. And having Christian Gunther along was a major bonus. Nobody was sharper than Christian. Certainly he felt himself no match for Christian's insights, even though he realized he was no slouch. He grinned and mumbled, "It's a shame that guy doesn't get into a legitimate business. He'd own it before anyone realized what happened."

He notified the acting foreman that he would be moving on. The foreman hated to see him go and offered Ben a promotion if he'd stay, but Ben declined, saying he just had to get away. The foreman understood. He knew that Bill and Ben were very close and that remaining at the warehouse was just too painful for Ben.

Like clockwork, Christian showed up the next Saturday, an old beat up satchel in hand. They headed over to keep their appointment with Brace. "So you boys are striking out in the world, huh? Frankly, I hate to see you go. Both of you could have been valuable to the Children's Aid Society if I'd just figured out how to get you involved. Christian, I know what you did when you were with the Bowery Boys. Bill never stopped talking about how helpful you were."

Christian smiled but said nothing.

Ben spoke up. "Reverend Brace, we're looking for information on a city called Bloomington. We think it is in the state of Indiana. My family may have moved there when they left New York. We thought you might know something about it."

"Well, certainly, Ben. I'm somewhat familiar with Bloomington, Indiana. But there are a number of cities of that name in the West, including towns with that same name in Illinois and Minnesota. There may be more, but those are just the ones I'm familiar with. You're sure it's Bloomington, Indiana that you're looking for?"

Ben gulped. "Actually, I'm not sure. My mother left a one-word message when my family disappeared. At least I think it was her that left it and I think it was a message. ..." But even as he spoke, he became more uncertain. "I heard my family talk about coming from Indiana, so I assumed the Bloomington in the message was there."

"Well, Bloomington is a relatively small city, maybe 3,000 people. There's a good university there and a lot of agriculture. It's in the southern part of the state. There's a rail line that runs through it, I'm quite certain. The presence of the university would dictate that. We may have even had an orphan group stop there once."

Christian asked, "How far away is Indiana from New York?"

Brace got up and procured a large folded map of the United States. "Let's take a look, shall we?" They poured over the map until it was familiar to both young men. Ben and Christian asked a few more questions, thanked the Reverend and wished him well. He did the same to them and they took their leave, heading for the train station. There, they bought two tickets to Bloomington, by way of Philadelphia, Pittsburg and Indianapolis. Their train was scheduled to leave early that afternoon.

Ben purchased a small suitcase to hold his belongings. He returned to the boardinghouse to thank Mrs. Sullivan for her kindness. He had already alerted her he would soon be leaving. The tough old lady surprised him by crying. She hugged him as he left.

He had saved $200, which he thought was a goodly sum and would be enough for the search. After that, he wasn't sure what he'd do to cover his expenses. He'd cross that bridge when he came to it. The train tickets had cost $30 and his suitcase cost $2. He tried to purchase Christian's ticket for him but Christian wouldn't allow it. He said that it was his adventure too, and he would pay his own way.

They boarded the train that stopped first in Philadelphia and then traveled on through Pittsburg to Indianapolis. There they would change trains and head south to Bloomington. They arrived in Indianapolis early the following evening, only a little behind schedule. They ate in the depot as they waited for the train to Bloomington.

They arrived in Bloomington near midnight and asked the station attendant where they could find a place to sleep. The attendant referred him to a boarding house a few blocks from the Station. They walked there and paid for a room for two nights. They assumed that would be sufficient time to see if they could pick up any leads regarding Ben's family. Bloomington was a very small town compared to New York. They laughed about that, but were actually greatly relieved. It would make their hunt easier.

They slept a few hours and were ready to begin the search. On the way out of the Boarding House, they decided to ask the owner how many bars or nightclubs existed in Bloomington. He raised his eyebrows at the question, assuming that the two young men were looking for a good time. "Not many here, gentlemen, but there are a couple. The best tavern is at Walnut and Second, but there's another one not quite so good east on Third Street about a quarter mile from here. You boys looking to do some drinkin?"

Christian replied, "Not really, but we are looking for a man who's known to do quite a bit of it."

"Oh, well what's his name? Maybe I know him."

"John McDonald."

"Well, there's McDonalds around, but they're not drinkers. One of them, by the name of Jake McDonald, owns the biggest business in town: the feed and implements store."

Ben's memory flashed and his heart skipped a beat. His father had once gone into a tirade about a brother named Jake. He addressed the clerk, "Thanks. Can you direct us to that business establishment?"

The clerk laughed and said, "Sure, it's hard to miss. Just go south on Walnut a few blocks. It's a big place. Jake'll be there at this time of the day. Come afternoon, he'll probably be out on deliveries."

"Thanks," said Ben. He and Christian turned to leave and had almost reached the door when they heard the clerk yell.

"Just a minute, boys." Ben returned to the desk. "I do remember something about a John McDonald now that I think of it. It was in our local paper a few weeks back. I don't think it was good news though. I recall that this guy got in a barroom brawl and there were charges brought against him. I think there may actually be some connection with this guy and Jake, but I don't exactly recall what it is. I've only been in town for a year. If they're related, they're as different as night and day, but I guess every family has its black sheep. Hope it's not him you're looking for, or at least, I hope he's not important to you."

"It probably is, but I wouldn't exactly call him important to me. Thanks again." Ben turned away and they exited the hotel. As they walked south on Walnut, Ben's mind was racing. He looked over at Christian. "It couldn't be this easy, could it?"

Christian shrugged. "Sometimes the simplest answer is the right one. If your family did come back here to this place, there shouldn't be too many John McDonalds around. You ever hear of this Jake guy before?"

"Yea, I think I have. He might be my uncle."

"Well, you said your mother and father talked about being from here. If Jake McDonald is your uncle, and if he owns one of the biggest businesses in town, it could explain why John came back. John probably thought he could get a piece of the action, or at least milk some money from it. I wonder if your dad was ever in the business to begin with, and if so, why he got out? I'd guess his drinking may've had something to do with that too. Shall we go see if Jake is your long lost uncle?"

Ben grinned. "Yep, that's a big lead to follow, isn't it?"

They headed down Walnut until they reached the large, prominent building with the big sign on the front that said, "**McDonald's Feed & Implements**". When they entered the store, it was crowded with people buying seed, fertilizer and other farm supplies and tools. It was even bigger than it looked on the outside and had all manner of equipment and supplies on hand, even clothing. Ben and Christian walked over to a wall where shiny black harnesses were hanging, pretending to inspect them, listening to the conversations around them.

"Hey, Jake, can you help me a minute out here?" a customer looking at plows yelled to an open door at one side of the store. "Sure," a voice shot back. "Be with you in a minute, Harry." Ben watched the door. In a few seconds a tall, well-built man appeared. He was about Ben's height, but heavier. He had a friendly, familiar-looking face, although Ben had not seen him before. After looking closely, Ben realized that this man had many of his own features. It would be easy to think that they were related.

The two men began to converse about a plow. Ben glanced over at Christian, who nodded. They waited for the conversation to conclude. When it did Jake hurried back through the open door before Ben or Christian could intercept him. They heard muffled voices from inside the room. In a short while, two men came out. Neither was Jake. They listened a bit longer, but heard no more voices from the office. Christian said quietly, "I'll wait here, Ben. Go talk to the guy. I don't want it to look like we are ganging up on him. From his looks, if he's not a relative of yours, it'll be a major surprise to me."

Ben went to the door, took a deep breath, and walked in. Jake was sitting behind a desk looking at some papers. He saw movement and glanced up. "Can I help you?"

"I hope so," Ben replied, not knowing just how to approach the subject. Jake observed that the young man was a stranger, but there was something strongly familiar about him. The boy seemed embarrassed and hesitant to speak.

"Sit down, son, and take a load off. Now tell me what you need. We should be able to help."

"I don't need any goods," said Ben. "I'm actually here looking for somebody. The hotel clerk thought you might know him."

"That right?" queried Jake. "What's the name?"

"John McDonald,"

A hard look flashed across Jake's face and his voice turned edgy. "Oh, what do you want him for?"

"I'm a relative and I haven't seen him or the family for a while."

Jake knew all John's relatives and he had never seen this boy before, but he looked so familiar! "A relative huh? What relation are you?" It was obvious to Ben that Jake had become wary.

"I'm Ben McDonald. John and Emily were—uh—are, my father and mother."

Jake's jaw dropped. Uncomfortable seconds ticked by before he spoke. "According to them, boy, you're dead; died of the measles back in New York City." But even as he said it, Jake suspected that it had been another lie. The shape of the face, the eyes and the mouth reminded him too much of Emily and his own family. If this boy wasn't her son, he was a first class forgery. "How old are you boy?"

"I'm 17," answered Ben, becoming somewhat agitated. "I'm their son and I'm obviously not dead, although they did abandon me six years ago, so they may have thought that was the case."

Jake was doing the mental arithmetic. "Well, I guess that'd be about right, if you're who you say you are."

"I am. And you're related to them too, right?" asked Ben.

"Yea I am, although I often regret having to admit it about him. I'm John's brother. If you're who you say you are, I'm your Uncle Jake."

Ben didn't know what to say next. Neither did Jake. After a long pause Ben finally said, "Well, Uncle Jake, I'm looking for my parents. My dad was horrible to my mom and us kids. I'm worried that he's continued to abuse them."

With that Jake realized that Ben was quite probably who he said he was. Jake began to shake his head. "Well, I'll be danged. I'm sorry I doubted you, boy. You definitely had good reason to worry. Your dad is a drinker of the worst sort, the kind that turns nastier the more he drinks; but then, I suspect you know that even better than me, don't you?"

Ben nodded.

He paused, reflecting, then went on. "Your dad wasn't always that way when he was young, although he did start early. He had every chance in the world. Good education, good parents—your grandparents are dead now—good jobs, and a spectacular wife." He hesitated at that phrase and looked away, sadly. Ben wondered why. A fearful thought flashed through his mind. Maybe she was already dead!

Jake went on. "He's destroyed everything he ever touched because of his damn drinkin. Then he blames everybody else but himself when things go sour."

Jake paused again, and then continued, the pain evident in his voice. "I have to tell you Ben, I find it hard to have any use for him anymore, even if he is my brother and your father. And I can't get Emily to leave him. It's just been a horrible situation to watch her and the children living the way they are. I know he beats them. There are scars and bruises all over them."

"So my mother is still alive?"

"Yes, if you can call living like that alive."

"Do they live in Bloomington?"

"Yep—uh—well actually not in the city limits. They live on an old farm five miles out of town. I own it. I'll take you there if you like, but I guess I should ask your intentions. And I have to tell you, it's not a pretty picture. The kids are a mess, and your mom looks twice her age. If I was you, knowin' what I know, I might be inclined to just move on and let it rest as it is. Doesn't seem to be anything anyone can do till he kills himself with his drink; that is, assuming he don't kill one of them first."

He stared at Ben. "You've sure got Emily's traits. You're probably more like her than him. You should get out of here now while you can. He eventually destroys everything he touches. She's pretty far gone herself."

Ben's eyes flashed and his face took on a hard set. He shook his head. "Not yet. I can't do that without seeing my mother and the kids, and I'll be seeing him too."

By the look on Ben's face, Jake knew he wouldn't be deterred. He suspected that he should probably worry about his brother when Ben found him, but Jake had lost all concern about John's safety long ago. Jake nodded, "Okay, but if you have any intention of trying to mete out your personal justice to John McDonald, he's not worth it, no matter how much he deserves it. Let me tell my people and we'll be on our way."

Ben remembered Christian. "I have a friend with me."

"And you want to bring him to see this?"

"Yea, I do. He's solid and I trust his judgment."

"Okay, get him and meet me out front in half an hour."

Ben nodded and walked out of the room. When he and Christian exited the store, they went across to a small diner to get some coffee and wait. Christian ordered a quick breakfast. Ben was not hungry.

"What did the guy say?" asked Christian as he took a sip of coffee.

"He said he's my uncle and he knows where my mother and father live. It's on some old farm five miles out of town. He says it's an ugly picture out there and that if I was smart, I'd just walk out of the store and hop on the next train."

Christian shook his head and smiled. "Well, we both know you're not that smart, don't we. He obviously doesn't know you very well."

Ben smiled. "He may know me better than you think. He didn't expect me to back down."

Christian nodded. "You want me to go?"

Ben looked at Christian and nodded.

"Okay, then. Let's go find your family."

"Jake says they're a mess."

"In what way?"

"Ben looked down at his coffee. "He says she's aged a lot. I'm not surprised. She's probably been beaten a thousand times since I last saw her. He says they all have bruises all over them."

"She'll still be your mother."

Ben nodded and then his voice turned hard. "I think I'm going to kill him, Christian."

Christian saw the deep hatred in Ben's eyes. "Get hold of yourself, McDonald! That's not smart talk. He's a drunk and far along. He's definitely not worth it."

Ben's eyes flashed hatred. "That's what Jake said, but I tell you this, he's battered them for the last time, Christian. I couldn't protect them before, but I'll be damned if I leave him alive to do more damage. He's killing them slowly and if he hasn't already, he'll cripple them in their minds and their bodies."

"Let's just take it as we find it and decide then. In the meantime, you need to keep your cool if you're going to help your mom and the kids." Christian's statement had an edge to it that snapped Ben to attention.

"Yea, I hear you, Gunther, but don't get in my way."

Christian smiled a little. "Why, I wouldn't think of it, Ben."

It took them nearly an hour to make the trip in Jake's wagon. It shouldn't have; the wagon was pulled by a team of spirited horses. But about a mile out of town, they turned onto a muddy, rutted path that slowed progress considerably. It had rained recently and that had turned the narrow dirt road to muck. The wagon became stuck twice and Ben and Christian had to get off and push.

Ben's stomach was churning. All these years he had dreamed of reuniting with his family. Now, he dreaded what he might find. But he had to see his mother, Julie, Alyssa and Matthew, and he also wanted to see John again, but alone for one last time. Ben detested him above all other human beings and decided he would make John pay for what he had done to his family. He would beat him slowly and make it as painful as he could, so his father would get a taste of what he had meted out to his family over the years. Then he would strangle him and see him gasp for breath till his face turned blue.

They finally arrived at a small, framed house with most of the paint peeled off, a broken fence and a yard full of weeds. Ben looked at Jake, his face reddening. Jake stared right back at him, knowing what he was thinking. "I couldn't help it, Ben. John destroyed every other place I tried to put them in and alienated everybody in the neighborhoods where they lived."

Ben's face softened a little and he nodded. "They've actually lived in worse."

Jake and Ben went to the door while Christian tied the horses to a section of the broken fence. Jake knocked. Ben stood back a little. There was movement inside and the door opened a crack. Julie peaked through the opening. Seeing Jake, she opened it wider.

"Hi, Uncle Jake," she said in a meek voice, looking first at him and then at the stranger beside him. Her face froze and she screamed. "Momma, come quick!" She continued staring at Ben as though he were a ghost. Ben heard rapid steps from inside and then Emily appeared, anxious at what had frightened her daughter. She looked at Julie to see what was wrong. It was dark inside and her eyes had not yet adjusted to the outside light. She saw Jake's familiar profile and someone else standing a little behind. She stepped out into the yard, putting her hand up to her face to shade her eyes.

"Why Jake, what in the world are you doing here this time of…" Her voice froze. She stared at the figure by Jake's side. She began to shake. Great tears began to cascade down her cheeks and her face turned deathly pale. She slowly sank to her knees. An involuntary sob convulsed her body. She looked up at Ben shaking her head. "Ben?" she cried, "Ben!" She put her hands over her face and leaned her head to the ground. Ben and Jake both started toward her but Ben was quicker and reached her first. He lifted her up. She was light as a feather—far too light. When he had pulled her up, she turned her head down and away from him in shame, but he wouldn't allow it. He lifted her chin. He had never seen so much pain in human eyes, even on the faces of children who had died on the streets. She was in a living hell.

"It's ok, mother. I'm here now. I'm just sorry it took me this long to get here."

Her body convulsed again. She looked as though she would faint or throw up. He held her up, fearing that she might pass out. She finally reached up to his face and took it in her hands. Then her arms slipped around his chest, squeezing him as tight as she could. Every few seconds she leaned back to look up at him, shaking her head, then clinging to him again. A dam in her soul broke and the flooding waters drenched the front of his shirt.

Jake and Christian watched quietly as Emily wept. The horses became nervous and began tossing their heads. Matt and Alyssa edged cautiously out of the house, watching this tall young man and their mother. They remembered, and felt the urge to run to him, but he was so much bigger than when they had last seen him.

Ben continued holding his mother as she wept. Matthew, now eight, and Julie and Alyssa, now thirteen and twelve years old respectively, finally found the courage to approach Ben and Emily. They tried to hug them both and then began to pat each on the back to comfort them. When Ben noticed them, he released his mother and knelt down to hug each one. He could see that all of them, including Matthew, had deep bruises on their arms and neck. They began to cry too and clung to him as he embraced them. He cried as well.

When they had exhausted their emotions, they went in and collapsed on rickety chairs around an old worn table. Emily took out tin cups to pour them water from a pitcher. "I would offer you some food or tea, but we don't have much right now," she said, embarrassed.

"We are fine, mother. We aren't really hungry," Ben said quietly. It was true. Hunger was the last thing on his mind.

She sat down beside him, moving her chair toward him until her knees touched his. "Ben, I didn't want to leave you. You probably won't believe me," her eyes searching his, pleading. "It is the most horrible thing I ever did in my life. I had to protect the other children. He threatened to take them away. I tried to leave you a message but I assumed you never found it." Her breath caught and she shuddered. She put her hands over her face to hide from the person she cared about the most, and the one she had most failed to protect.

"I know, mother," he soothed, putting his hands on her thin shoulders. "You did what you had to do. I'd have done the same." He glanced over at Christian, grateful for his insight. She shuddered and dropped her hands from her eyes, staring at him. She searched his face to see if he really meant what he said. Slowly, a look of relief washed over her. Except for still needing to protect the other children, if she died today, it would be in peace.

She leaned forward and leaned her head on his chest. She was shocked at how big and strong he was now. He pulled her to him and kissed her head. They held each other, a mother and her lost son, beginning a healing process that she had assumed she would never live to see. The other children sat watching with somber faces, tears in their eyes. Christian had to look away. This was all too close for him. He said he'd tend to the horses and went outside.

Eventually Ben released Emily and looked at her more closely. Jake was right. She had aged terribly in the past few years. She looked exhausted and spent. And there were numerous bruises on her face and arms; the same for all the children. Her hair was oily and straggly. There were aging lines around her eyes. Her face around one eye was bluish-black. "Where is he, mother? He has hit you and the kids for the last time." The sound of his voice signaled vengeance.

She became frightened. "I don't know, Ben! He's been gone overnight. He could get back any time. He's usually never gone longer than one night. When he is, it's always bad when he returns." She shuddered involuntarily.

Ben looked over at Jake. "Do you know where he is?"

"Of course I don't, Ben. Get hold of yourself. He's scum and he's not worth doing what you're thinkin. You kill him and you're just killing yourself. In a twisted way, it would be his last victory. I understand why you're angry and what you'd like to do. Don't think I haven't thought about it a hundred times myself. But he's not worth it."

Ben ignored the admonition. "You and Christian take my mother and my sisters and brother out of here. I have some money. I'd like you to get them a room at the hotel. Take them away now. I want them somewhere else when he comes back."

Jake looked over at Emily, then back to Ben. "Ben, I've talked to your mother a hundred times before about getting away, and she won't leave." He detested that his nephew thought he had not tried to help. "I'd have helped her as soon as they came back, but I couldn't get her to budge."

He turned to Emily. "Will you come away now Emily—do what Ben says?"

She looked at Ben. "Ben, I'll go back with you right now if you promise to come. But I won't leave unless you do. I won't leave you here and have him find you when he gets back."

Ben hesitated. He needed to get her and the kids away. He could come back—would come back soon—alone. There was time to do what he had to do once he knew they were safe with Christian. That was the most important thing now.

Emily looked at Jake in panic. She looked at Ben again. She realized the time for procrastinating was over. Ben had found them and he would not leave again without her and the children. If they stayed here now, he and John would come to blows. No matter how strong Ben had become, she feared what John might do to him. John always seemed to know how to cheat justice. She blurted out, "Let's go now, Ben. It's time we leave this place and get away from him."

Ben and Jake stood immediately. Jake said, "Don't worry about taking anything, Emily. We can get you all you need. And Ben, this isn't about money. There's plenty of that. If she's ready for help, everything else will be taken care of."

They walked outside to where the horses were standing. Ben helped Emily and the children into the wagon. The children moved as if they were in a daze. They couldn't believe they were leaving. Ben started to board the wagon, but then something caused him to glance at Christian, still standing beside the lead horse, holding his bridle. He didn't need to do that. Jake already had the reins in his hands. "Come on, Christian, let's go! I want them as far away from here as we can get as fast as possible."

Christian responded quietly. "You get up on the wagon, Ben. I'm going to stay here a while"

Ben froze in his tracks. "Stop joking, Gunther! We have to go now!"

Christian's face had a look that Ben hadn't seen since Hell's Kitchen. "It's time you take them out of here, McDonald. I'll be staying a while. I'll be there eventually." It was that deadly quiet voice again. Jake, who had no idea who this man was, felt a shiver run down his spine. He looked from Christian to Ben.

"Quit horsing around, Gunther. This is not your fight. Get on the damn wagon. I'm in no mood to talk. I'll put you on if I have to."

Christian smiled a little and stared at Ben. "You could try that, Ben, but you know you'd not get it done. It's not dark here and you won't be coming at my back. You couldn't have taken me then if I'd seen you coming and you won't be able to do it now. It'd just scare your uncle and your family. They'd try to stop it and somebody could get hurt. And after it was done, you'd still be riding back to town, but it'd be flat on your back and uncomfortable. You'll leave now, McDonald. I'll be there when I'm done here."

That was the most frightening voice Jake had ever heard in his life! It was a cruel voice—a killing voice. And those grey eyes were the coldest he'd ever seen. He implored his nephew. "Come on, Ben, we're wasting time. I am guessing your friend, if he is that, can take care of himself, and John deserves whatever he gets. Let's get out of here!"

Ben stared long and hard at Christian. For a split second, he toyed with challenging him, but then thought better of it. He sighed and nodded. "I'll be back as soon as I can, Gunther. And don't think for a minute that I'll forget this."

"Stay with your family, McDonald. You came here to protect them. Do your job." He turned away and walked toward the house.

Ben shrugged and climbed into the wagon. He yelled at Christian as he started to enter the house. "You are too damn' stubborn, Gunther!"

A tight smile appeared on Christian's face but Ben didn't see it. He turned at the doorway. "I've heard that before, McDonald." With that, he disappeared into the house.

Jake looked at Ben, who nodded. Jake turned the horses toward town.

Chapter 30

John arrived back at the farm at dusk. The shadows were deep and the path to the rundown rattrap was muddy and hard for him to navigate. He had slipped and fallen twice, his clothes a muddy mess. He was also exhausted from the walk. His boots and trousers were soaked. He realized that he wasn't as strong as he used to be, and these damned treks to and from town took longer every time. He needed a horse. He'd ask Jake for one on his next trip to town. Jake had lots of them. It wouldn't hurt the bastard to part with one for the sake of the family. He should move the family back to town, but it was embarrassing to be seen with his dirty, good for nothing wife and kids.

John was hungry. "That bitch had better have food on the table or she's going to be sorry, he thought. "She's worthless to me now for anything else but food and housekeeping."

He stopped at the edge of the yard. Something about the house seemed wrong. At first he couldn't put his finger on it as he staggered toward the door. As he drew closer it came to him. There was no light in the windows. She must have used up all the kerosene for the lamps while he was gone! And she would probably use that as her damned excuse for not cooking for him too! His simmering hatred for her was quickly rekindled to fine form as he covered the last few steps to the door of the house.

It was a pattern he had fallen into of late. Once a week, he would head to town to quench his thirst. He hated the long walk, so he tended to stay overnight after a drinking spree that was usually financed by making a scene at the feed store until Jake gave him a little cash for "groceries". That bastard of a brother now controlled all the family money and was as sticky as a hedge apple. But Jake had a soft spot. If John told him the family was out of food, Jake usually shook his head and ponied up a few dollars.

But it was never enough for his drinks *and* a hotel room, so he was forced to sleep on the ground in some filthy alley after an evening of drinking. He always woke up sore and miserable the next day. By the time the bar opened the next afternoon and he had a few more drinks, he was out of cash and in a foul mood. It just made the long walk worse, but it gave him time to build his case against the miserable woman who had ruined his life.

Things hadn't gone as well as he had planned after they left New York. He got back to find his old man and mother both dead, with Jake left in full control of the estate and the business. Jake had given him a job when he got back but he had become disgusted with it after a few weeks and quit. Jake was testy about his drinking and about some of the comments he had made to the dumbest of the store's customers. So he quit and it was obvious that Jake was relieved.

To assuage his guilt, Jake had paid the rent on two or three places in town for the family, but the neighbors kept complaining about noises they heard. That was the trouble with small towns; everybody was into everybody's business. Jake eventually moved the family to this miserable farmhouse. He wasn't doing them any big favor. John wouldn't have let his own dog, if he had one, live in this dump. Jake obviously didn't remember the Biblical admonition about being his brother's keeper, despite allegedly being such a fine Christian. A two-faced hypocrite was what he really was.

John staggered through the door and yelled, "Emily! Where are you, you bitch! I guess you used up all the kerosene again, didn't you. And you probably didn't fix dinner for me or the kids, did you?"

"Emily! John's voice had raised to a murderous tone. Where are you?"

Silence.

He staggered into the edge of the table, splitting off a splinter from its jagged edge into his hand as he tried to catch himself. Then he tripped over a chair that shouldn't have been there. She or the brats had left it out from the table. He had banged his knee painfully and that, too, fed his fury. He leaned on the edge of the table until the pain subsided. His bleary eyes, not so good anymore, slowly began to adjust to the dull light of the room. As he looked around the room, his eyes settled on something over in the darkest corner that shouldn't be there: a large figure that could not be Emily or any of the children, sitting in a chair. It brought him up quickly.

He thought a minute, a bit dizzy from his pain and his drinks, and then spat out, "Hey, you over there in the corner. What are you doing in my house and where are my wife and kids?"

Silence.

"Hey, you over there! Are you deaf and dumb? Who are you!"

The figure finally responded. "Hello, John. Finally made it home, did you?"

Something about that voice caused a chill to run down John's spine. "How do you know my name? Do I know you?"

No response from the figure in the corner. It was getting on John's nerves. He stood up straighter and began to feel around on the table with his right hand, hoping to find a stray knife or rolling pin. Nothing there, of course! There was never anything there when you needed it. He turned a little and reached for the back of the chair. He would use it as a weapon.

"I wouldn't try that, John. Why don't you just sit down in it instead and let's have a little talk."

But John didn't feel like sitting down. He felt more like driving this stranger out of his house. He tried to focus. If he could get the chair around, he could attack the intruder and smash it over his head. Whoever the intruder was, he was still sitting and would be at a disadvantage if John moved quickly.

Something about that voice caused John to hesitate and consider another option as well. He could simply run to the door and escape from the house. He knew he really didn't care what happened to Emily and the brats. But his pride and hatred of any form of resistance ultimately caused him to reject that option. By God, he would not run from his own house! People who thought they could mess with John McDonald on his own turf had to be shown! He hadn't been in a brawl in a while and now was as good a time as any. He swiveled around quickly to pick up the chair.

At least, he thought he had been quick. Drunk or not, he thought that he had always been pretty agile on his feet, and a sitting intruder was definitely at a disadvantage. But this time, it wasn't like that. In an instant, he felt himself flying backward across the top of the table, his body smashing into the kitchen cabinet.

One second the intruder had been sitting in the corner of the room at least ten feet away. In the next, John had been hurled violently over the table and against the cabinet, his back pressed hard against its sharp metal edging, his body arched painfully in an awkward limbo position. It passed through his mind as he fell that a mere mortal should not have been able to move that fast.

A knee smashed into his crotch, incapacitating him instantly, sending that unique horrible pain to his brain and deflating the air from his body. He went limp and would have fallen to the floor, but he couldn't. A huge hand had him by the throat and was lifting him back against the cabinet. His head smashed into the edge of the upper cabinet over the sink. Even in his alcohol-addled brain, he felt intense pain from all over of his body. The hand tightened around his throat, making him gasp for air.

All of this had happened in a flash. The pain was already intense and becoming unbearable. He gagged and choked. His back felt as though it was being crushed in a vice. A face appeared, not six inches from his own, as he was pulled back to an upright position. There was enough light coming through the window to give the face an utterly sinister appearance. He had never seen the intruder before and had no idea who he might be. But the intruder was big and powerful, and obviously knew him.

"Oh, sorry John! That must hurt." The intruder loosened his grip on John's throat and air came rushing back into his lungs. He gasped and instinctively started to reach up to free the hand from his throat. He saw the flash of the fist in the moonlight just before it smashed into the bridge of his nose. It felt like a post mall had hit him square in the face. He fell backward again, his head smashing into the corner of the window sill over the sink, his eyes blurring so badly that so he could no longer see. His body went limp. His arms dropped to his sides. He began to sag toward the floor.
Ever so slowly the intruder let John slip down, scraping his back painfully against the jagged metal edging of the cabinet. His legs splayed stiffly out in front of him as he sank to an awkward sitting

position. The hand released his neck. John had no strength to raise his head. He kept blinking, trying to reduce the sting in his nose and restore some of his vision. There was a loud ringing in his ears.

He was grateful that the attack was over and he assumed he could rest just a bit on the floor. But he was wrong. A heavy boot smashed into his solar plexus draining his lungs of air yet again. Try as he might, he couldn't catch a breath. He leaned over, his mouth opening and closing like a grounded fish. He felt his bladder release but he didn't care. He needed air. He gulped, trying to get his lungs working again, but no air would enter. Just as he was sure that he was going to pass out, a little air wandered into his lungs and he gasped and began to pant like a wounded dog.

The voice spoke again. "I bet that is really scary, isn't it, John. Not being able to get your breath like that." Then the boot smashed into the left side of his ribs. He felt, and heard, a sickening crack inside his chest, followed by intense pain as he tried to breathe. He felt himself floating blissfully away and he finally passed out.

When he awoke, he was sprawled in an awkward sitting position in the same chair he had tried to use as a weapon. He would have gladly slid off the edge to the floor but he was held up by his own stiff, splayed legs, each propped against a leg of the table. His crotch and ribs shot excruciating pain to his brain every time he moved. His breathing was ragged and shallow. Every breath hurt. He moved his arm across his ribs on his left side and held them to reduce the pain. He dared not move for fear he would pass out. His eyes were still watering and everything was blurred. It was also darker now. The voice spoke again from the opposite end of the table.

"Now, John, are you ready to have that talk that should have occurred before our little interruption? You can hear me, can't you? Or do I need to come closer?"

John groaned. "No!! No. I hear you! What do you want?"

"I'm here as a messenger. Your wife and children have been taken away. It's shameful for you for that to happen, but you were such an abusive little husband and father that you were putting them in too much danger. It was decided by the parties that I represent that you must be stopped. We can't have you doing what you already did to Benjamin, your firstborn son, now can we?

"That bastard wasn't my son. Who are you anyway, and how do you know about me and my family?"

There was silence for a long second before the intruder replied. "Why, John, I am your guardian angel just like you heard about in Sunday school. You do remember Sunday school from your early days, don't you, before you turned into the drunken, miserable little bully that you now are?"

John didn't respond.

"No? Well, it's probably the drink. It plays tricks with the memory after a while." The voice paused, as if reflecting. "Anyway, as I was saying, I am your guardian angel, sent to save you. That may be hard for you to believe, but I assure you, it's true. You weren't aware of it, but there were forces building that placed you in imminent danger. In fact, John, you might be dead by now if I hadn't intervened. Isn't it ironic that someone like you would have a guardian angel? But then you have been told that God moves in mysterious ways, haven't you."

The intruder paused to let John catch up. "You don't have to thank me for saving you John. I'm actually just doing my job, disgusting as that is in this instance. Now, I'm commissioned to give you an offer that you may decide to choose, or not. Your wife and kids are gone. You will never attempt to see them again. If you do, you will see me instead. Should that happen, I am commissioned to terminate you, which I assure you, I would enjoy a great deal. You and I both know that you are a little worm who doesn't deserve to live. However, it is within your discretion to avoid that outcome if you choose.

There was another long pause. The silence was maddening to John, yet he still dared not respond. The voice finally continued, almost whimsical this time. "Actually, I have been given the authority to eliminate you now if I decide that I can't trust you. And regretfully, John, my trust level is terribly low for human-kind in general, just as a matter of experience. I'm sure you understand why."

So I suppose I should be interested in what you have to say about the matter of trusting you. You may think that your honor demands that you resist my offer; that you still own your family and can abuse them as you please. If that's your position, I have no problem with that. A man should uphold his honor at all costs, no matter what the price. Don't you think that's true, John? Do you think you should defend your solemn right to abuse your family any way you please; even kill them if it suits you?"

John was growing more petrified by the moment, and dared not respond.

After another long pause, the intruder spoke again. "If you make that choice, John, as a reward, I'll terminate you quickly and with far less pain than I just administered to you. You can leave this world with your honor intact. Now wouldn't that be a valuable thing? Perhaps it could bring you a level of peace that might make your death slightly meaningful. Your one last great act of defiance, so to speak. And frankly, you haven't done any other great acts on this earth since you were a very young boy, have you, John? You have become a miserable little vermin in the terrible existence that you now live. And I can predict with absolute assurance as one who sees the future, that nothing will ever get better for you for the rest of your morbid life and that you will eventually come to a sad ending, whether now or later."

"So why not now, John? I can relieve you of all this pain and misery in mere seconds. What do you think? Shall I do that, or will you just reject your family and move on?"

The voice was so seductive that, for a split second, John caught himself considering the offer, but then realized its full implications. He panicked and began to stutter. "I....I have other things to do, places to see! I promise that...that I'll leave here if you want me to and I'll never come back. Where do you want me to go? I'll go wherever you say. You'll never see me again!"

It was now so dark in the room that he could barely make out the form across the table, but that voice was so clear and unearthly. It projected a level of casual violence that sent chills down his spine. He felt like an ant under a magnifying glass, waiting for a cloud to pass and the sun to come out. He needed to get away from whoever this was as soon as possible and find a drink. If he changed his mind, he figured that he could pick his own time to find this family and challenge this monster after he had planned it all out.

"So, you choose continue your miserable life, is that right, John?

330

"Yes! Yes. That's what I'm saying."

There was resignation, even sadness, in the voice. "Well, I'm sorry, John, but I just don't believe that I can trust you. I think you are already thinking that you'll just get away now and come back for your family when you think I'll be out of the picture. That is what you are thinking, isn't it. "

John saw the shadow rise from the chair at the other end of the table and start to move toward him. He slipped off the chair to the floor into a fetal position under the table. He started whimpering. "No, please don't. I don't want to die. Please! I'll do anything you want!"

The shadow halted. "Oh, John, you are such a pathetic little coward. You've beaten your wife and children to a pulp for years for no reason at all, but you whimper like a baby when it's your turn to take a little punishment."

The voice sighed wearily. "Bullies and cowards are all alike in the end. Pond scum like you would be better off removed, but you'll choose to cling to life as though it actually had something to offer. You'll delude yourself into thinking that you have a purpose other than just floating along polluting everything you touch. Life will never offer you anything more, John. It will only get worse for you. Deep in the recesses of your addled brain, you know that. But, if you think you want that, I'll grant it, even against my better judgment."

The voice spoke faster and took on a more positive, business-like note. "Alright then, here are the conditions. If you can make it to the train station, I'll give you a bottle of good whiskey to dull your pain and put you on a train. Then I'll monitor you to determine whether you try to come back. If you don't, you'll never see me again. If you do, you'll be terminated with no further discussion. Can I count on you to go directly to the train station and never come back?"

John responded quickly to the offer. "Yes! I'll leave and not come back; I give you my word!"

The voice laughed sarcastically. "Your word, John, has never been worth the utterance. You and I know that. Your word is as worthless as your soul. I wouldn't bother trading on either. But your fear—well that's another matter. I might count on that a little more. And I promise you, if you come back, your termination is assured. But I might decide to play with you a while, John, like a cat plays with a mouse. It will be very painful for a considerable time and you'd eventually beg me to put you out of your misery. You see, if you came back, that would be embarrassing for the parties that I represent. They would get very angry. It'd be more than just business at that point. It'd be personal. And I am the absolute best there is at delivering righteous justice, John. You should believe that with all your heart and fear it above all else."

John almost shouted his answer. "I swear to you, I'll never come back! If you let me leave, you'll never have to see me again!"

There was silence. The intruder didn't move or speak. John could only wait. He remained under the table, still in his fetal position, his head in his hands, his body quaking. Finally the voice spoke again. "Well, alright, John; I'm going to make this contract with you. I sincerely hope I'm not wasting my time. Time is precious, you know, even for those of us who have a lot of it. So here's what we'll do. I'll meet you in town at the railroad station under the water tanks in a couple of hours. You're familiar with the spot, John?"

John nodded.

"I'm sorry. I didn't hear you?"

"Yes, I know where it is!"

"Good, I'll bring you that bottle of whiskey and it'll ease your pain and make the train ride a lot smoother. I'll give it to you at the station when I put you on a train. You should start now. In your condition, it'll take a while to get there, and I'm generally not known to be patient. I really don't like you, John, and for your own good, we should part company as soon as possible."

"Remember, it's better that I'm not be seen, so don't stop to talk with anyone along the way. If you're late, it'll try my patience and I could easily change my mind. Remember, you'll go straight to the water tanks. If you go anywhere else, or if you talk to anyone at all on the way or in town, I'll know it and our contract will be broken. You understand?"

"Yes. I will do it....but I'm badly hurt and I don't know if I can make it that far." John groaned as he tried to move.

"Well, I hope you can. It will be a shame to have wasted my time and yours if you can't. I travel much faster than you, so I'll be waiting when you get there. Do you want to try to get up yourself or should I give you a hand?"

"No! I'll do it! I'll do it!" John crawled out from under the table and pulled himself to his feet by holding onto the table's edge. The exertion made him light-headed. John's pain was bad, but surprisingly not as devastating as he expected. He staggered to the door and started along the path, holding his chest, bent over a little at the waist.

Christian wasn't surprised. He had administered plenty of pain to John, but no major damage except for a cracked rib or two. A man lost all fight when he had a cracked rib, but he could still move if careful. Christian slipped outside and walked parallel to the lane but far enough away to remain in the shadows. He didn't care if John heard him. It would add to his fear. He could see John's form occasionally in the moonlight, stumbling along. Christian followed him in that manner for most of the way along the rough wagon road to make sure he stayed conscious, then circled ahead to reach the main road ahead of him.

Once Christian reached the main road, he jogged the rest of the way to town and entered the bar on 3rd Street. He quickly bought a bottle of their best whiskey. He had toyed with going cheap and then decided against it, figuring it could well be John's last good bottle. He slipped back to the edge of town to await his arrival.

It took John another fifteen minutes to appear, but when he arrived, he made the proper turn toward the railway station. Christian followed at a distance until John was within a quarter mile of the station, then lapped him again and headed for the water tower. It was getting late now. No one was stirring about.

Christian's main worry had been that there would be no freight train parked at the station. He intended to stow John away on a freight car to avoid purchasing a ticket. If there was no train, he would be forced to babysit John all night and then buy a ticket the next day to get him out of town on the first passenger train. That probably wouldn't be too risky, but the fewer people who saw him and John together, the better.

To his relief, a freighter was there, backed up along the side tracks, with livestock cars attached. The noises emanating from the cars told Christian the train was already loaded and would probably depart early the next day. He inspected it and caught himself smiling. The cars were full of calves and yearlings. That was good. Otherwise he probably couldn't have risked loading John into a car where he could be trampled by larger animals as he drank himself to oblivion. A ride with calves would be a fitting departure for John, and actually, it would probably be relatively warm.

Christian positioned himself in the shadows under the tanks. John staggered in. The pain in his side was getting worse. He was walking bent over at the waist. He leaned heavily against the large metal braces of the tanks, gasping. He tried to call out, but it hurt too much. He only managed a hoarse whisper. "I'm here like I said I'd be."

Christian slipped behind him. "I can see that."

John jumped in fright, causing him to double over again in pain. He tried to straighten up and started to look back. A hand on his shoulder stopped him. "Not necessary, John, you're pointed in the right direction. Here is that bottle of whiskey I promised you—my compliments." Christian handed the bottle over John's shoulder. Despite John's pain, he snatched it immediately.

Christian continued. "Now, cross over that track in front of you and walk to the nearest car of that train on the opposite track. Let's do it quietly, because if you're seen, it will not go well for you."

From his leaning position, John looked over at the cars. "Wait a minute! That's not a passenger train!"

"Getting choosey John? You don't like the train I've selected?"

John hesitated. He didn't want to ride a damn stock car! That wasn't the deal. He had obviously been cheated. But he felt the bottle in his hands and the big hand on his shoulder, very near his neck. The bottle was nice and heavy. It had a rich feel to it. He hadn't had a good bottle in such a long time. He decided to take what he could get.

He staggered across the tracks toward the cars. Christian followed closely behind. Once started, John kept his eyes focused on the goal. He decided that he didn't care to look at whoever it was behind him. That might lead to bad consequences. He just wanted to get out of reach of this monster and lie down with the bottle. They reached the nearest car. "Do you have the strength to climb up and open that door, John, or shall I put you on."

"No, no! I'll do it. He climbed the ladder at the end of the car and inched his way the brief distance along a six inch ledge to the reach the handle of the cattle door. He tried to shove it open. It was hard to do and painful, but the door opened enough for him to squeeze through. "There are a bunch of damned calves in here!"

"Why yes, there are, John. It's a shame they have to ride with you, but they don't have much choice. You'll suck up their warmth and offer nothing in return, I 'm sure. Now move to the front of the car and find a cozy place. And, John, I want you to listen very carefully. I'll remain here watching until you are on your way. If you try to come out, I'll be on you in a flash. Do you understand?"

"Yes, yes, I understand!" He shoved the calves aside as best he could and staggered to the front of the car. He leaned against the wall and inched his way down to a sitting position. The car stank. The calves stuck their snotty noses to him and sniffed, leaving their snot on his face and hands. He cursed and struck at them. They backed off as far as they could and left him alone.

He broke the screw cap loose on the bottle and twisted it open. He took a long swig. The warm liquor flowed easily down his throat. It was the first pleasant thing that had happened to him since coming home, and it really was good whiskey! In fact, it was some of the best he had swallowed in a long, long time. His eyes closed and he relaxed a little. He took another deep draught. The pain began to dull. One more swig and then he fumbled to close the cap. He placed the bottle carefully between his legs up close to his sore crotch. He didn't want the damn calves to step on the bottle and break it while he slept. Then, he quickly drifted off into a deep sleep.

The train left not long after daylight, heading to the Chicago slaughter houses. Christian watched it pull away, then turned and walked back to the hotel. John reached Chicago that day and surprised the stockyard workers as he staggered out of the car. He ambled off and disappeared into the city. The trip had been easier than he thought. The heat from the calves really had kept him warm, just like the guardian angel had said!

He decided along the way that he was done with his damn family and would not return. It gave him some comfort to know that he wouldn't have to worry about them anymore. They had disappointed him in every way and were nothing more than a drag around his neck. His brats were really no better than Emily's firstborn bastard. Good riddance to them all! It was just him now, unencumbered. Life would be so much easier! The guardian angel, or whoever the he really was, didn't have to worry about him breaking his word.

The following winter in Chicago was a bitter one. Many homeless people died on the streets. One of the bodies picked up by the undertakers was an emaciated, homeless drunk with a long jagged scar on his face. The body was consigned to the county morgue to await the proper time to be claimed. No one at the morgue figured that would happen. When the time had passed, they tagged his toe for burial in a pauper's grave. Since they did not know his real name they labeled him "John Doe." They were half right.

Chapter 31

Christian returned to the hotel to get some rest. Ben was in the lobby talking to his mother. Ben's sisters and brother were sleeping late in the wonderful comfort of a soft bed. Ben saw Christian come in and followed him to his room.

"So, you made it back okay." It was a statement, not a question. Ben was still sheepish from his behavior of the previous day.

"You doubted it?"

"No, not really." He paused, trying to decide what to say next. "Did he come back to the farm?"

"Yep." Christian took off his jacket and prepared to wash his face.

"You didn't kill him, did you?"

Christian's back was turned as he leaned over the washbasin. He smiled. "Nope".

"That's good, I guess. I would have though."

"I know."

"You figured I would have killed him?"

"Likely."

"And you chose not to."

"That's right."

There was another long pause. Christian continued to wash his face and neck. Then he wet his hair and pushed it back off his forehead.

"Where is he now?"

"He's riding a cattle car to somewhere with a good bottle of whiskey in his hands."

That confused Ben a little, but from the way the conversation had developed, Ben knew it probably wouldn't do him any good to ask for Christian to explain. "What if he comes back?"

"He won't."

"How do you know?"

"I just know."

Ben sat down on Christian's bed considering what to say next. Christian didn't offer anything else. Ben started to chuckle despite himself. He was sure that the encounter had not been good for John's psyche. Christian looked over and grinned.

Ben got serious. "Sorry I was such a bastard out there, Christian."

"I wouldn't have expected anything else from you. You're as stubborn as you are stupid sometimes. "

"So, you still think I couldn't have put you on the wagon?"

Christian laughed. "You wouldn't have had a chance."

Ben shrugged. "You're probably right. I'm glad I didn't test it.

Thanks for keeping me from confronting him. You're right; it would've gone bad. I was blind with anger. I hate him for all he did to us. I might have had to explain why I killed my own father, no matter how lousy he was. I doubt if people would've really accepted it. I'd have wound up behind bars, or at best, I'd have had to move on. You thought all this out, I suppose, while we were at the farm. You're a disgustingly smart man, Christian, even if you're a pain in the ass sometimes. You've saved my hide at least twice now. Do you ever get tired of doing that?"

"It's habit." Christian looked over at him and winked.

Ben laughed. "I hope you won't have to exercise that habit again. I also hope I can repay you in kind someday for all you've done".

Christian smiled. "For my sake, I hope you don't. That would mean I was in a bad situation. You don't need to repay me for anything, Ben. Friendship is enough."

Ben stared at Christian in shock. "You never cease to surprise me, Gunther. Thanks for calling me your friend. I'm very lucky you feel that way." He got up to leave. "When you are rested, come down to my room. I'll either be there or in the lobby with my family. You'll be hungry. I'm going to buy you the best steak in Bloomington when you're ready to eat it, no matter what time it is or what it costs. And thanks again for what you just did."

"Sure, and I'll take you up on the food. But there's one thing I have to tell you that John said."

"What?"

"He said you aren't his son."

Ben froze. "He said what! Did you believe him?"

"Yea, I think so. He was in a compromised position and in some pain. He had no reason to lie about it under those circumstances".

"Did he say who my father was?"

"No. It was a short conversation. I won't go into it, but it wouldn't have fit my little act to have asked him."

Ben stood at the door a few more seconds with his hand on the knob. "Thanks for telling me."

"Sure."

Ben opened the door and left. His world had just been radically reframed and he was unsure what to do with this new information. Then suddenly, he knew exactly what to do with it.

Christian closed the window curtains, took off his boots and fell onto his bed, slipping immediately into a deep sleep.

Ben went to his mother's room and knocked, calling her name. She came over and unlocked the door. She and the children had been playing a game with some dominos that Jake had provided. He had apparently just left. "Is your friend, Christian, ok?"

"Yes, he's fine. He saw John." It shocked Ben that he was already thinking of him as someone else than his father.

Emily shivered involuntarily. "Does he know where your father is now?"

"No."

"Then he'll be back!" She shivered again.

"I doubt it. I guarantee you that Christian scared him pretty good. He probably beat him up some and told him he would kill him if he ever came back. John has no idea who Christian is and how he knew him. I promise you, there is no one John ever met as frightening as Christian Gunther. I don't think John would ever want to face him again. No one but me ever crossed him and lived to tell the tale."

"But, believe me, he is also a very good guy for those he cares about. He saved my life when I didn't deserve it. He probably saved it again yesterday. He didn't want me to confront John because he thought I'd try to kill him, so he took care of it. He was right. I probably would have."

Emily nodded, but she didn't really trust what Ben said about John. He had been a destructive force in her life far too long for her to think he was gone forever.

"Mom," Ben cleared his throat, "John told Christian he was not my father. Is that true?"

He watched the color drain from Emily's face. She stared at him for long seconds and then looked away. "Can the children play in your room for a while?"

"Sure, I'll take them and be right back." He gathered the dominos and took the children to his room, telling Julie to lock the door and not to let anyone in unless it was their mother, him or Jake. They assured him that they wouldn't. They were still too frightened by the possibility that John might come back to take any chances.

Ben returned to Emily. She was sitting in a chair by the window, staring out. Ben sat down on the bed and waited. She sighed deeply and began, haltingly at first, still looking out the window. "This is a story I hoped never to have to tell you. You will hate me for it and think even less of me than you do now. It's a sordid story and I can't believe I'm telling it to my own son, but you deserve to know, no matter what you think of me when I'm done. So I'll tell it to you without sugarcoating it."

She sighed again and began her story. "When I was 17 and engaged to John, he coerced Jake into taking me to my high school graduation dance. Jake and I are the same age and were in the same class. John is five years older and he had already graduated from college by that time. He didn't want to go to my graduation ceremonies, or to any juvenile high school dance, so he said he had to be away on business. Jake and I knew that wasn't true. John had promised me earlier that he would take me, but he broke that promise, just as he had so many others before."

"Even then I realized that John wasn't trustworthy. My closest friends never liked John and told me to get away from him, that he had a reputation as a lady's man and could be violent. But John could also be gallant and persuasive, and I was a naive 17-year-old girl. He assured me that he needed me to help keep him on the right path. I was initially taken in by that as my heroic mission in life. But as the wedding date drew nearer, I began to have more doubts."

"Jake and I had been close friends since childhood, long before John had paid any attention to me. Jake was shy and sincere. I think he always liked me, but he never had much self-confidence about girls, and I now know that John tried to undermine his confidence whenever he could. John later told me that Jake had once talked to him about how to ask me out on a date. Jake admired John's 'sophistication' with women. He thought his brother might help him. John just laughed at him and told him spitefully that no self-respecting girl would ever want to date a big awkward buffoon like him."

Shortly after that, John came home, having just graduated with an accounting degree from the University of Indiana. He decided that, to humiliate Jake, he would ask me out as sort of a joke. Of course, I didn't know that at the time. He told me later." She looked at Ben, her face flushed with embarrassment. He nodded to her sympathetically.

"All the way through school, I always liked Jake more than any other boy and would've dated him in a second if he'd just asked. I assumed that he just wanted me as a friend and no more. Now I know that he was too shy to do so and too fearful I'd reject him. I would've never done that."

She paused again, looking out the window and then proceeded. "I must admit, at first John did sweep me off my feet. He was a smoother, more worldly version of Jake, and he was obviously an 'up and comer' with his new degree. John poured on the charm and made me feel like I was the most beautiful girl in the world. He introduced me to people his age and treated me like a princess at first."

"But by my graduation, I had seen some of his dark side. On that day of the dance, John insisted that Jake take me, even though I later found out that Jake told him he didn't want to go. After I'd started dating John, Jake always seemed to avoid being around me, which confused and hurt me. I didn't understand it at the time."

She sighed deeply. "I was pouting that night over John's latest broken promise. Jake saw that I was miserable and the tried to make it easier on me, but he was also fighting his own feelings. He surprised me by taking my hand as we were walking home after the dance. I shouldn't have let him, but I liked Jake and I was feeling sorry for myself."

"On the way home he blurted out, 'He'll only hurt you, you know! I don't think he really loves you. You're just another conquest to him!' The minute he said it, I knew he was right. But I still didn't know how to respond. I just squeezed his hand. He stopped right there in the middle of the path. I remember it was a full moon. He was so tall and handsome in his suit. He told me that he loved me—that he always had. Then he said, 'John only loves himself. I can't bear to think what he'll do to you!' He drew me close, and I let him." Her voice quivered and she sighed. "I guess I was just shocked and confused that he really did care after all. All this time he had never told me. If I had only known…." Her voice trailed off.

She resumed the story. "I remember thinking, 'I should tell John that I don't want to marry him. Jake is absolutely right about him. And Jake is just the opposite.' I realized that he was a far better person than John, just less polished. As he held me close, all these feelings overwhelmed me. He kissed me and I wanted him to do it. Before I realized it, we were lying in the grass on a little hill above the path. We made love right there and then he took me home, promising he would come to see me the next day."

"And he did, but I felt so confused and guilty about what we'd done that I had my mother tell him I was sick and couldn't see him that day. He was crushed. He'd assumed that night before had changed everything. He was humiliated. When I tried to talk to him later, he wouldn't let me near enough to be alone with him. John could tell something had happened between us. Instead of asking what, or ignoring it, he did all he could to make us both uncomfortable when we were all together."

"The wedding was supposed to be in October. As it drew nearer, I became depressed and nauseated nearly all the time. Within a month, I suspected that I was pregnant. By the next month, I knew for sure. I felt I couldn't tell Jake because I didn't want to get him in trouble. I was also ashamed and knew it was my fault. I had let Jake kiss and hold me."

"I finally decided that I had to tell John. I feared he'd be angry. I had not let him have sex with me even though he had pleaded with me to do it. I had hoped that he might understand the circumstances of that night and how I was hurt by him, but that was really naive of me. Of course, he was furious. He slapped me around three or four times—the first time he ever really hit me hard. Later, he told everyone that I had run into a door."

"John told me then that he'd never really intended to marry me and he sure wasn't going to do it now! His relationship with me started out as a joke on Jake, whom he now referred to only as 'that bastard'. He said he continued dating me just to see how long it would take to seduce me. He said the further he went the more infatuated he became with the idea of conquering a pretty, naive little high school girl. When it didn't work and I refused to have sex with him, he decided to ask me to marry him so he could get me in bed during the engagement. Once he did, he planned to dump me before the wedding. Since I still refused to have sex with him, he'd just about decided to call it off anyway when I told him about the baby."

"He swore again that he'd not go through with the wedding, and that I could rot in hell with Jake's bastard child. I pleaded, but he didn't care what I said. I panicked and told my parents that I was pregnant. They assumed that John was the father and I didn't correct them. They were furious with him and told his parents. Things quickly got out of control. Everyone told John they expected him to do the 'honorable thing'."

"John was beside himself. He told his mother and father that Jake was the father. His parents were even more furious with him and told him that he needed to own up to his own actions and quit lying and always blaming everyone else for his failings. They said that if he ever tried to pin it on his little brother again, they'd disinherit him on the spot. But if he'd would act like a man and marry me, he'd inherit the company someday. If he didn't, they assured him that he'd lose his share of the business. He said they needed to confront me about who the father was, but they refused to do so, thinking that it was an insult to me. They were sure that Jake and I had never dated or been together and they were sure that John had seduced me and then felt trapped by my pregnancy."

"John never confronted Jake directly and never told him that he was the father. To this day, I have no idea why john didn't confront Jake. In some strange way, he must have been embarrassed that Jake had gotten me to have sex with him while John couldn't. He became furious with his parents. He felt trapped. No one had believed him. That hurt his pride more than anything else."

"Both sets of parents insisted that we marry immediately. He said no, but his father bribed him. If we would go away for a little while, just a year or two until the child was born, he could bring John back to take over the business. His father found him employment through connections in Chicago and gave John plenty of money to make our lives easy during the pregnancy. He refused to give John a choice, threatening numerous times to disinherit him."

"But it didn't work out as John's father had planned. John started to drink heavily and began to beat me. He was so bitter all the time. His boss in Chicago got tired of his drinking and his sour attitude and fired him within six months. John began to gamble. He lost heavily. His father found him another job. He lost that as well. After that, his father refused to help him anymore and said he was on his own. He told John that it was time for him to grow up and that from that point on, he no longer had a silver spoon to eat out of."

"After losing three more jobs in Chicago, John and I became destitute. All of his father's money had been gambled away. Jake had long since stopped talking to his parents and he refused to allow me to go home to see mine. He decided to head for the greener pastures of New York City. He drank even more heavily in New York and beat you and me on a routine basis. Of course, he detested you. He blamed you and me for ruining his life. He wasn't wrong about me. That's what I couldn't explain to you when you were younger and asked why he hated you so."

Tears formed in Emily's eyes. "Jake heard of the pregnancy from his parents and wondered if you could be his, but then, he dismissed the thought. He was just 17 and didn't really understand that much about sex. What he had learned was from his brother. John had repeatedly bragged to Jake about his many conquests, including some after he was engaged to me, and that he had never once been caught 'knocking a girl up'." Jake probably assumed a couple had to have sex a lot to make a baby. He assumed I had slept with John a lot more times than the one time I had sex with him. He was sure now that our one time together had not been that special to me and that I had done it regularly with John. He was totally humiliated."

She shook her head and wiped the tears from her eyes. "Jake

apparently dated a few other girls in town after John and I left, but he never married." So I had ruined his life too. When I finally came back to Indiana with John, Jake was kind and tried to help, but he still kept his distance. I know now that he still had feelings for me but he remained somewhat remote in his dealings with me. I knew that I had made my choices and all of us, including him, were living with the consequences."

"He hated what John had done to me. He offered to help me get away from John's torture numerous times, but I had to say no without explaining why. I knew what John would do to the kids and how nasty it would be if Jake tried to intervene. John hated him so much that I'm surprised he didn't try to kill him. I think he might have if he hadn't wanted to hit Jake up for money for his drinks. "

She looked at Ben and paused. "Anyway, I could never have asked Jake for help. I had left his only son on the streets of New York. How could I ever tell him that?"

Ben had listened to all this in silence. "How do you know all this about Jake? Does he know now?"

Emily nodded. "We talked a long time last night."

"How does he feel about it?"

"He's still taking it in. It's a lot for him to understand and accept. It's a lot for both of you. So, now that you know, do you hate me even more for what I have done to you and Jake?"

Ben smiled and went over to kneel in front of her chair. He touched her face tenderly with his hand. "No mother. I never hated you and never will. It's a relief to me. It all finally makes sense. You made some big mistakes and then you compounded them. But you didn't know what else to do. And now I understand a little better why John was so bitter toward me. It was harder for me not knowing or understanding. I'm just glad Christian kept me from killing him. Bad as John handled it all, he probably doesn't deserve my hatred toward him. It'll be okay now."

Chapter 32

That night, Ben McDonald treated Christian Gunther to the biggest steak in Bloomington. And early the next morning, he went to talk to the father he never knew he had. Jake greeted him warmly, which was a relief to Ben. He told Jake about John's encounter with Christian.

When he had finished, Jake said, "Wow, you have a really great friend in Christian Gunther! He must really care about you."

He continued. "John was the bad seed in our family, Ben. I still can't figure it all out. He had everything he wanted. Your grandparents were well off. Your grandpa was a lawyer who made his money in real estate transactions and then in this business. They were good people, but John wasn't like them. I guess we'll probably never really know why."

"My mother and father eventually disowned John and left their full inheritance to me. They indicated that I could do as I saw fit with John's share, but expressly didn't want him to have it if he was just going to use it for drink. I've always been torn about what to do. Over the last five years, he was constantly asking me for money. I was tempted, hoping it would help Emily and the kids. But I couldn't bring myself to do it. It would never have reached Emily, and he would've probably taken them away again if I gave him enough to do it. He had no reason to stay if he got his inheritance. As long as I could keep them near, I hoped to find some way to help the family. You and Christian have become the answer to my prayers."

"It was killing me to see them live in those conditions. So I invested his share and hoped for him to die." His eye's misted.

"Isn't that terrible? I hoped for my own flesh and blood to die!" He paused, looking away, and with great effort, got control of his emotions. So you see, you don't have to worry about upkeep for Emily and the kids. I'm giving your mother the full share of the inheritance. It's a large amount. She can build a good house and put the children in school where they belong. She'll be set for the rest of her life."

"You know she was such a beauty when she was young," he murmured, more to himself than to Ben. "She was just about as wonderful a person as anyone you ever met. He's done some terrible damage to her and I'll never forgive him for that as long as I live, but there's hope for her if he stays away."

Ben nodded. He waited, thinking Jake might speak of him, but Jake was lost in thought and didn't say anything more. Finally Ben swallowed hard and said, "John told Christian he was not my father."

Jake looked at him, startled. "Oh? And did he tell Christian who is?"

"No, but my mother told me yesterday."

"Oh, my goodness, Ben! I am so sorry for not talking to you about it immediately. I didn't think you knew and I wasn't sure when Emily would tell you. I'm not really sure what to say. It's all so new to me too. He came around and sat on the edge of the desk close to Ben's chair. "But I can tell you this. If I'd known I had a son, your life would have been entirely different. I'd have gotten you and Emily away from him as soon as I knew, no matter what I had to do. I hope you can believe that. You've turned into such an impressive young man despite all that's happened to you. I was confused and scared, but so proud when Emily told me yesterday!"

A lump formed in Ben's throat. His father—his real father—was proud of him. He responded. "It'll take us both a little time to get used to it, I guess; but I'm looking forward to that. It's a relief for me to know that I don't carry his blood. And I'll admit, my life has been difficult sometimes—even horrible, I guess. But there have been special things about it too. It would've been nice having a father that cared for me, but then I'd probably have never met some of the special people that I have, and I think that I may be stronger than I would've otherwise been. So who knows, maybe it had its purpose."

His dad took his hand and held it. "Thanks, Ben. I appreciate you saying all that. And I can't tell you how excited I am to get to be your father and to make up for some of that lost time."

Chapter 33

Months later Ben and Christian were still in Bloomington helping Jake with the business and assisting Emily and the children piece their lives back together. The children were in school and adjusting pretty well, although they needed a lot of help to catch up. Fortunately, their teachers were understanding and supportive, and Emily could afford after-school tutors. Jake was a highly respected member of the community and all who had known Emily when she was young had remembered her fondly. Once the full story became known the town rallied around her and the children with their good wishes and support.

Emily and the children were still terrified that John might return. The whole family held its collective breath to see if he would reappear unexpectedly. Each of them had nightmares during the first few months after John's departure, but eventually the nightmares receded. As John's absence grew longer, life for them became brighter with each passing day.

With proper nourishment and reduced stress, Emily began to look a lot more like her old self. Jake could see the beauty returning. She was embraced by some of her old classmates and by the Church her family still attended. Jake kept commenting to her about how attractive she was and how great the children were coming along. He spent all his spare time with them.

With Jake's help, Emily built a new house in the best neighborhood in Bloomington. She, Ben and the children moved in. They had a terrific time furnishing it. The inheritance Jake had reserved for John's family would provide a comfortable life for Emily and the children. Ben and Emily invited Christian to join them in the new house but he chose to rent his own apartment.

Jake talked with Ben about an equity share of the business and was increasingly impressed with Christian's skills as well. It was apparent that he was extremely smart and an exceptional leader. Jake had already made him supervisor of the grain mill. Ben began to handle much of the company's sales and marketing activities. Jake paid them both well.

It was an ideal time in the life of Christian and Ben, these two orphans who had been through so much. It seemed like the happy ending to a difficult story, but Ben couldn't shake an uneasy feeling that something was still missing. One beautiful spring evening in 1888, Ben, Emily, Jake and Christian were sitting on Emily's spacious new patio after finishing a meal. Ben, as a passing thought, murmured to Christian, "I wonder if her weather is as good as this."

Christian knew who he meant. Ben hadn't mentioned Anna's name for nearly a year and Christian thought he had gotten past her, but obviously not. "Don't know, Ben. Hopefully her life has taken as good a turn as ours."

Ben reflected. "Yea, I hope so too."

Emily's ears perked up. "Who are you talking about?"

So Ben told them the tale while Christian listened. It included the stories of their time on the streets of Hell's Kitchen, of Ben's assault on the Bowery Boys and how Ben and Anna had escaped. Ben also told them of Bill Chambers, Charles Brace and Emma Mason. It was midnight when he finished. By that time they had moved back into the parlor out of the chill.

Emily was simultaneously enthralled and shocked by the story. "My God, boys! Why haven't you told us all this before. No wonder you're so close. And Christian, this family owes you a debt that it will never be able to repay! Somebody ought to write a book about all that has happened to the two of you! She turned to Ben. "Anna sounds like a once-in-a lifetime girl, Ben."

Ben nodded, and that haunted look returned to his face. "You know, maybe I could move past my feelings for Anna if I just knew what happened to her and that she was safe and happy. It's the not knowing that's hardest for me. I still don't understand why she never wrote. I thought she cared for me as much as I did for her, but I guess we were both just kids. She was younger than me, and maybe it was easier for her to forget."

Emma queried, "So you were never able to communicate with Anna and you have given up the possibility of ever seeing her again?"

Ben nodded.

"Well, Ben McDonald, that's not the son I know! You'll never put this to rest until you find out what happened to her and how she's doing. I think you're more scared of knowing than not knowing. You're afraid she really has moved on. And if she hasn't already, she'll have to eventually. You've never backed down from anything in your life before, Ben McDonald, no matter how painful. But now you're doing that very thing because you are afraid of what you might find out. I think I am ashamed of you! You should know better! You can look tot Jake and me as an example of how wrong that can turn out."

Jake chimed in, "She's right, Ben. You said Anna was taken by a family in Rolla, Missouri. I've been through on business. It's not that far away; it's less than 12 hours by train. Why don't you go see if you can find out what happened to her? I bet it won't take

357

you over a week to know."

Ben was shocked and a little defensive at their reaction. "But I don't have any idea where this family lives who took her in, or even if she's still with them. From what Reverend Brace said, families flocked in from all around, sometimes from 50 miles or more. It's likely to be a dead end. She remembered their name was Lowe, or something like that. But that's all I'd have to go on."

Emily pushed back. "Well, you came all the way to Bloomington just because of a word on the floor that I left you, Ben, and you didn't have much difficulty finding us again, did you? What would be the worst thing that could happen if you went to Rolla to look for her?"

Ben thought a second, "I suppose I could hit a dead end and not find out anything more than I know now."

"Or?"

"Or, I could go there and find out that she's settled in with some family, has a boyfriend or husband, and would be embarrassed to see me showing up."

"Do you really believe she would be embarrassed?"

"I don't know."

"Can you think of any other outcome besides those?"

Ben thought again. "Well, I guess I could go there, find her, and find out that she was as anxious to see me as I am her."

"Given all those choices, would any be worse than not knowing and not trying to find out?"

He thought about it for a minute, then shook his head and smiled ruefully. "No, nothing could be worse than it is now."

Emma laughed. "Ben, given what you've told me, I can't understand what you're waiting for. I know she was very young when you both met, but you had experiences together that most people wouldn't have in a lifetime. This girl's feelings for you may have changed. But would it be so bad knowing that? And if you have described her accurately, she may be as lonely as you, wondering the same things about you as you are about her. It is a horrible thing not to tell the person how you really feel. Believe me, you will regret it the rest of your life if you don't try to find her."

They finally went to bed, but Ben didn't sleep. He was up before daylight and found his mother sitting in the kitchen. She greeted him, got him some coffee and then said, "I saw your light on under the bedroom door when I got up this morning. Have you decided what to do?"

Ben laughed. "I'm going to go find out what Rolla, Missouri looks like."

She clapped her hands in delight. "I knew you would. And I'll pray every day while you're gone that you'll find her."

He laughed and hugged her. "Probably good I made that decision. Everybody who now knows the story would think less of me if I didn't."

Emily laughed and said, "By the way, you're taking Christian with you. I'll feel better knowing he's along with you. He may catch some clues that you miss."

"But, mother, he is busy and I hate to pull him away from Jake. It's planting season!"

"Jake and I talked about it last night after you went to bed. He went to talk to Christian. He came over already this morning to tell me that Christian wants to go and not to let you talk us out of it. I think he wants to resolve this almost as much as you do. Jake'll do just fine while you're gone. He's getting your tickets for you as soon as the station opens this morning. He says there's a morning train headed in that direction at 9 a.m. He and Christian will meet us at the station. Let's get you some breakfast."

Ben was astonished. "What if I had said I wasn't going?"

Emily laughed. "Jake and I talked about that too. He said, 'Our son would never say no to a proposition like that'." Ben laughed and his heart swelled. It was such a good feeling having parents who actually trusted you to do the right thing.

Emily and Ben were at the station at early, but Christian and Jake, were already there. Jake had just purchased the tickets. He handed each of them one. He also handed Ben an envelope. "Open it when you are on the train."

Ben looked at the envelope and back at Jake. He guessed it was travel money. "Jake you don't need to do that. We both have money of our own."

"I know, but it'll make me feel better. Humor your old dad a little."

Ben smiled. "Thanks, dad, I appreciate it."

They chatted until the train arrived. Emily hugged both Ben and Christian as they boarded. Jake shook Christian's hand but surprised Ben by hugging him. It was a little awkward. They'd get better as time went on. The boys boarded the train and headed west toward Illinois.

Emily and Jake walked back to her house, hand in hand. "He'll be alright, won't he, Jake? We did the right thing by encouraging him to go find Anna, didn't we? How will he feel if she really has found someone else?"

"We did the right thing, Emily. Not knowing leaves scars that don't heal. Once he knows, one way or the other, he'll be better for it. Let's just hope it's not too hard to find her and that she's really the girl he thinks she is."

She nodded, and they walked on in silence. She wanted more than anything for her son to find happiness. He had already seen far too much betrayal and sadness in his young life. Hopefully Anna Murphy would not be part of that pattern.

Chapter 34

The train was only half full so Christian and Ben could spread out. Ben was grateful. He was in a reflective mood and didn't really want to talk much. Christian, sensing this, remained silent. Ben thought about everything that had happened since Bill Chamber's death. It had taken the shock of his loss and Christian's advice and support to spur him to action. He looked over at Christian, who was now staring out the window at the moving scenery. Ben thought again that no man ever had a better friend.

His thoughts returned to Bill. He knew from their conversations that Bill had never experienced the joy of having a family who loved him. Bill had been respected and admired by everyone who ever met him, but he didn't have family. Ben knew that Bill was a lonely man. He also knew that Bill had never come to grips with the reasons he had been abandoned in Hell's Kitchen. Bill's family had been as dysfunctional as Ben's, but without the love of a mother. His mother had died at his birth and his father, also a mean alcoholic like John, had blamed him and never shown any affection.

Suddenly it occurred to Ben that he had never heard why Christian was on the streets! The thought shocked him. Christian knew almost everything about him and his family, and yet, he really knew nothing about Christian's story. He decided to remedy that on this trip if Christian would tell him. But Ben decided to wait a little longer before asking, still unsure that Christian would be comfortable enough to share that much personal information. Close as they had become, Christian seldom talked about himself.

Ben was still anxious about what he'd say if he really did find Anna. "Hi, Anna, remember me? I was in the neighborhood and thought I'd drop by to see how you're doing…" He laughed at himself. What did it matter what he'd say, really? But what if she had a boyfriend? In fact, what if he found out that she was now married? Should he go to see her, or just return to Bloomington? He wasn't sure. He decided he probably wouldn't really know until it happened—if it happened.

He knew her feelings for him had been strong, but she was just a girl—only 13 years old. Actually, it made little sense to think that a 13-year old girl would still harbor the same feelings at age 17, which was now her age if he remembered correctly. She was now definitely at the courting age, and even the marrying age, and he already knew how beautiful she had been. She was probably twice as beautiful now, which meant that she would have plenty of suitors, some who could likely offer her a good life. It would actually be surprising if she was still unattached.

He shuddered to think about it. Maybe he was just being a sentimental fool to think that things might be the same with them? He had a good job and a great family back in Bloomington. Did he really need to do this? Certainly there would be attractive girls to date in Bloomington if he could just get past his feelings for her. But he decided that he wouldn't go back without at least going to Rolla to ask about her, if nothing more than to save appearances with his family and Christian. He would at least do that. If they uncovered some good leads, he'd talk to Christian and make his decision then about whether to follow them. With that resolution, he relaxed a little.

Their train stopped at the elaborate Union Station in St. Louis where they would change to a southwest express bound for Springfield. Rolla was one of the stops along the way. There was a mechanical problem there that delayed the train for a couple of hours. It gave him a little time to quiz Christian as they waited. "It occurred to me today that you know everything about me and how I wound up in Hell's Kitchen, but I know nothing about how you did."

Christian smiled. "It's not much of a story, really."

"I'd like to hear it anyway, if you're willing."

Christian looked at him, and after a long pause, began to speak softly. "Well, when I was nine, my mother died. My dad, who was a foreman at the docks on East River near the lower end of Manhattan, took to drink. It was a shame, really. He was supposed to have been a top notch foreman. He apparently knew how to get people to do what he wanted and to like it. He was good to me before she died, but he turned inside himself afterward. He had always been a little blue, prone to the "melancholies" as he called it. But as long as my mother lived, she would snap him out of it. He was a big guy. My mother told me that nobody on the docks ever thought about crossing him. My mother was also tall, but slender, and I remember her as very graceful. It may have just been because I was still a kid when I lost her. But I think that she had a bearing that I haven't seen in too many women."

"I was their only child. She couldn't have children after me. I'm not sure why. Some medical problem. I was close to them. They doted on me. My mother spent all her spare time teaching me things. She read to me a lot. I took that up. I still like books."

"Anyway, I went out to play one Sunday morning not long after she died. I was in the yard—we had a nice house with a big yard. We lived near 2th Avenue. I heard a loud bang from inside the house and ran in to see what it was. I didn't find anything at first, but then I went into the den. He had blown his head off with a shotgun."

Christian paused and went silent for a minute, then resumed. "I panicked. My family didn't really mix much or make friends. We had no relatives in the city. I heard them talk of some in Pennsylvania, but I'd never met them. Apparently mom's kin didn't approve of the marriage and so my parents had run away together when they were young." I just started running. I couldn't get the picture of my dad's head out of my mind. I ran west till I hit the Hudson River; then I ran north. I never made it back." He stopped talking and looked out the window. After a few seconds, he resumed. "I never figured out why I wasn't good enough for him to hang around to be with me, even with my mother gone. I still haven't really figured that out. I knew he had issues, but you'd think he would have wanted to hang around for his own kid. I thought he cared about me. I guess he probably did, but not enough to stay. I guess it hurt me inside and made me cautious about trusting people. I still deal with that a lot."

Ben interrupted. "God, I'm sorry Christian! Your situation was far worse than mine."

Christian laughed. "Every orphan's story is bad if they wind up in Hell's Kitchen. It's all just matter of degree. I got taken in quickly by the gang and I adjusted. We all did, except for the few misfits like you. Now I am adjusting in a different way."

"But I'll admit that I was angry on the streets. I couldn't believe he'd do that and just leave me there with no one. I was bitter for a long time. I stopped talking and I didn't play or have fun anymore. I did some bad things in those days and every bad thing tied me closer to the gang. That's when I got my reputation on the streets. I wanted everyone else to hurt as much as I did."

He stopped talking and turned back to the window. After a few minutes, Ben realized that was all he'd get. It was more than he had expected.

"Thanks for telling me. Your mom and dad did a lot of things right or you wouldn't be what you are today. I wish you hadn't lost them."

Christian looked over at him and smiled sadly. "Yea, me too. Thanks for listening. I am new to this friend thing, but I am learning it has some pluses—although you still talk too much." He turned to look out the window. The conversation was over.

The train departed Union Station in the early afternoon. Ben fell asleep. He was still groggy when they pulled into the Rolla station. Christian had to shake him awake. They retrieved their bags from under the seats and exited.

They were in Rolla! Until now that had been just some mythical town representing the last known link he had to Anna. He had never even looked up what part of Missouri it was in or asked what the town was like. He hadn't really even known where the whole state fit in the geography of the United States. Now he knew.

What had she seen on the day she arrived? What did she think of the town, or wherever she now lived? She had completed her orphan train ride and probably stepped down onto this very platform. He imagined how she must have felt, travel weary and probably confused about what would come next.

Now that he was here, it looked like many other small towns they'd passed along the way. Jake had talked about the engineering college located here, called the Rolla School of Mines, where they apparently trained students to work at lead mines in the state. So it was a college town that would probably be full of handsome and successful young men interested in her if this is where she stayed. Maybe she'd already met one of them. A sign on the platform said Rolla had a population of 1,431 people. That was even smaller than Bloomington.

After they exited the train station, Ben turned to Christian. "Where do you think we should start? Should we get a hotel room first?"

"We could, but if she didn't stay here, we may need to go to another town. We know orphan trains came through here and we know the name Lowe. This won't be like finding John. Why don't we go to the newspaper office and see what they know?"

"Ah, good idea! I knew my mother sent you along for some reason."

"You're mother sent me along to keep your butt out of trouble and you know it."

Ben laughed and went back into the train station to ask directions to the newspaper office. It was only a few blocks south of the station. They headed there, hoping it would still be open. It was, but barely. A young lady had just come to the door to lock it to close for the day. She was friendly and reopened it for them. "May I help you, gentlemen?"

They explained that they were seeking information about orphan children who had come to Rolla and been taken in by families in 1884. She said she didn't know much about that and asked them to wait a minute. She disappeared to the back. A few minutes later a white-haired man came toward them. He extended his hand as he spoke, "Hello, I'm Ed Harris, the editor of this paper. I hear you're looking for orphan children."

Ben responded, "Yes—well, not exactly—we're actually looking for one particular orphan girl who was a friend of ours. She's from New York City and was brought here by the Children's Aid Society. Her train would've come through Rolla in late 1884. Miss Emma Mason was the Children's Aid representative on the train. We heard she was adopted by a family named Lowe. I'm not sure of the correct spelling of that name and I don't know much else."

Mr. Harris thought about it. "The name Lowe doesn't ring much of a bell with me and I know just about everybody in Rolla. There is a single man named Lowe who lives in Rolla, but he has no relatives here that I know of. All of that doesn't mean a lot, though. Families from all around these parts took in orphan children. I could look through our files from late 1884 but we seldom reported specifics on the Placements."

Tell you what; I think your best bet is to go over to the Baptist Church on 4th and Main. That's the church that sponsors the work of the Children's Aid Society now and organizes the orphan placements for this area. Maybe Pastor Casey might know something about the family. The church is just down the street."

They thanked him and headed to the church. When they got there they found it locked and empty. They were uncertain where to go next. They were about to leave and search for a hotel room when a passerby saw them standing at the front doors of the church. "You looking for the Pastor?"

"Actually, yes. Mr. Harris at the Newspaper office thinks he might have some information we need."

"Well, he's probably out visiting the sick, but that's his home right next door there. Maybe Mrs. Casey could tell you when he'll be back."

Christian said, "Thanks, much. Appreciate the help." They walked down the sidewalk to a small, neat white-frame house. Christian used the knocker on the door and they waited. A very dignified, attractive lady came to the door. "May I help you young men?" she asked.

Ben answered. "I hope so, thank you. My name is Ben McDonald and this is Christian Gunther. We're looking for a girl who was one of the orphans brought out this way by the Children's Aid Society in late 1884. We understand from Mr. Harris at the newspaper office that your church sponsors such events. The young lady is a friend of ours and we want to know how she's doing. The newspaper office thought Pastor Casey might know how to find her."

Mrs. Casey said sympathetically, "Well, Pastor Casey wasn't here in 1884, so I don't know if he'll be of much help, but he'll be back in a short while, and you can ask him yourself. You may wait on the porch if you like. Would you like some water or tea?" They were thirsty and said that they would, so she went off to the kitchen.

After a few seconds her voice came from the kitchen, "What was the name of the girl you're looking for?"

"Her name is Anna Murphy."

In a few minutes she came back onto the porch carrying a tray with two cups of tea and cookies. She sat the tray down on a porch table and handed them each a cup. "Would you like a cookie?"

They thanked her and each took one.

She looked a little puzzled, as if trying to remember something. "Well now that I think of it, the name does sound somewhat familiar. Pastor Casey told me about a year ago that one of our parishioners, a man named Sam Kofahl, had relatives near Salem who were seeking a Reverend's mailing address in New York. It had something to do with finding a man who ran a warehouse. Apparently someone in Sam's family from around Salem had been trying to reach him. I'm sure Pastor Casey will be back anytime and we can ask him the girl's name. He'll probably remember the story better than me."

Ben gripped the cup in his hand so as not to drop it. He took a small sip to calm himself. Christian looked at him and nodded. After what seemed hours, during which Mrs. Casey asked all sorts of polite questions that only Christian could answer coherently, a large friendly man came up the walkway. Ben hoped it was the Pastor. It was.

Fred Casey was a friendly man who always had a twinkle in his eye and a smile on his face. It was easy to see why he'd be a good minister. He shook hands with them as though it was perfectly normal to find strangers sitting on his porch late in the day, which it actually was. "Well, gentlemen, I'm Fred Casey. Who might you be?"

Ben liked him instantly. "Good afternoon, sir. I am Ben McDonald and this is Christian Gunther. We're from Bloomington, Indiana. As I told Mrs. Casey, we are looking for a girl who arrived in Rolla among a group of orphans from New York City four years ago. Her name is Anna Murphy. Mrs. Casey thought you might know of her."

Pastor Casey laughed. "Matter of fact, I have heard of her. Actually, anybody who knows Sam Kofahl has probably heard of Anna Murphy. She's this exceptional young teacher down past Salem. Supposed to be the prettiest girl around and smart as a whip to boot. Sam can probably tell you everything you want to know about her whereabouts. If I might ask, why exactly are you looking for her?"

Ben's face flushed red and Fred suspected he already knew why, but he was surprised at the answer from the other young man. "Anna and Ben were both on the streets of Hell's Kitchen in New York together and were fortunate enough to escape. She received help through the Reverend Brace and a man named Bill Chambers to ride the orphan train. Ben had to stay in New York for a few years."

"Ah, and now he wants to find her to see how she's doing. Must have been pretty hard on the streets from what I hear."

Christian responded. "Yes sir, it was."

"Well, finish your cookies and tea and I'll take you over to see Sam."

Ben ask nervously, "Begging your pardon sir, I wonder if we could just go right on over."

Christian smiled at Pastor Casey and winked. Casey laughed heartily and said of course they could. They walked east to a large lumber company, no more than ten minutes away. When they arrived, Fred yelled to a man in back of the showroom. "Hey, Sam, I've got someone you need to meet up here."

"Okay, Pastor. Hold your horses. Be there in a minute."

When Sam finally came up to them, he stuck out his hand to Christian and then Ben. "Hi, I'm Sam Kofahl. What are you boys doing hanging out with this character?"

Pastor Casey laughed. "That's going to cost you extra in the contribution plate, Sam. Boys, why don't you introduce yourselves?"

"My name's Ben McDonald and this is Christian Gunther and we are…" but before he could say more, Sam Kofahl's face broke into a wide grin and he interrupted Ben. "So you're the famous Ben McDonald, eh? I was beginnin to believe that you were just a figment of the imagination. But here you are, bigger'n life. It sure took you long enough to get here boy!" He slapped Ben on the back like he was some long lost friend. Ben was completely confused. Christian grinned. Sam read the expression on Ben's face and laughed. "Ben McDonald, you said, right? *The* Ben McDonald from New York City? Anna's long lost friend?"

Ben swallowed hard and nodded. "Then you know Anna?"

"Yep, sure do, boy. And she's been waiting a long time to hear from you. Myself, I can't figure why she didn't give up on you a while ago. She must think you're real special. Goodness knows she's had all the choices a girl could want."

Ben was speechless. Christian spoke for him. "He's been waiting a long time to see her too, Mr. Kofahl. Does she live near here?"

"Well, that depends on what you mean by 'near here'. Considering how far you boys have come, it's near here, but it's still some miles away. But she'll be as anxious to see you as you are to see her, and we can't keep fate awaitin too long, can we. You come here about seven in the morning and we'll head down

372

that way. It's a pretty long haul and it would be nice to get there in plenty of time for Bessie to cook one of her suppers. You boys got a place to stay? There's cots in the back if you need them."

Christian responded, "Thanks anyway, Mr. Kofahl, but is there a hotel near here? I suspect Ben will want to clean up a bit."

Kofahl laughed. "Sure there is, and a good one too. We get engineers and other bigwigs through here all the time. It's up Pine Street near the college. I'll walk you over there and introduce you to the owner. Pastor, we'll see you later. Thanks for bringing these gents over. It'll be a big day in Jadwin tomorrow, that's for sure!"

Pastor Casey smiled and shook their hands. He turned to Ben. "Well, Ben, looks like you've found what you're looking for. I'll leave you with this old bag of bones. Don't let him embarrass you too much with all his teasing. He talks a big game but he's harmless." He slapped Sam on the back and headed home.

Sam walked them to the hotel and introduced them to the owner. He put them in two of his best rooms at a discount. They had dinner in the hotel. Christian thought it was good, but he knew that Ben would never remember the meal. Ben just pushed the food around the plate a little. Christian was merciless. "You seem a little nervous, McDonald. You think you'll make it through the night without having a heart attack?"

Ben, whose face was still somewhat pale, gulped. "I don't know. This is all too easy. Mr. Kofahl acted like Anna was waiting for me. That's not really possible is it? And did you hear him say she was a teacher now? That's not surprising, I guess, but she's so young! I mean, she would be capable of that if she set her mind to it, but she was not much more than a child herself four years ago.

How did she get to be a teacher so fast? And what exactly did he mean when he said that she had all the choices a girl could want?"

Christian chuckled. "That's a lot of questions I don't know the answers to. I think you may just have to wait and ask the girl yourself."

"You think she's really been waiting for me, Christian?"

Christian knew Ben needed some reassurance, so he answered straight this time. "Sure sounds like it, Ben. If she has, she must be as set on you as you are on her. If that's true, you will be a very lucky man."

Ben nodded. They finished supper and went up to their respective rooms to rest. They would need to be up early in the morning. Rest came easy for Christian Gunther. Ben McDonald didn't sleep a wink.

They left for the lumber company at 6:30 a.m. Christian was waiting for Ben in the hotel lobby when he came down. He knew Ben would be restless and would want to get there early. They walked to the lumber company to wait for Sam. When he showed up, the first thing he asked was if they'd had breakfast. Christian said no and to Ben's horror at the delay, they went on to Sam's house for breakfast.

Sam introduced them to Martha, who promptly hugged Ben like he was family. She set about making a big breakfast. The time that took nearly drove Ben mad. When they had finally finished, Sam told her to keep the boys company while he hitched the team to the wagon and to fix up some food for the trip.

While he was gone, Ben asked "How far exactly is Jadwin from here, ma'am?"

"Oh, it's about 30 miles, Ben. It'll probably take seven or so hours, depending on road conditions. That should get you there just about the time school's out."

Christian said, "We're sorry to impose on you and your husband like this, ma'am. We'll be glad to pay him for the trip."
Martha laughed loudly as though he had told a joke. "Why, Christian, we'd have paid to have Ben come all the way from New York if we could've found him. Anna's such a wonderful girl and Jess and Bessie have been so worried about her not being able to contact you, Ben."

Ben asked, "Who are Jess and Bessie, ma'am?"

"Oh, my goodness! You don't know anything do you?"

Ben shook his head.

"Well, never you mind. Sam'll have plenty of time to fill you in on the way. I guess you do have a lot of catching up to do. I assumed you got here because you finally received some of Anna's letters."

So she'd written! "No ma'am, I never received anything from her, and my letter never got to her either."

Martha suddenly looked as though she was about to cry, "Oh, no, Ben. She never got anything from you! It's so sad....but if you didn't get any letters, how did you find us?"

Seeing Ben's panicked look at the thought that he might have to relate the whole story before being allowed to leave, Christian answered for him. "It's a long story, ma'am, and maybe not so important now. It's just good to know that Anna tried to reach him."

Martha said, "Oh, yes. From what I'm told, she wrote you over a hundred letters. It's such a shame they didn't get to you, Ben. No matter now though. All's well that ends well, you see. Here comes Sam. You'll see Anna soon enough. She's waited a long time for you to come."

Ben realized that someone had told the Kofahls a lot about him. He was grateful. It had made their search so much easier. He had forgotten all about making a decision about what he would do if he had the opportunity to see her. He was ready to ride, the sooner and the faster, the better!

Martha hugged Ben and shook hands with Christian politely as they boarded the wagon. Ben's face turned red as she hugged him, but she just giggled and didn't care one whit. She kissed Sam and told him to get going and be careful. "You have precious cargo on board, you know."

They finally left the outskirts of Rolla by 8:00 a.m. headed south. They made reasonable time between Rolla and Salem. There had been rain, but those roads were good. Along the way Sam told them the story of Anna and Zachary's arrival and how they met Jess and Bessie. Ben asked how to spell the last name and learned that it was "Lough", not "Lowe". Sam expounded. "It's an Irish or Scottish name, boys. We don't know which. It means something like a body of water—like a lake maybe."

Sam filled in the last four years of Anna's life and Ben grew more and more excited. And as he listened, it became clear how fortunate Anna and little Zachary had been to find Jess and Bessie.

Sam was a great storyteller, and in the hours it took them to get from Rolla to Salem, Ben and Christian were fully immersed with descriptions of Jess Lough's family, as well as every detail Sam knew about the saga of Anna's life in Missouri, including the fate of the letters she'd written to Ben.

Along the way, Sam figured out who Christian really was. He had been told that someone in Hell's Kitchen had saved Ben and Anna at great personal risk. He just didn't realize that the hero was the young man riding on his wagon. From that point on, he was in awe of Christian Gunther.

Sam stopped for lunch and allowed the horses to take a breather. He and Christian ate the meal Martha had packed. Ben just paced around the wagon looking agitated. They started again, soon passing through Salem and eventually turning a little southwest. The roads became narrower and more rutted. The going got slower. About five miles past Salem Sam said, "Won't be too long now boys!" Ben was grateful to hear it. He had tried not to prod Sam about how much distance they had covered too many times along the way, but it had been difficult.

Chapter 35

It was a beautiful spring day, just before 4:00 p.m. at the Jadwin School. The sun had passed its zenith and started its downward arc toward the western horizon. The school day had just ended a half-hour ago and Anna was still at her desk grading papers.

The school year was nearing its end. It had been a good one and she was already looking forward to the next. She loved teaching even more than she had anticipated. She would have additional pupils next year with the new families moving into the area, many of them to work at Charlie Schafer's sawmills and flooring operation.

The west-facing door of the one-room schoolhouse was bathed in a bright light. The yard was still glowing in the afternoon sun except under the big tree where Anna and Bessie had eaten their picnic lunch on that day she was tested by Brad Fletcher. That didn't seem too long ago, but it was over three years and now she was the teacher. She smiled a little thinking about all that. It had happened so quickly.

Each spring afternoon, as the sun moved toward the horizon, it cascaded a shaft of light through the door, creating a great, bright whitish-yellow rectangle down the aisle between the seats, almost all the way to her desk. It always reminded her of a picture in one of Bessie's Bibles where a bright Angel was announcing Christ's birth to the shepherds.

She realized that she should leave soon to help Bessie with supper but she had just a little more grading to do and she knew Bessie wouldn't mind. She was grading a geography test about the United States. One of the questions asked about the largest city in the United States. She paused momentarily, daydreaming. She knew that answer from personal experience.

She lost herself briefly to the daydream, remembering that city, wondering where Ben McDonald was at this very minute. Was he back there now, or had he found his family? She hoped that he had and that it had turned out well for him. She shook her head impatiently, disgusted with herself for the distraction. She knew she was wasting time to lost memories. She returned to her task.

As she leaned over her work, her long brown hair flowed around her shoulders almost touching the desk in front of her. During the school day she wore it up in a bun in the proper schoolmarm fashion dictated by the expectations of the community, but she didn't really like it that way. After the children left, she usually released the pins and let it out. She had no reason to expect mid-week visitors, particularly this late in the afternoon.

She heard a wagon on the road but paid no attention. Wagons passed occasionally at this time of day. But a moment later the shaft of light danced, and she looked up. She assumed it might be Jess passing by and offering her a ride home, but it wasn't. The silhouette in the door was far too tall for him, and didn't enter.

The figure was bathed in blinding light, just like one of Bessie's angels. But unlike the picture, the glare made it impossible for her to see the stranger's face. She felt a touch of fear, but it passed quickly. The people of the Jadwin community had never given her reason to worry about her personal safety. "May I help you?" she asked, lifting her hand to shade her eyes.

"Well, I hope so," said The Voice.

She hadn't recognized silhouette. But that voice she would never forget in her lifetime, no matter how long she lived. She had heard it first in a graveyard. Her heart stuttered, caught, and then began to beat rapidly. She stood slowly and walked around her desk toward the isle. Her mind was racing. Maybe she had drifted off to sleep. Maybe this was just a dream. Despite the sheer foolishness of it, she pinched the inside of her hand with her fingers. She wasn't dreaming.

The Voice came again. "I'm told by a reliable source that there's a teacher here who can help just about any fool learn to read, no matter how slow he might be. I was wondering if you would be interested in trying me."

She had kept inching forward down the aisle trying to make out the face. The figure had not moved from the open door. Then she saw it. That was all it took. She bolted forward, crashing into him with the full force of her embrace, catching him by surprise and almost knocking him back down the steps. Her arms encircled his chest and she squeezed so tightly that she forced air out of his lungs. He teetered precariously, then regained his balance and lifted her off the ground as he brought her face up to his. Nothing in his life would ever match the thrill of that moment.

They clung to each other, two lost orphans, reunited now in body and spirit. She began to weep and, truth be told, so did he. He had found her. He vowed to himself at that moment that he would never lose her again in his lifetime. Wherever she was, that was where he'd be. He finally set her gently back down to the floor. She wiped her eyes with the sleeve of her dress and then took his hand, leading him to the front of the schoolroom. She pulled a chair up beside her desk.

"So you still need those reading lessons, huh? Well, we must work on that. There are some letters that have been waiting a long time for you to read."

"I know," he said, smiling. She looked up at him, puzzled, but didn't ask. There would be time for that later. She opened a primer and they began their first lesson right then and there.

Sam and Christian, watching from the wagon and hearing what they said, smiled at one another. Sam turned his wagon down the lane to the Lough homestead. This was their moment and he didn't need to spoil it. Ben and Anna could walk home when they were ready. Besides, Sam wanted to see the look on the faces of Jess and Bessie when they found out who was coming to dinner that night! It would send Bessie into an absolute tiz!

Ben McDonald was an exceptional student and learned to read those letters very quickly. He memorized each one by heart and always kept them close to him until the day he died.

Made in the USA
San Bernardino, CA
12 December 2016